PENGUIN BOOKS

Worst Idea Ever

By the same author

Getting Rid of Matthew
Got You Back
Foursome
The Ugly Sister
Skeletons
Strictly Between Us
My Sweet Revenge
Faking Friends
Tell Me a Secret
Queen Bee

Worst Idea Ever

JANE FALLON

PENGUIN BOOKS

PENGUIN BOOKS

UK | USA | Canada | Ireland | Australia
India | New Zealand | South Africa

Penguin Books is part of the Penguin Random House group of companies
whose addresses can be found at global.penguinrandomhouse.com

First published by Michael Joseph 2021
Published in Penguin Books 2021
001

Printed and bound in Great Britain by Clays Ltd, Elcograf S.p.A.

The authorized representative in the EEA is Penguin Random House Ireland,
Morrison Chambers, 32 Nassau Street, Dublin DO2 YH68

A CIP catalogue record for this book is available from the British Library

ISBN: 978–0–241–51533–4

www.greenpenguin.co.uk

Penguin Random House is committed to a
sustainable future for our business, our readers
and our planet. This book is made from Forest
Stewardship Council® certified paper.

Dedicated to the wonderful staff of Mayhew
for their tireless work with animals

https://themayhew.org/

Prologue

I stare at the message. Read it again.

'No good ever came from listening at closed doors,' my mum always said. 'If you were meant to hear what was being said about you behind your back then the door wouldn't be closed in the first place, would it?'

My mum is a living, breathing encyclopaedia of pointless sayings. An idiom for every occasion.

But sometimes she's wrong. Sometimes you can never really know a person until you hear the way they speak about you when they assume you can't hear. Sometimes the lure of an insight into what someone really thinks about you is too much. It's irresistible. Not that any of this started out with that intention. I thought that I was doing a good thing. I wanted to help, to support my friend.

That was my first mistake.

Part 1

Chapter 1

Three weeks earlier

'All I want is something that's mine. I mean, is that too much to ask?' Lydia dabs at the underneath of her eyes with the heel of her hand. We're drinking in the Princess Louise, near her Holborn office, crammed in with the after-work crowd, valiantly clinging on to the corner of a table that is slowly being taken over by twenty-somethings intent on getting noisily wasted. Every now and then one of them gives us a hungry stare, willing us to leave so they can achieve total table domination, but scared to actually say anything because one of the middle-aged ladies seems to be crying into her Pinot Noir. Lydia flaps her hands at her face like a primitive air dryer. She's always telling me off for rubbing my eyes. 'You'll give yourself wrinkles,' she says, as if they're a disease that can be avoided with a little self-restraint.

Lydia is my longest-standing friend. My surrogate sister. We have an unbreakable partnership that began more than twenty years ago when we were art students together, a stone's throw from here. Both studying illustration. A double act from the moment we first met, although I'd never understood why she even noticed me among our cool, confident contemporaries.

We'd both chosen the sensible art path. One that could actually lead to a career. Later Lydia had landed on a steady road upwards at a small publisher producing educational books. Not doing the illustrations but commissioning and overseeing those who did. I had played the role of starving artist in a garret to perfection for a few years before somehow lucking out when the animations I sometimes placed on Twitter, featuring a wallaby with a penchant for filling up his pouch with random shopping, caught the eye of an editor whose kid loved it. There have now been six books featuring Wilbur. They make no sense. Wilbur is clearly a boy, but he has a pouch. He spends most of his time at the shops. He apparently has an endless supply of money. None of this seems to matter in the children's publishing world. Cats become mayors. Dogs work in offices. It's a world we'd all love to live in, let's be honest. They've all sold well. I'm by no means rich but I'm doing OK. More than OK. And I'm managing to make what I love my full-time job. I know that's enviable. My problems are firmly in the First World.

I just have terrible imposter's guilt.

They're the most simplistic drawings I've ever done. No real skill necessary. Wilbur is a few strokes of the pen – as are his friends Walter the wombat and Olga the opossum – no perspective, no elaborate backdrops. There are very few words. And those that there are are mostly lists of goods he's decided to purchase, but in rhyming form. I have basically turned my weekly shop into a living, with added marsupials. I am better than this. I have talent. More to the point, other people – Lydia included – have way more talent than me. But apparently no one has noticed.

I've just signed a contract for books seven and eight. Life is good.

Lydia, on the other hand, hates her job. She loathes the relentless routine. The lack of any creativity. 'When you've seen one illustration of the ventricles of the heart you've seen them all,' she said to me once. Her company produces a lot of medical textbooks. She hates having to get up in the mornings, having to get on the tube, having to eat a sandwich lunch at her desk to avoid the small talk of her colleagues. She hates not getting home till quarter to seven on a good day, knowing she has to do it all again tomorrow. Whenever I moan about the fact that I think I'm selling myself short – which I try not to do too often – she tells me she'd kill to be in my position.

She's recently opened an Etsy shop. A sideline to try to keep her sanity rather than a money-making scheme. She wants to be able to show she's more than just someone who works in an office showcasing other people's talent. Her speciality is line drawings in ink. Scratchy, darkly beautiful depictions of faeries and trolls. Nothing cutesy. They're gnarly and more than a little evil-looking. Underworld spirits. Beneath her polished exterior Lydia hides murky waters. Deeper than you'd think on first glance. It's one of the things about her that I love. She's created a whole world of intricate detail: family trees, relationships, maps of her creatures' homes in the forest. They deserve a book of their own. Instead, they are printed to order on T-shirts and greetings cards. Hours of artistic endeavour embossed on a tea towel: £7.95 plus postage and packing.

The Etsy shop was my idea. I thought it might get Lyd's work noticed. At least get her some kind feedback. What it

7

has actually got her is nothing. So far she hasn't sold a single item. I set her up with a Twitter account so that she could promote it – she's Instagram through and through, but she doesn't think it fits with her 'brand' to be trying to flog stuff on there. I have no idea what that means. 'How are you a brand if you're *not* flogging stuff?' I'd asked her. But she told me in all seriousness that you need to stay on message. 'It's not real life,' she said. 'It's a fantasy you're selling.' I restrained myself from reminding her that she wasn't actually selling anything, that was the point – but so far she only has seven followers, and that includes me and my eighteen-year-old twins Edie and Joe, both of whom think Twitter is lame and never look at it. I thought about placing an order but she gave me a stern lecture about not patronizing her, so I didn't dare. It hurt me to see how disappointed she was, though. I don't think she thought she was suddenly going to be Tracey Emin, but she did hope she might get a bit of affirmation. Nothing.

'It'll get better. These things just take a while. Word of mouth and all that . . .' To be fair I don't really know what to say. I have no idea how to help.

Lydia sniffs. 'Word of mouth between who? You and Joe?'

She's got a point. 'What about the other four?' I say, referring to those of her followers who aren't basically family.

'My yoga teacher, Kira who does my nails, my hairdresser and my auntie Susan's dog walker.'

'Dog walkers need greetings cards too,' I say, in an effort to be funny. Lydia just rolls her eyes.

'It was a stupid idea. I don't know why I thought it would work.'

I hate it when she gets like this. She has a tendency to put herself down. Be defeatist. It's as if all the fight has been knocked out of her over the years. I know she compares herself to me – dream career, happy marriage, kids – and I know it hurts. Not that she would ever want me not to have any of those things, or that she even wants the same – well, apart from the career – but she wants her own version of fulfilment. And I want that for her too.

Which is why I've just had what might turn out to be the worst idea of my life.

Chapter 2

Meet Patricia.

Patricia has just followed Lydia on Twitter.

Told her that her art was exceptional.

Ohhed and aahed over every piece she's ever posted.

Said she was dying to place an order, she just had to wait for payday.

Lydia has responded with happy emojis. Hearts.

Told me happily – and only half jokingly – how she has a fan.

The only problem being that Patricia is me.

I created her on a slightly drunken whim, three pub-sized glasses of Merlot down. After we left the Princess Louise – out into the freezing early-January night, misty rain clinging to our faces, coating our clothes, forlorn Christmas decorations still dangling limply from the trees – we said goodbye at the corner of High Holborn and went our separate ways, she to Hammersmith, me north to the leafy gentility of Primrose Hill. The house that Wilbur built. Or bought.

I fretted about Lydia's mood. I watched as she headed down into the tube, belting her chic raincoat tightly around her already too tiny waist, her shoulders slumped. I hated seeing her so down. If I'm being honest, not just because

I felt bad for her but also because I no longer felt I could celebrate my own success when I was with her. I would hesitate before I told her any work-related good news, play it down, try not to show the excitement I was feeling that there was talk of Wilbur becoming a TV animation or that the Japanese translations were apparently flying off the shelves in Tokyo. I couldn't be honest with my best friend. So how did I handle it? By creating a whole other layer of deception.

Here's what I decided about Patricia. I knew I had to get her story straight in my head if this was to work. She's a couple of years older than Lydia and me. Forty-seven to our forty-five. She works in retail. Divorced. No kids because her husband never wanted them and she cared more about making him happy than being a mum – he now has three under six with his inappropriately young wife, aka his former assistant. Lives in Buckinghamshire. Two cats. Not that I was probably ever going to share any of this information with Lydia, but I'd watched enough episodes of *Catfish* with Edie to know how important it is to keep track of any info you let slip. Consistency leads to believability. And one thing I was sure of, if I was actually going to do this, was that I would never want Lydia to find out it was me. It was a crime of compassion, but one she would find it hard to forgive.

I scrolled through my phone and picked out a generic photo of a pair of kittens, one ginger and one black and white, as Patricia's profile pic. A blood-orange sunset as her header. Kept her bio short. *Love animals, art and reading.* Added a quirky detail – *Wycombe Wanderers. Come on the Blues!!* – for authenticity, spent way too long wondering whether I really believed Patricia would be a rabid football fan – and then deciding that was the point. It was so unlikely, why would anyone have made it up? – and hit the button to create the account just as Nick arrived home from his evening playing squash followed by a couple of pints with his best mate Dom. We're not the kind of couple who socialize separately all the time. Our lives are completely blended, our friends shared; we're happy in each other's company. But Nick sometimes has to work in the evenings and every week or so he likes to play squash, something at which I am entirely useless, not to mention a somewhat dangerous liability, and so I usually meet up with Lyds either at one of our homes or in a bar or restaurant.

I didn't tell him what I was doing when he walked through the door. I don't know why. Maybe because I thought he'd tell me it was a bad idea (it is). Despite my wholly good intentions it still felt like an underhand thing to do. Sneaky. Or maybe it was just because I still wasn't sure myself whether I'd go through with it. It felt like a good plan to sleep on it. Reassess when I was 100 per cent sober.

'Good game?'

He leaned down and kissed the top of my head, stubble grazing my brow. Nick always has perfect three-day stubble. I have no idea how he achieves it. I haven't seen his face fully shaven for about eight years. Every now and then he threatens to scrape it all off, buffing up his skin to shiny-apple consistency just to see my horrified reaction. He knows how much I love his artfully dishevelled look.

'One set all.' He smelt of shower gel. The Body Shop grapefruit he keeps in his squash bag. He unloaded a wet towel and sweaty clothes, wandering through to the utility room to deposit them on the laundry pile.

'Did you eat?' I shouted after him. 'We didn't. There's a pizza in the fridge I could heat up.'

'And that . . .' he said as he came back in and reached over to the rustic wire rack for a bottle of wine, '. . . is why I love you. How was Lyds?'

'Fed up,' I said, rooting around in the cupboard for glasses. Our basement kitchen is that old cliché: the hub of the house. The place where the kids did their homework while Nick or I cooked (Nick usually, if I'm being honest), or sat with their friends round the big rough wooden table. It backs on to our tiny garden, patio doors allowing the afternoon sun to stream in in the summer months. I love it. It still blows my mind that I live here.

'Still?' Nick is by nature a kind soul, but he doesn't really get Lydia's frustration. He's sympathetic but not empathetic. He has a good job – working in events for a downmarket but hugely successful holiday company – but he doesn't need it to define him. He needs it to pay enough with hours that are not crippling and a commute that doesn't kill him. He needs it as a foundation on which to build the life he wants. He could be doing anything that fulfilled those criteria; he doesn't really care what. I used to find this frustrating – not because I thought he needed to do better, but because I couldn't understand it. How could you be happy not having a passion? A drive? Now I find it enviable. Nick is as chilled, as content as he is precisely because his job starts and ends during work hours. The minute he puts his coat on to come home it's forgotten until the next day. His life is his own.

'I get it,' I said. 'I just wish I could help her somehow.'

He reached round me from behind to pour the wine and I leaned back into the comforting solidity of him. I know how lucky I am.

When I woke up early next morning, before it was light, the first thing that popped into my head was Patricia. I was both relieved that I hadn't sent a series of tipsy tweets to Lydia before bed, and excited that I had a plan to cheer her up. Usually once Nick has left for the office I potter around 'working from home'. The truth is that each Wilbur first draft takes me only a matter of days to produce. What rhymes with aubergine, or is it irresponsible to have him carry a hot takeaway coffee in his pouch being the most challenging questions I face generally. That day I sat and tried to bring Patricia to life. I decided that she would follow a variety of arts and crafts people, some authors and a few well-chosen celebrities, some funny cat accounts and a couple of news feeds. A newspaper local to her supposed home town in Buckinghamshire. The interests of a nice woman. Bland and unthreatening. I composed a couple of anodyne tweets – her message to Lydia mustn't be the first she'd written. Too suspicious. So she posted a cute picture of some cats, retweeted a funny dog video, admired the work of an artisan bag maker. That last one elicited a like. I whooped for joy.

Buoyed up, I had her send a few more compliments to small-time artsy enterprises. When I returned from a break to make a cup of tea and hunt out a biscuit, one of them had followed her back. I exploded with pride like a mother on sports day. Patricia had a follower! She existed! It was that easy. I decided that she couldn't contact Lydia until she had at least ten. Otherwise she'd just look like a desperate saddo. Patty no mates. Was she a Patty? I wondered. No. Nor a Pat. She was a Patricia through and through. Dignified.

I built her up over a few days and then, when she'd flattered her way into follower number ten's orbit, relentlessly following anything that moved in the process, I made my play. Lydia had posted a photo of a section of one of her drawings – a map of an area of the forest inhabited by gnomish creatures who live in the hollows of trees. Layers of twisted flora. Sinewy fauna. There were annotations about the habits and behaviour of her characters. It was blackly cartoonish in the best way. Black and white. I've seen the original and it's gorgeous. Dark. Disturbing almost. Different every time you look because of the layers of detail. Patricia gushed.

Omg that is gorgeous. I've just looked at your Etsy store and I want everything. No exclamation marks. I didn't think Patricia was an exclamation mark kind of woman. Unlike Lydia, whose motto is why use one when you could use three.

How could Lydia not bite? I waited, pacing around the kitchen half-heartedly wiping down surfaces, checking my phone every few seconds, until I remembered that Lydia was so disheartened by the lack of response to her virtual offerings that she almost never logged on. I forced myself up to my little office on the first floor. Anyone else would call it the spare bedroom – it's still the room guests stay in when they visit – but it has a desk and a floor-to-ceiling bookshelf with copies of all the Wilbur foreign editions. Nineteen different languages and counting. When we have guests I have a tendency to pile other books in front of them so as not to feel as if I'm showing off; I don't want to look like one of those Hollywood stars who bashfully admit they keep their Oscars in the downstairs loo, as if none of us are going to realize that that's the most likely place their guests will get a good look at them. I occupied myself with admin. There was talk of a toy company making plushy Wilburs with a line in consumables that would fit into his pouch, a query about a visit to a primary school to talk to the Reception-aged kids, a couple of bits of fan mail to be answered. I managed to occupy myself until lunchtime without looking at Twitter. When I picked up my mobile the first thing I saw was that I had a text from Lydia.

I've got a fan haha!!

I clicked on the message, knowing what I'd see, and there was a screen grab of Patricia's tweet. Lydia had added smiley emojis with heart eyes.

See, I texted back. *I told you!*

Not that she's bought anything! Lydia replied.

Van Gogh never sold a single painting in his lifetime, I sent, knowing it would make her laugh.

I looked at Twitter and saw that Lydia had responded to Patricia's compliment. *Thank you so much! I do commissions too!*

I waited a decent amount of time until I decided Patricia might be on her lunch break and then I responded. *I'll have to wait for payday but then I'm definitely ordering something.* Then I hit follow. I didn't even think I'd really have to do anything else. Throw Lydia the odd new compliment every time she posted a picture. Hint at a purchase in the future. It was hardly going to change Lydia's life but I felt happy knowing it had made her day.

If only things had stayed that simple.

Chapter 3

They do for a while. Patricia gushes. Lydia basks in her compliments. She gains a few more followers because Patricia raves about her work to anyone who'll listen. Someone orders a card featuring an evil-looking elf. It's Lydia's first order. A whole £3.41. But it's validation. Someone likes her art enough to buy it.

'Do you think that means I can finally call myself a professional artist?' she laughs, sipping tea in my kitchen. Lydia is a sipper. I am more of a gulper. This, I feel, is an appropriate metaphor for our lives. Did you ever see those memes that went round of a cat delicately picking its way through a series of obstacles without knocking a single one over and then a dog steaming through and scattering the lot? That's Lydia and me. It's not just that she's more slightly built than me – five foot two, tiny-boned, a pale angular face with high cheekbones, huge, shockingly blue eyes (made all the huger by the fact she is bordering on too thin at the moment and her love for Charlotte Tilbury eyeliner), dark, almost black hair. Whereas I am more robust, much taller. Also blue-eyed and pale-skinned, although not as blue or as pale. Also dark-haired, although not as dark. The budget version; the one that's been through the wash a few times. If you had to pick an adjective to describe each of us, I'd probably get 'strapping' or, on a good day, 'sporty', whereas she'd get something far more interesting like 'waif-like' or 'gamine'. She's more cautious, careful. She takes her time and gets things right. She's meticulous in everything she does. She loves working through a magnifying glass, scratching tiny particulars into her drawings that probably no one will ever even notice. It's why her work takes so long but is so satisfying to look at. You'll always find something you missed the first time. I scrawl a dozy-looking marsupial in twelve strokes of the pen and I'm the one who ends up with all the attention. I can see why it stings.

'Definitely. You'll need to file a tax return.'

She gives me a grin. 'I might have to move to the Isle of Man.'

It takes me a moment to get what she means. 'I think there are nicer tax havens. Less rainy.'

She knocks back the last of her tea. 'I have to go. I have a date tonight.'

'What? Wait. Who—'

She shrugs. 'Just some bloke I met through work. He got us tickets for *Hamilton*. He seems like a nice guy but I'm not really interested . . .'

Lydia has been single forever. She has left a field hospital of broken men in her wake. I've never known anyone have so many suitors. So many proposals of marriage, come to that (I have had precisely one in my whole life. Nick, on one knee in the park with a hastily plucked half-dead daffodil between his teeth and me laughing uncontrollably at the ridiculousness of it). She's just not that bothered, not unless the perfect man suddenly comes along. 'Anything less is doing myself a disservice. I deserve better,' she said to me once when I queried why she'd walked away from another budding relationship. 'I'm fine on my own.' And I believe she really is. I've always envied how self-contained she is.

'Still, *Hamilton* though . . .'

'Exactly,' she says, shrugging her arms into her cardigan. I would rather be doing literally anything other than going out. It's dark already at four o'clock. Grey, with sludgy half-snow. Damp frozen drizzle in the air. I have wine and Netflix and a log burner. Nick is at Morrisons right now, filling the boot with bags of chopped wood. In an ideal world I think he pictures himself in the forest, axe in hand, not pushing a trolley filled with the other haphazard items I shouted at him as he left: Quorn mince! Toothpaste! Miso paste! Lemons! A leek! It's like that game where you keep adding random products and the other person has to remember them all in order. 'Fizzy water!' I yelled as the front door shut. I have no idea whether he heard me.

'Have fun,' I say, giving her a hug. 'Let him down gently.'

'I already have,' she says, hugging me back.

That's the thing. Lydia's not a user, luring unsuspecting hopefuls into her net just to fleece them for their *Hamilton* tickets. She's always upfront. Honest. She tells them in advance that this is it, a companionable visit to the theatre or an art gallery or a restaurant. Just friends. Nothing else. But still half of them end up lovestruck and wounded. Retreating, confused, to nurse their injuries.

While I wait for Nick to get back, I call Joe. When the twins were babies Nick and I used to have a running joke about how we couldn't tell them apart. 'Which one is that?' I'd say when he appeared with a freshly woken infant on his hip. 'The needy one,' he'd say. 'The one who takes after you.' Or he'd come in when I was feeding them both at the same time and do an exaggerated double take. 'There are two of them? I thought we just had one who ate a lot.' The truth is they have always been different: not just in the obvious way that they're a boy and a girl, but their temperaments are polar opposite. Edie breezes through life with an enviable confidence that she must have inherited from some ancient ancestor neither of us remembers. She has a wide circle of friends, both at home and at uni in Bath. She fits in effortlessly wherever she goes. Her life is full of colour: pink hair, blue nail varnish, violet lipstick. She can go days without calling and it never worries me. It just means she's off having a good time somewhere. Joe is far less self-assured. His twin has always been his security blanket – someone he could hide behind at parties – and it took him longer to settle into life in Brighton. There was a moment a few weeks ago when I worried he wasn't even going to go back for his second term, but then he sat us down on Christmas Eve – Edie was at the pub with her school friends – and told us he had something to say to us: that he was gay. I think our underwhelmed reaction must have confused him; afterwards Nick said to me, 'We've known for years, haven't we?' and I'd felt terrible that yes, we had, but maybe we'd never communicated that adequately to Joe. It had seemed like one of those things we all just knew and no one batted an eyelid about, but clearly our son hadn't picked up on our vibes. 'Does that make us awful parents?' I'd said. 'Should we have talked to him about it before?'

'God, no,' Nick said. 'He'd have been horrified if we'd brought it up, wouldn't he?'

'That's what I always thought. I mean, I just thought he knew we knew . . .'

They really should hand you a set of rules when you have a child.

Anyway, long story short, Joe went back to uni last weekend a much more confident, easy version of himself and is currently having a blast. But he's still the one I worry about the most. Still the one who never likes to go too long without checking in.

He answers on the second ring. 'Ma!' he says in an exaggerated *EastEnders* accent, one the four of us used to use to make each other laugh when the kids were younger.

I settle back on the sofa. 'All right, son?' I say in a voice so gruff I make myself cough.

Later, once Nick and I are slouched in front of the TV for the evening, glasses of wine on the go, one episode of *Ozark* down, I half-heartedly check Twitter. I haven't even looked at it since yesterday. Now that Lydia is a bit happier and she has a few genuine followers who like her work – even if most of them seem to be other artists also looking for validation rather than potential customers – my job is pretty much done. It's then that I see the DM. The private message Lyds has sent to Patricia. I know I shouldn't open it. I know that Patricia should just recede into the background now and let Lydia's community grow organically, however slowly, but I'm torn. Will she be slighted if Patricia ignores her? Suspicious even? It can't hurt to at least see what it says.

Apologies for the DM! I just wanted to say how much I appreciate you supporting my work. I was about to give up when I got your first message!

I decide that a short acknowledgement is all that's needed. Patricia would politely respond, but I don't have to open up a whole dialogue.

Gosh

I have no idea where that came from. I have never said gosh in my life. Patricia, though, is definitely a woman of the gosh, darn, fudge variety. Nicely brought up.

Gosh, not at all. I meant it when I said your work was wonderful. Never give up.

Send.

And then I turn back to my husband, the TV and the wine, and forget all about it. Oblivious to what I have set in motion.

Chapter 4

Like most couples Nick and I have couple friends and, like most couples, in most cases we infinitely prefer one half of those duos to the other. His brother Phil and his 'I'm so quirky!' wife Lianne, my school-gate buddy Kim and her 'I think you'll find you should do it like this' husband Dean, our neighbour Mart and his 'Have you seen my new bag, it's Louis Vuitton. Three thousand pounds' partner Alana. When we got friendly with our then-neighbours Harry and Anne Marie about ten years ago, and realized we both liked both of them equally, we clung on for dear life, so precious a commodity were they, so rare. Thankfully they seem to feel the same way – we have all told each other this at the end of drunken evenings in the throes of a soppy group hug – and so we spend at least one evening together most weeks. At ours, at theirs or – when we can be bothered – at a restaurant. Anne Marie has become one of my closest buddies, my default choice for a quick coffee or a walk in the park. We still live within five minutes of each other and her flat is almost as familiar to me as my own house. She's one of the most straightforward, straight-up people I know. She's the living definition of 'what you see is what you get'.

Tonight it's our turn to host. By turn I mean they walk over to us rather than the other way round. And by host I mean there is no other effort involved on anyone's part beyond calling out for Deliveroo and making sure there's wine in the fridge. We've long since got beyond the need to impress each other with cooking.

By seven the living room has had the quickest of once-overs, there are plates stacked in the kitchen and I've had a shower before dressing in something that closely resembles pyjamas but can officially get away with being described as yoga wear if pushed. Not that I think either Harry or Anne Marie would care if I was in a nightie and slippers so long as there was takeout and alcohol.

We flop on the sofas – automatically gravitating to the same seats, that's how long we've been friends. Nick and I sit in our usual places, Anne Marie opposite me and Harry opposite Nick. We all know it's ridiculous but we feel somehow powerless to change it. One evening, feeling rebellious, I flopped into Harry's spot and it almost caused a collective meltdown. So now we just accept it. We're all in a rut but we're in it together and it makes us happy.

Tonight, because it's icy outside, we have the fire lit and orange-scented candles lining the mantelpiece. Our living room is all throws and cushions, the epitome of *hygge*. Comfort. Home. I think – not for the first time – how incredibly lucky I am to live here. Our house isn't grand, don't get me wrong. When the twins were still at home it felt as if we were all tripping over each other. In fact, we didn't just feel it, we actually were, once they sprouted both their father's and my long limbs seemingly overnight. It was always a given that Nick and I would sire giraffes. I used to lie awake at night worrying that they would be subjected to the same name-calling at school that I had been, thanks to my height, but the fact that there were two of them, and that they were easy in their own skins, thankfully meant they were spared that particular horror. Or maybe kids just pick on different things these days. The house is a terrace, but not one of those grand mansion-sized ones they specialize in round here. Three bedrooms. Kitchen in the basement. Tiny office. Tiny garden. But it's in one of London's prettiest areas. I never would have thought we'd be able to afford to buy a place anywhere near here when we were renting round the corner, pre Wilbur. Harry and Anne Marie still live in the flat a couple of doors down from the one that used to be ours. If they're envious they've never let it show. They're that rare breed: friends who are genuinely happy when things go well for you.

'How's work?' This to Anne Marie. She pulls a face.

'Same.' Anne Marie loves what she does but hates her job. She's a music teacher in a school where the majority of the staff and parents consider music a complete waste of time and money. The school my twins attended for five years. She seems to spend most of her time battling budget cuts and the threat of her role being axed altogether. 'You?'

'Wilbur bought a hammer,' I say, rolling my eyes. 'I'm thinking about revealing he's a serial killer in book seven.' Nick always tells me off for downplaying my success to our friends. Or not so much downplaying it as avoiding talking about it if I can.

'It's not as if you were handed anything on a plate. You should be proud of it,' he said once after I'd failed to mention the fact that one of my books had finally found an American publisher when Anne Marie asked me how things were going shortly after. The advance was quite hefty and pretty much all I'd had to do for it was change the word courgette to zucchini. And then think of something to rhyme with it, obviously, so suddenly Wilbur was sporting a rather risqué bikini. I have an all-expenses-paid trip coming up to promote it when it comes out in the summer, by the way. Not as glamorous as it sounds. No five-star hotels and dinners in my honour. A short book tour of strategic cities, staying in motels and appearing in shops to an audience of probably five kids and their parents in each, if I'm lucky. A long train ride in between. If I'm honest I'm beside myself with excitement, something that I've shared with Anne Marie although not with Lydia. With Lydia I've played it down ('It'll be miserable, just me and some PR person I don't even know in a grotty motel. No one will turn up . . .'). All of this is probably true but I couldn't care less. It's a dream. An adventure of a lifetime. I can't wait.

'I am,' I'd said. 'Of course I am. But I'm hardly going to drone on about how brilliantly my career is going while she's struggling to keep her incredibly pressurized and underpaid job.'

'It's not just with them. You do it all the time.'

I'd shrugged, not wanting a row. We were clearing up after an evening at ours. Stacking plates and glasses into the dishwasher. 'What can I say? I'm saintly in my modesty.'

Nick wasn't having it. 'I'm just saying don't sell yourself short. I'm proud of you. You should be proud of yourself.'

'I am,' I said, looping my arms round his waist from behind and resting my forehead on his broad back. 'It's just . . . you know . . .'

He turned round and enveloped me in a hug. 'And, I mean, if you ever get bored of drawing Wilbur, Anne Marie could probably ask some of the year sevens . . .'

I shoved him away, laughing. 'I'm going to pretend I didn't hear that.'

'Is he going to do DIY?' Anne Marie asks now.

'God knows. I'm running out of . . .' I stop as my phone starts to buzz. Pick it up. 'It's Lyds. I'll just tell her I'll call her tomorrow.' I walk into the hall as I answer to get away from the chatter.

'Hey.'

'Evening. Oh . . . have you got people round?' She must be able to hear them in the background. Harry is doing an impression of his boss who has a voice like a foghorn, making even the most trivial things sound vitally important. 'HAS ANYONE SEEN MY FUCKING COFFEE MUG?' I can hear him booming.

'Harry and Anne Marie. I've got a minute though. You OK?'

'Totally. I just phoned for a catch-up. Shall I ring you tomorrow?'

'Lovely. I'll be here. No date tonight?'

I can hear the smile in her voice. 'Just a drink with Tom from work. I'm on my way.'

'Have fun,' I say as the doorbell rings to announce the curry has arrived.

Once they've left – Nick and I waving them off from the doorstep, laughing as Harry slipped on a patch of ice and had to grab Anne Marie's arm to steady himself, nearly pulling her over in the process – and we've done a bit of cursory clearing-up, we slump back in the living room, both too tired to make it to bed. I scroll lazily through my phone. Check my Twitter and answer a few Wilbur compliments. He's a big deal with the three-to-fives and their mums and dads. I check Patricia's almost out of habit. Notice that she has another private message. Lydia of course. It's a continuation of the conversation from the other day.

The thing is that I hate my job and doing this on the side reminds me of who I really am. Especially when I get lovely responses like yours. Does that sound sad? It does, doesn't it?

She's added a laughing emoji to show she's joking but I feel a tug on my heartstrings because I know that actually she isn't. There's a second message underneath.

What do you do, Patricia?

I'm a bit pissed. I know I shouldn't engage in this conversation. Sober I'm sure I'd think twice. But in the happy afterglow of an evening with friends, I think what the hell? Lydia's second message was only minutes ago. She's obviously still up.

I work in a shop. Boring, I know. A haberdashery. But we do classes and tutorials so it's not just selling.

I can picture Patricia pottering around a dark-wood-lined store, measuring out fabric and cutting ribbon. Do haberdasheries still even exist? I'm not sure I've seen one in years. But I know it's not a field Lydia is remotely interested in so hopefully she won't ask any awkward questions. Her reply is almost immediate.

Sounds lovely! So does that mean you're a whizz with a sewing machine?

28

God, she really must be bored. I wonder if she really was having drinks with someone from work or if she just told me that to make me feel better for not having invited her over, and instead she's had an evening home alone. She's only met Anne Marie and Harry a couple of times and, although she'd protested that she liked them, I'd felt there was a snippiness on her part that pervaded the whole dynamic. She's never liked hanging out with couples – Nick and me aside, of course; I think because she was there for the early stages of our relationship, we didn't come as a pair – she always feels as if she's being judged for her singleness, she says, and she has a tendency to get defensive and start seeing smugness and pity where there is none. She's a virtuoso in micro-aggressions. Tiny digs said with an innocent smile on her face. It's a trait that's always made me uncomfortable, if I'm being honest, but I know she only resorts to it when she's feeling under siege. On the back foot. In the end, though, I decided we would all have much more fun if we met up separately, but I still sometimes feel bad for excluding her.

I went to fashion college. Ooh, Patricia, you old dog you. You have hidden depths. *A lifetime ago, obviously.*

Amazing!! So do you teach the classes?

Why not? *Some of them. There are two of us. Me and Dinah the owner.*

Omg I love that. Do you make your own clothes too?

'Who are you chatting to?' I jump. I'd completely forgotten Nick was even in the room.

'Oh. Lydia,' I say, sticking as close to the truth as I dare.

'She's up late.' He yawns. 'I'm going to bed. I told you three times already but you were completely absorbed.'

'I'm coming.'

Occasionally. I don't think I'll be appearing on Sewing Bee anytime soon though. What about you?

Well, I'm currently in an Uber that's being driven by an absolute psycho!! If you don't hear from me ever again he's got me in his basement!!

I have to resist the urge to phone her and ask if she's OK. Patricia would be concerned too, though.

Oh goodness. Are you all right?

Just about!! In the daytime I work for a publisher commissioning artists. It's soul-destroying.

One day that will be you! I have faith.

'Do you think Lyds gets lonely?' I say to Nick through a mouthful of toothpaste.

'Where's that come from?'

I wipe my mouth on a towel. 'I don't know. Just a feeling.'

'She has loads of friends, doesn't she? She always seems to be out.'

Lydia leads an Insta-perfect life. Carefully curated. No sticking up a drunken, out-of-focus selfie for her. Every image is cropped and filtered. Perfectly framed. Her make-up is always impeccable, her outfits agonized over. Showing a glamorous, fulfilled existence. All friends and cocktails and art and perfection. I take the piss out of her for it sometimes. 'What? This old thing? I just threw it on,' I said in my best impersonation of her smooth Home Counties vowels when she showed me one photo of her lounging on her sofa in a cocktail dress and spiky heels. She had taken it on a timer, she told me. She'd rewarded me with a smile. 'Oh, you took me by surprise. I've just got out of bed,' I deadpanned in response to another picture, this time with artfully messy hair that I knew had taken her hours to perfect. 'Stop,' she'd said, laughing. 'Don't.'

'Who are they for?' I'd asked her. Not meanly, I was genuinely curious. 'What's the point?'

'Everyone does it,' she'd said as if that was a good reason.

'Well, if everyone does it then that makes it even more pointless. Because they all know everyone else's lives are being staged same as theirs.'

'You just don't get it,' she'd said and I'd agreed. I really didn't. Nick, on the other hand, seems to have been taken in by it all.

I clatter my toothbrush back into the holder. 'She doesn't have this though.'

He raises a sardonic eyebrow and I know I'm not going to get a serious answer. 'Fighting over who gets to spit in the sink first?'

I roll my eyes. 'You know what I mean. The mundane stuff. The stuff that doesn't take any effort. She has a lot of people she can go to the theatre with or the cinema or whatever, but they're not people she can really just relax with. Say anything to.'

He takes the towel from me. Folds it over the radiator. 'That's what you're for, isn't it?'

'I suppose. But it's not the same. Not really.'

'She's fine,' he says, heading to the bedroom. 'She likes being on her own, that's what she always says.'

'Maybe,' I say, but suddenly I'm not so sure.

Chapter 5

When Lydia and I were in our third year of college her parents died. One minute she had a loving home. People who adored her unconditionally. We were both only children and had bonded over the pressure – but also the privilege – of being the sole focus of your family's hopes and dreams. And the next she had no one. An absentee aunt. It was the single most shocking thing either of us had ever experienced. Probably ever would in her case.

They were alive – she had spoken to them both the night before, queuing for the payphone in halls for forty-five minutes as a girl from our floor snivelled accusations at her wayward boyfriend. They were on their way out, she'd told me. Off to see a play at their local rep theatre. Like Lydia, they were culture vultures. They loved nothing more than a show or an exhibition. An excuse to dress up and have fun.

And then they were not.

Lydia and I were hanging out in her room – a condition we had made for ourselves when we'd applied to go back into college accommodation in our final year was that we got into the same hall. We had lived together for a year at that point and we had no desire to be separated. In fact we'd ended up on the same corridor. Two rooms separating us. She was pasting henna on to my hair, laughing as the thick brown clumps slipped on to the oatmeal carpet. The air was filled with the cloying smell. I still can't stand it to this day.

I remember so clearly that we were crying with laughter about something that had happened that morning – her with a hand on my shoulder – when there was a knock at the door. She was still smiling when she opened it.

They had lost control of the car on the way home from the theatre, the sympathetic policewoman told her. There were two of them, a young woman and an avuncular older man, and the warden of the halls standing behind them ashen-faced. They had taken a bend in the road too quickly – her father at the wheel – and maybe had to swerve to avoid a fox or a rabbit. There were no witnesses, of course – the country lanes were deserted – but the tyre marks suggested a sudden change of course, a loss of control. Straight into the path of a tree.

They had been found by another driver, how much later no one knew. They were both dead before an ambulance even arrived. There was an implication in there that I tried to block from my mind, that I desperately hoped Lydia hadn't picked up on, that they were still alive when that random stranger came along. That if the road had been busier, they might have been found in time.

I remember the utter disbelief. Lydia saying that of course her father would have tried to avoid hitting an animal. He loved animals. The cliché of the policeman making us both a cup of too-sweet tea. If it felt unreal to me, impossible to grasp, I couldn't even imagine how it was for her.

The officers asked her if she had anyone she could stay with. Any family they could call.

'I'll stay here with Georgia,' she had said, clinging on to my hand.

I'd helped her organize their funeral. Liaising with her devastated aunt Susan, who had flown over from her home in Florida. I'd travelled down with Lydia the night before, stood by her side on the day as their seemingly endless friends and acquaintances paid their respects, and then Susan and I had gone into a frenzy of organization, clearing the house to get it ready to sell, parading a series of personal items in front of Lydia so she could decide what to keep. It felt callous. Disrespectful. But Susan was adamant. 'All she's set to inherit is their debts,' she'd whispered to me in the kitchen when we were alone. 'I loved my brother but they were terrible with money. We need to sell the house otherwise Lydia'll be saddled with it all before she's even had a chance to start earning money to pay them off.'

I'd been there before, of course. Twice during the previous summer holidays alone. My mum hadn't yet met Frank – my dad was long gone, moved up north and out of our lives. I saw him now and then but we weren't close – and she was still living in the tiny, boxy 1970s house that I had grown up in. Everything was new. By that I don't mean my mum spent lots of money on the most up to date and best of everything. She didn't have any money to spend. I mean that nothing had any history, any soul. The house had no features, no personality. All our furniture came from catalogues. I had tried to persuade her many times that she could get more beautiful – and potentially cheaper – items by checking out the second-hand shops, but she said she hated the idea of having other people's cast-offs, as she called them. She didn't see the beauty in the past. She wanted new, convenient, disposable. She wanted neat and clean. Lydia's home could not have been more different. It was like a treasure trove. Stuffed full with things her parents had collected; every surface held a trophy, a shared memory. It could have felt oppressive but what it actually felt like was home. I would potter around picking up a wooden sculpture, a glass bowl, an antique fan and asking where they came from while Lydia rolled her eyes. Her mum and dad loved having an audience to tell their stories to and I loved to listen. Their life had been full of colour. Of, well . . . life.

After a week we had travelled back up to London with the three boxes of personal mementos Lydia had opted to keep, and her childhood home – her only home – was on the market. Susan had gone back to the States, issuing an open invitation to buy Lydia a ticket whenever she needed one. From then on my mum had made it clear that whenever I visited, Lydia was welcome too. She had nowhere else. And so we became inseparable. Not just friends. Sisters.

Wilbur has been nominated for an award.

I'm going to say that again. Wilbur, my shopaholic wallaby creation, is on the shortlist for the 'Best Illustrated Book for Age Six and Under' category of the annual children's book awards of one of the biggest bookshop chains in the country.

I am speechless.

Blown away.

Overwhelmed.

And not a little embarrassed. I can only assume that only four picture books for the under sixes were published last year. That I made the list by default. Nothing like this has ever happened to me before. OK, so it's hardly the Booker and it probably won't even make the papers, but someone somewhere picked me, fought for me to make the list, considered me worthy. And there will be a do. At a posh venue. With free champagne and fancy outfits. At least I assume so. I doubt we'll all be in jeans sipping Evian. Authors don't get to go out much; we have to make the most of any occasion. I definitely won't win (I google the other nominees and the level of skill is mind-blowing) but I couldn't care less about that. I am a nominee and no one can ever take that away from me.

I reread the email from my agent just to make sure it's true.

I need to call Nick. It goes straight to voicemail and I don't leave a message because I want to hear the reaction in his voice when I tell him my news. There are only a handful of people in the world who I know will be as thrilled for me as I am. My mum won't be up yet and you could call her to tell her she'd won the lottery but she'd still be furious that you woke her. The kids definitely won't be awake; or, if they are, they'll be like the walking dead, unable to grasp what I'm saying. That leaves Lydia and Anne Marie. Lydia has been there for every significant moment of my adult life but something holds me back from phoning her. Because this isn't just my dream happening, it's hers too.

If I'm being honest, my friendship with Anne Marie has always been — what? Easier? Less competitive? — more straightforward, maybe, than mine with Lydia. We have different ambitions. We were on completely separate paths when we met. Lydia and I were always striving for the same thing and, when I achieved it and she didn't, it added a filter to our friendship that wasn't there before. I couldn't always be 100 per cent truthful for fear of hurting her feelings. I learned quickly to edit what I said before I said it.

With Anne Marie there's no second guessing, no need to tiptoe delicately round any subject. We truly want the best for each other, whatever that best may be. If that sounds disloyal to Lyds it's not meant to. I adore her. Apart from Nick, the twins and my mum she's the person I care about most in the world. She's family. But families can be complicated.

I send Lydia a text. I feel guilty that she's not going to be the first person I tell my news to, so I want to send her some love to make me feel better. *Did you get home OK in the end last night? I was worried about you and the crazy driver.* x

I get a reply a few minutes later. *Yes! All in one piece!!* xx

'Oh my fucking God!' Anne Marie squeals. 'Oops, hold on. That was in front of two year sevens. Let me just walk round the corner.' I check the time. It must be morning break. I can hear screaming and squealing. It sounds like the soundtrack of a horror film. 'I'm on playground duty,' she says. 'Right, where was I? Oh yes: OH MY FUCKING GOD! That is incredible.'

'It's not like a big prestigious thing. And I won't win . . .' I say hastily. I always do this, prepare myself for failure. You know that saying 'Fail to prepare and you prepare to fail'? Well, mine would be more like 'Prepare to fail because you're probably going to anyway.'

'You so do not know that,' she says. 'If I was judging it you definitely would.'

'Are you?' I say, laughing.

'Well, no, but let's not get bogged down in the details. When is it? Tell me everything.'

'Not for a few weeks. At a church in Mayfair. An ex-church, I mean. It's a venue now; I looked it up.' I think about asking her to help me find something to wear but I know that Lydia will want to do that once I can bring myself to break my news to her. She loves an excuse to go clothes shopping.

'We need to celebrate.'

'OK, don't get carried away.'

'My friend the award-winning author,' she says and I can hear how genuinely happy she is for me. 'It has a nice ring to it.'

'Award-nominated.'

'Who cares? It's still brilliant.'

I suppose I just feel unfulfilled. It's hard. My best friend is super success-ful. She writes and illustrates children's books. I'm really proud of her but sometimes it's hard not feeling a little bit envious. Do you know what I mean?

I snap to attention at the mention of me. Lydia and Patricia's conversations have become more in depth over the past few days. I should have anticipated this. Lydia loves to make new friends. She's the person who gets on a train in London and has swapped numbers with her seat mate by Birmingham. Who sits next to someone in a theatre and, by the time the curtain goes up, has arranged to have a drink with them in the interval. Maybe being on your own keeps you on your toes. You can't sink into the isolated complacency of a couple, safe in the knowledge you always have a plus-one on standby.

We've talked about music and books (Patricia is a big fan of Carole King and the Brontës. I thought I should stay on safe ground and stick with things I have at least a grass-roots knowledge of), family (Patricia's only sister lives in Canada. *Vancouver. I'm planning a trip there next year. I've been saving up my holidays*) and hobbies (Patricia is a big walker and crafter. I worry that I'm making her sound old before her time, so I throw jiu-jitsu in there: *I've been doing it since I was in my twenties. I'm a brown belt*. It's the anomalies that make her credible, I think, adding to my – ever-growing – notes). We've talked about Patricia's love of football (I struggled a bit here; I should have picked passions I'm more knowledgeable about) and the time she met David Cameron at a local function (*Ghastly entitled man. Thinks he's better than the rest of us*). Patricia is very definite about her likes and dislikes, unafraid in her opinions. I'm a little envious, I have to say. I'm inclined to edit myself before I speak so as not to offend. Patricia just breezes right on in there (*Jeremy Corbyn? Overgrown student. Strictly Come Dancing? Load of people strutting around like they've got rods up their backsides, or wiggling about like they've got nits! I don't get it*). I'm trying to only respond when Lydia asks a question or when it would look rude if I didn't, but she's always very keen to chat, and I can't say I'm not intrigued by the insights into my friend's state of mind.

Really? Who is she? I might have heard of her . . .

No. Delete. That'll make her feel even worse. (I finally told her about my nomination last night, on the phone: 'Oh, by the way, I got nominated for some little award, just a stupid thing and they obviously couldn't find enough eligible books to make up the numbers so anyway, yeah . . .'

There was the tiniest hesitation. A millisecond of silence. A pause that gave away how much this must sting. Then: 'George, that's amazing! How brilliant! Really. Wow.' Because of course she's pleased for me. She just had to bury her personal disappointment first. I understand. Totally.)

That must be tough. One of my friends from college became quite a successful designer for a while soon after we left. I remember having very mixed feelings. I was thrilled for him but it stung more than a little. It's natural.

Send.

That's exactly it! I couldn't be happier for Georgia but that doesn't mean I don't wish it was me it was happening to sometimes. Does that make me a bad friend?

Not at all. Wishing something good would happen for yourself doesn't mean you want to take it away from anyone else. Patricia is quite the philosopher. *I bet Georgia would love it if you were published too.*

Her response takes ages, as if she's thinking about what to say. *I don't know. Sometimes I think she would hate it. That our friendship works because she's super successful and I'm not.*

Wait. What? I have only ever wanted the best for Lyds. OK, so I admit there's a deeply buried fear in me – that I am most definitely not proud of – that if Lydia were published people would compare us (people who know us both anyway) and I would come up lacking. That behind my back they would all say she had been the real talent all along and my success was just luck. But I had absolutely no idea that Lydia had ever picked up on this. Ever. Before I can reply there's another message from Lydia.

I don't mean that! That sounds awful!! Forget I said it. God, Patricia, what must you think of me?

I'm devastated. Have I really made Lydia feel like this? That I would ever want anything but the best for her?

Gosh, don't worry, it's understandable. But from everything you've ever said about Georgia it sounds as if she's a good friend. I'm sure she would do anything to support you.

I know, you're right. I just feel like such a failure. I've been sending a book of my own out recently — you know, the characters from the cards — but getting rejection after rejection. I haven't even told Georgia that bit!

I've always known that Lydia must find what's happened to me quite tough, however much she protests otherwise. It's both odd and strangely fascinating to hear her talk about it so openly, though. And I'm not going to lie, it makes me feel seriously uncomfortable hearing something she doesn't want me to know. I understand why she doesn't want to confide in me – the *real* me. She would never want to rain on my parade. But I don't think I realized it was still so raw for her, that she was harbouring her own ambitions to be published even now. I mean, I know she hates her job, but did I really think she was holding out for her own publishing deal still? I don't know. Maybe I've been burying my head in the sand because that makes it easier for me to enjoy my own success. Once again my guilt racks up. My insecurities hovering at the edge of my consciousness. I'm sitting in my office, pretending to work (I often count hours spent in here as work just as I count hours spent wearing gym gear as exercise), surrounded by images of Wilbur on book covers, on a poster on the wall. It's his simplicity, my editor once told me, that makes him so appealing to pre-schoolers. I think she meant it as a compliment but I stewed on the comment for days.

I would love to see it one day. I actually did see her book a couple of years ago. She handed me a copy one night, saying she wanted some feedback, leaving it till the last minute when we were hugging each other goodbye in the street after an evening out before thrusting the large brown envelope into my hand and fleeing into the tube station. I'm sure it's changed since then if she's still working on it, but I remember thinking it was exceptional. Magical. I can't remember what I said to her about it. I know I would have been complimentary but did I encourage her enough? Did I realize how important it was to her?

Maybe I can help her. She obviously has connections in publishing of her own but I doubt she wants her employers to know she's trying to get her own deal on the side. I should show her work to my editor. I still have it somewhere. Lyds has skirted around the idea before that maybe I could, but my relationship with my editor is complicated to say the least so I've always deliberately failed to pick up on her hints. I feel terrible. I hadn't realized she was having such a rough time. I wish she felt she could confide in me about this stuff. Before I became successful we told each other everything. All our fears. Our ambitions. At least, I thought we did. Maybe it was always just me pouring out my heart. Maybe I was always so wrapped up in myself that I didn't notice her lack of openness.

One day, Lydia writes. I imagine for a second the two of us published side by side, celebrating together, before the old panic sets in. My career fading while hers goes stellar.

What do you think of her books? I press send before I can stop myself. Curse myself for being so stupid. I leave my phone on the desk and head down to the kitchen to make a coffee before I see her answer. No good can come of hearing what people say about you when they think you can't hear, remember, even your best friend. Actually, though, I know Lydia better than that. I know how generous she always is. I stir in some oat milk and wander back up, telling myself that that's the last time I ask a question like that. It's not fair. Patricia needs to stick to her remit – a cheerleader for Lydia's art – and nothing else. I can see there's a new message before I even pick the phone up.

They're great for little kids. They do really well.

That's it. Damned with faint praise. No 'I love them' or 'They're gorgeous'. This, I remind myself, is why I should leave well alone.

Is she a good illustrator?

What the fuck is wrong with me? I throw my mobile back down on the desk. I need to delete Patricia's account. I can make some excuse to Lydia about her giving up social media or pretend she's ill or something. I'll do it now. I'll just wait for Lydia's reply . . .

Fabulous, she says and I breathe a sigh of relief. I don't know what I was waiting for.

Nick is out for the evening. He's the Events Manager for a chain of leisure parks. Eleven sites from Dorset to Inverness boasting static caravans each with a large clubhouse hosting entertainment every evening during the holiday season, which runs from March to the New Year. Nick helps to organize tours that seem to comprise mostly of former *X Factor* finalists and *Britain's Got Talent* rejects as well as one-off

43

events and even smaller acts local to each venue. The guests expect something every night and don't seem to care much what. Nick works in the London headquarters – Diamond Leisure are raking in some serious cash and have offices in the new development behind King's Cross, chosen for its proximity to the Eurostar in readiness for their proposed expansion into Europe – and tonight is attending a team-building dinner. Every year they spend a lot of time in the off season discussing ways to improve the company's slightly tacky image and every year they end up back where they started and Nick's team are checking out Gareth Gates's availability the following day.

I'm in Manna with Lydia eating veggie bangers and mash and drinking a large glass of red wine. Lyds has just confessed that she's been on a second and then a third date with Vince – he of the *Hamilton* tickets – and that, shock horror, she thinks she might like him. I put down my fork.

'This . . . no . . . it can't be true . . .' I can't remember the last time she had anything but the most passing interest in a man and a third date is unprecedented.

She raises her thin eyebrows. 'I know, right. I'm not saying we're about to move in together but it's been nice.'

'And . . . ?'

'What?' She takes a tiny sip of wine.

'Are you seeing him again? Don't make me beg for details.'

'Oh.' She laughs. 'Yes. At the weekend. It's my turn to decide what to do. I'm thinking maybe the cinema. They're doing *The Sound of Music* singalong at the Gate.'

'Jesus Christ. If he wants to see you again after that he's definitely a keeper. And have you . . . ?'

44

A pink flush creeps up from her neck, something that always happens when she's put on the spot. 'I have no idea what you mean,' she says, laughing.

'I'll take that as a yes.'

'Take it any way you like, I'm not saying anything.'

'Lydia Somers! On the third date!'

'Second actually. Right, let's talk about something else . . .'

'No way. I have questions. Second *and* third? If not, why not?'

She slices a piece of sausage, agonizingly slowly. Lydia is the only person I know who always uses both a knife and fork, to neatly parcel out each bite before she starts eating. I wait. Finally she finishes.

'Nope. Not telling.' She pops a chunk of sausage into her mouth as if to say 'Case closed'.

'Spoilsport,' I say, just as a woman at the next table – half of a couple who were already eating when we arrived – says, 'Just when it was getting good. Don't leave us hanging,' which results in Lydia nearly choking on her morsel, laughing. Sadly I don't get any more details, but we do end up chatting to our neighbours – Shaz and Dave ('No, really. We met at speed dating, and once we introduced ourselves to each other we knew we had to go on a date just on the basis of our names. I mean, it would have been like being called Ant and Bec and not giving it a go') – who turn out to be both sweet and hilarious, for the next hour or so. By nine o'clock we've moved our tables together and we're sharing a bottle. They've been together for four months and they're like a couple of proselytizing Jehovah's Witnesses about the speed-dating club they met at. 'You meet people you'd never

45

encounter anywhere else,' Shaz says. 'I mean, most of them are probably psychopaths, but at least you only have to spend three minutes with them . . .'

'How cute were they?' Lydia says as we pick our way through the ice back to mine.

'I wonder how often that happens. Someone meets their absolute soul mate at one of those events.' I squeak as my right foot slides away from me. Clutch at Lydia's arm. I have an out-of-proportion fear of falling over in weather like this and I never seem to have the right shoes on to ensure it doesn't happen.

'That's the thing . . .' Lydia says, wrapping her scarf round her face three more times so only her eyes are visible. It makes it hard to hear what she's saying. 'Vince's nice and all that. But he's one hundred per cent not my soul mate, so what's the point?'

This is what she always does. Talks herself out of relationships before they've even started. I put it down to the fact that her parents met when they were sixteen, married at twenty-two. From what she's told me they never had a cross word, they did everything together, never spent a night apart, and neither of them would have wanted it any other way. She has picked an impossible role model to aspire to. And not necessarily a healthy one. I mean, I love Nick. I couldn't imagine sharing my life with anyone else. But we're not joined at the hip. And we wouldn't want to be.

'You don't know that yet.' We've reached my front door. I dig around in my pocket for the keys. 'Give it a chance.'

She sighs. 'I do though.'

'Not all couples are soul mates.' The warmth from inside

rushes out to greet us as the door opens. 'Coffee before you go? Nick'll be back any minute.'

She shakes her head. 'I've got an early start. You should aim for that though, shouldn't you?' She pokes around on her phone. 'I don't want to settle. I'd rather be on my own.'

'I know,' I say. 'But the two things aren't mutually exclusive. You can have a bit of fun with Vince without it having to lead to anything serious. I mean, why not?'

She shrugs. 'I suppose.' Her mobile beeps. 'Oh, my Uber's nearly here already. It must have just dropped someone off round the corner.'

'Text me when you get in,' I say, as I always do when she's about to be driven across London by a strange man who's only requirement for the job is that he owns a car. Or knows someone who does. She hugs me, her nose a block of ice on my cheek.

'Will do.'

Nick stumbles in, merrily drunk, while I'm in the bathroom, scrubbing my face with a wipe. He's a textbook good drunk. Happy and affectionate. In love with the world.

'Was it fun?' I say, attacking a particularly persistent blob of mascara.

He catches my eye in the mirror and gives me a lazy smile that still makes my heart flip. 'Boring as fuck. I'm just happy to be home. How was Lyds?'

'Good,' I say, slathering on moisturizer. 'Trying to talk herself out of dating a man she actually seems to like.'

I check in on Patricia's Twitter while I wait for Lydia's text, and Nick to have a shower. Send out a banal tweet about having been to a local theatre production just to keep the myth alive (*So wonderful. Theatre at its best*) and then, just as I'm about to log out, a 1 appears on the little envelope in the corner. A direct message.

Hope the theatre was fun! I've been for a delicious meal with Georgia. Manna in Primrose Hill. Do you ever come up to London, Patricia?

I hesitate before I reply. Do I really want to get into a conversation now? I hate to leave her hanging though. *Not if I can help it!*

I don't blame you, comes the response. I'm surprised. Lydia usually professes to love the city and all it has to offer.

I can hear Nick singing away to himself in the bathroom. I need to wrap this up quickly. *Well, I hope you had a fun evening.* I press send and then wonder if I should have said *Night* or something that indicated the conversation was over. I start typing again, one ear open for Nick's movements. As I do a response pops up.

It was great to see her. It's just . . . it's difficult at the moment. I feel awkward around her.

What? What does that mean?

In what way? I start to write and then realize that sounds too nosey. I delete it. *I'm sorry. Nothing to worry about, I hope?*

I sit there willing her to reply, one eye on the bathroom door. I can't imagine how people with illicit lovers cope with the stress of secret communication. This is bad enough. I'm staring at my phone when Nick breezes out of the bathroom, dressed only in a towel, a slightly comedy wolfish look on his face. He leans over me. He smells of citrus and mint, with an undertone of booze. He always gets amorous when he's had a few beers. He gently takes the mobile out of my hand and kisses me.

'She didn't text me yet,' I say, when we come up for air. He knows I always demand Lydia let me know she's safely home. I will him not to look at the phone. Not to ask who the hell Patricia is. He puts it on the bedside table and I breathe a sigh of relief, but my head is full of a million questions I want to ask Lydia. What is she talking about? Why does she feel uncomfortable around me? Why didn't she say anything to my face? And what's she going to think about Patricia abandoning her halfway through a confessional conversation? Nick has peeled back the covers and is nuzzling the inside of my thighs, something that would usually make me forget anything else that's happening in my life. I can't concentrate though. I go through the motions, but my mind is elsewhere. Probably she's just talking about the inequity of our careers. A continuation of the conversation she started with Patricia the other day. I try to remember the exact wording of what she said. Force myself to resist the urge to pick up my phone and check. Faking it is one thing, but looking at Twitter while my husband gives it his all might be a step too far.

Ten minutes later, once Nick is snoring lightly, one arm draped heavily over my stomach, I slide out from under it and take my phone to the bathroom. Lydia has replied.

God, I shouldn't have said anything. That's what a couple of glasses of wine do to me! It's just . . . I found out something and I feel terrible about it. I'm really having trouble pretending everything is normal. But I can't tell her because what if it's not true? What if I blow her life up by telling her something that turns out to be a made-up bit of gossip?

I sit down on the bathroom floor, which is damp from

Nick's wet feet. I stare at the message. Read it again, hoping I might have missed something, that I've misread it, that Lydia is actually talking about a play or a film she's seen and not real life. My life.

There's only one response I want to write:

What?

What have you found out?

For God's sake tell me.

Delete. Delete. Delete.

I don't have it in me to write an anodyne Patricia response but I know that if I don't find out what Lydia is alluding to I'll never sleep. I have to tread carefully, though. Eventually I manage a reply.

That's an awful position to be put in. Poor you. I hope it's nothing serious.

While I wait I check my texts. One from Lyds about fifteen minutes ago, confirming that she's home in one piece. I send a kiss in return. Back on Twitter there's a message. I jab at the envelope icon.

If it's true, it's the worst. Hopefully it's not though. Thanks for listening, Patricia. I really shouldn't be burdening you with all this! Night night.

Shit. Of course she's not going to tell Patricia the details. She barely knows her. I don't know what to do. My heart is racing. I think about waking Nick up and showing him the messages, asking what he thinks Lyds knows that is so awful. But he'd never get past the whole 'So, I set up a fake profile pretending to be someone called Patricia' issue. And what if it's something about him? I read her message again:

If it's true, it's the worst . . .

I need to find out what that means.

Chapter 6

Sleep is impossible. I lie there, listening to Nick breathing, running through all the possibilities in my head. What would be the worst thing that could be happening to me? That my children were dying. Nick. Lydia herself. Me. This clearly doesn't come under the heading 'gossip'. And why would Lydia ever know before me, except about herself, and then she would be certain. What else? That my publishers are going to drop me? Lyds works in publishing so she might have tapped into the grapevine. I consider it on the devastation scale. Of course it would be traumatizing but Wilbur's success would surely mean that someone else would step in and make me an offer. And if they didn't, I'd survive. I force myself to run through a list of children's book publishers in my head, consider each one and whether they might take me on. It's as much a calming exercise as a practical one. The career equivalent of counting sheep. I start to feel heavy behind the eyes. Finally I'm drifting off. I try not to jinx it by acknowledging it. Focus on breathing slowly, four counts in, hold, eight counts out. Infidelity! The voice in my head is back with a vengeance and I jolt awake. Gambling? Drugs? I look over in Nick's direction but it's too dark to see anything except the vaguest outline of the duvet. The familiar comfort of him. Could that be it? It's almost impossible to imagine.

Almost.

But could there be unfounded gossip about him? Maybe. That could happen to anyone. It doesn't mean he did anything to deserve it. I roll over, drape an arm over his waist. He mutters in his sleep, takes hold of my hand on autopilot.

That must be it. Whatever it is is just rumour. Unsubstantiated. Lydia has blown it up in her head to be something it isn't. I wish she wasn't talking about it to complete strangers over the internet – even ones who don't exist – but apart from that there's nothing to worry about. I fall asleep, almost convinced.

Lydia and I are in Selfridges, browsing the candles and interiors floor, our favourite. I suggested it. I wanted to see her face to face and try to edge her into telling me whatever it is she is afraid to tell me. Alcohol would have helped but she's out tonight on the unprecedented fourth date with Vince, so sober daytime will have to do. I know she wants to protect me from anything bad, and I love her for it, but not knowing what it is is eating me up. You can't fight an enemy you can't see. (Another one from my mum's lexicon of useful sayings.)

I'm in the middle of telling a long – and entirely made-up – story about someone I know who is struggling to keep a secret she's been burdened with. Hardly subtle, but I didn't say I was good at this.

'I mean, it's not fair, is it? Telling someone something huge and then asking them not to do anything about it . . .'

Lydia shrugs. Turns over a small wooden bowl in her hand. 'Everyone does it all the time. How many times have we told each other something and said "Don't tell anyone"?'

'It's not the same though, is it? I'm talking about . . .' What am I talking about? I need to be careful not to be too specific here or I'll give myself away. 'I think if someone told me a bit of bad news about a person I loved and said don't tell them I'd still have to. I mean, I'd want to know if it were me, wouldn't you?'

'Depends what it was, I suppose.' She doesn't look flustered by my question, although she's not catching my eye. 'Is it bad? The thing your friend's been told?'

'What? Oh . . . Well, I think so. That was the implication.'

'Better to stay out of it, I think.'

I can't let it go. 'But if you cared about the person the story was about more than the person who told you it . . . ?'

Lydia considers. Puts down the bowl and picks up another, slightly larger one. Surely that's got through to her. 'I think I'd ask them not to tell me whatever it was in the first place, if that was the case.'

'What if they don't give you the choice?'

She laughs, showing her tiny white teeth. She did a whitening treatment recently and ate nothing but cottage cheese, yoghurt, white rice and chicken for ten days. Now they glow in the dark. 'So someone just runs up to you and says, "Your brother-in-law's a paedophile, don't tell your sister," out of the blue and then expects you to keep it to yourself?'

I force myself to laugh along. 'Maybe not quite like that.'

'No good ever came from inserting yourself into the lives of others. Isn't that what your mum used to say?'

'Well, yes, but she also told me that if you eat apple cores a tree grows inside you, so she couldn't always be relied on.'

'I miss your mum,' Lydia says.

'Me too.' Mum moved to the south of Spain four years ago with her boyfriend Frank – technically now my stepdad since they got married out of the blue one day. I have no idea what he does for a living, but if you told me he was a bank robber I would believe you without a moment of surprise. He has a huge bouffant of white hair, pockets stuffed with cash, an arm full of gold bracelets and a bunch of expat friends who look like a showroom of outdated mahogany furniture. Mum seems blissfully happy, but I always make excuses not to go and stay with them. I'm worried I'd be carted off in a dawn raid for starters. Gunned down in a revenge hit. If I'm being honest, the truth is that I find it awkward. Acquiring a step-parent in your forties means that every time you visit there's a virtual stranger in the house. One who doesn't love you unconditionally and who might be pointing out all your faults to your doting mother the minute you leave again. It's impossible to relax. 'I'd want someone to tell me if they heard something awful about me, wouldn't you?'

She waves the bowl at me. 'I'm getting this. Not necessarily. Definitely not some random bit of gossip. It would just make you completely paranoid.'

There's no point pushing it. I don't want to make her start wondering why I'm suddenly so obsessed with what people are saying about me.

Later, once we've said goodbye, both laden down with decorative tat we don't need, I invoke Patricia from the privacy of the bathroom. Nick is cooking – the heady aroma of garlic wafts up from the basement – and I know he'll have a glass of red on the go, alternately taking a swig and sloshing some into whatever it is he's making. He's a better chef in his head than in reality, but I don't care. I'm just happy he's doing it and I don't have to. I can't help it, I've been watching him for the past couple of days, ever since Patricia's conversation with Lydia about the big secret. Trying to spot any signs that something is wrong. The problem is that once you start doing that everyone's smallest move looks suspicious. Why did he offer to nip out to the greengrocer's for ginger? Was it because it's next door to the betting shop? (Or just because we needed ginger?) Why do his pupils look dilated? (Because the overhead lights are off, and it's dark in here?) Why did he turn away when he read that message on his phone? (Because he just did? Sometimes people just turn around.) I'm in danger of sending myself mad.

Patricia hasn't messaged Lydia since. I couldn't trust myself. And besides, I thought working on her in person might prove more fruitful than hoping she'd confide in a stranger. Clearly not.

Hope you're feeling a bit better now.

I don't want to refer to the big secret directly, not having badgered her about it in person all afternoon. But I'm at a loss. If she won't tell me, Georgia, then I have to find a way for her to tell the other me, Patricia.

I wait. Nothing. Clearly she's not on Twitter right now. Hardly a surprise. There's a limit to how long I can sit in the bath and hope to hear from her. And then I remember it's singalong *Sound of Music* night. Lydia will be busy getting into her nun outfit. At least, I'm guessing she's going for that and not full-on Nazi. I wonder what poor Vince has been steamrollered into wearing. A dress made out of curtains probably. I'm not likely to get a reply for hours. I plaster on a happy face, ready to be thankful for the meal Nick has cooked me.

By bedtime there's still no response. I check her Instagram page, more for something to do than because I think I'll find any insight there. A new picture has been posted. The wooden bowl, now filled with shiny cherries and placed on the striated walnut of Lydia's kitchen counter, a fat glass of rich red wine beside it. A paperback – *Living Your Best Life: The Power of Positivity* – lies face down and open, the spine carefully cracked, the reader halfway through. *Treats!* says the post and then about fifteen hashtags including *#LiveYourBestLife*, *#BeYou* and *#LoveYourself*. I like the photo (me and thirty-eight others) and restrain myself from leaving a comment: 'Those cherries and that wine will stain your teeth, you know,' or even 'I have no idea how I can be friends with someone who posts this kind of nonsense.' It's not that I don't think they would make her laugh, it's that I know she'd rather I didn't put things like that up there for other people to see. It would ruin the conceit. Instead, I send her a text: *Did you just buy that bowl so you could Insta that picture??*

I resist the temptation to plug my phone in by the bed instead of downstairs as usual. Manage a fitful sleep. In the morning there's still nothing so I send Lydia a text: *How was last night?* She replies almost immediately, even though it's only about 8 a.m. and I'm assuming she had a late night: *Fun. Well, I enjoyed it anyway. Vince was bored stiff and showed it! So, no date number 5!*

Not really? You're dumping him??

Really!!! I ended up going for a drink with a bunch of women on a hen night who were sitting next to us and he went home in a huff!

Honestly, she's her own worst enemy where love is concerned. *But you like him, don't you?*

Liked!!! That extra letter should tell you everything!

When the kids went to uni Nick and I joked that we should get a dog to fill the void. At least, I think we thought we were joking. But now here we are at the Mayhew on a Sunday morning, meeting Igor, a huge, sad-eyed hound whose picture we both fell in love with when we were idly browsing their website one night. Just window shopping, we told ourselves and each other, but somehow we've made an appointment to take a look at him in person and I think we both know how this is going to end.

Igor is enormous. Black, brown and white with half-sticky-up ears and big brown eyes. He's four years old and has been through two homes already. 'He's a bit clumsy. You'd need to bear that in mind,' Fay, the friendly girl who has done the introduction, tells us. He plonks his paw heavily on Nick's shoulder when Nick crouches down to say hello and hefts his enormous rudder of a tail back and forth a couple of times when I rub the top of his head. We walk him round on a lead for a while and he sits when I tell him to and I feel as if my heart is going to burst. I'm gripped by a sudden panic that they might not let us take him. You can't just waltz into a rehoming centre and flounce out with a pet on your arm these days. There are procedures. They need to make sure we're the best match. That we'll treat him right. There's a home visit. And so there should be. I know that. I just want to swoop him up and take him with me now.

'What if someone comes in tomorrow and says they want him too?' I ask nervously once Nick and I have agreed he's the one.

'We can reserve him for you till the checks are done,' Fay says. 'Don't worry.'

'Don't let anyone take him,' Nick says. 'Please, I mean . . .'

She laughs. I imagine they get this a lot. 'I won't. It gives you time to make certain you're doing the right thing too. He's a big boy. A lot of responsibility. His size has been a problem in the past . . .'

'We are,' I say. 'But, yes, of course . . .'

We take photos, WhatsApp Joe and then Edie to show them their new brother. *Does he get a share in the will??* Joe writes and I reply, *He's getting all of it.* I cry in the car on the way home in case it doesn't work out. I hadn't realized I was so desperate to fill my empty nest. I was full of bravado when the kids left, telling anyone who'd listen that I was thrilled to get them off my hands and have more time for me. Nonsense, it turns out.

We stop at Pets at Home and buy a dog bed so big we could sleep in it ourselves if we wanted. A couple of toys the size of large babies. I stop short of stocking up on food. I don't want to jinx anything. We're as excited as a couple of kids on Christmas Eve, breaking down in a fit of giggles as we try to fold the bed into the boot of the car, and it keeps springing out as if it has a life of its own. I'm overwhelmed by endorphins. A wave of love for my husband. Everything is going to be OK. Whatever Lydia has heard, we can get through it together.

I hardly even realize what I'm doing when I sneak a look at Patricia's Twitter in the car. I'm feeling defiant. Bring it on. Give me your worst.

I'm still laughing at something Nick's said when I read the message.

Chapter 7

Patricia, can I tell you something? There's no one else I can talk to who doesn't know Georgia too. Obviously it's top top secret! But I need some advice. If you found out your best friend's husband was having an affair, what would you do? Would you tell her?

I stare at the words, tuning out whatever it is Nick is telling me. I'm sure he must be able to feel the change in atmosphere. My heart is pounding so hard my temples must be visibly throbbing. I feel my face flush red and a wave of nausea overwhelms me. I can't look at him. All I want to do is confront him. Demand to know if it's true. If we're talking about playing happy families with a giant dog while all the time he's screwing someone behind my back. I close my eyes, trying to calm myself down. So Lydia has heard a rumour. So what? Ninety-nine per cent of rumours aren't true. They're vicious, mean gossip and nothing more. People love to bring other people down, to imagine their lives are flawed, because it makes them feel better about themselves.

'Are you OK?' We're stopped at the lights and Nick is looking at me, concern etched on his face.

'I feel a bit sick.'

'Shit, I'll pull over. Shall I pull over?'

I shake my head. 'Let's just get home.'

'You don't think you're allergic to dogs, do you?'

'No,' I snap. 'Of course not.'

The car behind us beeps. 'Go,' I say. I stay silent for the rest of the journey, the joyful atmosphere deflating around us. I daren't even respond to Lydia. I need to be on my own, think straight, work out what to do. I can't confront Nick yet. What would I say? So, Lydia heard a rumour about you. She told it to a woman who doesn't exist because she's actually me. I need to find out exactly what Lydia has heard. Work out if it can possibly be true. And I need to give Nick the benefit of the doubt until I've done that.

'Sorry,' I say. 'I just suddenly feel really rough. It must be a stomach bug, I think. I need to lie down for a bit.'

He reaches over and puts a hand on my knee. I feel myself stiffen. I don't even want to look at him at the moment. 'You poor thing,' he says. 'We'll be home in five minutes. I'll bring you peppermint tea in bed.'

'I just want to sleep. I'll be OK.' The last thing I want is him fussing over me.

Safely shut in the bedroom, I pull up Patricia's profile and try to decide what to say. Lydia is probably already regretting saying anything and I don't want to scare her off completely. After a few false starts I come up with something I'm happy with. Hold my breath and press send.

Oh no, that's awful. Is that what it is? The secret? Do you definitely know it's true though?

I take my jumper off and get under the covers, just in case Nick looks in on me. The response comes almost immediately.

I'm pretty sure. I don't think the person who told me would make it up.

I blink back tears. *Maybe they believe it but they've got it wrong. Or whoever told them has. People do like to exaggerate gossip.*

I know. That's the main reason I haven't said anything to Georgia yet. But they were pretty adamant. I feel really disloyal even telling you. You won't ever tell anyone, will you?

Of course not. Who would I tell anyway? But I'm happy to be here as a sounding board if you want to offload.

Tell me! I want to write. Tell me who told you and exactly what they said.

Thank you! Really appreciate it. I'll try and not bore you stupid with it though! Talk to you soon.

She's obviously not going to divulge any more yet. I sign off, telling her to look after herself, and then I pull the covers over my head and sob. Nick is cheating on me? We're the ones everyone always cites whenever there's a conversation about whether marriage can last these days. Look at Nick and Georgia. Look at how happy you can be.

In a second I go from sorrow to anger. Who is she? How the fuck can he do this to me? To us. I want to storm downstairs and throw things. Tell him he might think he's sneaking around and getting away with it but I know. My phone buzzes and I see it's Lydia. I can't face talking to her. I wouldn't be able to pretend everything was OK. I turn it face down and ignore it. I need time to think.

He looks the same. He sounds the same. He puts a mug on the bedside table. Lowers a hand to feel my forehead.

'How are you feeling?'

'OK.' I'm really not.

'You've been asleep for hours. I thought I ought to wake you.'

62

'Have I?' I flap a hand around for my mobile. It's nearly three o'clock. We got back from the Mayhew before twelve. Outside it looks as if it's thinking about getting dark already, the sky slate-grey and heavy. I hate this time of year. Hate the sad, oppressive light. Christmas is over and spring's not coming for months. It's a time to be endured not enjoyed. 'I'll get up.' I just want Nick to go and leave me alone. I don't want to talk to him. Don't want to look at him.

'Do you want anything to eat?'

'No. I'm fine.' My stomach growls in protest. 'Later.'

'In that case I'm going to go for a quick run,' he says and leans down to kiss me. I freeze. 'Sure you'll be OK?'

'Yup.'

Once I hear the front door bang I leap out of bed. I've never wanted to be the kind of person who checks their partner's phone but it seems like as good a time to start as any. I look in all the obvious places first – on the coffee table, the sofa, plugged into the charger. I can't see it anywhere. I start turning over cushions, moving piles of papers aimlessly. Has he taken it with him? Why would he do that? Is he phoning her? Hiding round the corner and muttering sweet nothings about how his wife doesn't understand him, and then faking breathlessness when he gets home? Or maybe just talking to her makes him breathless, who knows?

I jump when I hear the front door click. Nick walks in, sweating lightly, phone in hand, headphones hanging from one ear.

'Great, you're up.'

'Why did you take your phone?' It comes out of my mouth before I can stop it.

He looks down at it, confused. 'Spotify,' he says, a tiny frown line appearing on his forehead.

Right. Of course. He always takes his phone when he runs. He has a specific running playlist on there.

'I know. I meant . . .' What did I mean? God knows. I need to get a grip. I need to get some perspective. I need to know what I'm up against.

I've been thinking about your friend. Maybe you should tell her? Not that it's any of my business but I think if it were me I might be grateful for being told. I hope you don't think I'm poking my nose in. Do tell me to mind my own business.

I'm in the bath. I don't trust myself around Nick at the moment. I managed to get through dinner being fairly mono-syllabic and allowing him to put it down to me being unwell. The dog bed suddenly seemed tragic, dominating the kitchen in the corner he had cleared for it. A symbol of a happier, more innocent time. Only a matter of hours earlier. I knew we should be planning for Igor, laughing at the absurdity of the idea that this giant mammal would soon be living in our house, imagining the beautiful life we would give him to make up for his traumatic start. But I couldn't bring myself to play along.

I've been staring at my message for half an hour now. If Patricia can persuade Lydia that coming clean is the noble thing to do then I can flush it all into the open. Have it out with Nick. Demand the truth.

I top the hot water up again. Will it to be tomorrow so Nick will be out at work all day. Although doing God knows what. I'm not sure I can bear it. We even joked about being left alone together, before Edie and Joe moved out.

'What if I realize you're actually really boring?' I'd said, trying to keep a straight face. 'And that once we don't have to organize who's picking Joe up from track practice or taking Edie to dance we don't have anything to talk about at all?'

'We can discuss the weather,' he'd said. 'Or take up a joint hobby like brass rubbing or flower arranging. I imagine they're good conversation starters.'

'What did we talk about before the kids?' I'd said, in a moment of seriousness. He'd laughed then.

'I have no idea. How much we fancied each other, I suppose.'

'Well, good luck keeping that one going now.'

Everything had – has – always been an in-joke with me and Nick. It has always been 'you and me against the world', our own little exclusive club that let in two – and only two – more members eighteen and a half years ago.

I check Twitter again. Lydia has responded. I almost drop my phone in the water in my rush to read it.

I would never think you were poking your nose in! I value your advice. But I don't think I can. Apart from anything else she would definitely shoot the messenger!!

Would I? *Would she?*

Probably! If I knew for certain it was true then yes, I'd tell her in a heartbeat.

Does it seem likely to you? I mean, you know him well, I assume?

Why have I asked her this? Fuck. But I want to know the answer. I jab at my phone impatiently, in and out of direct messages in the hope that will make a response appear more quickly.

Yes I do. And, honestly, no, it doesn't surprise me. Not at all.

For fuck's sake. What does that mean?

Has he done it before? I write, knowing the answer. I close my eyes, will myself to press send. Wait.

He has!

Because that's the thing. That's the reason this rumour, this gossip, whatever it is, bites so deep.

Nick has form.

Everything I've said about our relationship is true. We're best buddies. Soul mates. But about six years ago it was almost all over. Maybe it was the first flush of my success – not that I have ever thought Nick was jealous of that in any way, but I've often wondered if he felt he might lose me. That my new life might sweep me off my feet. Or perhaps it was a midlife crisis or even just plain old lust, although I don't like to think of that too often. In retrospect I think it's as much of a mystery to him as it was to me. But whatever the reason, it happened, and nothing can change that.

He was working at a conference centre in Islington, looking after the day-to-day needs of the clients. What I remember most – apart from the shock, the feeling that my world had collapsed – was the absolute ordinariness of that time. That's what was – what still is, if I ever allow myself to think about it – so shocking. There were no furtive phone calls, no sudden attention to grooming or the way he dressed, no tell-tale aroma of a strange woman's perfume. Nick was Nick. We laughed, we had fun, we revelled in the kids. And then one night, after they'd gone to bed, he'd paused the episode of *Spiral* we were watching and said those fateful words: 'I have to tell you something.'

66

It was over by the time he told me, but it had gone on for a couple of weeks. An attendee at a two-day summit on joint health. They had got talking, ended up having a drink . . . I can't bring myself to think about the details even all these years later. He had come to his senses and ended it. He was horrified with himself, with what he had done to his family. My first instinct was to throw him out but he had begged to stay, to try and work it out. And we did. Slowly. Sometimes it would all be too much and I would bombard him with questions, details I needed to torture myself with. He went above and beyond to prove himself. He wore his guilt on the surface, his fear that he had ruined everything, his desire to make it up to me, to rebuild my shattered, already fragile, confidence. It took a long time. Months. And for most of that it was touch and go. If we hadn't had the kids I think I would have given up, thrown him out, but eventually, weirdly, it brought us closer, solidified that what we wanted was each other. I can honestly say I have never doubted him since. Not once. It's become a distant memory. Something that happened to someone else.

The only person I'd confided in was Lydia. I couldn't bear for people to know. I didn't think we had a chance of getting through it if we became that couple who almost broke up because he cheated. But I couldn't process it all on my own either. She let me vent, told me she would back me up whatever I decided, helped me see how hard Nick was trying. I don't know what I would have done without her.

I'm a little thrown that she's so quick to share my secret with Patricia, but then Patricia is not supposed to know who she's talking about. I remind myself that Lydia is looking for help here, not gossiping.

As for me, I need something. Some kind of steer. It took me a long time to curb the urge to interrogate Nick every time he got home from work late, not to bristle every time he mentioned a female colleague, but I knew that if we were going to survive I had to learn to truly trust him again. I had to be able to move on and look to the future. I can't risk everything we've worked so hard for by blundering in now and accusing him without evidence.

Is there any way you can find out more? What about the person who told you?

I pretty much told them I didn't want to know! But, yes, I suppose I could ask them to tell me the details. God, Patricia, do I really want to hear them?

Good idea, I write, ignoring Lydia's anxiety. Patricia needs to sound decisive. There's no doubt this is the correct thing to do. *Otherwise it's just going to eat away at you.*

She replies almost immediately. *You're right. OK. I'll do it.*

Now all I can do is wait.

Chapter 8

I find myself watching Nick as he gets ready for work the next morning. Is he taking extra care over how he looks? Does he seem more eager than usual to get going? The answer to both is no. Nick on a Monday morning is always a slow-moving, slightly sulky train.

'I'm at that thing tonight, remember?'

I snap to attention. 'What thing?'

He catches my eye via the mirror. 'The presentation about the new site in Suffolk.'

It does ring a bell. Not that that matters. A lie is a lie: it doesn't matter when you tell it. 'Right. What time shall I expect you?'

He shrugs. 'Ten? We'll probably have a quick drink after.'

'OK. Have fun.' I hate myself for being like this. But I hate him more for giving me cause. He takes my comment at face value, thankfully.

'I won't.' He bends down to kiss me and his mouth grazes mine. I'm struck with a sudden urge to hold on to him. To beg him not to go. I settle for looping my arms round his neck. He hugs me back. 'I'm glad you're feeling better.'

Work is impossible. In the end I give in to all the voices in my head and check through Nick's coat pockets and the little desk in the living room where he keeps his bits and pieces.

Finding nothing, I turn on his laptop. I know his password because I just do. Same as he knows mine. We've asked each other to look for things on our computers before. We're an open book. That's why I know I won't find anything on here either – his work email stays strictly on his computer at work – but I won't rest till I've looked. There's nothing more from Lydia and I don't know what else to do.

I'm saved from myself by the phone ringing. I don't recognize the number but I snatch it up, eager for the distraction. It's a woman's voice.

'Mrs Shepherd . . . ?'

For a moment I think she's going to say: 'I'm having an affair with your husband. I thought you should know.' It would be a relief. I could get answers at least. But what she actually says is, 'It's Jules from the Mayhew. We have a last-minute cancellation, so I was wondering if it was convenient to do your home assessment this morning?'

'Oh . . .' I should probably say no. Now is not the time to be taking on a responsibility like this. But what if Lydia's got it wrong and in the meantime someone snaps Igor up? And how would I ever explain that to Nick? 'My husband's at work. It's just me, if that's OK?'

'Absolutely,' she says. 'I just need to see the space and talk you through a few things.'

We arrange for her to come over in an hour, which gives me time to shower and tidy up a bit. I try to imagine what might be considered hazardous to an outsize hound – a delicate pottery ornament, a thin-legged spiky floor lamp, shoes he could swallow in one gulp – and shove them all in cupboards out of sight.

Jules is a smiley young woman in her twenties. I show her the kitchen and the garden first, talk her through my day. She keeps reminding me of Igor's size, showing me a video on her phone of him on one of their daily walks, playing with a beagle. It looks like a dog being chased by a bouncy pony. Every time I look at him my heart melts and by the time Jules leaves I know I'll do anything to keep him. No matter what happens with Nick. He needs someone to love him and I need something to love. Now more than ever, it would seem.

Jules tells me she'll let me know, but I feel as if it's a done deal. Ordinarily I'd call Nick straightaway, tell him the good news, but I feel as if he doesn't deserve to know. I try Lyds (having first checked whether she has any news for Patricia – there's nothing, but while I'm on there I like a couple of random tweets and retweet a touching story about a couple who have married nearly seventy years after they first met. Patricia is a bit of a romantic, I think), but her phone is off, which probably means she's in a meeting. So I call Anne Marie and manage to catch her on a free period.

'You'll never guess,' I say when she answers.

'Well, obviously not,' she says. Anne Marie does a great line in dry retorts. 'And I only have eight minutes till my next class, so tell me.'

'OK. We're getting a dog. A rescue.'

She laughs. 'You called me at work to tell me you're getting a dog?'

'I may have done, yes.'

'Well, congratulations. Is this because the kids have moved out?'

'Probably.'

Anne Marie and Harry's eldest, Gino, is leaving in the autumn to study at MIT – on a prestigious scholarship that will transport him halfway across the world – but they'll still have two at home. When the kids were young we'd joked about Gino and Edie growing up and falling in love. Or even Gino and Joe, come to that. But both my kids wrote him off as a nerd early on so it was never going to happen. They tolerate each other but they aren't friends. I adore Gino. He really is a nerd through and through but he embraces it. He's sweet and funny and he loves nothing more than astrophysics. And to tell you about it if you'll let him. Not that I ever do – and he never ever takes offence. I remember when he saw the first Wilbur book – he must have been about ten or eleven – and he very sweetly asked me probing questions about where he lived and how he got to the shops, because if he was in a zoo he couldn't just hop out whenever he wanted and, anyway, wouldn't the other customers call the police and report a wild animal on the loose? And what did he do with all his purchases? ('I don't think he would be able to cook, Georgia, even if he had access to a kitchen. Also, he'd be a herbivore, so I'm not sure why he'd be buying bread.' 'Because it rhymes with bed,' I told him and he'd replied that kangaroos sleep on the ground actually, so it was unlikely Wilbur would waste his money on a mattress.)

'I'm not even going to have a goldfish once mine have all gone,' Anne Marie is saying. 'I want no responsibilities. Nothing. Just me and Harry doddering down to the pub any time we feel like it.'

Something clenches in my stomach at the thought that that was what I'd wanted too. Well, not the pub so much, but

Nick and I had always looked forward to it just being the two of us again. All the things we could do. The ways in which we could please ourselves. I suppose that is what he's doing. I'd just always imagined we'd please ourselves together.

'Do you think anything's up with Nick?' I say before I can help myself. 'Does he seem OK to you?'

'Well, I haven't seen him for a week or so but . . . what . . . is he ill, do you think? Shit.'

'No. Not . . . It doesn't matter. He just doesn't seem himself, I suppose. I'm probably imagining things.'

'He hasn't said anything?' I can picture her frowning, her dark eyebrows pulled together under her heavy electric blue fringe. Anne Marie has a very expressive face. It sometimes seems as if she has no control over it. She would be the world's worst poker player. She still looks exactly like she did when I first met her ten years ago – long, thick hair, all knees and elbows in her floaty dresses and Doc Martens. I was drawn to her because all the other mums wore Boden uniforms. Not that there was anything wrong with that except that I could barely tell them apart in their Breton tops, linen trousers and subtle blonde highlights. I've always been wary of those gangs of cookie-cutter women. I remember them as teenagers. So petite. So perfect. So mean. I'm sure most of them are nice enough, but they weren't. Not when they were thirteen. They were part of an exclusive club that barred me at the door. Now they reeked of helicopter parenting, Pilates classes and privilege. Self-styled yummy mummies. Anne Marie screamed rock and roll and subversion. We bonded over the fact that neither of us would care if we never tasted balsamic vinegar ever again. I once heard one of the mums refer to us slightly sneeringly as 'those artsy ones'. I took it as the compliment it wasn't meant to be. This was pre Wilbur. Afterwards I was suddenly a desirable commodity. A trophy to have on your sofa when your friends called round. But it was too late by then: I'd seen their true colours.

I had a part-time job, a few hours a week, running life-drawing classes at the local adult education centre. During the days, while the twins were at school, I sketched. Anne Marie was already teaching music, but privately. Guitar and singing lessons. Her neighbours must have loved her. We lived on the same street, it turned out – more Chalk Farm than Primrose Hill – and we used to walk home together most days, four kids trailing along behind and her little one, Nina, due in a couple of months.

'No,' I say now. 'Forget I said anything.'

I hear a bell ring in the background. 'Shit, I have to go,' Anne Marie says. 'Are you sure you're OK?'

'Yes. Absolutely. Everything's fine.'

'I'm happy for you about the dog . . .'

'Don't mention what I said when you see Nick –'

'Of course I won't,' she interrupts. 'But I'm here if you want to chat.'

'The Mayhew did their home visit yesterday,' I say to Nick at breakfast. Last night, when he got in at a quarter past ten, I was already in bed, pretending to be asleep. I could tell he was a bit pissed. He made a lot of noise in an attempt to be quiet, fighting with one of his socks in the effort to take it off for far longer than a sober person would have.

'You're kidding? How did it go?'

'Good, I think.' I busy myself making more coffee. I've been biting my tongue all morning, desperate to ask him how his evening was. Who was there. 'Oh my God. And you're only just telling me now?'

'You weren't here,' I snap and Nick's expression drops.

'I was kidding,' he says. 'What is up with you at the moment?'

'Nothing,' I say, picking up my coffee and stalking up the stairs. He can pour his own.

'Did we pass?' he calls up after me. 'Can we have him?'

I pretend I haven't heard.

I hide in the bathroom till I hear him shout that he's leaving, calling out a half-hearted 'See you later' in response. I resist the temptation to crawl back into bed. I just want it all to go away. Instead, I make more coffee and sit at the kitchen table with my mobile clutched in my hand. If Nick's up to something I need to know. I need to work out how I possibly could have found out – so I don't get Lyds in the shit – and confront him. When I get up the courage to look, there's another private message on Patricia's Twitter.

So it's definitely true! The person who told me has heard it from the horse's mouth. Hers not his. Oh God! I can't tell Georgia!!!

I put my head in my hands. What do I do now?

Chapter 9

I swallow the lump in my throat. Lydia's message was only sent ten minutes ago. She's probably still on the bus on her way to work, hopefully browsing through her phone.

Who is it? I type and then I remember I need to be more subtle. More Patricia.

Oh no! Your poor friend. Is it someone she knows? That's what happened to me. It makes it even worse.

Her reply comes back straightaway. *Oh, I'm so glad you're there!! I've been awake all night worrying about what to do!! It's so awful! Poor Georgia!*

Shit. I feel terrible for Lyds. It must be a horrible position to be put in, and I love her for agonizing so much about me, but I just need her to tell me what she knows. There are only so many times Patricia can ask for the details and get away with it.

So what did your friend tell you exactly? Maybe I can help you work out what to say.

Please, Lydia. Please just tell me. An image of Nick thrashing around on a bed with another woman flashes into my head. It's unthinkable. Unbearable. Does Nick have a type? I have never seen Felicity. The woman from all those years ago. But I made him describe her to me over and over, and then my imagination added 20 per cent to how attractive he made her sound. He made her out to be ordinary, nothing special. I don't know if that made it better or worse. He had a few girlfriends before me and I've seen the odd photo but nothing stands out. And even if it did, tastes change over the years. Maybe after all this time with me he yearns for diminutive. That would almost feel like the worst betrayal, that he had been powerless to resist someone of five foot nothing. I feel a visceral, physical need to know who it is. What she looks like.

She swore me to secrecy — that's the thing. And I can't land her in it!

So it's a woman. The passer-on of gossip. I rack my brains for who Lydia might know who knows Nick. I'm sure she's never mentioned anyone, or if she did I wasn't paying attention. That should be easy enough to find out.

How does your friend know Nick? What I mean is, is she actually in a position to know if it's true or not?

Definitely. She works at the same company.

Ah. So does that mean the woman he's seeing does too? It would make sense. It's not as if he's out every night meeting random new females.

You wouldn't have to tell Georgia how you knew.

Oh my God, she'd get it out of me! You don't know her!

I groan in frustration.

Yes, you do need to tread carefully. You don't want to get your friend or yourself in trouble. Did she tell you who Nick was seeing? Maybe you can find another way to let Georgia know?

I wait.

Come on.

Tell me.

I stare at my phone, willing it into life. My heart is pounding so loud I can feel it in my ears.

A new message pops up. I drop my mobile in my eagerness to read it. Scrabble around and pick it up again, terrified I might somehow have deleted what she's said.

This is my stop. Talk later!

Fuckssake.

How hard can it be to find out exactly who works in Nick's office? Maybe I can work out a connection to Lydia? I know he's in charge of about twelve people, but there are literally thousands of employees across the whole company. All I can do is start close to home and work outwards. I google Diamond Leisure. Their website promises 'Feelgood family fun' in 'spacious homes away from home'. There's a photo of a beautifully sunny and exceptionally quiet beach. The sea turquoisey blue and calm. The sand pristine. I wonder how many weeks they had to wait to get the perfect conditions. And on a day when it wasn't crammed with a hundred families dropping litter and glowing crimson from lack of sunscreen. I click on the 'About' section but it's just a potted history of the company and their ethos: 'Affordable luxury for all budgets', which seems like overkill. I click out and on to the 'Company Info' link. There's a 'Key Staff' subsection but all that gives me is five photos and the phone numbers for the Managing Director, the Head of Sales, Human Resources Manager, Marketing Manager and Nick, the Events Manager. It's like an identity parade of different versions of the same white middle-aged man. Nick looks positively bohemian next to the others, but they could all be members of the same extended family. Or the Ku Klux Klan. Clearly diversity is not a big priority at Diamond Leisure.

I try to remember what Nick has ever told me about the people who work with him. Precious little, it turns out, because he's never been interested enough in his job to want to talk about it when he gets home. I know he has an assistant, Sue. It doesn't sound like the world's most glamorous name but I'm not sure I can rule her out on that basis. Not every mistress can be called Tiffany or Crystal. I google 'Sue Diamond Leisure' and get a million photos of women – presumably called Sue – in swimwear, eating barbeque, on a dance floor. A whole host of Sue Diamonds. So I add 'Nick Shepherd' and get a seemingly random selection of Sues and Nicks with diamond rings, in leisure centres, a couple of Alsatians and a man in Wales herding sheep. I only know Nick's direct line so I look up the number for the main headquarters and jab it into my phone.

'Diamond Leisure?' It's a question, not a statement, as everything seems to be these days. I try to imagine the face that goes with the voice. Twenty-five. Big hair. Fishy lips. Flappy eyelash extensions like a pair of marauding spiders. Is it her?

'Oh. Hi. I wonder if you could help me . . .' Get to the point, Georgia. Sound authoritative. 'I've been dealing with Nick Shepherd's assistant Sue about something and I've forgotten her surname . . .'

I wait for her to take the hint. Nothing.

'. . . so I was wondering if you could give me it?'

'Oh! Right. Of course.' She has a silky Welsh lilt. 'Brown. Sue Brown.'

Great. That's going to narrow it down. I end the call and google it for the hell of it. There are over 500 million entries for Susan Browns. I'm not even kidding. Even if half of them are for the same mega-famous Susan Brown that I've somehow never heard of I'd be checking the rest for the next ten years. I try it with the combinations I tried before and find a couple of references to what looks as if it might be the correct Sue but no obvious photos or links to social media.

I rack my tired brain. I think he mentioned a Janice once. Or was it Janet? I google both, along with Diamond Leisure. Nothing. I need something more concrete than vague recollections. I toy with the idea of calling Eyelashes back and asking for a staff list but I can't think how to explain why I want it.

I need a distraction, so I walk up to the top of the hill, even though the wind is biting and the ground is slippery underfoot. There are only two other people who have braved the elements, and they both seem to be wishing they hadn't. Heads down like charging bulls. There's no way to enjoy the view even if it was visible through the cloud. My hands are going numb in my pockets.

'God, I'd give anything to be an author,' someone – actually many people over the years – said to me once. 'Not having to go out to work. Sitting around waiting for the muse to strike.' And they were right. It's an amazing privilege to be able to do what I do. But it's also lonely, stressful and paranoia-inducing. I would love to draw a book about something other than Wilbur, to show off my real talent, but would anyone be interested? Almost certainly not. And what if Wilbur goes out of fashion, or someone decides there are already enough stories about him to last a lifetime? What if a character called

Kevin the Kangaroo comes along with better rhymes and more interesting shopping? As for waiting for the muse to appear, well, a deadline is a deadline and it doesn't care whether you feel inspired or not. I'm always aware my career is not a given. Yes, we live in a lovely house in a smart area but we have a huge mortgage. What if we get divorced? What if Nick leaves to set up home with Janet or Janice or Sue? Or all three of them? I stomp down the hill and straight back up again, trying to drive away my demons. I have to believe Nick is innocent until proven guilty, although the evidence is stacking against him. To calm myself down I do what I always do in times of stress. I look around for inspiration for objects Wilbur might buy in the next book. Scarf? What does it rhyme with? Laugh? Barf? Forget it. Ooh! Giraffe! That might be good.

Anne Marie once asked me if Wilbur was a shoplifter, and it's true that we have never seen him pay for anything. Never seen him with cash or a credit card. I love the way Anne Marie will take the piss out of my success. Most people – Lydia included – tread on eggshells around it. It's as if they don't know how to deal with that side of my life. Maybe they're scared of sounding critical or envious. Of accidentally letting slip a judgement on my talent. Anne Marie just blunders straight in, making me laugh at the absurdity of the world I now live in. She's the most straightforward person I know. Almost without filter, but never unkind. It occurs to me that I could confide in her about Nick. I could fudge the whole Twitter Patricia thing. I know that she would give me honest advice. But would it make things too awkward for the four of us? Worse, would she feel compelled to tell Harry? I've always thought that if someone tells me something and asks me not to breathe a word to anyone they're accepting that Nick is the exception to that rule.

I do need to talk to someone though. Speculation is making me crazy. Absence of the facts is making me feel stupid. Laughed at. Poor old Georgia has no idea what's going on behind her back. It takes me right back to the playground. Standing a head above all my classmates. Shoulders stooped to try and take up less space. The odd one out by virtue of my ungainly height and chronic shyness. Listening to the other girls whisper about me, hearing only the sibilance, none of the words, unless, of course, they wanted me to. Cruel sniggers when I knocked over my drink at lunch or tripped during netball, my overlong limbs seemingly out of control. My mum used to tell me that they'd all be jealous one of these days when they aspired to be supermodels but their lack of inches got in the way. And it turned out she was right. Those were a long few years to wait, though, and by then my insecurity was too ingrained to ever completely go away. I didn't even end up outsized. Five foot eleven and a half. I just did most of my growing early on. And anything that makes you stand out when you're young is a curse, even something that turns out to be enviable later on. Surviving adolescence is all about blending in. Not handing out ammunition to be used against you. The alpha bully – a neat Barbie lookalike with a mouth like Joan Rivers without the jokes – used to call me Bigfoot. And so they all started. It sounds harmless enough now, but when it was accompanied by mocking laughter and a distinct lack of invitations to parties it was like a long, slow death. These days I've truly embraced my stature. I stand with my back straight, head high. Limbs toned by yoga and Pilates. But one cruel remark and I crumple in on myself again like an armadillo. Hard shell protecting the soft inside.

A couple of years ago, right after Wilbur four, my breakthrough book, was published, Alpha Barbie – aka Heather Chambers – sent me a friend request on Facebook. Being friends with her was the last thing on my mind as I accepted. *My little girl loves Wilbur!* she sent the next day. *She's so impressed that we were at school together! I'd love to catch up and hear all your news x.*

Heather, you made my teenage years a fucking misery, I sent back. *Why you think I would want to have anything to do with you now is beyond me. I hope you're bringing your daughter up to be nicer than you were.*

And then I blocked her. That was a good day.

I slip-slide down the hill again and walk along Regent's Park Road out into Chalk Farm. Anne Marie's school is a ten-minute stroll towards Kentish Town and I know she'll be coming out any time now, unless she has a rare after-hours lesson. I'm still not sure what to do but I decide to leave it to fate. If I bump into her it's meant to be.

Everyone I pass looks tired and angry. The fun part of winter is gone and now it's the long dreary slog to spring. Have you ever met anyone who said that January was their favourite month? No surprise there. I pick my way along Anne Marie's most obvious route, but when I get to the school it's too quiet for the kids to have already been set free, so I give up on fate and lean against the fencing. There are a few parents hovering about ready to embarrass their offspring by insisting on collecting them in front of their mates. Year sevens only, I imagine. Or maybe there's some poor year-ten boy who still has to walk home holding hands with Mummy.

An ear-splitting bell rings out and within about a millisecond upwards of a thousand teenagers come piling out of a set of double doors. I hate crowds. Hate the knife-edge between good-humoured and full-on riot. When my two left school all I felt was relief that they'd got through it alive. Teenagers en masse are terrifying. I honestly don't know how Anne Marie can cope with the sheer bravado of them. The desire to push the boundaries of their newly discovered strength. She loves them though. She finds them hilarious and stimulating but also sad and challenging, she told me once. I stand to one side of the gate, out of the direct path of the stampede. It passes almost as quickly as it arrived. A living, breathing organism with four thousand limbs.

In the calm after the storm I'm the only person left. An occasional adult – a teacher or support staff, I assume – comes out and either walks past me or heads for the tiny car park. I know I can't have missed Anne Marie but I'm starting to wonder if she left early. I decide to give it up as a bad job. As I turn away from the main doors to walk back the way I came I catch sight of someone round the side, near the car park. I recognize the blue hair immediately and I'm about to call out when I realize she's not alone. There's only one car still there – not Anne Marie's, she doesn't drive – and leaning against it is a middle-aged man. By which I mean about the same age as me. He's quite tall with thick hair swept back, a neat beard and dark features. Black square glasses. They're laughing at something. I start to walk over towards them, but then there's just the briefest second where they lean their foreheads together. Actually touching. It's such an intimate gesture that I almost gasp. Turning on my heel I walk off as quickly as I can, not looking back.

Chapter 10

My mind is racing. What did I just see? I try to dissect the moment in my mind. Two people, friends, sharing a joke. So far so harmless. Then both of them leaned forward, wordlessly, like muscle memory. Because they've done this many times before. It's not as if it was a kiss, I tell myself as I cross back over the main road. But this almost felt worse. More meaningful.

I've never seen the man before. I've met quite a few of Anne Marie's colleagues over the years, at parties or concerts that her students have given. I assume he's a fellow teacher. My heart aches for Harry. Does he suspect? Has he confided in Nick?

Shit, Nick. Nick is the person I burn to tell about Anne Marie and what I've just witnessed. But Nick isn't Nick any more. Have I walked into some kind of parallel universe? Not only is my husband having an affair but now it looks as if one of my best friends is too. And not even with each other either. What are the odds? Maybe Harry has a bit on the side as well. Maybe they all compare notes behind my back. I think about Harry. Big, solid, kind Harry. There's no chance.

Suddenly I realize I'm in exactly the position Lydia is in. Do I tell him? I can't even begin to imagine the opener to that conversation, let alone how I'd feel if there were even a billionth of a chance that I'd got it all wrong. Of course he'd shoot the messenger. Who wouldn't?

A cyclist shouts a tirade of abuse at me as I step out into the road without looking. I jump back, calling out my apologies and then, humiliatingly, I burst into tears. This is like one of those horror films where you don't know who to trust. All the people you loved and relied on have been taken over by alien life forms. They're no longer the people you thought you knew. I have to forget about Anne Marie, I decide, sighing with relief as I reach the steps to my front door. Just be thankful I didn't confide in her. She would hardly have given me impartial advice. Finding out what is going on with Nick has to be my priority.

This is definitely a bad idea. I have never visited the offices of Diamond Leisure before. Never had a reason to schlep to King's Cross just to drop in on my husband unannounced. Today I am going to use the excuse that I've been to a meeting with my publishers in Queen Square and have time to kill before I'm seeing my agent for tea in nearby Fitzrovia at three. Surprise! I thought we could have lunch!

None of this is true. Instead, I travel from home straight to the confusing new development at the back of the station, and wander round for half an hour before I can locate the correct building. I assume Nick usually goes for lunch at about one. (Isn't it odd, these details about our partners that are such ingrained parts of their lives that we don't even know? Does he eat a sandwich at his desk? Sit in Leon? Wander round the Camley Street Park? I have no idea. Maybe he closes the blinds on his office windows and straddles Janice across the desk while eating cheese and tomato on granary.)

Diamond Leisure is housed in a shiny anonymous-looking glass building, occupying – so the floor plan in the ground-floor reception area tells me – floors four and five. A security guard waves me through to the lifts. Everything about the main atrium says success: the koi pond (although I can only see one fish; maybe no one can agree whose job it is to feed them), the acer in an island in the centre, the complicated metal wall art. The Diamond Leisure reception on the fourth storey, on the other hand, is strictly utilitarian. No frills.

I'm hoping that the receptionist – Eyelashes, I assume – will let me go on up to Nick's office so I can have a nosey round. That's the whole point of this exercise. Get a look at the potential suspects. Of course, I'm taking a leap of faith that not only does Lydia's friend work here, but the woman Nick is apparently seeing does too. Although the truth is she could know her from anywhere. But I need to start some-where. Need to begin to narrow down the list from 'all the women in the world' to something more manageable. And maybe a small part of me is hoping that Nick will somehow give something away.

Eyelashes, however, is having none of it. I know it's her from the voice, but my detective powers clearly need work because she's fifty if she's a day, with a short dark mullet and minimal make-up. She wears a badge declaring that her name is Karen.

'If you take a seat, I'll call his assistant,' she says. She's smiley enough, but it's professional not genuine.

'I was hoping I could surprise him. I'm his wife.'

'I can't just let you through, I'm afraid. He might be in a meeting.' The steely look where her smile doesn't reach her eyes tells me she's not up for persuasion.

'Could you ask his assistant if I could go on up regardless? I'm sure there's somewhere I could wait up there.'

'Of course,' she says. 'Now if you'd like to take a seat . . .'

I do what I'm told because she intimidates the shit out of me. I sit close enough so that I can hear her conversation with Sue, which goes something along the lines of 'Nick's wife's here to see him . . . No, he's not expecting her . . . OK, will do.' She clunks the phone down and turns back to me.

'She says to wait here.'

I want to say, 'Well, of course she did because you didn't ask her if I could go up', but I know that challenging Karen won't get me anywhere. I have a feeling she gets off on the power of being the gatekeeper. Instead, I try Nick on his mobile. I've lost the advantage of surprise now anyway. If there's lipstick on his collar he'll already be cleaning it off.

'Hi,' he says almost immediately. 'Are you downstairs?' He doesn't sound like a man who's just been caught doing something he shouldn't. He sounds pleased.

I try to mirror his tone. 'Yes. I have to hang around for a couple of hours before I meet Antoinette. I thought we could have lunch or something . . .'

'Great,' he says with a smile in his voice. 'I'll come down.'

I have to try. 'I was going to come up . . . see your office . . .'

'There's nothing to see. It's a shithole, to be honest.'

'It's just . . . I've never been here before, you know . . .'

He hesitates for just a second. 'Sure. Come on up. I can only take an hour though really, so it'll have to be quick.'

Nick is the Events Manager. Is he really bound to an hour lunch break? It seems unlikely. 'Can you tell the receptionist? She won't let me past.' Clearly I have lowered my voice here so as not to be overheard. I'm not stupid.

Nick laughs. 'Do I have to? She terrifies me. I'll get Sue to do it.' He sounds just like Nick. My Nick. I wait, trying to look innocent until Karen answers the phone and then turns to me with her big old fake smile and says, 'Mrs Shepherd? You can go up. Fifth floor.' If she knows I dobbed her in she's keeping it to herself. I look for some stairs, given that it's only one flight up, but there's no obvious sign of them, so I wait an age for the lift, conscious of Karen's judgemental eyes boring into my back. When I finally get out an attractive young woman — early twenties probably, slim and incongruously tanned for January with a high, swishy, caramel ponytail — is there to greet me.

'Mrs Shepherd? I'm Jasmine . . .'

Ah yes. Jasmine. Not Janice or Janet.

'. . . I'm the department assistant. It's so nice to meet you.'

'Hi. Georgia,' I say. I'm trying to sound friendly but really I'm thinking: Is this her? Is this the kind of woman Nick would go for? And then I'm hit with a wave of self-loathing. Jasmine's smile is open and friendly. How would I feel if women reacted to Edie like this? Seeing her as a predator, a threat, just because she's pretty and young. I have never been that kind of person. And I never want to be.

'Jasmine! Nice to meet you at last,' I say, at least doing a convincing performance of someone who is happy to be there.

'It's through here,' she says, leading me past a bank of open-plan desks towards a row of offices at the back. I rack my brain for conversation but I'm too preoccupied with scanning the personnel. There are at least thirty people out here, half of them female. I try to commit them all to memory so I can forensically examine the images later. A couple of them look up, faintly curious, as I pass. I'm conscious of the fact that my cheeks are flushed red from the cold, my nose shiny. Why am I doing this?

'The managers' offices are all at this end,' Jasmine says with a wave of her hand. 'Can I get you anything? Tea or coffee?'

'No. Thank you,' I say and plaster on a smile again. Hopefully she thinks I'm friendly at least.

Nick gives me a wave when he sees me through the glass. His office is plain. Unloved. This is not the environment of someone who enjoys being here. He stands up from behind his desk, arms out. 'Well, this is a nice surprise.'

He looks relaxed. Unfazed.

'It was probably a stupid idea, but I was hanging around—'

'No,' he interrupts. 'It's great.' He grabs his coat from a peg on the wall, wraps his chunky-knit scarf around his neck. 'Is it freezing out there?'

'Miserable,' I say.

'Where do you want to go?'

I can't say, 'Actually, I was hoping you could take me round and introduce me to all the women who work here,' but I do need to make this trip worthwhile somehow.

'Show me round first.'

Nick laughs. 'Show you round?' He waves an arm. 'This is it. Not very exciting.'

'Right. What's on the other floor?'

'You saw it. Reception. More offices. Honestly, it's really

not worth seeing.' He looks at his smart Fitbit. 'And I have a meeting at two, so . . .'

'Oh. Of course. Well, let's go then. Where do you usually go?'

He shrugs. 'Jasmine just picks me up a sandwich. She gets everyone's . . .'

I seize on that as though he's thrown me a life jacket. Maybe I can salvage something from this after all. 'We can do that. If you'd rather. I don't want to disrupt your routine, and I'm not bothered about eating. I can get something later . . .'

'No, don't be silly, this is an occasion,' he says, striding out. 'I'll be back in an hour or so,' he calls to a woman – Sue, I presume – as he goes. She has a round face under long, stringy hair. Pale pasty skin and owlish glasses. God strike me down for being so judgemental but I don't think it's her.

'You have Jeff at two,' she says sternly.

'I'll be here,' he says with what I know is an insincere smile. He's told me before that he finds Sue both overbearing and irritating and now I've met her I believe him. I flap a hand at her as both hello and goodbye.

'I'd like to meet some of your colleagues,' I say, slightly desperately, as I follow.

'God, why?' he stage-whispers as he presses the button for the lift. 'I don't even want to talk to most of them myself, so I'm not going to subject you to it.'

So that's that. Now I'm just having lunch with my husband, who is about the last person I want to be spending time with. I can't be normal with him. Can't think of anything to say except 'Who is she?' or 'You're a bastard.' I've been weighing up whether telling him about Anne Marie would be useful or not. A week or so ago I would have called him straightaway. We would have agonized together over what to do next. Now I'm only interested in his opinion because it might give me an insight into his own state of mind. I hold back, though. Whatever Anne Marie is up to it doesn't seem fair to use her as a pawn in my own relationship.

We buy sandwiches and drinks in Leon but there's nowhere to sit so we huddle on a bench outside.

'Jasmine seems nice . . .' I say, for lack of any other inspiration.

'Yeah, she's great.' I listen for an edge but I'm pretty sure I can cross Jasmine off my non-existent list.

The wind suddenly whips up, funnelled between two high office blocks. It's so cold it takes my breath away. I pull my scarf up over my nose, clutch both hands round my coffee.

'Well, this is pleasant,' Nick says with a laugh. Despite everything, I join in before I remember I'm furious with him.

'Is everything OK?' I ask a few moments later. Maybe he'll just tell me. Maybe whatever he's doing is burning a hole in his conscience again and he's been waiting for a moment to unburden himself. He was brought up a Catholic, after all. I'm not sure this freezing, bleak square is the place to inspire confessions though.

His brows knit together. I can't see the rest of his face under its woolly layers but I know exactly what it's doing. I know it as well as my own. 'Yes. Why?'

'Nothing . . . just . . .'

I try to give him a meaningful look but my eyes are red and watering from the chill. He looks even more confused.

'I'm all right. Are you all right?'

I nod unconvincingly, unsure what to say. I'm saved by my mobile ringing. I have to scrabble inside my coat into the pocket of the cardigan I'm wearing underneath to find it. 'The Mayhew,' I say, holding it up so he can see.

'Answer it, quick!' he says.

'Mrs Shepherd?' a woman says once I've said hello. 'It's Jules from the Mayhew. About Igor?'

'Yes?' I manage. I raise my eyebrows at Nick and suddenly we've reconnected. We're in this together.

'We've done all the checks and we're happy to let you have him if . . .'

I don't hear the rest of what she's saying because I'm shouting, 'It's yes!' at Nick at the top of my voice. He whoops with pleasure, flings his arms round me. I can hear Jules laughing on the other end of the call.

'Sorry. Sorry. We're just excited . . . How soon can we pick him up?'

'Whenever you like. Tomorrow? That'll give you time to get any bits you need.'

'Yes. I can come at ten. Does that sound OK?'

'That sounds fine,' she says. 'And congratulations. I'm thrilled for you. And for Igor.'

I say goodbye and then Nick and I stare at each other, eyes wide. 'I need to go to the pet shop,' I say eventually, standing up. 'What haven't we got? A lead. Food. That's all for now, isn't it?' I feel euphoric, like this dog is going to save our lives. Like those people who think having a baby will repair their broken marriage. Like that ever worked.

'I think so. Poo bags.'

'God. Yes. Big ones. Right. I'll go now and then I can tidy up a bit this afternoon. Make room for him.'

'Don't you have to meet Antoinette?'

Shit. Yes. I mean, no I don't, but I told him I did. 'Of course. I mean, after, on the way home.'

I hug him goodbye. Maybe it's all going to be OK. Maybe Lydia's friend heard what she heard but it was a flirtation that was never consummated, or – God forbid I would think of this as a relief – a one-night stand that he'll spend the rest of his life regretting and never repeat. A drunken fumble. I could never accept another affair. Once is a regrettable mistake. Twice would be a habit. But maybe there is no new mistress, only a faint black shadow of remorse. I could live with that. Just.

Chapter 11

I know without a molecule of a doubt that there's no way I am going to mention what I saw to Harry. I can't even imagine how I would crowbar that into a conversation. Nice jacket, and by the way, I saw Anne Marie dry-humping some bloke in the school car park the other day. I try to justify my decision to myself: I may have misinterpreted a friendly but innocent gesture (no way); maybe it was her brother (she doesn't have a brother); he'll be better off not knowing (yeah, right). I'm closer to Anne Marie than I am to Harry so I try to convince myself my loyalties should lie with her if push comes to shove. Of course I can see why Lydia can't bring herself to tell me about Nick. It's a lose–lose situation. All I can do is try to forget what I witnessed.

I now know that Lydia will never tell me about Nick, by the way. Not on the basis of hearsay from her friend. Not without concrete proof. And I can't leave it. There may be people who can turn a blind eye to this kind of thing. Wait for it to blow over. I am not one of them.

My only hope is Patricia.

We haven't communicated for a couple of days, not since Lydia cut the conversation short on the bus. Anne Marie threw me, and it made me realize I have to approach this differently if I'm to have any chance of getting answers. There's no point spending time trying to persuade Lyds that telling me is the right thing to do. I have to convince her to confide in Patricia.

How are you doing?

I leave that there and try to distract myself with other things which, given Igor's impending arrival, isn't as hard as it could be. I've been to the pet shop on Regent's Park Road and stocked up on everything I can think of, including some kind of harness for the car that would fit a Shetland pony. I've moved anything breakable out of harm's way and lined up his new bowls on the kitchen floor. I snap a photo and WhatsApp it to the kids.

I suddenly remember that I've arranged to meet Lydia tomorrow night, while Nick – apparently – plays squash, but we can't both go out and leave Igor home alone on his first evening here. He'll be scared. He'll probably wreck the place. I don't like calling her in office hours, so I send her a text telling her we've been approved and I'll be collecting him in the morning so does she want to come over to mine for takeout instead of the pub?

She must be bored because she replies straightaway. *Isn't Nick going to be there?*

Of course, she probably doesn't want to bump into him at the moment if she can avoid it. That explains why she was so keen to jump into an Uber the other night too. She knows his big secret. Maybe she's worried she'll give herself away.

Squash, I reply. *Won't be back before ten.*

Ah! I can see why you can't leave the house then! I'll get to you about six thirty xxx.

It'll be the first time I've seen her since I found out about Nick. I'm a bit nervous about it, if I'm being honest. I don't know how I'm going to restrain myself from just asking her outright after a couple of glasses of wine. I need to make sure I drink slowly – more slowly than her, at least. That I keep my wits about me. Of course, I could just not drink at all but – at the moment – that feels out of the question. There's too much flying round in my head. I've decided I'm going to tell her about Anne Marie, the dilemma I'm in. It's the closest I can get to the subject of Nick without actually asking her about him. And then, if that fails, I'm going to try and find a way to get out of her who it is she knows who works at his company. I feel bad about using my friend for information but I need to exhaust every lead I have before I give up and confront Nick, dropping her in it in the process and potentially driving a wedge between me and her too if I find myself having to explain about Patricia.

I text her a row of kisses in return.

Nick takes the morning off work to come to the Mayhew with me. Rather than feeling grateful I'm slightly resentful, as if he's muscling in on my big moment. I no longer feel as if we're in this together. Igor will be *my* dog. I'm the one who'll spend all day with him, who'll take him for most of his walks. I've never thought about things in this way before. Territorial. Nick and I pool everything. What's ours is ours. The idea of unravelling all that, twenty years of building a joint life, is mind-blowing. It occurs to me that maybe my subconscious is already laying the groundwork for a separation. Cushioning the blow.

Still, we do a good impression of a couple united in excited anticipation. Some kind of autopilot kicks in, arranging my

face in an array of happy expressions that perfectly complement Nick's.

Igor is waiting in reception with Jules, a purple ribbon
tied round his collar in a bow. He definitely remembers us
and he jumps to his feet, straining to come and say hello.
Ludicrously, humiliatingly, I burst into tears.

'Hey,' Nick says gently. He puts an arm round me and I
fight the urge to shrug it off.

Jules gives me a smile. 'Don't be embarrassed. This often
happens. It's a big step.' She passes me a folded tissue that she
produces from somewhere. I blow my nose, nodding as if to
agree, but really she has no idea. It's loss that's making me
cry. For the moment that this should have been.

By the time Lydia arrives bearing wine, I'm frazzled,
wondering if we've done the right thing. I clearly under-
estimated the height of the wagging tail because I'm a mug
and a glass down, Igor obliviously stomping through the
mess he'd made and me having visions of having to rush
him to the vet on day one with a bleeding paw. I daren't take
my eyes off him for a second. When I go upstairs to have a
shower he follows me and, when I come out, he's asleep on
the bed, passed out like a hyperactive toddler at the end of a
long day at nursery.

'Stair gate', I write in Notes on my phone. And then I add
'× 2'. And then I delete it again because he'd probably just
step over them like a minor inconvenience. A pebble in the
road.

When Lydia rings the doorbell I'm there in seconds before
she can press it again, just like when the twins were babies and

my main concern – after keeping them alive – was keeping them asleep.

'Shh,' I say dramatically, giving her a hug.

Lydia looks round. 'What?'

'Don't wake the dog.'

She hands me the bottle and follows me into the hall, unravelling her scarf as we go. Lydia is always cold – I put it down to her being so thin – and on a day like today it looks as if it hurts. Her nose glows red against her pale skin, eyes rimmed with crimson.

'It's freezing out there,' she says, unravelling layer after layer. 'Where is he, by the way?' Static pulls her hair up on end as she peels off her woolly hat. She smooths it down.

'Igor? Upstairs. I need to let him sleep, I'm knackered.'

We wander down to the kitchen. She piles her things on a chair. 'Won't he be up all night if he sleeps now?'

'He's a dog, not a baby. Do you want to sit by the radiator?' I pull out the chair nearest to the warmth and she flops into it gratefully.

'I definitely want to see him before I go. I brought him a toy,' she says, reaching into her bag and producing a tiny rubber bone that he'll probably swallow accidentally in three seconds.

I pour a large glass of the red she brought and hand it to her. 'Oh, you will. He's hard to miss.'

We chat about nothing much, filling each other in on our week, although there's a lot of detail I have to omit from mine.

'Oh, I forgot . . .' I say, casually, once we've exhausted that topic. 'Nick mentioned that someone he works with is a friend of yours . . .' I wait to see if she bites.

She takes a sip of her wine. 'Oh. Well, I do know someone who works at Diamond Leisure. I didn't realize she knew Nick though . . .'

She's lying, obviously. 'I've forgotten what he said her name is . . . ?'

'Emma,' she says quickly. No offer of a surname. How many Emmas can there be? Lots, I imagine. It hits me suddenly that there's no reason to think she works at the London office. She could be at any one of the regional sites. They employ hundreds of people. Thousands even.

'How do you know her?'

'She's a friend of a friend. What's that?'

As luck would have it, Igor has chosen this moment to wake up and go into a frenzied panic, presumably not knowing where he is. Either that or my house has just been struck by a meteor. The building rumbles and he appears at the foot of the stairs. Does a perfect double take when he sees Lydia.

'It's OK, Igor. Come here.' I tap the arm of my chair and he comes over and slumps beside me. I stroke his ears.

'He's . . . well, I mean, he's gorgeous but he's huge . . .'

'I told you.'

'Yes, but I thought you meant like a big dog, not an average-sized horse.' She holds a hand out and lets him sniff it. Tickles him under his chin. 'What a sweetheart.'

'God, I hope we've done the right thing . . .'

I top up our glasses. Lydia is being deliberately cagey about her mole so I have to move to Plan B.

'Something funny happened this week. I don't know if I should tell you but I really need some advice.'

Obviously no one can resist a lead-in like that. Lydia has

never been a salacious gossip though. I've consciously steered away from those kinds of people. I know how much it hurts to be on the other end. To be the one that all the other girls whispered about. Made up stories about. My mum used to tell me it was because I was too pretty, that they were jealous. God love her. I wasn't (not even slightly) and they weren't. I was just different enough – due to my height, my big feet, my clumsy limbs – to give them a target. And that's all some people need. Because the bigger the gang you join in pursuit of a common enemy, the less likely you are to be singled out yourself. Lyds is too frustrating for a tattletale to confide in. She always questions the source. Tries to look at all other angles. Leaves no room for reasonable doubt. Of course, I realize now, she will have cross-examined Emma. She must 100 per cent believe that her intel is reliable or she would have dismissed the story altogether. She would never have felt the need to confide in Patricia.

I tell her what I saw. Anne Marie in the school car park. I don't embellish, I just give her the bare facts. She sits back in her chair, legs crossed. 'Cousin?'

'When did you last rub foreheads with your cousin?' Too late I remember how tiny her family is. Basically just the one aunt at this point.

'I don't have any cousins. But some people are very close to them. Old friend?'

'Maybe.' Igor sighs and leans his head on my leg.

'He likes you,' Lydia says, smiling. 'Maybe I should get a pet.'

'You should. I just know there was more to it. The way they looked at each other. Something. Should I say anything?'

'To her?'

'Or Harry. I don't know.'

'God. No. What if you're mistaken?'

I need to approach this carefully. 'What if I found out I was definitely right? How could we all hang out together as if nothing was wrong? I wouldn't be able to look at her. And what if I couldn't stop thinking about it and then I let something slip? It's a nightmare.'

'They've got kids, George. You can't just blunder in there. Maybe she is having an affair but Harry's OK with it so long as no one else knows? Or they have an open marriage but they know you wouldn't approve so they keep it to themselves?'

'Anne Marie and Harry? No way. We've talked about all this kind of stuff over the years. I know. Same as you know me and Nick would never be OK with something like that.'

Is it my imagination or does she look just the tiniest bit uncomfortable?

She's quiet for a moment. 'But would you want me to tell you? If I found out something about Nick?'

'Yes!' I almost shout it. 'Yes. I would. Of course I would.'

We sit there for what seems like an age. I don't want to break the silence because I feel as if she's on the verge of saying it and I don't want to ruin the moment. I steady my gaze on her, slow my breathing.

Suddenly she flicks a glance at the oversized vintage railway-station clock on the wall. 'Shit, is that the time? I need to call an Uber. I've got an early start . . .'

And just like that the chance is gone.

Chapter 12

Nick and I lie at the edges of the bed like two sentries guarding the beast in the middle. Our resolve not to let Igor into the bedroom lasted less than ten minutes, the pitiful howling from the kitchen both heartbreaking and terrifying in equal measure. I could imagine one of our neighbours calling the police: 'There's a wolf on the loose in Primrose Hill.' Now he's sleeping like a baby with a very noisy sinus condition. I'm not going to lie, I like it. Nick came home tipsy and a bit amorous. He shoved his kit in the washing machine and turned it on so I have no idea whether it really was sweaty, whether he had indeed been playing squash. He'd definitely had a shower though.

'Lyds was saying she knows someone who works with you. Emma something,' I said as he made himself a snack of peanut butter on toast. I thought I'd strike while the iron was pissed. Catch him off guard. I watched him for a reaction. Did the idea of my best friend having a spy in his camp make him nervous? It was impossible to tell.

He shrugged. Twisted the lid back on to the peanut butter, missing the thread so it went round and round without catching. Tonight the comedy drunk act wasn't endearing, it was grating. 'Emma who?'

'I don't know. Do you know any Emmas?'

He handed me the jar as if it was a puzzle he was never

going to solve. 'Not that I can think of. What department's she in?'

'I don't know.'

'What does she look like?'

'No idea. You either know an Emma or you don't,' I snapped.

Now I can't sleep. My mind is whirring with frustration. All I want is a straight answer, whatever that answer is. Let me know the worst and I can find a way to deal with it. I slide out of bed, trying not to wake either of my sleeping companions, but Igor senses my movement immediately and throws himself off to follow me. Nick sleeps blissfully on, one arm thrown above his head, lips parted. I grab the throw from the foot of the bed and wrap it around me, carefully closing the bedroom door as I go. Down in the basement I make myself a cup of tea and take it and my phone to the soft cream sofa. Igor flops on to his bed and starts snoring almost immediately, his sweet face resting on his paws. Lydia is right, he likes me. I feel a rush of maternal affection and tears spill down my cheeks before I can stop them.

Once I've cried myself out I open up Twitter. Patricia needs to up her game. There's a message from Lydia from earlier. Heart pounding, I open it up.

I've just seen Georgia. Honestly, Patricia, I can't bear it. I'm finding it so hard!! And I think she suspects her husband is up to no good now too. She kept bringing the conversation round to people having affairs. Do you think she knows I know something???

I check the time it was sent. Twenty-five past eleven. So much for Lydia rushing home because she needed an early night. My theory that she's avoiding bumping into Nick gains weight. I know she won't be up now and neither would Patricia so I resist answering.

In the morning when I wake up before it's light – still on the kitchen sofa, shivering under the thin throw – I send the response I've spent half the night composing.

Poor Georgia. The not knowing is the worst. Especially if you suspect. You feel as if everyone is laughing at you behind your back. All I wanted was for someone to be straight with me, however bad the news.

And then I drag my big coat on over my pyjamas, pull on my warmest boots, stuff my pockets with poo bags and take Igor out for a walk to the top of the hill.

'Don't forget it's Anne Marie and Harry tonight,' Nick says when I get back. If he thinks it's odd that I've already been out he doesn't say so.

'Wait . . . when did we arrange that?' The last thing I want at the moment is to be in a room with the two of them.

'A few days ago. I told you.' He offers Igor a bit of his toast and he scarfs it down greedily.

'We shouldn't feed him crap,' I say huffily.

'Look at the size of him, he's hardly going to get fat.'

'I was hoping for a quiet weekend. What with Igor and everything. Shouldn't we just let him settle in?'

'They want to meet him. It'll be fine. It's too late to cancel them now anyway.'

'Can't we say I'm ill or something? I don't know . . . food poisoning?'

He looks at me with concern. 'Do you really want to? Wouldn't I just have them over anyway if that were the case?'

He's right. It's happened before when one of us has been genuinely unwell. The others have still met up and popped in and out to visit the patient.

'Something catching then.'

He kisses the top of my head. 'You'll enjoy it once they're here. And if you still don't feel like it you can feign illness then and hide in the bedroom, how's that?'

I shrug. 'It doesn't feel as if I have a choice.'

'It's Harry and Anne Marie,' he says, heading for the stairs. 'It's not as if we have to be on our best behaviour.'

I'm so sorry, Patricia! It sounds like your husband was a dick!!!

I'm in the bath. Igor sits in the corner of the room, staring at me. It's unsettling to say the least.

I think that's a fair assessment. He had an affair with his assistant. Always one to go for the cliché. When I think about all those times I spoke to her on the phone. The humiliation was the worst thing. If I'd known at least I could have spared myself that.

Come on, Lydia. Bite. Put me out of my misery.

I follow my message up with another without waiting for a reply.

Is that what Georgia's husband is doing?

I sit there for an age, waiting for her to respond. Igor comes over and puts his paws on the side of the bath, thinks about getting in.

'No. Sit.'

He sits.

'Good boy.'

It is someone he works with (I didn't tell you that!!!!). Not his assistant though. Don't think G knows her.

107

So the mistress is a colleague too. At least I now have one fact. I can't think of anything to say so I leave it for now. Concentrate on getting through the evening.

The first thing I notice about Anne Marie is that she's glowing. Not in a 'might be pregnant' way. More 'getting a lot of action'. It's the middle of winter. No one glows in the middle of winter. It's against the natural order of things. It makes me angry. Doesn't she realize what she's doing? What she's risking?

'You look really well,' I say as she hugs me hello. She's almost as tall as me but the naturally bony version. She smells as she always does of Diptyque. Something floral but not girly. Green and heady rather than pink and fluffy.

'Really?' She produces a bottle of white from somewhere. Harry has already followed Nick down to the kitchen. 'I don't know why.'

I look her dead in the eye. She looks away.

'I came to meet you from school the other day.' I don't know why I say it. It just comes out. It's as if, if I can understand why she is doing what I think she's doing, it'll give me an insight into Nick.

I don't imagine it: she flushes. 'Oh. Which day? I must have missed you.'

'I saw you,' I say, although I try to keep my voice light. Just a statement, not an accusation. 'But it looked as if you were busy. You were talking to someone in the car park.'

'You should have come over,' she says, recovering her composure. 'Why didn't you?'

'You didn't look like you wanted to be interrupted. Is he another teacher?'

She clears her throat. 'Could have been anyone. What day did you say it was?' We're interrupted by Nick and Harry on their way to the living room, glasses in hand. A white for me, a red for Anne Marie. If they detect the slightly frosty atmosphere they don't show it.

'He's amazing,' Harry says. 'The dog.' Right on cue Igor lopes up from the kitchen after them. Anne Marie makes a show of making a fuss of him, but I know she's feeling rattled. She wants to know what I know.

'Did you order yet?' Nick says as he hands me my drink.

'No. Could you?'

'Sure.' They go on through and I hear him rattling around in the drawer where the takeout menus are stuffed in a pile. We try to patronize one of the local restaurants whenever we can. Whichever one they choose they'll know exactly what Anne Marie and I would want to order.

'About our age. Tall. Beard. Glasses,' I say once I'm sure they're out of earshot. 'I'm not having a go. But if I picked up on it then anyone could have.'

She nods. Closes her eyes briefly. 'Moment of madness. Please don't say anything.'

'I won't. I wouldn't.'

'I'll tell you all about it. Him. But not tonight.'

'I think Nick might be seeing someone,' I say quietly. Her face gives away that this is definitely news to her.

'What? No way. How do you . . . ?'

I shrug sadly. 'Not now.'

I watch her and Harry as we eat. On the surface they're the same as ever, but I feel as if I can see it's a bit forced on her part. A show for my benefit, maybe. Is she seeing the same when she looks at me and Nick now? I wonder. Do the cracks show once you know they're there?

The evening feels flat, and we're all ready to call it a night by half ten. Nick suggests that we walk them back, at least part of the way, so Igor can do his business before bed. I feel as if Harry is the only one of us who still thinks everything is the way it's always been. He clowns around, letting himself be dragged along by the dog, mimicking being on a sled. He seems oblivious to the tensions around him and I'm thankful for that at least.

'Anne Marie was quiet. Is she OK?' Nick says once we've turned back. Without saying anything we've walked past our turning and up over the hill. It's completely deserted. Eerie in the frosty lamplight. London laid out in front of us like a jewelled banquet.

'Just tired, I think.'

'I couldn't do her job. Can you imagine?'

'Mmm,' is all I can come up with.

He slips on a patch of ice. 'Oh, I have to go to the Inverness site on Monday. Check out the new clubhouse. I told you they've been building a new one . . .'

First I've heard of it but then it's not exactly hot news, so I might not have taken it in. 'Right.'

'I'll stay over. Come back in the morning.'

Ah. My heart splinters. 'I'm freezing. Let's go back.'

Chapter 13

Nick does indeed have a plane ticket to Inverness, so that part at least is true. He prints it off as we get ready for bed on Sunday night, and leaves it lying on the hall table along with his passport. I stare at it, wondering who else is doing the same. Who is checking her legs for stray hairs and packing her skimpiest underwear. Maybe she's bought something new for the occasion. Hit up Victoria's Secret. Trussed herself up like a sweaty turkey in the name of sex. Their first whole night together. I imagine it's a big deal. I think about slipping something of mine in his overnight bag. Something personal that will pop out when he unpacks, reminding him what he's risking losing, pricking at her conscience if she has one. But I can't think of anything poignant enough. A pair of my old M & S knickers won't really deliver the message I want to send.

While he's in the shower in the morning, tired and grumpy from the early start, I scrawl a quick note – 'Igor had a bathroom emergency! Taken him out. See you tomorrow. Have a good trip x' – grab the dog and rush him out of the front door. I take him down towards Regent's Park instead of up and over Primrose Hill, just in case Nick decides to find us and say a proper goodbye, and I walk with him until we're both exhausted and I know my husband will have left the house if he's not going to risk missing his plane. When I get back he's scribbled something on the bottom. 'Hate not saying goodbye!! Call you later! Love you!' I tear it up. Then I worry what if his plane crashes and it's the last thing he ever said to me, so I fish the pieces out of the bin and put them on the side.

I spend a fretful day alternating between trying to work and googling random things to do with Diamond Leisure in the hope of a breakthrough. I think about calling Sue or Jasmine and asking who else has gone to the Inverness site today, but I'm guessing she's there in an unofficial capacity so they wouldn't know. The chances of the woman he's sleeping with also being someone who legitimately could be accompanying him on a routine visit seem low. Too convenient. Unless, that is, it's an affair of opportunity not passion. More Ms Right Under My Nose than Ms Right. Or maybe I should call and ask who's called in sick or booked two days' holiday but, even if they had the faintest idea, why would they tell me? And I'm keen to try and preserve some iota of dignity in all this if I can. I don't want to add 'sad suspicious wife' to the list of things they can gossip about behind my back.

Just as I'm about to force myself out to the gym at about five to four, the doorbell rings. I recognize Anne Marie's willowy form through the rippled glass panels of the front door. Shit. I don't want to talk to her. I should never have said anything. Never have involved myself in her business. Igor starts barking helpfully, so she'll know I must be at home. No creeping back down to the kitchen and hiding for me.

I hold on to his collar and open the door. I live in fear of him bolting and not yet knowing where he lives to find his way home.

'Hi,' I say, a question in my voice. It's not unusual for her to pop round without notice, but after our brief conversation on Saturday night this doesn't feel like a casual visit.

'Have you got a sec?' She looks anxious. The glow waning.

I think about saying, No, I'm in the middle of a work emergency. But she'd probably just laugh. My work is never urgent. The world will not end if I don't come up with a rhyme for shampoo before tomorrow. The global publishing industry will not collapse.

'Sure.'

She follows me in and down to the kitchen and I flip the kettle on without even asking if she wants anything. Anne Marie is a coffee addict. I don't think I have ever witnessed her refuse a cup. She's the kind of person who indulges in two lethal-looking after-dinner espressos and then sleeps like a baby.

'So . . . um . . . what you said on Saturday night—'

I interrupt. 'Sorry. I shouldn't have. It's nothing to do with me.'

She sits down at the table. 'It's not . . . It's over. But . . . you won't say anything to Harry, will you?'

'No,' I say too quickly and then immediately regret it. I don't want to end up making a promise I can't keep. I should have waited till I heard what she has to say.

She exhales loudly. 'He's another teacher. Obviously. Jez. Teaches English. He's divorced. We've been friends for a little while – he only started in September – but lately it's got a bit more . . .'

She leaves it hanging there.

I put the coffee down in front of her. 'You don't have to

tell me. I'm not sure I want to know, to be honest. Sorry if that sounds harsh; it's not meant to be.'

'I need to get it off my chest. I know you won't tell anyone. Anyone. Not Harry. Not ever.'

I shake my head. 'Of course not.'

'You remember I went to that conference thing at the beginning of the Christmas holidays?' She doesn't wait for me to respond. I actually do remember. Some kind of teenage developmental thing. Up in Yorkshire, I think. We'd invited Harry and the kids over for the evening because he's a useless cook. And when Anne Marie's not around he tends to mope about like an abandoned puppy.

She exhales loudly. 'There was no conference. We just went to a hotel. I knew as soon as we got up to his room that it was a terrible mistake. Fantasizing about it is one thing but actually doing it . . .'

'Shit, Anne Marie . . .'

'I went through with it. That's what I can't forgive myself for. I should have just got out of there. Anyway, Jez knew my heart wasn't in it. It was pretty much a disaster. But it still happened . . .'

'Then what?'

'I didn't see him till the start of term. I told him I had to concentrate on my family over Christmas – that he shouldn't phone or text or anything – and he agreed. What you saw . . . that was the first chance we'd had to really talk about it . . .'

She stares at her hands, twists her wedding ring round and round. I have no idea if she knows she's doing it. I wait. The atmosphere feels weighted. Heavy. Igor finally breaks the silence by doing the loudest fart known to animalkind. He sighs happily. It's impossible not to laugh. I flap my hands around, open the patio doors even though it's minus one out.

'Sorry,' I say. 'He's not quite got etiquette down yet.'

'I'm going to stop it before anything else happens. Tell him it was a mistake, that I love Harry and my family,' Anne Marie says, snapping out of her reverie. 'I just want you to know that.'

I lean over and put my hand on her arm. 'Like I said, it's none of my business, but I'm glad. How do you think he'll take it?'

'I think he'll be OK. He's a nice bloke . . . He's probably expecting it, to be honest.'

'So that's it?'

She nods. 'It was a moment of madness. Not even a moment. A fraction of a moment – whatever that is.'

'A nano moment,' I say helpfully and she smiles.

'Please don't hate me,' she says.

'As if.'

She shivers and I lean over and shut the door.

'If I thought . . . If there was any way it was ever going to happen again I'd tell Harry. I absolutely would. But it won't. Not with Jez. Not with anyone. If anything, it's made me appreciate what I have more. But I know if he found out he would never forgive me, however hard he tried. Not completely. It would ruin everything. It would break his heart.'

It would, I have no doubt about that. 'You're right. There's no reason for him to know.' Do I actually believe this? I think I do.

'Thank you.'

We sit there saying nothing for a moment. I feel as if a huge weight has shifted off me. Of course what's happened would devastate Harry if he ever found out; I haven't forgotten that. But he won't and, for the first time ever, I understand that that's a kindness more than a deception.

Anne Marie sighs. 'Tell me what's happening with Nick. I don't believe he's seeing someone. He's the last person . . .'

I can't tell her about his history. I don't want her to think our relationship was already broken, because it wasn't. Just fractured. Healed. 'I would have said the same about you a couple of days ago . . .'

'Don't . . .'

'Sorry.' I take a sip of my coffee. 'That was cheap. Someone told me that he's having a thing with a woman at work.'

The shock on her face tells me she really had no idea. 'No way. Who told you?'

'It doesn't matter. Just a friend of mine who knows someone he works with. I don't know what to do.'

'Have you asked him?'

I shake my head emphatically. 'No, because then he'd want to know how I'd heard and I'd have to drop her in it. What if he fires the person who told her?'

'Shit. I just can't see it.'

'He's gone up to the Inverness site tonight. He's staying over . . .'

She looks at me. 'You don't think . . . ?'

'I don't know. Yes. Do you think he might have confided in Harry?' On balance I think this is unlikely. Nick would know Harry'd feel duty bound to tell Anne Marie. His mate

Dom is far more likely to be his confidant and Dom and I have never had the greatest relationship. We get on fine on the surface, we just don't gel. If he comes round and Nick leaves the room we never seem to have the faintest idea what to say to each other beyond 'How's work?'

'No. I think he'd know . . .' She stops, sighs. 'I think he'd know Harry would be horrified. That he hates that kind of thing.'

'Anne Marie . . . while you were . . . you and Jez . . . did you feel as if you'd fallen out of love with Harry? Was that it?'

She grabs my hand across the table. 'No! God, no. It was nothing to do with Harry. It was like I got taken over by the bodysnatchers. Honestly, George, if it's true about Nick it's nothing to do with how he feels about you. It's a mid-life crisis or something. Some kind of subconscious rebellion against ageing. I know it's awful but maybe he just needs to get it out of his system.'

I drain the last of my drink. 'It's a deal-breaker. I didn't sign up to be the pitied wife at home while my husband fucks about.' As I say it I realize it's true. Two strikes and you're out. No more chances.

'Just find out what's true before you damn him,' she says. 'Don't write him off yet.'

Which is why I'm soon to be sitting in a King's Cross pub, feeling like an exhibit. Feeling as if everyone is looking at me, judging me. The spare part at Nick's department's weekly drinks. Nick usually just buys his team a round, stays for one, and is home by half seven. It's not something to which partners are invited, but they're not not invited either. It's more that they would never think to come unless they happened to be passing. There's nothing duller than work drinks for anyone not intimately acquainted with the offensive personal hygiene of Ian from Marketing or the passive-aggressive power plays of Vera in Sales. No one ever talks about anything other than their colleagues, their work grievances, their perceived slights. Why does X always ask me and not Y to do her photocopying? Why does Z never listen to my ideas but if Martine pipes up he's all ears, probably because she bats her eyelashes at him and acts all giggly so he thinks she's up for it, lecherous bastard. No one ever has a conversation, it's all gossip and innuendo. But gossip is exactly what I need right now. One drink too many and someone might let something slip.

Nick went straight to the office from the airport when he got back from Inverness. He'd phoned me a couple of times the night before: when he arrived and before he went out for 'dinner with the resort manager'. We've always laughed about the way Diamond Leisure refer to their sites as 'resorts' with all that word promises. Palm trees and sandy beaches. Mojitos and spa treatments. Diamond Leisure parks are more ball pits full of snotty toddlers and two pints for the price of one on Mondays. At about ten past ten I'd called his mobile and it rang out. So I sent him a text saying *Just tried to call you to say goodnight. I'm still up for a while xx*. Then I sat up waiting. When he hadn't phoned by five to eleven I tried again. Still no reply. In the morning I woke up to a text: *Reception up here is rubbish. Only just got your text. Won't call now because it's way too late! X*. Sent at twenty to one. No explanation of what he was doing up in the early hours. Had she just sloped back to her own room? Or was he sneaking around texting me from the bathroom while she slept?

I asked him how it had gone when he got home and he said 'good'. That was it. Good. I had to resist the urge to sniff him like a forensics dog. He must have brought trace evidence home. I quizzed him as subtly as I could. 'Who's the resort manager again?' All I wanted to know was whether it was a man or a woman, although the practicalities of him having an affair with someone who both lived and worked at the other end of the country rendered it pretty unlikely.

'Mal Reeves,' he said and then proceeded to tell me an anecdote about Mal that I had no interest in hearing. I hurried him along, laughing before the punchline in an effort to speed the story up.

'You were up late,' I said, trying to be casual. He looked at me, confused. 'Your text . . .'

'Oh. Yes, sorry about that. I'd had a few too many beers and I couldn't sleep. I didn't realize how late it was. Did it wake you?'

'No. Where did you go? The bar?'

He shook his head. 'It's all closed for the off season, isn't it? We went to his house. Fucking awful food so I had to get pissed.' He laughed.

We. That word hung in the air between us. 'Who else was there?'

'Just a few others from the company. No one interesting. I'm going to have a shower,' he added. Subject closed.

I know that he and his colleagues always head to the modern open spaces of the Lighterman in Granary Square. In the summer they gather outside, by the canal, but I assume that's off limits in winter except for the most diehard of smokers. And I know that they all leave work a bit early to get seats before the six o'clock rush. When Nick first started working there he used to beg me to come down and meet him.

'I don't know what to say to them all. It's torture.'

'Well, if you don't then I wouldn't have a clue,' I remember saying, laughing. 'You're on your own.'

Over the years – he's been there five – he's stopped asking but I've always known that if I'd ever offered he'd have been thrilled. It just never seemed that big a deal but maybe if I'd made more of an effort to get to know his colleagues we wouldn't be in this situation now.

'Stop it,' I say out loud to no one. I often do this. Say words out loud. It comes from working at home, I think. Sometimes you just want to hear a voice even if it's your own. Now, of course, I have Igor as an excuse. 'Talking to myself? Of course not. I was saying something to the dog.'

I chastise myself inside my head this time. None of this is my fault. This is Nick's bad behaviour, not mine.

I'm going to surprise Nick at his work drinks, I text Lydia as I get ready. We haven't spoken much this week. I'm worried she's avoiding me because she's nervous about what she might give away. I'm pretty sure this text'll make her panic on my behalf, but I want to see how she reacts.

What's brought that on!!!

I don't know. I thought it'd be nice to make an effort. He's working really hard at the moment, so I'm not seeing much of him. Thought it'd be nice!

I wonder if she gets rolling news from her friend Emma.

Updates as they happen. If she already knows he spent the night in Inverness and who with. Knowing Lyds she will have asked for no more information until there's solid proof.

Is he expecting you?? You don't want to give him a heart attack! She adds a smiley face to take the edge off.

No. I only just decided. I'll text him on the way. I won't, but she doesn't need to know that. I know I will have worried her, but I want to provoke a reaction. I text her a row of kisses, promising to call her tomorrow and then I head straight for Patricia's Twitter page. While I wait I have her like a few more arty enterprises. And then, there it is, the little number one in the bottom right-hand corner that tells me I have a private message.

Oh God, Patricia, I hope you're there!!! Georgia is on her way to surprise Nick at his work drinks!!! I don't know what to do.

Of course Patricia is there. Good old reliable Patricia. *I'm here. Oh my goodness. Do you think SHE will be there?*

She works in his department!! She's bound to be!!

Fuck. My heart pounds. This isn't someone who he's met at one of the regional sites. It's a person he sees every day. And I'm going to be in a room with her in less than an hour. I'm not just going to hear a random bit of gossip about her. I'm actually going to meet her.

Another message pops up. *Should I let him know somehow?? Just casually mention she's on her way??*

Really? No. No, you should not. I'm just about to have Patricia give her a stern rebuttal for that one when there's more.

No! Forget I said that! That would be awful. Like I was colluding in his deception! I just don't want George to get hurt!

The only thing you can do is tell her, Patricia says. *Or just wait and see what happens and then be there to support her.*

Thank God I've got you to talk to. What would I do without you!!

I don't reply. I can't think what to say.

Chapter 14

The doorbell rings and I know it'll be Anne Marie, come over to babysit. She's the only person who knows where I'm going; in fact, she offered to come with me but there was no one else I could ask to keep an eye on Igor. He's been watching me get ready – making much more of an effort than I usually would – with his big, sad, accusing eyes. Abandoned again so soon.

'You look gorgeous,' she says when I open the door.

'Not too much?' I'm wearing skinny jeans with lace-up ankle boots that mean I'm now grazing six foot two, and a soft slate-grey fitted cardigan. I watched an Instagram tutorial on smokey shadow and, I think, I've copied it pretty successfully. So long as I can remember not to rub my eyes. Or cry. My hair is down in shiny waves, parted in the middle. I think I look as good as I can, which is all any of us can hope for. It's not for Nick, it's for me. To give me confidence. Actually, let's be honest here, it's for her. I want her to look at me and feel intimidated.

Of course, she might just look at me and think I look like her mother.

'Perfect. Are you really sure you want to do this?'

I nod in what I hope is a convincing way. She puts her hands on my shoulders. 'Remember: smile, look happy, don't drink. It's a fact-finding mission, nothing more.'

'Yep.' My mouth is dry. I want to go down to the kitchen and get a glass of water, but I'm scared if I do I'll never come up again.

'And even if she's not there, or you can't work out which one she is, Nick'll see you and come to his senses . . .'

'Because he's scared he's going to get caught?' I'm about to say I don't want him to end it with her just because he thinks I'm on to him when she interrupts.

'Because he'll realize what he's in danger of losing. Trust me. I know.'

I hug her goodbye. Wait for her to grab Igor's collar before I head out of the door to my taxi.

By the time I reach the pub my immaculate façade is fading fast. My face is red and blotchy from concentrating on not slipping on my way across the square. My hair frizzes damply. I find the toilets and lock myself in a cubicle, sitting down on the closed lid and breathing deeply. Not the greatest of ideas. I put my hand over my nose. I hear voices and a pair of laughing women clatter in. I sit very still. Wait for what seems like an age before I hear two flushes and the tap running.

'Fucking cheek of it,' one of them is saying. 'You should have fucked her up.' Jesus, I hope she's not my rival. I'm a full-on, card-carrying coward when it comes to physical violence. I once offered a bloke my mobile because I thought he was going to hit me. Turned out he was just swiping an angry wasp off my arm. Once they've gone I emerge and do what I can in front of the mirror. I brought a few emergency supplies in my bag so I smooth down my hair with argan oil and press Bare Minerals powder on to my shiny face. It'll do.

I head out to the bar. There are a couple of large groups having shouty conversations. That kind of manic energy that you get when people who work together let loose together. The knife-edge potential that you might say something to your boss after a few drinks that'll get you either promoted or fired. I scan them both for Nick and spot him over by the window, penned in by nine or ten people. I have a moment to scrutinize them before there's any danger he will see me. It's tempting to stay here and just observe. Get a true picture of how he behaves when I'm not around. Seven of the group are women. I recognize Jasmine and Sue. Nick is flanked by two of the others. Both around mid-thirties. Both attractive. The one on his left is talking to him intently, leaning in to say something for his ears only. I feel a sharp pang of jealousy. I've never been a possessive person. Not even in the post-Felicity world. But this is different. This is not unfounded suspicion. This is fact.

I force a smile on to my face. Pull it back a bit. Happy to be there, not unhinged. And then I push my shoulders down, stand as tall as I can, take a calming breath and stride towards my husband.

He's deep in conversation with suspect number one – long, poker-straight dark blonde hair, low-cut top – and so he doesn't see me approach. I hover awkwardly. A couple of people give me a passing glance and then go back to their chats. I'm about to slope off and try again later when Jasmine spots me and greets me warmly.

'Georgia! Hi.' Twenty-plus eyes all swivel to look at who it is she's talking to. Out of the corner of my eye I see Nick double take, and – I would swear – his first, unconscious reaction is a frown that he swiftly buries and replaces with a smile.

'Hi, Jasmine,' I say, just as he says, 'Georgia? What are you doing here?' He stands up, maybe to put some distance between himself and one of the women he was sitting between. I feel myself colour as if they are all waiting for me to explain myself.

I unravel my scarf. 'You're always saying come down, so I thought I would,' I say lightly. 'I was bored stiff at home.'

'Great,' he says. 'Brilliant.'

Someone fetches a stool for me to sit on, opposite Nick. The perfect vantage point.

'Would you like a drink?' a woman to the left of me says. I can see that they all have full glasses. She waves a half-full bottle of white at me.

'Oh. Yes, that would be lovely.' She produces a glass from somewhere and hands it to me. I pour myself a tiny measure.

'I'm Elaine, by the way,' she says. 'I'm Logistics, but don't hold that against me.' I think Elaine may have had a couple before the others got here. Perhaps she has a flask in her desk drawer. I don't think she's drunk, but she's on the way. She's in her late fifties. Frizzy hair. Shiny suit jacket. I don't think she's my rival, but who knows.

'Oh. Yes,' Nick says. 'I should introduce you. Everyone, this is Georgia, my wife . . .' Does he imbue that word with gravitas? Is he making sure that whoever it is knows to dial down the flirty looks? 'You know Jasmine and Sue. This is Martin,' he says, indicating the man to Sue's right. He carries on counter-clockwise as I smile, smile, smile. 'Si, Danny, Elaine you just met, Abigail . . .' Abigail is thirty-odd, pretty.

Big blue eyes. Girl next door in that way that gets more attractive the more you look at her. A possible. He jumps over me and Jasmine. 'Anil, Jess . . .' Jess is another possible. A bit younger than the others, dark-eyed, full-lipped. My grin is becoming a rictus. Finally he gets to the woman on his left. The one he was deep in discussion with. 'Lou. And' – indicating the woman on his right who has rich red hair and a pale porcelain complexion. Delicate. Tiny. I'd bet she's not more than five foot. I feel like a wardrobe next to a bedside table – 'Siobhan. That's it.'

'No one is expecting you to remember all that,' Elaine says, topping up her own glass.

'Hi, everyone,' I say. They all mutter hello and then there's an awkward silence where, I think, they're weighing up whether they need to be seen to entertain the stranger or if they can carry on with the conversations they were having before I arrived. I'm an inconvenience. I know I have to make the most of this opportunity though, so I can't worry about that. I turn to the nearest of the women I haven't met before. Abigail.

'What do you do?' I ask and then I cringe at my lack of originality. If I was hoping to show them that Nick has an attractive, smart, funny wife who they can never truly compete with, this is not the conversation-opener to go with. Luckily the rest of them are so relieved to be off the hook that they pick up where they left off when I showed up, so they're not listening. Abigail looks like a rabbit caught in the headlights, forced to talk to the stranger.

'I'm one of the bookers,' she says.

'Oh, right,' I say, grasping for what to ask next – 'Are you having an affair with my husband?' not being a viable option.

In my peripheral vision I can see that Nick has turned to Siobhan on his right. Does that mean something? Is he no longer talking to Lou because I'm here? They seemed pretty cosy when I arrived. Is he telling Siobhan to act casual, not to give herself – or him – away?

'It's lovely to meet you at last. You're a novelist, aren't you?' Abigail says, making an effort.

'Not really. Picture books. For kids.'

'That's amazing. I wish I had a talent like that.' I like Abigail, I decide. I really hope it's not her.

We're interrupted when Lou pipes up. She has a braying voice, like an agitated donkey. 'So, Georgia, what's Nick like at home? Surely we're allowed to pump you for his deepest, darkest secrets as you're here? What's his worst habit?'

Lou, on the other hand, I do not like. I smile faintly. Nick is looking stricken, the focus of potential ridicule from his team. And maybe his mistress too. 'Oh no,' I say, forcing a laugh into my voice. 'My lips are sealed.'

'Come on, you have to!' Flame-haired Siobhan, on Nick's other side, joins in. I catch a flash of her eyes, a vivid emerald green. Even from across the table they're startling.

'Leave the poor woman alone,' my new best friend Abigail interrupts.

I remind myself that part of my mission today is to play the happy, friendly wife who might just prick someone's conscience enough that they'll want to tip them off after a few drinks. 'He's a model husband, aren't you, darling?' I say sweetly, and just about avoid vomiting. Nick just looks confused.

I'm pretty sure I can eliminate Elaine and Abigail as well as Jasmine and Sue from my enquiries. Lou and Siobhan are definite possibles. Jess is the only one I haven't yet interacted with, so I turn to her, completely ignoring Anil who is sitting next to her. I'm sure he's a nice guy, but I don't have time to waste on him at the moment. 'How about you, Jess? What do you do?' She looks at me as if I'm her teacher and I've just singled her out to read her homework aloud.

'Events. Same as the rest of them.'

'Oh. You're all in the Events Department?'

'It's department drinks,' she says with a – probably sub-conscious – sneer.

'Right. And what do you do? In the Events Department?'

'Jess is our sunny Budgets Exec,' Anil says. 'She lives to tell us we're offering the Cheeky Girls five pounds more than they're worth.'

'So you end up offering them nothing?' I say, attempting a joke. Luckily he gets it, and lets out a yelpy laugh. Jess just sits there stony-faced. Out of the corner of my eye I can see that Nick is trying to get my attention, leaning forward while Lou and Siobhan chat animatedly behind his back.

'Is this the whole department then?' I say to Anil, ignoring my husband. 'Are you all here?'

He looks around. 'Not quite. Camilla's gone home, I think. She's the graphics person. Does all the artwork . . .' Shit. I need to add Camilla to the list. Anil gets to his feet. 'It's my round. What can I get you?'

I hear Nick saying my name. He's shrugging into the sleeves of his jacket, obviously keen to go.

I pretend I haven't heard, keep my eyes focused on Anil. 'Thanks. Vodka and tonic, please.'

'Ooh, Nick, that means you'll have to stay for another,'

Lou purrs. 'He never stays for two,' she says to me as if I have no clue what my husband gets up to. Well, actually, she's right, but not on that score.

'We can't leave Igor this long,' he says to me, pleadingly.

'Anne Marie's babysitting him. Come on, I've only just got here.'

'OK. Just one more, though. I'm knackered.'

'Sure,' I say, not mentioning that Anne Marie has agreed to stay till half past ten. I need to be here for long enough for them all to get pissed and lose their inhibitions. 'It'll be fun.'

Famous last words.

Chapter 15

We don't speak a word to each other for most of the taxi ride home, as if we've silently agreed to delay our row until we're alone. I send Anne Marie a text so that she won't be there to pick up on the atmosphere when we get in. *Home in 5 so you're off the hook! He'll be fine on his own till we get there. Thanks so much again. I owe you! Xx*

Any time, she texts back. *He's been an angel. Except he ate my scarf. Well, a bit of it. How did it go?*

OK, I lie. I can't get into it now. *I'll tell you all about it tomorrow.*

It was all going so well. Halfway through drink number two I started to feel more relaxed. Anil was friendly and easy to talk to, but I was still more interested in the women of the group. The alcohol meant everyone started to loosen up a bit and, although I still felt like an intruder, I was able to sit back and watch the dynamics between them all. There was a definite frisson of sexual tension between ghastly Jess and the bloke called Si – a young hipster with a bushy beard and tattoos who was drinking frothy pints of dark ale and smacking his lips loudly like, I imagine, he thought an extra in *The Last Kingdom* might – and it made me think that she wasn't the one, unless it was all an act to make Nick jealous. I have a vague recollection of them leaving together later in the night, although by then things had started to go a bit hazy.

At one point Nick got up to go to the loo and my phone beeped with a text. I knew it would be him. We have always sent each other jokey messages when we've been out together. *Toupee at two o'clock* or *Check out the waiter's facelift*. Stuff like that. This one just said: *Let's go after this one. I don't want to spend all evening with this lot. We can go and eat somewhere.* I ignored it. Accepted the offer of a third drink for the two of us.

'Ready?' he said when he came back and I feigned ignorance. 'Abigail's just getting a round in.'

'I'll tell her we don't want one,' he said, turning away just as she appeared with my vodka and his red wine.

I remember, later, the group shifting. People moving seats to find someone different to talk to. I remember nabbing an empty stool next to Lou, who was still clamped to Nick's side, when Jess vacated it to clamber on to Si's lap. It was getting messy. I was feeling a mixture of heady confidence and crippling insecurity. I was hilarious, fun, sparkly. They thought I was sad, old, frumpy. They were all storing up embarrassing anecdotes about me to share in the morning. I leaned into Lou, aware that all my double vodkas were making me slur.

'What do you do, Lou?' It seemed to be the only conversation starter I had.

She looked at me down her perfectly straight nose. 'Talent liaison.' She turned back to continue her conversation with Siobhan. Nick was deep in discussion with the one called Danny. I wasn't letting her off that easily. 'Do you get on well with Nick?'

'Sorry?' she said, and I noticed Nick flick me a look. I knew he was tipsy too, because he hadn't objected to staying for the previous round. Everyone was. That's something at least. 'It's just you look as if you get on well, the two of you.' Shut up, Georgia, a voice in my head said. Go home.

She turned to Siobhan and gave her a 'get a load of this' look. Siobhan sniggered. 'I'm not sure what you're saying.'

Shit. 'Just . . . it's nice. That you get on with the boss.'

'Right,' she said, and then I think she decided to give me the benefit of the doubt briefly. 'It is. We all do.' I was aware of Nick glaring at me.

'It makes a big difference, doesn't it?' I rambled on, trying to claw some dignity back. Lou smiled at me in a way that I interpreted as patronizing. 'It's a happy department, what can I say?'

'And it's nice that you all socialize together. Do you get to travel round to the sites?' Did you go to Inverness recently, is what I really wanted to ask.

She arches an eyebrow. 'Of course. That's my job, looking after the acts, making sure they have everything they need.'

'Doesn't each resort have their own person to do that?'

'They do, and I oversee them all.'

I didn't know if I was imagining it but it seemed as if there was a weird competitive edge to our chat. Did that mean Lou was the one or was it just because she felt under attack from me? I had no way of knowing.

'Not in the off season, though? Or do you . . . ?'

I tried to tell myself to drop it, but I wasn't in any state to listen.

I have a vague memory of her rolling her eyes at Siobhan. 'Do I . . . ?'

'Visit the resorts in the off season?'

'Sometimes.'

'That must be nice.' Apparently nice was the only adjective I knew.

'If you like that sort of thing,' she said.

Suddenly I was convinced she was the culprit. Something about her sneering tone gave her away.

'Did you go to Inverness when Nick went?' I knew I shouldn't ask it. I knew it made me look sad and jealous and paranoid but, at that moment, I was all those things.

Lou snorted. I can still remember the sound. Dismissive. 'Is that a problem?'

'So you did.'

'No, actually. But who knows? I might have to in the future. Do you have an issue with that?'

I knew I should try to save face a bit, but I was past caring. I loathed this woman. All my frustration and anger of the past few days was suddenly focused directly on her and her sarcastic sneer. 'Of course not. You don't have to be so aggressive . . .'

'So sorry. It's just not every day someone's fucking wife starts giving me the third degree about my relationship with their husband . . .' she said, way too loudly.

Siobhan touched her arm. 'Lou . . .'

Of course I knew I'd gone too far, knew that everyone's eyes were suddenly on us. 'I was just making conversation.'

Lou laughed. Looked round at her colleagues for approval. 'Well, poor Nick then, if that's your idea of banter.'

'No need to be so fucking rude . . .' I said. Suddenly I was aware of someone taking me by the arm and handing me my coat.

'Time for us to go,' Nick said brusquely. I hadn't even noticed him stand up. I wriggled out of his grasp.

'No. Not yet. I'm in the middle of a chat—'

He ignored me. 'See you tomorrow, everyone. Come on, Georgia, our Uber's here.'

'When did you order an Uber? I don't want to go yet.'

He glared at me in a very un-Nick-like way. 'It's waiting.' I got to my feet reluctantly, knocking my stool over in the process, and struggled into my coat, choosing the wrong armhole at first. I was aware of Jasmine giving me a sympathetic smile.

'Bye, everyone. Lovely to meet you,' I said, waving a hand as I tottered after Nick, still trying to dress myself for the cold. I heard a burst of laughter coming from behind me. Willed myself not to look round. I caught Nick up by the door to the corridor. 'Hold on a sec.'

'What the hell was that all about?' he hissed. His tone shook me.

'What? What have I done?'

'Getting pissed. Giving my colleagues the third degree . . .'

'I was just talking. Anyway, you're pissed too—'

'Because you insisted we stayed!' he barked. 'I wanted to go home after one as usual. I've got to face them all at work tomorrow.'

'Well, I'm sorry I invaded your lovely drink. Of course, I know why you're really upset.'

'What are you talking about?' he said, slamming out of the door and striding across the square. I hurried to keep up with him and slipped on the ice, almost hitting the ground.

'Where's the Uber?'

He didn't even turn round. 'There isn't an Uber. We'll flag a taxi on the road.'

'Sorry that I wanted to meet the people you spend all day with. I thought you were keen for me to make more of an effort. Or was that before?'

'Before what?' he said. 'No, don't answer that.' He flapped his arm at a cab and, thankfully, it stopped. We threw ourselves in the back. Sat there in furious silence, neither of us wanting to give the driver a show.

'Did Lou go to Inverness with you?' I say now, unable to stay quiet.

'What? Is that what this is about? The answer's no, but so what if she did? We work together.'

'I don't like her,' I say, on the verge of tears. 'She was laughing at me.'

'Because you were making a fool of yourself,' he snaps and the driver's ears visibly perk up.

'I know something's going on.'

'With me and Lou? I'm not going to have this conversation. You're drunk.'

'Just tell me, Nick,' I sob, all pretence of dignity gone. Even as I'm talking I know I'm going to regret this in the morning. It's clearly too much for the driver now because he turns up the radio and starts to hum along tunelessly to 'Nessun Dorma'.

'I'm not even going to dignify that with an answer. What the fuck has got into you?'

'I *know*,' I say, but he's leaning forward to point out the turning. 'I know what's been going on.'

Chapter 16

There's that brief, blissful moment when I wake up before the hangover kicks in. Before it all comes flooding back. I turn over. Nick's side of the bed is smooth and un-slept-in. Then I remember that he stomped off to the spare room as soon as we got back. I look at the clock. Ten past nine. He will have left for work already.

Next to the clock is a glass, standing on a piece of paper. There's an arrow with the words 'Drink this, it'll help' written on it in Nick's scrawl. He must have crept in and left it for me, putting a coaster on top to stop Igor from drinking it. He can't totally hate me then. As if on cue the dog appears in the doorway and then clambers on to the bed next to me. I know I need to get up and take him out but moving is out of the question. I knock back the concoction – Alka-Seltzer – and flop back on to the pillows.

Images come flooding back. Lou's smirking face as I quizzed her. Siobhan's look of amusement. Nick's confusion, irritation, anger in rapid succession. Me slurring my goodbyes. Struggling to put my coat on. Did we start arguing in front of everyone? Or did we at least have enough dignity left to wait till we got outside? The shame is too much. I pull the covers over my head and attempt to sleep it off. I can't deal with it yet.

I wake up I don't know how much later because my phone is ringing. I do know that even if I were capable of making a dash for it I wouldn't get there before it rang out, so I crawl out of bed slowly, heaving Igor off my legs as I go. He takes this as a sign that he might finally get to go outside and leaps up, asleep to hyper in 0.5 seconds. My head is no longer throbbing, but there's a solid block of pain lodged behind my left eye. I unplug my phone in the hall and stagger on down to the kitchen, flicking the kettle on before I open the patio door and let the dog out into our tiny back garden. I stagger around finding a clean mug, spooning coffee into it, getting the milk out of the fridge, before I finally remember my missed call.

In fact, there are three. All from the same number. My publishers. It hits me like a bolt of lightning. I have a meeting there today at – I check the time – now. Actually, twenty-five minutes ago. Shit. Fuck. How could I have slept till nearly midday? I jab my fingers at my phone, play back my messages. It's Kate, my editor's assistant, wondering if I'm on my way, if I've forgotten, if I want to call and reschedule, in that order. I hit the button to call her back.

'Kate! It's Georgia Shepherd. I am so sorry. I've got food poisoning and I've been up all night. I finally fell asleep about half six this morning and I've only just woken up again,' I jabber as soon as she answers.

'Oh gosh, you poor thing,' Kate says. She sounds as if she believes me, and why wouldn't she? I'm sure I do sound awful and I have never let them down before. Never been flaky. 'I'll let Bibi and the rest of them know. Drink lots of water. Do you need anything?'

A reset button, I think. A do-over. Anything for last night not to have happened. 'No. Thank you. I'll be fine. And I'm so, so sorry again.'

'Don't worry about it,' she says. 'We knew there must be a good reason. I'll email you to rearrange for next week.'

I make a strong coffee and sit sipping it, looking at Igor bouncing round the garden. He can cover the whole thing in two strides, but that doesn't stop him. Totally caught up in the moment. No existential angst for him. He sees me watching and comes bounding towards the glass door. I manage to open it just in time and he flings himself in, followed by a blast of icy air. I know I need to confront last night head on. Force myself to remember what I can. It's too painful though. Too shaming.

My phone beeps. Lydia. This often happens. One of us randomly reaches out to the other just when it turns out they need them most. We've laughed about it over the years, our almost telepathic connection. I read the message.

How was last night?

Bit shit. Too much to drink and then me and Nick had a fight.

Oh no!! What about?

Maybe I should just tell her. Make up some story about where my suspicions came from. God knows I could do with her advice. I don't want to tell her another whole raft of lies though. Patricia is bad enough.

I don't even remember. Nothing probably. But he's pissed off with me for showing him up in front of his workmates. And then I overslept and missed a meeting.

Oh no!!!! What did you do?

God knows! I'm just not used to drinking that much! His whole department was there. They must think I'm awful. I can't even re-member what I said!

You poor thing!!! I'm sure it's nowhere near as bad as you think. I'm here if you want to call me!!

Too hung-over to talk, I write. *I'll try you tomorrow. Love you x.*

Love you too!!!

And then fifteen seconds later: *Drink water!!!!*

I sit and stare into space. Every image that pops into my mind is too raw, too painful. The idea that I'm a laughing stock. The subject of whispered gossip behind Nick's back. Or maybe even to his face. Maybe Lou or Siobhan or even Camilla, whoever the fuck she is, is sharing her feelings about what an embarrassment I am with him over a cosy coffee. Maybe he's agreeing. And then I wonder if that's why Lyds texted when she did, because her friend Emma had heard what a fool I'd made of myself and taken it upon herself to share the news.

I need Patricia. It's like picking at a scab. You want it to heal, to go away, but you need to face up to how bad the pain is first.

I open up her Twitter account, like a few random things while I compose a message in my head. Lydia has posted a photo of a new batch of cards featuring a woodland wedding between a warty troll and a faerie princess. *They're stunning*, Patricia tells her as she retweets the picture. Hashtag: *MyFavouriteArtist*. She can't just go straight in with talk about me, it would look suspicious, so when she moves to DMs, her first is anodyne.

Those new cards! Goodness, how beautiful. How are you today?

If Lydia wonders why Patricia hasn't ordered anything yet she's too polite to say. I can't figure out a way to do it without setting up a whole fake identity with PayPal and an address for them to be sent to and that feels like a step too far, however desperate I am.

I wish I could buy something but I'm still horribly overdrawn since Christmas! To be honest, Lydia, I've struggled a bit financially since Steven left. I've never told anyone that. I'm not very good at confiding in people, but I find you so easy to talk to.

I don't think she'll care. I think they – Patricia and Lydia – are way beyond that now. They're no longer artist and potential customer. They're friends. I force myself to go and have a quick shower while I wait for a response. Knowing Lydia, it could be hours. Part of me wonders whether I should phone Nick. Or send him a text: *Are we OK?* Except that I know we're not, whatever he says. Last night I more or less accused him of having an affair with Lou. He denied it, of course, played indignant that I would ever think he'd do something like that again, but now he knows I know. OK, so I might have got the details wrong. It might not be Lou – although I think the smart money would be on her or Siobhan – it might be one of the others, but he stands accused. And now it's up to him to decide whether to seize this moment to tell me, to confess all, and then we can deal with the fallout, or whether to dig his heels in and keep lying.

By the time I come back down, feeling better for at least smelling fresh, and clutching a bundle of washing in my arms, Lydia has already replied.

Oh Patricia you poor thing!! You can always confide in me. It's hard making ends meet on one income, isn't it? I'm very bored at work today, so doing some sneaky drawing at my desk!!!

I know I need to make polite conversation but the urge to ask her if she's heard anything is almost overwhelming.

I feel your pain! The shop is deserted today and it's all I can do not to shut up and go home.

Well, this will give you something else to think about!!! My poor friend surprised her husband at his work drinks last night and basically got rather tipsy and made a bit of a fool of herself. I feel so awful for her. I tried to stop her going but short of saying 'You might catch him with his mistress' there wasn't really anything I could say!! I hope you don't think I'm gossiping telling you this btw! You're the only person I can talk to.

I blush to the roots of my hair. No, not blush. Blush is a delicate word. I flush red, a wave of nausea making me double over. I can't bear it. I stick my finger a bit deeper into the wound.

Oh poor woman! I feel so dreadful for her. Was she there? The other woman? She works with him, doesn't she? As if that piece of information isn't imprinted on my brain.

Yes. And yes!!! But, of course, Georgia had no idea!!!

I steady myself on the back of a chair. Sink into it. So I have met her. That means Camilla is off the list. It's Lou or Siobhan. Possibly Jess. Maybe even Abigail. Jasmine. Sue. Elaine. I have my definitive list of suspects, Lou and Siobhan at the top in bold.

Chapter 17

'I'm going to confront him.' Anne Marie is over and we've left Nina and Igor staring lovingly at each other down in the kitchen and decamped to the living room. I tell her about the disastrous evening before. 'I might as well now. Strike while the iron's hot and all that.'

She furrows her brow. 'What if he just denies it?'

I shrug. 'What else can I do? I've basically accused him anyway. I can't believe he'd be that cruel not to put me out of my misery.'

She thinks about this for a second, runs her finger round and round the rim of her mug. 'God knows. You just have to be happy that once you open that box you can't close it.'

'I know. But I don't think I have any alternative. Well, live in ignorance and just let him get on with it, but that's never going to happen. I do have some pride.'

She tells me – unprompted – that now she's told Jez they need to cool things down, that she's not in the market for an affair, she's beyond relieved that she ended it when she did. It was like being under a weird spell, she says, a look of confusion on her face. And as soon as it was broken no trace of it was left. 'Nick will probably feel the same once he comes to his senses.'

'Was he OK? Jez.' It's not that I give a fuck about Jez but I want to make sure he's not some kind of vengeful maniac who's going to make life difficult for her and Harry.

'Yeah . . . I mean, upset. It's going to be awkward . . .'

'And you don't think anyone else has picked up on it? None of your colleagues? He didn't tell anyone?'

She shakes her head emphatically. 'God, no. Definitely not.'

'Then it's over. You can forget about it. Don't feel bad.'

She hugs me as she leaves. 'Good luck. I'm here if you need me.'

'I'll call you tomorrow,' I promise, planting a kiss on the top of Nina's dark head.

The house smells stale, fusty. Despite the cold I open a few windows, clean up the kitchen and make the bed. Then I have another shower and wash my hair. I want to give Nick the impression that I'm together. That I wasn't so wasted last night that I'm still feeling the effects (even though I am. My mouth is fuzzy no matter how many times I brush my teeth and I still haven't been able to face eating more than a slice of toast). I want him to take what I'm saying seriously, not put it down to the ramblings of an insecure drunk.

Usually when we fight it blows over before it's really begun. A bit of alone time in different rooms, a sheepish sorry from the instigator and an immediate forgiveness by the other. We've evolved a routine over the years and we both know the steps. Since . . . well, since . . . we've both shied away from full-blown confrontation, as if we're scared to rock the foundations too deeply. We worked so hard to rebuild them that we can't risk a stray jibe shattering them again. We negotiate. We reason. This time is different, though. This time the issue hasn't just gone away, splintered to dust by being aired out loud. If anything it's grown stronger.

I have no idea what mood Nick will be in when he gets home. All I can control is myself, so I rehearse what I want to say in my head: I'm sorry for embarrassing you in front of your colleagues, but I need you to tell me the truth. You owe me that at least. Calm. Reasonable.

By half past six I'm sitting at the kitchen table, ready. I assume he's coming straight home after work but I have no way of knowing, short of calling or texting him, and I worry that would make him think I'm spoiling for a fight or checking up on him. I play with Igor's silky, half-up half-down ears absentmindedly while I wait. Force myself to breathe in and out slowly, trying to calm my rising anger. Why hasn't he contacted me? When I check the time on my phone I automatically click on to Twitter and Patricia's account before I really think what I'm doing. There's a new message. Do I really want to read this now? Of course, now I know it's there there's no way I can ignore it.

My friend just texted me again. Apparently the woman Georgia's husband is seeing is now telling everyone about their affair! It must be because of whatever happened last night!!! Maybe she thinks Georgia suspects anyway, so what the hell!

I sit there with my blood boiling. The embarrassment, the humiliation, the shame. More than anything, more than what Nick is actually doing, that is what stings the worst. I rush to the toilet and throw up. How the fuck dare he put me through this? I lean a hand on the wall to steady myself, shaking with anger.

And it's at this exact moment that Nick arrives home.

* * *

I'm on him before he can get his coat off. I'll never know if he was hoping that all would be forgotten and forgiven, put down to alcohol and insecurity, because I don't give him the chance to get a word in.

'Hi,' he says warily. I think of all the times we've laughed about WAGs whose husbands have been caught doing something terrible and next thing the wife is wearing a huge new diamond and all seems to be forgiven, and I'm irrationally angry that Nick hasn't brought home so much as a bunch of flowers. I mean, I would have thrown them in his face, but even so.

'Tell me the truth,' I say. Igor clearly hasn't got the memo and he's bounding around happily at the sight of his dad. It's hard to conduct an argument over sixty-five kilos of bouncy dog but I'm going to give it a good go.

'What? Oh, come on, George. Not this again. I thought you might have calmed down by now.'

'Calmed down? You're shagging some woman you work with and you think I should have calmed down?'

He places his keys on the hall table. 'What is up with you? I came home ready to just forget about last night and move on. Even though I've had people making smart-arse comments all day about—'

I don't let him finish. 'You came home ready to forget about it? That's very big of you.'

He stomps up the stairs towards the bedroom. 'You know what? I'm going to have a shower.'

'No!' I shout. 'You don't get to just walk off. Just tell me the fucking truth. I know what's going on, don't you

146

understand? I know about you and Lou. Or Siobhan. Or whichever fucking one it is.'

He turns back, hovering halfway up. 'Ah, so you one hundred per cent know I'm having an affair but you don't know who with?'

'Why are you being like this? Why can't you just admit it?'

'Admit what? There's nothing to admit. I would never . . .'

'Again,' I snap. 'Never again, isn't that what you mean?' I hadn't meant to bring up his history. Felicity. Hadn't meant to drag this argument back into the past. I made a rule for myself when I decided to stay that I had to forgive him 100 per cent. Had to believe he was as penitent, as regretful as he claimed. Otherwise what was the point?

His face drops. 'Exactly. I would never do something like that again. I thought you knew that.'

'Well, it's not as if it's impossible to imagine . . .'

'So that's what this is about? I did it once so I must be guilty again? I've spent six years trying to make it up to you . . .'

I can feel the tears coming. I try to hold them back but it's impossible. 'I just want to know the truth. You have no idea what it's like feeling as if you're being lied to and laughed at.'

'Do you know what? I do know what it feels like to be laughed at. Because my wife showed up at my work drinks last night, got absolutely shitfaced and made a complete fucking fool of herself. And me. Maybe you should be apologizing to me.'

I feel like tearing my hair out. I know I've probably handled this all wrong but I have to keep reminding myself that I'm the wounded party here.

'I don't understand why you're being like this,' I say, faking calmness now. Maybe I can appeal to his better nature, if it's still in there somewhere. 'OK, I admit it must have been embarrassing for you last night but I didn't set out to humiliate you. Unlike what you've been doing to me.'

'Georgia. I have no idea where this has come from. No idea what you think you know. But I am not having an affair. And if you don't believe me then that says more about you than it does about me.'

He stomps down the stairs again, grabs his coat. 'I'm going to Dom's.'

'No . . . Nick. We need to talk about this . . .'

'There's nothing to talk about,' he says. He has never stormed out in anger in the whole twenty years of our marriage. Then again, I've never accused him of repeat offending before. I want to say don't go round to Dom's. At least try Anne Marie and Harry first. People who like me. Who like us, as a couple. I know Anne Marie would do her best to persuade him to come clean. But what if he then decides to go to Lou's or Siobhan's . . . ?

'Oh yes, run off to your Neanderthal of a mate. You can go out on the pull together,' I say before I can stop myself.

'Why would I want to do that when I'm already having an affair with Lou and/or Siobhan apparently?'

'Just tell me which one it is.'

'Jesus Christ, Georgia! Where the fuck has this come from?' He's shouting now. Igor lets out a little whine and slopes off down to the kitchen. I feel awful for him, but I can't follow him now.

'I know, Nick! I *know*. Don't you understand? There's no point in trying to deny it any more.'

He grabs his phone and his keys. 'You have lost your mind.'

Then he walks out of the front door and slams it behind him.

He doesn't come home all night. I have to stop myself from calling Dom to ask if he's really there. What difference does it make? We're past the point of no return.

Obsessively I google Lou – Louise is my best guess – Talent Liaison, Diamond Leisure. And there she is: Louise Carlyle. There are even a couple of photos. Work-related. I find her Instagram and she's there in all her glory, pouting at the camera, holding her cockapoo, hugging her mum. Her bio just says *Loving Life!* so I know she's pretty much an idiot. No sign of Nick but then no sign of any other suitor either. Lots of friends – sunbathing, skiing, drinking. Her Twitter page is easy to find because she's with the same little dog in her profile picture. I scour her photos but I've already seen most of them. I search the word 'Nick' on her timeline and there's nothing. I check I'm on Patricia's account, like a couple of photos of the dog, and hit follow.

Next up is Siobhan. There only seems to be one at Diamond Leisure. Siobhan Farrow. Events Coordinator. Her Instagram account is private but her profile picture is of the same red-haired, pale-skinned woman I met. Her Twitter is harder to find but I cross-reference possibles with people Lou follows and eventually there she is. I hunt through her pictures. There are several with the same man, a striking white-blond Viking. The most recent is from two weeks ago. Not that that means anything. If Nick had a Twitter account he would probably have pictures of him with me on there.

Patricia follows her too. Hopefully she and Lou aren't sad enough to discuss new followers but, just in case, I take Patricia on a random following spree adding twenty-odd un-related strangers to her list.

While I am getting ready to go to bed – it's barely even nine o'clock but I just want this day to be over – Joe rings. Like every parent, calls from my kids are the only ones I can never ignore. It's out of the question that I let it go to voice-mail, but it's also out of the question that I allow him to pick up on what's going on, so I tell myself to get a grip and an-swer in my happiest voice.

'Maaaaaaaate!'

'Maaaaaaaaaaaaaaaaaaate!' he replies, so I know that all is well.

'Why in't you down the pub with some sort?'

'Early night, innit?' he replies. Sometimes our whole con-versations are like this. It's as if we silently dare each other to give up first. It's become like a code. If we're both playing along then all is right with the world. Usually I'm the one to crack, desperate to hear the real goings-on in his world, but tonight I could stay locked in our in-joke forever.

'Put the old fella on,' he drawls.

'He's at Dom's,' I say, breaking character.

'Ah. Lovely Uncle Dom.' Joe and I have bonded over our lack of enthusiasm for Dom before. Always jokingly, and always in front of Nick, of course, because I didn't want my kids to think I'd be disrespectful to their father like that. Joe once described him to Nick as 'your unreconstructed lunk of a friend' and I think that sums him up pretty well. He and Nick have been mates since college – Dom is my Lydia equivalent – and they don't have much in common these days except a shared history, which, to be fair, you really can't underestimate. Dom is divorced and refers to his ex-wife as 'that bitch'. Her crime? Realizing what a 1970s throwback she'd married and wanting out. I can imagine him now, encouraging Nick to come back to the single life. He's always wanted a wingman on his nights out.

'I'm surprised you didn't go along,' Joe says.

'Maybe next time,' I say and we both laugh, knowing that would never happen.

I manage to get through the call without giving anything away and, despite everything that's happening, I feel a lot better by the time we say goodbye. Somehow I sleep, arm draped over the comforting heft of my dog. He uses Nick's absence as an opportunity to conquer more of the bed, sprawling out across the whole space, sighing contentedly. For a blissful moment when I wake up everything feels normal until the memories come crashing in. My world has gone to shit and I have no idea how to fix it.

Chapter 18

Of course I've completely forgotten that my mum is coming to stay. Of course I have.

She comes for two nights every February. One with us and one with my auntie Liz in Leigh-on-Sea. Usually the dates are imprinted on my brain. Except that this year isn't like any other year. I barely even know what day it is.

'Mum, could we maybe put it off for a few weeks?' I say tentatively when she calls first thing to remind me what time she's arriving at Stansted. 'Things are a bit fraught here. I'm really behind with work . . .'

'I always come at this time, Georgia,' she says, as if this is news to me. 'I've got all your Christmas presents.'

Mum and Frank spend Christmas Day at 'the Club' these days, with their cronies. They took me there the one time I went to stay and it was like walking on to the set of a film about the Kray twins. I was terrified someone would light a match because the heady combination of hairspray and Old Spice would have killed us all in a second. Their friends were all very pleasant, if a bit bemused by my job ('What's your old man thinking of, making you work like that?') and my personal style ('You could be a stunner if you dressed a bit more ladylike'). 'She's a famous author,' my mum kept saying to anyone who'd listen, me cowering with embarrassment, but once they'd established I wasn't Len Deighton they all pretty much lost interest.

'Frank's booked to play golf with the boys.' By boys I assume she means his bunch of seventy-five-year-old friends, most of them made up entirely of joint replacements. There's not a real knee, hip or elbow among them but nothing will keep them from their eighteen holes in the blistering sun.

'It'll just be me, I'm afraid. Nick's had to go away for a work thing, he had no choice about the dates. And obviously the kids aren't here this year.' There's no point fighting it, and I don't want to upset her. I can't bring myself to tell her the truth though. She'd probably get Frank to organize a hit on Nick.

'Well, we'll have a lovely girls' night in. Or out. We could go into town. Where's good these days?'

'I'm knackered, Mum.' Sometimes I feel as if I'm the parent in this relationship. My mother would be out partying every night if I let her. 'We can stay home and chat. I'll cook you a roast.' That gets her. She loves her little corner of expat Spain but she misses a traditional roast by a fire. Snow outside. 'The weather's awful; you'll love it.'

'Ooh, good. I'll pack a scarf.'

I send Lydia a quick text. *Mum over tomorrow! I completely forgot. Can you come?? Nick and kids not here and I need reinforcements!*

Of course!!! she texts back. *I have a thing at 8ish but I'll come up first.*

A date???

Sort of. Gallery opening in Westbourne Park. With that Simon I met in Pret.

I do remember. Not Simon but 'Seeemon'. French, I think

she said. Only Lydia could go to buy a lunchtime sandwich and come out with a number in her phone and an entry in her diary.

Are you sure you can face coming up here first?

Definitely!!! I wouldn't miss your mum for the world! And it won't matter if I'm late the other end xx.

Clearly poor old Simon's days are numbered before they've even begun.

At three o'clock the following afternoon I'm waiting in arrivals, trying to spot my mum's bottle-blonde heavy fringe. She'll be dragging a wardrobe disguised as a carry-on bag and I know that in there she'll have a carefully coordinated outfit for every possible occasion. Just in case. Finger- and toenails pristine. Thick black eyeliner. I don't think I've seen her without make-up since she had food poisoning when I was about twelve. Even then she tried to get me to help her apply some before my dad came home from work. She'll be clicking along on high heels, tan the colour of gravy.

Suddenly there she is – one advantage of us both being tall is that we can easily spot each other in a crowd – looking as if she's being sponsored by Louis Vuitton. As ever, when I see her I'm hit with a rush of love and guilt. I don't visit her often enough. I should make the effort to go over and see her, Frank or no Frank. I should insist she stays for longer. She always used to, but without meaning to I kept finding reasons to whittle the days down. Her face lights up. Big open smile, arms outstretched. I hadn't realized how much I wanted my mum.

On the drive back we catch up on everything with the

exception, of course, of Nick. I sent him a text last night. *Mum here tomorrow. Told her you're away for work.*

Fine, he sent back.

Talking to my mum in person is an entirely different experience to talking to her on the phone. She hates the phone. Conversations are an exchange of information only. A Q and A. Are you well? How's the weather? Did you finish your book yet? In real life she's garrulous and funny. A compendium of stories about her neighbours, Frank, our relatives. During the rest of the year I worry about her. Is she happy? Is her age starting to show? And then I see her and those worries just dissipate. I wish she'd come over more often. I've offered to pay her fare, not that she needs me to, but she says she doesn't like to leave Frank. And, unspoken in that sentence, is the fact that she knows I'd rather she didn't bring him with her.

It strikes me suddenly that I have no right to judge the man my mother is in love with on any other basis than does he make her happy? Does he treat her well? And the answer to both – unless she is a brilliant actress and, having once seen her in the Harrow on the Hill am-dram performance of *A Streetcar Named Desire* I am pretty confident she's not ('Aah have awlways deehpended awn the koyndness of strayn-geers') – is yes.

'How's Frank?' I ask.

She beams at me. 'He sends his love.' I'm guessing he didn't. He picked up on my disapproval early on. Kept out of my way.

'You should both come over sometime. In the summer maybe.'

'Really?' she says, and that one word breaks my heart. 'Well, we'd absolutely love that.'

We spend the rest of the afternoon cooking together like we used to when I still lived at home. She's still in her heels. Igor follows her around, staring at her feet as though he's never seen anything like it. Every time she moves he wags his tail. 'He's got a foot fetish,' my mum laughs. 'Weirdo,' she says affectionately, ruffling his head.

Lydia shows up just before six. Squeals when she spots my mum. 'It's so lovely to see you!'

'You're too thin,' is the first thing Mum says. 'We're cooking a roast.'

'I can't. I'm going out,' Lyds says, shrugging out of her coat. 'What time did you get here?'

'Don't try and change the subject. At least have a couple of potatoes.'

Because my mum has absolutely no filter she fires questions at Lydia that are so direct even I wouldn't ask them. Why don't you just pick a nice bloke and settle down? (Because I'll regret it. I'm holding out for the big one.) Why don't you look for another job if you hate it so much? (Because then I'll just be stuck doing something else I don't want to do.) Why don't you get George to show your drawings to her publishers? (Awkward silence.)

'It's not really the done thing, Mum. Me and my new editor don't really get along . . .'

By the time Lydia leaves – on her way to being at least twenty minutes late for poor old Simon – she looks as if she's just faced an inquisition, but I know deep down she loves it. Only someone who considers you family would badger you that much without worrying that it might piss you off.

Once she's left, Mum and I share a bottle and a half of wine, sitting on the sofa, FaceTiming the kids somewhere along the way. She tells me that Frank is having a bit of bother with his prostate, 'but nothing that can't be fixed'. I can tell she's worried. I squeeze her hand.

'If you want me to come over when he's in hospital . . .'

'No, no,' she says. 'You're much too busy. I've got a lot of friends. I'll be OK. To be honest, it'll be nice to have the house to myself for a bit.' I'm pretty sure she doesn't really mean it but I don't want to push. I've spent too many years avoiding going out there for her to feel she can accept.

As I hug her goodnight on the landing she puts both hands on the sides of my face.

'I know there's something wrong,' she says gently. 'But I'm not going to push.'

The temptation to offload, to spill out the whole story, is almost overwhelming. But all I'll do then is pass the worry on to her. I might feel better for a few minutes, but she'll be left having sleepless nights.

'I'm fine, Mum,' I say. 'Just work, you know . . .'

'If you say so, love.'

Just knowing she's in the next room – even if my traitorous dog has deserted me to occupy her bed (she's been sneaking him treats all evening, both of them acting as if they thought I had no idea. Nothing to see here) – means I have the best night's sleep I've had in weeks.

'I meant it,' I say when I steer her towards the Leigh-on-Sea train next morning. 'Both of you come and stay in the summer.'

'I'd love that,' she says. 'We both would.' I wrap her up in a hug.

'You know you can always talk to me if you need me,' she says as I let her go.

Chapter 19

'So, you see, if we can move Wilbur on. Bring him into the 2020s . . .'

I'm finding it hard to concentrate. 'You want Wilbur to be more woke?'

Bibi, my editor, nods. Her name is actually Julia, she told me once after a couple of glasses of Prosecco at a launch party, but she felt she deserved something more exotic. Bibi rarely drinks. She thinks it upsets her chakras. She lives in Hoxton and she drops the 'g's from the end of all her words, but she's actually landlady to her housemates in the five-bedroom terrace her parents bought her, and she went to Cheltenham Ladies' College. 'We want him to appeal to the millennials. So that when they start to have children he's their go-to book. We need to bulletproof his future.'

'He's a wallaby,' I say. 'He's not really political.'

She nods. 'And I wonder if we should think about his pronouns.'

Bibi hasn't been my editor long. She took over when Leah, who had looked after my first five books, got promoted. I 100 per cent know she doesn't have the emotional investment in me that Leah did and that if Wilbur's sales plummet for whatever reason she won't be putting her neck on the line to save me any time soon. We're having the rescheduled meeting that I slept through the other day. I'd assumed it was just of the 'When will the new book be ready, we'd like to publish in September?' variety, but it seems not. At this point I'm finding it hard to act as if I care. Nick hasn't been in touch since he stormed out. Yesterday, after I'd said goodbye to Mum, I called Lydia and she dropped her plans and came over after work – I didn't want to leave the house for more than about fifteen minutes in case Nick returned to collect more clothes and I missed him. I'd decided I needed to tell her about what he was up to. I mean, she knew, obviously. She knew more than I did. But we hadn't actually talked about it. At least, not as Lydia and Georgia. Now that Nick had moved out it made no sense for me not to fill her in. It had gone way beyond her confiding in Patricia. And besides, I was hoping maybe it would give her an excuse to tell me what she knew. To let a few things slip. I had to fudge what I said, obviously, but luckily she didn't seem interested in where my original suspicions had come from. Too much had happened since to eclipse the importance of that. And, of course, she already knew he was guilty, so I knew she'd definitely hear me out.

'Jesus. You poor thing. Shit, George, that's awful.' She was acting, obviously, pretending that what I had to say was news to her. 'Is that why . . . what you've been arguing about?'

I nodded. 'I didn't want to tell you till I was sure. Just in case, you know, I'd got it wrong and then you thought badly of him for no reason.'

'What a bastard. I can't believe it.'

'Me neither.' I filled her in on the past few days. She reached out a hand and took one of mine. 'Oh my God, you poor thing . . .' It was such a relief to finally be able to talk to her about it. I needed her advice, her unequivocal support.

'If he won't even have the decency to admit it then . . . well . . .' she said, filling the kettle for the third time. I felt sick from caffeine.

'I know,' I said. 'I just don't get it. If he wants to be with someone else why not just tell me? Then at least we can start to work out where to go from here.'

'Let's say for a minute you're right . . . maybe he's just too eaten up by guilt. He can't face seeing you . . .'

'Or he doesn't care any more.'

She thought about that for a second. 'Shit. I'll kill him. Really, though.'

'I'm finding it so hard to . . . It's like it's all been a lie.'

'Do you think . . .' She looked at the floor as if she might find the words there or perhaps she just couldn't look me in the eye. 'Maybe this is him. What he does. I mean . . . maybe Felicity wasn't a one-off . . .'

'I know,' I said quietly. 'Could you ever have imagined him doing it again?'

She shook her head emphatically. 'No. I mean he's always been a bit of a flirt but . . .'

Has he? I've never thought of Nick as being the slightest bit flirtatious. Maybe when I wasn't around. Maybe all my female friends have been fighting off his attentions for years, commiserating with each other about the awkward position it put them in and how sorry they felt for me. I was starting to wonder if I knew my husband at all. I said as much to Lydia.

'Don't over-analyse it,' she said.

I was wrestling with the idea of talking to Lou. And then, if that got me nowhere, Siobhan. Appealing to their better nature. Telling them that all I wanted was the truth; I wasn't looking for a fight. It would be humiliating but what the hell. I never had to see either of them again.

'Why would you put yourself through that?' Lydia said when I told her. 'Who cares which one of them it is? You'll find out eventually. If it's true . . .' she added hastily.

I nodded, unconvinced. 'You're right.'

'Listen, I was thinking. Do you want me to speak to him? Maybe I can persuade him to talk to you? Or, if not, maybe he'll tell me what he's up to, what he's intending to do?'

I thought about it for a second. Lydia and Nick have always got on in a way that Dom and I just don't. They're similar in lots of ways: kind, fair, empathetic. Lydia still was at least.

'Would you? I don't want to put you in an awkward position.'

She shook her head. 'Not at all. What have you got to lose?'

I leaned over and gave her a hug, feeling her bony ribs. 'I love you,' I said.

She squeezed me back. 'You too. It'll be OK. If the worst comes to the worst we can be two sad old spinsters doing jigsaws together.'

'Don't knock jigsaws,' I said, managing a half-laugh. 'Oh,' I added as a thought occurred to me. 'Do you want to come to the awards with me? No way am I taking Nick along now. Not that I imagine he'd want to . . . I mean, I know it's a bit of a busman's holiday . . .'

'No! I've never been to an awards do! Aldwych Press Reference Division do not get nominated for awards. Ever. And even if they did I wouldn't get to go. Nowhere near important enough. Are you sure?'

'Don't feel you have to . . .' Now I'd asked her I was

wondering if it was an insensitive thing to do. Rubbing her face into it.

'I want to. It's ages since we had a proper night out. Besides, I can Instagram the shit out of it.'

'That's my girl,' I said, giving her another hug.

Once she left – when I insisted I'd be fine and she needed some time for herself to get ready for work the next day – I sat down and weighed up the evidence. Lydia's comment about Nick being a flirt, being a different person when I wasn't around, had thrown me. Did I not know him at all, even after all these years? Had he been fooling me all this time? I made a list. What did I actually know? That someone he worked with had told Lydia he was having an affair with a co-worker. Could they be mistaken? Vindictive? There was the trip to Inverness. Obviously he has to visit all the sites all the time, but almost never overnight. Could you go all the way to Inverness for a day of meetings and make it home that night though? It's a long way. Not a straightforward journey. Why didn't he tell me who else was at the dinner? And why did he not text me back till the middle of the night? Why was he up so late in the first place? None of it was exactly a smoking gun, I had to admit. Laid out on the table it didn't sound like it added up to much. Except that I'd been told it was true by someone who knew. I didn't have much proof and some of it was pretty circumstantial, but that one point was incontrovertible.

I couldn't stop myself checking Patricia's messages every few minutes. Sure enough, at about nine o'clock, just as I was pouring myself a glass of wine, there was Lydia.

Oh Patricia! Georgia has found out about Nick somehow and they've had a huge fight. He's refusing to admit it and he's gone to stay somewhere else!! I feel so awful!!

Despite everything it made me feel better to see how upset she was for me. But I didn't want her feeling as if she had any responsibility for any of this.

Oh no, I'm so sorry. Don't be too hard on yourself though. There's nothing you could have done. If you'd told her what you'd heard the outcome would have been the same.

I know, you're right. But it breaks my heart!! She's so upset. What a bastard!!! I'm going to speak to him. Make him tell me exactly what he's up to. She deserves to know the truth at least!!!

She's lucky she has you, Patricia wrote. I wanted her to realize how much her friendship meant to me. I wanted to make her feel good about herself. That was what Patricia was supposed to be for, after all.

Bibi is still expounding on her theme. I know I should fight my corner, plead for Wilbur's integrity, but all I can come up with is 'The thing is, he's a 2014 kind of a wallaby . . .'

'Exactly!' She seizes on this, and I know I've said the wrong thing. 'And we need to bring him into the 2020s.'

'I like him as he is,' I say. The most pointless argument ever. 'Besides, he's a boy and he has a pouch. That's pretty diverse in my eyes.'

'But you're not our target audience.'

'I'm not four years old, no . . .'

Bibi's voice takes on a supercilious tone. 'Our target audience is the mums, Georgia.'

'Not the mums and dads? That's a bit discriminatory,' I say

facetiously. I can't help it. She brings out the worst in me. I should just shut up and get out of here. Go home and check if my dog has wrecked the house. Talk to my agent. 'Let me have a think about it,' I say in an effort to be conciliatory.

'Wonderful. That's all I ask,' she says, not meaning it for a second. 'And maybe think about making the rhymes a bit more sophisticated. Children are much more advanced these days,' she adds as I'm about to walk out of the door.

What, like 'are you having me on' and 'you trust-fund moron', I think but don't say. Luckily. Because then I remember what else I have to do. I fish around in my bag, produce the copy of Lydia's manuscript that she left at my house once. I may as well at least do my good deed for the day.

'Could someone look at this . . . It's my friend, she's an illustrator too. She's looking for a publisher.'

There's an awkward silence. It's not really the done thing to foist someone's work on your editor unsolicited. And it's not as if Bibi and I have the kind of relationship where we trade favours. Eventually, ever polite, Bibi stands up and takes it from me. 'Of course. Leave it with me.'

On the way home in a taxi I turn on my phone. It's the first time Igor's been left home alone and I installed a Ring camera in the kitchen this morning so I could check up on him if I felt I needed to. I figured he was most likely to be near to his food bowl at all times. There are 489 notifications. I watch the first three: he walks one way, he walks the other way, he walks back again. I don't have the stomach for 486 more. I skip to the most recent. He walks past, tail wagging. I delete the app.

I send Nick a message. *Are you still staying at Dom's?*
I wait for what seems like an age.
Yes, is the only response he sends.

Chapter 20

I try to distract myself with work. I know I've messed up with Bibi and I need to put it right. I can't afford for her to decide I'm too difficult to work with to be worth it. I know that Lydia is meeting Nick at half past six, though, and it's all I can do to keep from calling her to check she's on her way. Apparently he agreed readily when she sent him a text. I can't decide how to interpret that. That he wants some kind of absolution? That he wants to reinforce his lies?

I pour myself a glass of wine and at least turn my mind to coming up with more complicated rhymes so I can look as if I'm making an effort, but I get stuck on 'a set of mugs and some big butt plugs' which I'm not sure is entirely appropriate for four-year-olds, however sophisticated Bibi might think they are. Maybe I should write an adult Wilbur. Take him out in a blaze of glory buying guns and ketamine and having a three-way with his marsupial friends Olga and Walter. Blow up my whole career before it dies a slow death on its own. I down my wine, pour another. Lydia promised to phone as soon as she leaves the pub. I check my mobile. Twenty to seven. It won't be for ages yet. She's barely just arrived. I picture her confronting him. No, not confronting, that's not a Lydia move. Calmly putting the case for the prosecution and then stubbornly refusing to accept his woolly answers. Lydia is a quiet powerhouse. He won't see her coming.

Five minutes later my mobile bursts into life. I yelp with surprise; Igor howls. I grab it up only to see it's Anne Marie. I think about not answering: I don't want to be engaged when Lydia calls. But I could use the distraction. And besides, I haven't spoken to her for a couple of days so I may as well update her on what's going on.

'Nick's moved out?' she says as soon as I say hello. Clearly she doesn't need much updating.

'He's staying at Dom's. How did you know?'

'Harry called him this afternoon. Has it got that bad? What's happened?'

'What did he tell Harry?'

'That you were having a few problems. No details. Has he admitted it then?'

'No.' I talk her through it, repetitively stroking Igor's ears – my furry stress balls – as I talk.

'Oh, Georgia,' she says sadly once I finish. 'I'm so sorry.'

'It's . . .' I say. 'I don't understand it. How we've got to this
. . .'

'It's interesting that he's at Dom's and not at hers. Maybe she's already living with someone.'

I've thought about this, but then why – if Lou or Siobhan were married or whatever – would she be telling her colleagues about her new relationship? 'Maybe. Or maybe it's not even serious. Maybe he's willing to lose everything for someone he doesn't even want to take it further with. God, that's even more depressing.'

'The grass isn't always greener . . . Harry said he seemed miserable.'

'Good,' I say. 'That makes two of us.'

'Lydia will get it out of him,' Anne Marie says. She and Lyds are so different on the surface but they have the same values underneath. The same bullshit detectors built in.

I nod. 'I hope so. She's my last resort.'

Chapter 21

Lydia pats down her hair, using the screen of her phone as a mirror. The snow has melted, replaced by biting rain, and she got soaked walking the ten steps from the cab to the front door of the pub. She thought about going to the toilets and giving herself a proper once-over but she's already nabbed the best table – in the corner by the window, a two so no one could join them. Near enough to the roaring fire for it to be warming, but not so near that after the first few minutes of relief you started to feel as if your face was melting. She hadn't even paused to buy a drink once she spotted it, just in case someone else snatched it as she waited – the pub was crowded with after-work drinkers – and now she doesn't want to risk either losing it again or having whatever she left as a place-holder (her coat? A scarf could be ignored or tossed aside) stolen, so that would have to wait. Hopefully he'll be here soon.

She'd been surprised that Nick had agreed to come so readily. They'd been friends for over twenty years, of course, but never outside of the axis of him and Georgia. She could count the number of occasions she had spent time alone with him on one hand, although they had all holidayed together often in the early days. Even after the kids came along they had still always invited her but she hadn't wanted to end up as 'poor Auntie Lydia' tagging along like a spare part, so she'd started to make excuses. But he'd said yes immediately. Offered to leave work pretty much straightaway and meet her wherever. She'd picked a pub where she thought no one would know them. They needed the chance to talk undisturbed.

She looks up just as he walks in. He looks pale, as if he hasn't been sleeping. Which, presumably, he hasn't, given his life is falling apart. As if he's lost weight. It suits him in that annoying way that some people look better when misery has rubbed off their perfectly smooth edges. He's wearing a coat totally unsuited to the rain. Wool. No umbrella. She watches as he runs a hand backwards through his thick hair, flicking off the drops. Looks around. Smiles hesitantly when he sees her.

She stands up and offers him a hug. Doesn't even care that his coat soaks her top.

'How are you doing?' she says. 'Actually, let me get us a drink first. Lager?'

He nods. 'Thanks.'

He slides into the seat opposite hers and she pats his shoulder lightly as she passes. It takes an age to get served. She feels invisible next to the pushy young men and flirtatious young women jostling for the barman's attention. She looks over to where Nick is sitting, head low, staring at something on his phone.

'I was next,' she says forcefully as soon as the barman hands a tall lad his change. She's usually the last person to be pushy. She's all passive aggression and simmering grudges. Her lack of assertiveness has always annoyed her. She's full of opinions and ideas but most of the time too intimidated to express them out loud. Which is odd because she finds it easy to make connections with people, to strike up acquaintances. She'd thought about going on a seminar once – 'Claim Your Place in the World' – but when she'd looked more closely at the literature she'd worried it might be the gateway to a cult. Lately, though, she's started to feel as if life has begun to pass her by and she hasn't achieved any of the things she set out to achieve. It's time to stand up and take what she wants.

To her surprise it works and she's served next, much to the – loudly expressed – disgust of a woman a few feet along the bar who was definitely there first. Lydia gives her order and then looks down, avoiding making eye contact with the irate woman. Being more assertive is one thing. Getting into a fist fight in order to get your alcohol three minutes sooner is quite another.

'God, I didn't think it would be this rammed,' she says as she places Nick's beer in front of him.

'It's fine,' he says. 'Thanks.'

'So,' she says. Here goes. 'Tell me what's going on.'

'I was hoping you might be able to tell me,' Nick says, drawing circles on the table with his finger. 'Where has this even come from?'

Lydia lets out a long sigh. 'I have no idea.'

He looks up at her, eyes pleading. 'You believe me, don't you?'

She hesitates. She wants him to hear what she's saying. Really hear it. 'Of course,' she says gently. 'Of course I do. I keep telling her she's crazy. That there's no way . . . but she's convinced . . .'

He sighs, clearly relieved. 'I don't even know where she got the idea from. It's not like I've done anything different

– started going away more or drinking after work. None of that.'

Lydia considers this for a minute although she already knows exactly what she's going to say. 'She told me there are rumours. Someone said something—'

He interrupts. 'And she's willing to blow up our marriage because of a rumour? What happened to trusting me and believing me when I tell her it isn't true?'

'I don't know. I've tried to tell her . . .'

He lifts up his glass. Puts it down again without taking a sip. 'If someone told me something about her and she said it wasn't true I'd believe her. No questions asked.'

'It might just be a kneejerk overreaction. Because of, you know . . .'

Nick shakes his head. 'It's been years. Six years. We're over it.'

'Do you ever really get past something like that, though? I mean, I'm not trying to make you feel bad . . .'

He sighs loudly. 'She's decided it's true. She won't even hear me out.'

'Like I said, I've tried to make her see sense . . .' The rain starts lashing at the window outside. It makes the pub feel even more cosy, more of a haven.

'Who's even telling her this crap in the first place?' he says, angry suddenly.

Lydia sighs. 'Probably someone with an axe to grind. There's no point worrying about who it is, you'll drive yourself mad.'

'It must be someone . . . Oh, she was talking about you knowing one of my colleagues. Did you introduce her to

173

someone I work with? Maybe it's them. Maybe they told her some made-up story . . .' He runs out of steam.

She arranges her face carefully. She's been waiting for this. 'At Diamond Leisure? I don't think I know anyone . . .'

'Emma or something? I couldn't work out who she was talking about . . .'

'I can't think of any Emmas. Besides, when Georgia and I meet up it's always just us. I don't think I've introduced her to anyone. Did she definitely say it was me?'

He rubs at his eyes. 'I thought she did. I don't know. I don't know what the fuck is going on.'

'What are you going to do now?' she asks gently. She's nearly finished her drink already and it seems too pushy to ask if he wants to stay for another.

'I don't know. I want to go home. But I want to go home and it be like it was before all this started. If she's never going to let it drop then I don't know what to do.'

She fiddles with the stem of her empty glass, hoping he'll get the message. 'Maybe give her some time. Don't contact her for a bit. If she thinks you're trying to pressurize her into believing you she'll probably shut you out altogether. I can work on her if you want? Try to make her see sense.'

'Would you?' He looks at her so hopefully that she almost feels bad.

Almost.

Part 2

Chapter 22

Patricia had been the final straw. She knew Georgia had created her out of love. That she was trying to make Lydia feel better. But actually all it had done was illuminate once again how differently their lives had turned out. It was humiliating. Her mega-successful friend thinking that she needed a fake confidence boost, and to sell a couple of greetings cards and she'd be happy. And, to be fair, at first she had been. Patricia's enthusiasm for her work had buoyed her up for a few days. Made her feel valued.

And then, of course, Georgia had slipped up catastrophically. Given herself away.

After that Lydia had started noticing other little things. A turn of phrase here and there. Georgia obviously didn't even realize she was doing it. And Lydia didn't either until she read back through their messages to see if her suspicions could be confirmed. Idiosyncrasies in spelling that Lydia knew so well because she and Georgia used to copy each other's essays back in the day. That's what happened when you knew someone inside out: you could spot them anywhere.

To say Lydia was angry was an understatement. She was incandescent. It didn't matter that it was an act of kindness. In her eyes it was an act of patronage. But in the worst way. An act of being patronizing. Look at my poor failure of a friend, it screamed. Pity her. She can't make it on her own so

I'm handing her a few crumbs from above. See how generous I am.

Well, fuck it.

The thing is she loves Georgia. They've been best friends forever. More than that. Intertwined in each other's lives like two strands of ivy. But she's sick of Georgia having it all and her having nothing. She's sick of Georgia getting money and recognition for drawings that she could have done herself when she was ten years old. Younger even. And – if she's being really honest – she's sick of Georgia and Nick. Not because she doesn't want Georgia to have a happy relationship. She's not that petty, however it might look. She just doesn't want her to have it with Nick.

Because a few months ago Lydia realized that she was in love with Nick herself.

It had hit her like a bolt of lightning one night. The three of them were sitting in Nick and Georgia's patio garden, enjoying the early autumn heatwave. Nick was barbequing, swearing at the dying coals, laughing about the fact they probably wouldn't be eating till bedtime. It was just starting to get dark and the fairy lights were twinkling along the high back wall. It was hot. One of those evenings where the temperature never seems to drop. No delineation between day and night. The smell of the honeysuckle that spilled over the fence from the neighbouring house sweet and heady. She can even remember what she was wearing: a pale yellow halterneck dress and sparkly sandals. Can still see the purple polish on her toenails, her smooth brown legs. She had taken a photo – Nick's tanned hands with the tongs, the orange glow of the coals, the amber lights – and put it on Insta. *Evenings with friends are the best!!!* A slew of hashtags. She knew that most of her friends would assume she was on a date, some handsome suitor impressing her with his caveman fire-making skills, and she was happy to let that assumption fly.

She was tipsy. They all were. Just slightly. Just enough to soften the hard edges. In the near distance she could hear soft music, people laughing, the pop of a champagne cork. It was one of those evenings you never wanted to end.

'I absolutely love you both,' she'd said out of nowhere and they'd all laughed. She had a tendency to get sentimental when she'd had a couple of glasses.

'Ooh, here she is,' Nick had said. 'I wondered when she'd get here.' Georgia had reached over and squeezed her hand.

And then it had happened. Not because of anything he did or said. Nothing was different. Nothing changed from one minute to the next. Except that she had looked at him and smiled and he'd smiled back and her whole body had tingled. She'd had to catch her breath, will her heart to slow down. She knew this feeling. She was prone to crushes. Fierce and all-consuming for a couple of days and then gone as quickly as they arrived. It was just lust, she knew that. Not love. Usually she enjoyed them. Welcomed the feverish excitement. But that's because usually they weren't this inappropriate. She told herself to ignore it. Crushes needed to be fed. Ignored, it would die of starvation in a few days.

Except that it never did.

It grew.

She had no idea why, where it had come from. She and Nick had always got on well. He was funny. Good company.

Loyal to Georgia in a kind of quiet, effortless way that felt a hundred times more authentic than the men she always met who felt the need to make over-the-top protestations of love while secretly texting other women snapshots of their dicks when she wasn't looking. Even more so since he'd had that – totally out of character – midlife crisis and Georgia had managed to get past it. He'd been like a rescue dog, overwhelmed with gratitude for its second chance in life. Determined to prove it was worth saving.

Lydia could only put it down to some kind of cumulative effect. A slow build that took twenty years to reach a critical mass. The world's slowest avalanche.

Now she would find herself thinking about him when she couldn't sleep at night. Weaving elaborate fantasies. At first just sexual (she would blush whenever she saw him from that point on, although luckily neither he nor Georgia seemed to notice) but then deeper, about a future she knew could never happen. About a perfect home. Her sketching, him cooking. She hated to cook and he loved it so that made them an ideal fit. Her career taking off to incredible heights, success, recognition, but all reflected in the pleasure it would give him. How proud he would be of her. They were adolescent fantasies, she knew that, but they were also what she wanted. She wanted the dream.

Georgia would feature in her imaginings too. Sidelined but happy for them. Somehow having come to the realization that this was for the best. Lydia sometimes got caught up in trying to imagine the details of this. Georgia had fallen out of love but wanted Nick to be happy? She had met someone else but Nick was OK with it? She wanted to fulfil a lifelong dream to travel without the burden of having to worry about anyone else's needs? Some nights she never got beyond this part of her waking dream. It was critical that she get the foundations right. She couldn't relax and enjoy the later part without knowing that her friendship with Georgia was intact. That Georgia was as content as she and Nick were. That the three of them could still hang out. She knew it made no sense but she seemed powerless to lose herself in it any other way.

As the months went by her fantasies became more and more elaborate. Movies. Then mini-series. Then full-on five-times-a-week soap operas. No other man she met came close. She wondered if she had loved him all along. Deep down. If that was why she always knew her liaisons were doomed from the start. Why put herself or anyone else through it? She would never have acted on it though. Not in a million centuries. When the confines of her (single-income and not a very big one at that) flat felt stifling – cold and lifeless, show-home clean because there was no one else there to mess it up, and tidying gave her something to do on lonely evenings and weekends – imagining her alternative life comforted her. She was sick of going out, meeting seemingly random men in pubs and theatre foyers, making small talk and then excuses. She wanted someone to stay in with. To eat with and argue over what they were going to watch on Netflix. And she wanted that person to be Nick and only Nick. She was powerless over how she felt. There was no point feeling bad because there was nothing she could do about it. Or so she'd thought.

And then, in her fit of anger about Patricia – and one too

many glasses of wine down – she had sent the message about the big secret. She couldn't take it back. The next day she had thought about backtracking, shame washing over her like sweat. She could say it was about a different friend, fudge it somehow. Had she given away that it was Georgia she was talking about? She'd checked back, scared to look. Shit, she had. OK. She could make up some anodyne rumour that Georgia wouldn't care about. It didn't even have to involve Nick. Georgia would write it off as a hopeless overreaction on Lydia's part and it would be forgotten.

But then a tiny voice in her head had said why not finish what she'd started? If she played it right Georgia would never know that it was all a lie. She would never blame Lydia for anything. It probably wouldn't work anyway, she told herself. Georgia would almost certainly believe Nick when he protested his innocence and forget all about it. All she was doing was opening a tiny crack. If it grew into a fissure that meant there was something fundamentally unstable in the first place. In which case . . .

So she threw herself head first into the deception. Held back just enough to fuel Georgia's paranoia. Made a point of avoiding bumping into Nick (that had been hard! She'd been aching to see him) so that Georgia would believe she felt uncomfortable being around him. And she waited.

She tried to forget that she knew Georgia's Achilles heel. Her fear of being laughed at behind her back. Her absolute obsession with truth and transparency. Georgia had always believed she could deal with anything so long as everyone revealed all their cards. She had an almost pathological hatred of being lied to, of being the butt of the joke, as she saw it. Nick hiding something from her again would be a deal-breaker. The ultimate betrayal. Lydia had pushed that thought to the back of her mind.

'I need to go home and collect more stuff,' Nick says now, and she notices for the first time that the shirt he's wearing is a shade too big. Cut for rugby-playing Dom's oversized shoulders. The sleeves are rolled up to the elbow, thick dark hair on muscular forearms.

'I think she mentioned that she's going over to Harry and Anne Marie's tomorrow night. If . . . I mean . . . I'm not trying to say go when she's not there because you probably want to talk but it might be better . . .'

'Do you think it'll make things worse if I see her at the moment? Shouldn't we be trying to thrash it out?' he says.

'Just until she's calmed down a bit. I think that's why she asked me to act as intermediary . . . she doesn't want to talk to you yet. Beyond the essentials, I mean . . .'

'I guess she's not prepared to give me a fair hearing, anyway,' Nick says, worrying at a scratch on the table. 'So I should probably stay away. I don't want to say something I'll regret.'

'Exactly. Just for a while. Like I said, I'll work on her,' Lydia says kindly, shrugging into her coat. He hasn't taken up her hint of another drink. He's too preoccupied with his failing marriage, she thinks, and who could blame him? She can't begin to imagine how confused he must be feeling.

'I just want things to be back how they were,' he says, and Lydia has to resist the urge to slide her hand over the table on top of his. She needs to move slowly. Not crowd him. Just be there when he decides to accept that it's hopeless and he's ready to move on. Right place, right time. Right man, right woman.

'They will be,' she says. 'Just give her space.'

Chapter 23

Anne Marie and Harry's flat is comfortable chaos as usual. Worse than usual (or should I say better?) because I've added Igor into the mix. He greets Nina like the old friend she is, places his paws on Gino's shoulders which, considering Gino has shot up to five foot eleven over the past couple of years, is no mean feat, and even their middle child, Billie, who is going through a serious emo phase that precludes enthusiasm about most things, gets caught up in trying to teach him how to cover his ears with his paws if she says the words Ed Sheeran. The flat smells of baking and cinnamon. There's some kind of one-pot wonder bubbling away on the stove and home-made bread cooling on a rack. It's like *The Waltons* with fewer children but more attitude.

Harry grabs me in a hug before I've even taken my coat off. 'Are you OK?'

I nod into his shoulder. Harry is a bit like a human wrapped in a duvet. He has a soft outer covering that gives him a kind of cuddly appearance. Blurry round the edges. Edie once told him he looked like her teddy bear and I haven't been able to get that image out of my head ever since – round-faced, reddish-haired, big button eyes. The last couple of years he's been sporting a full-on beard and it gives him the appearance of a benevolent giant. Which is exactly what he is.

The idea that Anne Marie cheated on him makes me shudder.

'Yeah. No, but . . . you know . . .'

'I can't believe it,' he says, and all I can come up with is 'Me neither.' I need to remind them not to say too much in front of the kids because my twins are still clueless. Mobile phones can hide a multitude of deceptions. If I call them while I'm out on a walk with the dog why would they ever wonder why I wasn't passing the phone over to their dad? This morning I sent a text to Nick: *I haven't mentioned anything to the kids. Please don't.*

Of course not, he'd sent back, which made me wonder if he was still hoping we could work things out. I knew he was still staying at Dom's, or at least, that's what he'd told Harry. Maybe this was all too much too soon for Lou-stroke-Siobhan. Maybe the idea of commitment had sent her running to the hills. A casual fling had suddenly turned into something life-changing and she wasn't sure that was what she wanted. Well, boo hoo.

Anne Marie appears with a large vodka and tonic. She knows without asking that I only like one cube of ice. Lots of lemon. Harry hands me over to her like a pass the parcel and she swoops me up, the lonely ice cube rattling in the glass.

'Come into the kitchen.'

The two of them follow me in and shut the door. A scuffed wooden table fills up most of the available space, six mis-matched chairs set around it. Harry clears a space in the detritus of homework, some kind of bead craft and food preparation. I move a flute – Billie's – from a chair and sit down.

'The kids are on strict instructions to stay out of the way and keep Igor amused till dinner,' Anne Marie says, plonking herself into the seat next to me. 'I haven't told Harry all the . . . you know . . .'

I look up at Harry, who's hovering anxiously. 'What did Nick say to you?'

He shrugs. 'Not much. Just that you were having some problems and he'd moved into Dom's . . .'

'Did he say "moved into"? Not just he was staying there?'

Harry looks at the floor, like a guilty toddler. He has no guile. He could never get away with deceiving anyone. 'Yes.'

'Well, that's that then, I guess,' I say, trying to sound offhand.

'It makes no sense,' Anne Marie butts in. 'Can I talk about it in front of Harry?'

'You don't have to . . .' he says quickly.

'It's OK.' I nod. I fill him in with the edited highlights. His face is a picture. A kaleidoscope of shock, horror, revulsion.

'There's no way . . .' he says when I finish.

I shake my head. 'That was my first reaction.'

'I'll fucking kill him,' Harry says, and I almost laugh. The idea of Harry killing anything is ludicrous. He once spent half an hour in a pub garden trying to revive a bee while the rest of us sat shivering in the car and waited to go home. In the end we persuaded him to bring it with him and then, when it perked up, he started to fret that it would never find its family again, so he chauffeured it back to the pub and let it go there. And what thanks did he get? It never wrote. It never called. 'I mean . . . if it's true, if he's . . . then he's the lowest of the low. Lower.'

'I just can't see it,' Anne Marie says. I can't look at her. I stare out of their third-floor window as thick snowflakes start to tumble past.

'And he seemed really down when I spoke to him. I assumed it was your decision for him to leave.' Harry is warming to his theme. 'He actually made me feel sorry for him.'

I suddenly feel overwhelmed. I shouldn't have come over. I should have stayed at home licking my wounds, not be having to deal with anyone else and their shattered illusions of my husband. Managing my own disappointment is hard enough. Harry is like a child who's just found out that Santa doesn't exist, that Superman is nothing more than a bloke who likes to play dress-up.

'I can't move on till I know the truth,' I say, only realizing as it comes out of my mouth that that's what I need. To move on. My marriage is over regardless of whether Nick is regretting his actions. Not even because of the affair itself but because of the way he's dealt with – is dealing with – it. Lying to me over and over again. Letting me beg and plead. Refusing to put me out of my misery. It's a side of him I've never seen before. A cruel, calculating side. Whatever happens I can't be married to that person. Joe and Edie pop into my mind. Ridiculously, I think about Christmas – where we'll all go. Will they have to split their time? Lunch at mine and dinner at his? – even though it's still only February. Tears rush to my eyes.

'Oh, Georgia.' Anne Marie reaches out a hand to stroke my arm.

'Don't . . .' I say. 'If I start I'll never stop.'

To distract myself I tell them about Lydia's drink with Nick. She had called me on her way home from the tube at about a quarter past eight – by which time I was tearing my hair out for news, pacing round the kitchen aimlessly, Igor following me back and forth, back and forth, his nails tapping on the wooden floor.

'Sorry, sorry! I couldn't get any reception before I got on the tube so then I had to wait till I got off.' I could hear her clicking down the street. Lydia always wears heels to work. She believes that looking smart keeps your mind focused on the job. My home office uniform is sweatpants. Socks if I'm making an effort.

'It's OK. So . . .'

She sighed. 'I don't know what to say, Georgia. I tried to persuade him to talk to you, but he was adamant there was no point . . .'

'Did he admit it?'

'Not in so many words . . . Hang on, I just have to find my key . . .' I heard her rattling around and then some unidentifiable noises and the street hum was gone. 'I'm back.'

I could picture her walking up the stairs to her first-floor flat. Past the little table in the hall where the three residents of the house leave the mail. She's lucked out with her neighbours. Two other single women, one in her fifties and Mrs Morgan on the ground floor who must be approaching seventy. Both quiet, both considerate. Lydia's flat is bright and airy. A large bay window overlooking the street from her sunny living room. Kitchen and bedroom at the back, with a view of Mrs Morgan's neat garden and the backs of the houses in the neighbouring road. She's decorated in muted Farrow & Ball colours. White sofa because there's no one to leave grubby marks all over it. It exudes Zen-like levels of calm, but I would miss the mess of family life. I like a home to feel lived in. Although, of course, mine is only lived in by me and the dog at the moment. All those times I counted down the moments till the kids left for school and Nick for work, revelling in the prospect of a few hours of blissful silence. But it was only blissful because I knew it was finite. Turns out unending hours of silence just means loneliness. What will we do with the house? I thought suddenly. If Nick was gone for good where would we both live?

'He didn't want to talk about it, but he didn't deny it either.'

My heart sank. 'He didn't?'

'He just said there was no point talking to you. I told him all you wanted was the truth. I even said he could tell me if he'd rather, but he didn't bite.'

'So, do you think that's it? He cares so little about me that he won't even give me that?'

'I don't know. I'm so sorry, George. I wish I could have been more help.'

I sank down in a chair. Rubbed at my eyes with the back of a hand. 'Don't be silly. I love you for trying.'

'Are you going to be OK? Should I come over?' I heard the cork pop out of a bottle of wine.

'No! I mean yes. And no. I'll be fine. You've done enough.'

'I'm not giving up.' She laughed ruefully. 'I'm going to make him come clean with you.'

'I don't understand why he won't,' I said, not for the first time. 'He's clearly made his choice.'

'Because he knows everyone will think he's a shit,' she said. 'He can't bear to lose his nice-guy image.'

* * *

When I let myself into the house at about half ten, having shrugged off Harry's offer to walk me home, I can feel that something's different. The air has shifted. I know, even before I see the note, that someone has been here. If I were in any doubt Igor's nose goes into overdrive and he snuffles round the hall as though he's hunting for truffles. For a moment I think that Nick is home and, despite everything, I feel a crashing sense of relief. Then I see the sheet of paper. A4. Snatched out of the printer. Written on it in black Sharpie: 'I came to pick up a few bits and pieces. N x'.

That kiss. Probably added without even thinking. I try not to read too much into it. Had he been waiting for me to go out before he came home? Had Harry mentioned that I was going round to theirs? Given him an opportunity without realizing it? It seems like way too much of a coincidence otherwise. What a coward. Scared to face me in case I bullied him into the truth. I dig out my mobile to call him. Decide on a text instead. *Really? You're sneaking in when I'm out now?*

I wander down to the kitchen as I wait. Give Igor some kibble. And then there's a reply.

I thought you wouldn't want to see me.

So he did know that I wasn't going to be there. *What? You're just going to avoid me forever??*

Tell me what you want me to do. I'm not being sarcastic. I mean it. Anything. I miss you.

THEN TELL ME THE TRUTH!!! I respond, shouting on the screen.

He responds immediately. *For fuck's sake! I am! I have!!! This is why I didn't want to see you tonight. Forget it.*

I turn my phone off. Plug it in and stomp up the stairs.

Chapter 24

When I get up in the morning, dragging myself down to the basement to make a cup of tea and taking it straight back up to bed, there are no more messages. I haven't looked at Patricia's Twitter for a couple of days – it feels a bit pointless now that Lydia is talking to me about Nick's affair in real life. But she's still not telling me everything she knows. Not yet.

There are two private messages. Both from the night before last. The night Lyds met up with Nick. I nestle into Igor's broad back for warmth and open them up.

Patricia, are you there?? Need a bit of your sage advice!!!!

And then:

Met up with Georgia's husband tonight to try and prise the truth out of him!! Help!!!

Shit. How could I have missed this? Nick obviously said far more to Lydia than she's letting on to me. I type quickly. Force myself to read it through carefully before I hit send.

I'm so sorry not to have been there in your hour of need! I went to the Cotswolds for a short break and no reception. What has happened? Can you tell me? I'm here now if you need me.

It's early. I'm not even sure Lydia will be up. She has her morning routine down to the absolute minimum length of time before she has to leave the house. She is not, and never has been, a morning person. Two sips of tea later there's a response though.

Oh Patricia! Thank goodness. How was your break?

I don't have time for niceties. *Lovely, thank you. Just visiting my mother. Are you OK?*

I wish I'd never met up with him, to be honest. It's as if he couldn't care less about Georgia any more.

I calm myself with a deep breath. I have to go through the motions. Patricia would ask the right questions even though I already know the answers. *So he owned up?*

He did!!!

Wait. What? She told me he didn't. *Really?*

Yes! But not even like he felt bad about it. I begged him to talk to her, but he said there was no point.

And he's still seeing the woman? What's her name again? I figure Patricia's allowed to be a bit nosey at this point.

She doesn't bite. *That's the impression I got.*

What did you tell Georgia in the end?

Just that he was cagey. I couldn't bring myself to elaborate. How can I tell my best friend that her husband couldn't care less that their marriage is over?

'Why is no one being truthful with me?' I wail to Anne Marie on the phone. She's on her way to school. I can hear car horns and angry raised voices. Just another rush hour in north London.

'What don't you think Lydia is telling you?' I knew she would ask this and I've already decided I'm going to fill her in on everything. I'm going to go insane if I don't confide in someone and Anne Marie won't judge me for Patricia. She'll understand the reasons behind why I did what I did.

'It's a long story. Can I pop over later? Before Harry gets home?'

'Of course. Any time after four. He won't be back till seven.'

'Thanks. Brilliant. Apologies in advance that I'm just going to drone on about myself.'

'Drone away,' she says, and I can hear the unforced warmth in her voice.

'Can I bring Igor?' I've started to panic that Nick might go to the house when I'm out and decide that he wants to take the dog to live with him. Who knows what he's capable of now?

'Nina would never forgive you if you didn't,' she says.

I go back to the beginning, taking great pains to stress that Patricia was a kind gesture, not some weird kind of catfishing con. We're sitting in her kitchen. Nina is entertaining Igor in the lounge, having been banished from the bedroom she shares with Billie. Gino is at an after-school chess club. He loves chess. He has tried patiently to teach me many times but I've never got beyond learning how the pieces move. Sometimes I ask him annoying questions just to see if I can get a rise out of him. 'Which way does the horse go again?' I said once, and he'd very calmly explained that it was a knight. 'The horse is symbolic, Georgia.' Unlike the girls, he has never called me Auntie, just Georgia, as if I were the child and he the adult. Another time I asked if 'the prawns' could go backwards, and he gave me such a withering look I had to tell him I was joking before he wrote me off completely.

'OK,' she says a couple of times. 'I mean, crazy, but OK.'

I show her Patricia's private exchanges with Lydia, sit there in silence while she reads them all through.

'A haberdashery?' she says at one point and we both snigger. Me more from nerves than anything. 'God, you really have got into character.'

I wait for her to finish reading. 'Why didn't she just tell me what he said? I mean, what was the point . . . ?'

'She's just trying to protect you,' Anne Marie says. 'To be fair, it's got to be hard for her—'

'It's just so frustrating,' I interrupt. 'She knows I'm going crazy not knowing. You won't tell Harry, will you?'

'Maybe you just need to give her time. It's a shitty situation she's in.'

'I've started making plans in my head.' I pick at a sliver of wood that has detached itself from the table. 'How we'll tell the kids. What'll happen to the house. It's as if I've accepted that my marriage is over without even sitting down and talking about it with Nick.'

'It's self-preservation,' she says. 'You need to know you're going to be OK. Edie and Joe have no idea?'

I shake my head. 'We agreed not to say anything, but I don't know how long we can keep that up for.'

'Shit,' she says. 'Don't risk them finding out any other way.'

'I know,' I say decisively. 'I'm sending him a message.' I pick up my phone and send a text. *We need to talk about the kids.*

Anne Marie gets up to put the kettle on. I can hear music from Billie's room. Something I recognize. Some band Edie likes too. My Chemical Romance maybe. My mobile beeps with a response.

So, is that it? You're giving up on me?

I hold the phone out for her to see.

I'm not the one who gave up, Nick, I reply.

Chapter 25

It's only been a couple of days since Lydia met up with Nick but she feels as if she needs to make contact. Remind him that she's here if he needs her. She sends him a text. *How are you doing?* Georgia called her, incandescent with rage, after she discovered he had been home while she was out to collect more stuff. Lydia couldn't deny it, she was pleased that he'd listened to her, taken her advice. Maybe now he would confide in her more, use her as a shoulder to cry on. That would be enough for the time being. Until he's ready.

Patricia has also been in evidence, asking thinly disguised questions about what she knows. Hedging around the subject in a way that Georgia obviously thinks is subtle. Lydia is tempted to elaborate more in her replies, but she has to stay within the bounds of what Georgia might believe she would tell a stranger. Lydia has always made a virtue of her dismissal of gossip. It's one of her best qualities and one she's worked hard to cultivate. Not to mention the fact that she doesn't want to tell Georgia anything she could fact check. So no real specifics. She's pretty confident she'll never be able to check there is no Emma at Diamond Leisure. Of course there is an Emma. There are probably twenty-five. But there is no Emma who is friends with Lydia. There is no Emma at Diamond Leisure that Lydia has ever met. She picked the name for its popularity among women their age. There were six in her year at school alone.

It's almost funny watching Patricia flounder. She can't imagine how frustrating it is for Georgia not to be able to ask the question she really wants answered outright. Who is it that Nick is seeing? Lydia knows that Georgia has narrowed it down to two suspects – Lou and Siobhan – and that suits Lydia perfectly. She has no intention of steering her in the direction of one or the other.

She works on the illustrations for her book – it's for children but it's dark, an underworld world. 'It's *Game of Thrones* for eight-year-olds,' she imagines herself saying to prospective publishers, giving a little laugh. 'But with gnomes. *Game of Gnomes.*' Obviously there's no gore, no murders, but it's a cute description. They'll remember it. Especially if she plays it like she's just come up with it. An off-the-cuff remark. She hasn't yet heard back from a few of the publishers she sent it to, so she still has hope. But deep down she's scared. It's all very well telling herself she could be as successful as Georgia if she tried; it's another thing altogether to actually try and have that dream shattered.

She loses herself in her task. It's like therapy. The only time that her brain quietens. She's scratching away at the roots of a tree, her magnifying glass propped up in front of her, when her mobile buzzes.

Not too bad, Nick says. *Have you talked to George lately?*

Yesterday. She's still not budging I'm afraid x.

OK. Thanks, is all he says. She doesn't want to leave it like that. She needs to make the most of every opportunity.

Well, I'm still here if you need someone to talk to xx.

She waits.

Thanks Lyds x.

That diminutive, that kiss, will get her through the rest of the day.

Later she needs to get ready. She has a date with Wes, a man she met at her yoga class of all things. Lydia only ever meets men IRL. She has never even looked at Tinder or Bumble or Hinge. Dates just seem to present themselves to her in the least likely of places. Maybe because she gives off an air of not caring. She's a challenge.

Wes seems nice. He's flexible, she'll give him that. And he wears long trousers to class, which is a bonus. No way would she date one of the tiny-short-wearing men who like to let it all hang out – literally – while they do their sun salutations. Power yoga seems to attract them. The excuse to strip down to next to nothing and stand at the front of the class watching themselves and their hairy legs sweating in the mirror. Leaving everyone behind not daring to look up when they're in the downward dog for fear of what they might see. She and Wes have ended up at the same classes twice a week for a good few weeks now, while most of the clientele have changed around them. It was inevitable that they would get talking. Inevitable, it seems, that he would ask her for a drink one evening. As usual she'd explained the lack of any kind of potential for an actual relationship and, as usual, he'd smiled, thinking she was being cute. Portraying herself as a wild spirit, hard to pin down when, in fact, the truth was simply that she was in love with someone else.

She can't face it, really. It all seems so pointless except that she needs to get out of the house. She'd suggested to Wes that they do something other than just go to the pub. She doesn't want to spend the evening listening to him talk about his family or his job (what is it he does again? Something hipstery. Runs a microbrewery or a plant-based cheese company). Not because she didn't think it would be interesting, but what was the point? Getting-to-know-you evenings were a necessary evil when you were thinking about starting a relationship with someone. You had to fill in the surface blanks before you could progress deeper. But she has no intention of ever progressing deeper.

Thankfully he'd agreed, and they were going to see an exhibition of graffiti art at a gallery in Shoreditch. Every night was like opening night, apparently. Music. A bar. She'd been wanting to go since it opened a couple of weeks ago, but she hadn't felt she could face trekking over there on her own. And what was an art exhibition if you had no one to talk over what you'd seen with?

She could have asked Georgia, she thinks now. She's at home alone every evening. Maybe she would have jumped at the chance to get out. Lydia puts her phone on hands-free while she makes up her face.

'So who's this one?' Georgia asks, laughing. Lydia can tell the laugh is fake: Georgia's attempt to make her think she's doing OK.

'Oh, forget about him,' she says. 'How are you doing?' She knows it's odd, this genuine concern for her friend's well-being when she's the cause of all her problems in the first place. She can't really explain it, except to tell herself that she's doing what she's doing not to hurt Georgia but to give herself a future. It's her turn.

'Yeah. OK,' Georgia says.

'Anything from Nick? Did he contact you yet?' She gives herself a second coat of mascara.

Georgia sighs. 'Nothing. We're going to have to tell the kids something soon. I'm sure Joe's getting suspicious.'

'Well, definitely tell them before they find out some other way.'

'It makes it so final though, doesn't it?' Lydia can hear Igor clicking about on the wooden floor in the background. She's glad that Georgia got him when she did. Glad that she has company. Something that loves her and she can love back.

'But, I suppose . . . I mean, I don't want this to sound wrong, George . . . I suppose it kind of is final, isn't it? If he won't even discuss it with you and he's still seeing whoever she is . . .'

'It's just . . . it's too much . . .'

'I know. But the twins are grown up, more or less . . .'

'Maybe I can get them to come home for a weekend. Maybe Nick and I can talk to them – together, you know, lessen the impact a bit.'

Lydia isn't sure it's a good idea for Nick to be in the same room as Georgia at the moment. She's relying on them not having any in-depth conversations any time soon. Of course, she hasn't really thought through what she'd do if he decided to replay their conversation from the pub line by line for Georgia's benefit. Deny, deny, deny is as far as she's got. He's hardly seen as a reliable witness at the moment. 'Mmm. You don't really want them to see the atmosphere between the two of you. I'm not sure that's such a great idea.'

Georgia is quiet for a second. 'You might be right. So, where is it tonight?'

Lydia fills her in. When they've said goodbye she snaps a selfie. Filters it. Crops it. Posts it on Instagram: *Another fun night out!!!* She looks good. She looks like a woman who, as the hashtag says, is leading her best life.

Chapter 26

Joe is home for the weekend. I wasn't expecting him, didn't have time to prepare him for the fact that his father wouldn't be here. I just answered the front door and there he was, having forgotten his key as usual. God knows what he would have done if no one was in. Shivered on the doorstep waiting. Maybe taken himself round to Anne Marie's. All his friends are away at uni. My first reaction is utter joy at seeing him there – my handsome, six-foot-tall baby. And then, of course, I panic. Nick and I still haven't agreed on what or when to tell the kids. I need to call him.

'Oh my God,' I squeal, grabbing him into a hug. 'What a lovely surprise.' I don't want to let go. The familiar feel of him floors me. He smells faintly of cigarettes and something clean and citrusy. It suddenly hits me that maybe something is wrong. 'Are you OK? Is everything OK?'

He untangles himself from my arms. Kisses the top of my head. 'Everything's fine. I just thought I'd pop home. Get my washing done.'

'Did you bring washing? Give it to me. Let me feel as if I have a purpose in life again . . .'

He laughs. 'Of course I didn't. There's a machine in halls. Where's the dog?'

'Sleeping. He's the world's worst guard dog.' He follows me in, dumping his holdall on the floor. We're halfway down the stairs to the kitchen when Igor wakes up and storms to my defence, pinning Joe against the wall.

'Jesus, Mum. Couldn't you have found a bigger one?'

'He's a softy,' I say, just as Igor launches a licking offensive. It's as if he recognizes that Joe is family.

I flick the kettle on, trying to think fast. Maybe I can fudge it, tell him his father's away on a business trip. And then I think about him finding out that I lied, and I know I can't. He slumps on to a kitchen chair, all arms and legs. It's as if he and Igor are stars in a film with a set that's just a tiny bit too small for them. The result of someone scrimping on the budget by scaling everything down just a fraction. Almost imperceptible. His hair has grown since I saw him at Christmas. It suits him.

'How's Brighton?' I say pointlessly, trying to buy some time. I speak to him pretty much every other day, so I know he's having fun. And even if I didn't I could tell all was fine within a minute of clapping eyes on him. Joe wears his mood on the surface like an overcoat. He always has.

'Yeah. Good.'

'Are you here for the whole weekend?' I say hopefully.

He gives me a big grin. 'I have to leave first thing Monday. Basically I've run out of food so, you know, I thought I could get in a couple of days' eating here.' He picks up Igor's giant cow toy and they wrestle with it for a bit. I should warn him that he'll want to give up many hours before the dog will get bored. Igor is foaming at the mouth with determination. 'You meant to get one with rabies, right?'

'Of course,' I say. 'It's very in at the moment.'

'Gwyneth Paltrow recommends canine drool as a rejuvenating face serum, apparently.'

'Oh. I bought one of her candles. "This smells like my dog's farts".'

That gets him. He laughs. I've won.

'What time's Dad back?'

Ah. I put his mug of tea down in front of him and sit in the seat opposite. I need to be truthful, but I need to try and underplay it at the same time.

'Dad's . . . um . . . he's staying at Dom's for a bit . . .'

Joe, of course, picks up immediately that something is very wrong. I never could hide anything from him. It's as if he tuned himself to my feelings when he was a baby and never tuned out. And Dom only lives in Somers Town. It's not as if Nick would have gone there on holiday. 'Right . . .'

'Just for a few days. If you ring him I'm sure he'll come over though . . .'

'What's going on, Mum?'

'I'm . . . We're . . . having a little break. It's nothing . . .'

'A break? You and Dad? What the fuck? How long's he been gone for?'

I reach out a hand and put it over one of his. 'Only since last weekend. We need to sort a few things out, that's all.'

He pulls his hand away. Sweeps it back over his head in the exact same way his father always does. 'What's happened? Everything was fine at Christmas. Wasn't it? Or were you putting on an act for me and Ede? Does she know?'

I shake my head. 'No. We . . . we were going to tell you both. It only just happened. We were waiting to see . . . you know . . .'

'So, what? He just upped and left? You kicked him out? You've secretly hated each other for years but you were biding your time till we left home? What?'

'No! Not that.' I hate seeing that his mood has shattered. Shit, we should have laid the groundwork for this. I don't want to turn him against his father – Joe has very black-and-white ideas of what's right and wrong. Edie has always been better at seeing the grey areas – but I don't want to take the blame for this either. 'Something happened. Your dad . . .'

'Has he got someone else? No way. I don't believe it.' He stands up, sits down again.

'I don't know if he still . . . he did. I think. Well, I know, but he won't . . . He doesn't want to talk about it . . .'

'And he just left? After twenty-whatever years? That's it?'

I shrug. 'I don't . . . It's complicated.'

He stands up again. He looks, at the same time, so grown up, tall and strong, and like a little boy. Confused. Shattered. 'What the fuck is complicated? Dad's seeing some woman? Fucking hell, Mum.'

'I know . . .'

He comes round to my side of the table, leans down and grabs me into a hug.

'We didn't want to say anything till . . . He's still insisting it's not true,' I say when I emerge.

Joe sits on the chair next to mine. 'You don't know for sure?'

'No. I mean yes. I do. But Dad isn't ready to discuss it. He won't . . . I can't get him to . . .'

'Wait . . . So you didn't, like, catch him in the act or find an incriminating text or anything?'

I shake my head. Tell him the same potted version I told Lydia, leaving out Patricia.

'So it might not be true!' he says, clutching at straws, when

I get to the end. Neither of the kids has any idea about Nick's earlier indiscretion; I made sure of that. They have no idea what he's capable of.

I sigh. 'It is. I believe the person who told me one hundred per cent.'

Joe leans over and grabs his coat. Igor jumps to attention and Joe reaches down and ruffles his head. 'This is ridiculous. I'll be back later. For dinner or whatever. I'll call.'

'Where are you going?' I say with a sinking feeling. I think I know the answer.

'Dom's. He really is there, right?'

I nod. Do I actually know that's true? I only have Nick's word for it. Checking with Dom would be too humiliating and, besides, he lives by some sad bro code that would mean he'd lie for Nick in a heartbeat if he thought he was about to be caught out doing something wrong. 'So far as I know anyway.'

'No way is he going to be able to lie to me if I ask him straight out,' he says, leaning down and kissing me. 'I won't be long.'

I know I should try to stop him but I also know I'd fail. And, to be fair, his father does deserve to be put on the spot. He got us into this mess. For Joe's sake I text him though.

Joe home unexpectedly. I had to tell him. He's on his way to see you.

Less than a minute later I get a reply.

What did you tell him?? That you've kicked me out for no reason???

This is not about you. Just think about what's best for Joe. I'm going to call Edie before he does.

Her phone goes straight to voicemail and I know I'm too late, that Joe will have phoned her on the way to the tube.

While I wait I make up Joe's bed. His and Edie's rooms are in the eaves, a shared bathroom between them, the toiletries lined up with rigid precision, his on the left, hers on the right. Edie's room is a riot of colour, reds and purples. Fairy lights and photographs. A clutter of hairbands and bracelets. Joe's is painted a steely grey with white furniture. No less cluttered but somehow more airy. There's a gap where his turntable used to be and his prized vinyl collection, now adorning his student accommodation. I pick up my mobile to try Edie again and see that Nick has sent another message: *Don't try and make me look like the villain in this.*

Grow up, Nick, I send.

Chapter 27

Lydia can't believe it when her phone rings and it's Nick. She's had enough of the graffiti artist's exhibition. Not that it's not good – it is. But she's tired and Wes is a bit of a bore . . . No, that's not fair, he's not a bore; she's just not interested in what he has to say. It's not his fault. If she fancied him she'd probably be hanging on his every word. She knows she's not exactly being sparkling company herself but – now she can see a glimmer of hope in the future – these dates are beginning to seem more and more pointless. She's taken a few good pictures. Urban and edgy. Warm Prosecco and a scuffed skateboard someone has left in a corner become a juxtaposition of privilege and grit when photographed together. A snapshot of an enviable life. But, if she's being honest, she's tired. Her feet hurt. She wants the evening to be over. The memory is always far more interesting than the reality.

'Sorry, I need to get this,' she says to Wes who, even though he was warned, is clearly finding the evening a bit of a washout too. She indicates that she's going out on to the street as she says 'Hi!' Of course that's a mistake. Her coat is in the cloakroom and it's sub freezing out there, so she hovers in the doorway, trying to keep the shiver out of her voice.

'Sorry, are you out?' he says, and she would have recognized his voice anywhere even if his name hadn't popped up on her screen.

'Yes, but wishing I wasn't. How are you doing?'

'Joe just came round,' he says. 'Georgia told him every-thing apparently.'

Lydia feels a rush of guilt. She adores Joe and Edie. Always has. She's godmother to both of them. They'll need her when they find out their father has left for good. She's always been a good shoulder to cry on and, so long as there's a decent enough gap between him leaving and – hopefully – shacking up with her, she still can be. Better for them that he ends up with someone they already call family. 'Why did she do that?'

'I guess it wasn't entirely her fault. He came home unex-pectedly. Wanted to know where I was. But she's told him I've been having an affair. I don't . . . This is like some kind of nightmare that I can't wake up from. Why would she do that?'

Lydia sees an in. Maybe the night – the hair, the make-up, the sleekly fitting boho dress – isn't a write-off after all. 'Where are you now? At Dom's?'

'Yes. He just left. Joe. I thought he was never going to speak to me again.'

'I'm coming over. Is there a decent pub nearby?' She doesn't want to run into Dom. He once made a pass at her in the days when they would occasionally – disastrously – meet as a four, and he hadn't taken it well when she'd rebuffed him. Then, out of the blue, years later, he'd called her in the wake of his separation and tried to persuade her to go on a date with him. She wasn't keen on being used as a middle finger up to his ex-wife, she'd told him, and he'd basically told her to go fuck herself and that he wouldn't be interested in her if she were the last woman alive. 'It'd be like sleeping with an ironing board,' he'd said, angry with embarrassment. 'Trust me,' she'd said calmly. 'It would be more like sleeping with the iron if you ever put a finger anywhere near me.'

Nick doesn't even argue. 'The Lord John Russell's OK. Marchmont Street.'

'I can be there in half an hour,' she says.

'Great. Thanks.'

She's tempted just to leave without even bothering to say goodbye to Wes, but he doesn't deserve that and, besides, she doesn't want to have to give up power yoga just to avoid bumping into him. She pushes her way back in through the crowds of hipsters and would-be Banksys and finds him chatting to a couple by the bar.

'I'm so sorry,' she says breathlessly. 'I've got a bit of an emergency. I have to go.'

His face falls. 'Is everything OK? Can I do anything?'

He's a nice bloke, she realizes. Kind. 'No. Thanks. You stay.'

'Only if you're sure. I'll come and help you find a cab.'

He walks her out without his coat, having waited for her to collect hers. He asks her again if she wants him to come with her but she tells him it makes no sense, he lives much nearer to here than to where she's going. 'Can I call you?' he asks just before he shuts the taxi door. 'At least so I know you're OK.'

'Of course,' she says. 'I was having a lovely evening, thanks.' She can let him down gently when the time comes. Maybe lay it on thick about whatever tonight's emergency turned out to be. A sick family member. A suicidal friend. 'I just don't have the space in my head for a relationship right now.' She can hear herself saying it. Regretful. It's ridiculous really. There's no reason not to go out with him again. No reason, that is, except Nick.

He's standing at the bar with his back to her when she gets there, after a seemingly interminable journey with a cabbie who wanted to talk about bike lanes at every opportunity. 'Empty, see?' he said every time they turned a corner and there was a new one. 'Fucking ridiculous, excuse my language.' Shoulders hunched over in his big coat. Her heart flips. Is she really doing this? She's just meeting a friend in need, she tells herself. The fact that she's in love with him and he's married to her best mate is neither here nor there.

'Hey,' she says. He turns round. There are shadows under his eyes and it almost looks as if he's been crying. He gives her a weak smile.

'Just in time. What can I get you?'

'I think I'll make my first one a Diet Coke,' she says, laying the groundwork for a second drink. 'I've had too much Prosecco already.'

'Where were you?'

She fills him in on her date with Wes.

'God, sorry, I didn't mean to ruin your evening,' he says, handing her her drink. The pub is half empty and they have their pick of tables. She leads him towards an intimate two in a corner.

'No. I was glad to get out of there. We'd pretty much run out of things to talk about.'

He drapes his coat over the back of his chair. 'How was the show?'

She shrugs. 'OK. Good. Not mind-blowing.'

There's an awkwardness. She can feel it. She's had this before when she's liked someone and suddenly she can't think of anything to say to them. She doesn't want him to think she's dull company even though, surely, after all these years of being friends, he must know that's not usually true. She remembers why he called her. Not for a date but a mercy mission.

'So, tell me what happened. Joe just showed up?'

He nods. 'I can't believe Georgia would tell him like that. I mean . . . I know she had to say something, but the whole affair story? She must have known what that would do to him.'

Lydia nods. Clearly Georgia must have been put on the spot. And, although she would never want the kids to think badly of their father, she also wouldn't want them to think that she was the one to blame. It was completely under-standable. 'It does seem . . . well, a bit unnecessary,' she says now. She has to be careful not to bad-mouth Georgia. She just needs to drop enough insights to reinforce Nick's own conclusions.

'It's completely out of order. Joe came round ready to rip me to shreds.'

'Oh God, you poor thing. And him. I mean, both of you. I don't know what is going on with her at the moment.'

He stares at the table. 'You don't think . . . ?' He exhales. 'You don't think she's been wanting to break up and so she's decided to use this as the excuse? Like maybe she never really got over . . .' He leaves it hanging but she understands what he means. Felicity. The truth is that Lydia knows Georgia *was* over it. Had been for years. Nick had proved himself time and time again, even when he no longer needed to. But, of course, the fact of it was still there somewhere. Buried so deep it was all but forgotten until she helped to unearth t again.

'No! No, I'm sure that's not it. She obviously believes what this person's telling her . . .'

'Did you find out who it is yet?'

He looks up and she stares him dead in the eye. 'No idea. She just keeps saying it's someone who works at Diamond Leisure. Could be anyone. How did you leave it with Joe?'

'OK, I think. I asked him just to believe me until he has definite proof that he shouldn't and he agreed.'

'I'm so sorry, Nick,' she says, briefly touching his hand. 'Let me get us another drink.' She's not leaving it up to him this time. 'Same again?'

Chapter 28

'I think I believe him.' Joe is wolfing down the pizza I prepared as if he thinks he might never see food again. Whenever he thinks I'm not looking he flicks a bit into the dog's bowl. Igor gazes at him as if he's met his god. 'He seems really fed up.'

I'm feeling bad that I blurted out the truth. Edie had called me back, tearful, after Joe had broken the news. 'Is it really true?' she'd said hopefully, as if I might be able to tell her that Joe had got it all wrong. I'd gone through the whole story again, as gently as I could. Nothing good can come of pitting them against their father. I murmur now something about it all working out in the end. I don't mean it, obviously. I'm desperate to quiz Joe about what exactly his father said but I know that's probably item 41 in *The Bad Parenting Handbook*, so I leave it be. 'Well, I'm glad you saw him, anyway.'

'Dom's place is hideous,' he says, folding a slice of pizza in half and then quarters. 'Imagine somewhere Donald Trump might live if he had no money and even less taste. Lots of black and chrome.'

I laugh. 'Has Dad got his own room?'

Joe shakes his head. 'On the sofa. He looks a mess.'

Despite everything that's happened it still hurts to think of Nick like that. I'd hate him to be living in the lap of luxury, don't get me wrong, but I get no pleasure from imagining him sleeping in someone's front room like a student couch-surfer. 'Was Dom there?'

He pushes his plate away; then remembers the dog and puts it on the floor in front of him. 'Joe!' I say over the ecstatic slurping.

'What? No point it going to waste.'

'Honestly. I'm trying to teach him manners.'

Joe ruffles Igor's head. 'Good boy.' Between the leftover pizza and the praise I think my dog might explode with happiness. He thumps his tail on the floor and the whole room shakes. 'He was out, thank God. Dom. I didn't have to go through the whole "What would I give to be back at college, all those fit birds. Are you pulling?" routine.'

'Yes, because they'd all be fighting over a fat, sweaty, bald-ing forty-five-year-old man, I imagine.'

'It's all muscle,' Joe says in Dom's booming public-school tones. Sometimes I've felt a bit sorry for Dom. His glory days are firmly behind him. All that wasted privilege, everything handed to him on a plate and nothing to show for it. Just memories of his time at school and university when he thought he was someone special. Obviously that thought disappears as quickly as it comes every time he opens his mouth and spouts some unreconstructed piece of nonsense. I can only be so tolerant.

'It's so lovely to see you,' I say, tears springing to my eyes. I turn away to the freezer and rummage around for something I can conjure up a dessert from. I know the way to my boy's heart.

*　　*　　*

Once Joe has left on Monday morning, weighted down with home-made biscuits that I got up at six to rustle up, and every carton of toothpaste, bottle of shampoo or tin of beans I could lay my hands on ('This is like Buckaroo,' he said, protesting as I handed him a stuffed carrier bag for each hand), I go through my Twitter ritual, making sure I'm on Patricia's account in case I accidentally like or respond to something. There are no private messages. No enticing little '1' in the corner of the screen. I check Lydia first. She's put up a couple of photos of the graffiti exhibition she went to last night. Of the artwork, not of Wes, her date.

Cool, Patricia says, as if she would have any idea.

Next up is Siobhan. There's a comment about the weather (Really, Nick? You've left me for a woman who tweets about the weather?). I work backwards and there's a photo of her and the Viking at a party. They make a striking couple. Her petite and red-haired, him the size of a shipping container and pale blond. Big old beard. He's good-looking if you're into brawn. Which I'm not. I've never seen the appeal of being with someone who could squash you in the throes of passion. Who has bigger breasts than you do. They seem to have a dog that looks a lot like him. Large, golden and a bit thick. It's cute. I have to admit they look happy. Well suited. He has a protective arm around her and they're both beaming at the camera. If I'm being truthful it's hard to picture her sneaking off and meeting my somewhat metrosexual husband. And would he risk being torn apart by this monster if they were caught out? Would it be worth it?

I've saved the best till last. I open up Lou's page. There's something about Lou that I find compelling in the worst way.

She's so awful. Such a type. Every tweet is about Prosecco, girls' nights out or Chris Hemsworth. She loves a meme with a pithy saying. *Wake me up at wine o'clock* or *Of course I have my 5 a day. Wine is made from grapes!* She's like an overgrown teenager. There's a new picture of her on a night out, arms drunkenly round her friends, sticking her tongue out at the camera. I expand it as much as I can, looking for Nick's face in the background, but there's not a man in sight. *Before things got messy!!* the tweet reads, followed by a variety of incomprehensible emojis. *Hashtag LoveTheseLadies.* I have no doubt this woman would steal your husband soon as look at you.

As if by magic I'm saved from stalking Lou when I notice a message has popped up. Lydia.

Patricia, are you there???

Hello! I was just looking at your pictures of that graffiti exhibition. It looks fabulous. I must try to get there.

Shit, maybe I shouldn't have said that. I don't want her to think Patricia being available to come up to London to look at art is a possibility. Knowing Lydia she would suggest meeting up. I crank the radiator up while I wait. Flick the kettle on.

Have you got a moment to dispense some Patricia wisdom?

Always, I type.

It's an age till she responds. I potter about tidying the kitchen. Joe has left a tsunami of devastation in his wake and I'm glad of something to do. This morning he and I took Igor on a long trek round Regent's Park and we all trailed mud and God knows what else back into the house. Joe seemed calmer. Happier now he'd seen his dad and declared a potential mistrial.

I saw Nick the other night. I was on a date of all things and he called me sounding so angry. Georgia had told their son (he's 18, they have twins) that he's having an affair and he – the son – had stormed straight round there. He was furious (Nick)!!! And then at one point he said, 'What if she'd been there when he came round?' Meaning the girlfriend!!! He admitted there is one!!!! But he managed to convince Joe there wasn't. Which, I suppose, is a good thing for now. Sorry, I'm rambling! But what do I do??? I don't want to be put in this position where I know things I shouldn't. I don't want to be the one to tell Georgia that it's definitely true. And that he's basically told me while he's still refusing to be straight up with her!! God, he's such a bastard!!!!

I reach out a hand to cling on to the back of a chair. So he's still seeing her. And he's prepared to admit that to anybody except me and our kids, it seems.

I sit in my office and stare at my drawing pad, Igor at my feet. I need to do something proactive. I can't just let myself be manipulated like this. Now that the kids know at least part of the story I have nothing to lose except my dignity, which actually seems to be long gone. Usually I find sketching calming. Therapeutic. Today it feels like pulling teeth. My computer pings to tell me an email has arrived. Bibi. *I wondered if you'd had any thoughts re our chat the other day?* I think about responding *Yes, I did. It was absolute bollocks*, but instead I slam the lid down and leave the room.

So you'll talk to Lydia about it, but not to me? I text to Nick. I know he's at work and probably won't read it for ages, but it makes me feel better. I pace around the house, unable to settle to anything. This is the problem with working from home. No one else is around. I can't just call Anne Marie or

Lyds for a debrief. I have no colleagues I can distract myself with. It's just me and my own brain. And my dog. I've never found it lonely before but now I feel desperate for company.

We need to talk about what happens next, I send an hour later when I haven't heard from him. *You and whoever can run off into the sunset. I don't care any more. We just need to sort out the practicalities and we can only do that if you'll stop playing games.* I feel better once it's gone and then immediately much, much worse. What have I done? Apart from anything else I've probably dropped Lydia right in it.

I pace the house. This is agony. Why isn't he responding? I decide to walk up to the shops, just for a change of scenery. It'll give me an excuse to get dressed, apart from anything else.

Fifteen minutes later I'm halfway to looking human but it feels like too mammoth an effort to actually leave the house. I circumvent the front door and head down to the kitchen. I'll just have a coffee first.

Eventually I drag myself out, Igor straining at the lead. We walk past the shops and just keep going, up the hill through Steeles Village and Belsize Park. I'm sweating despite the cold but I keep pushing the pace, trying to drive the thoughts out of my head. We walk for what feels like hours before we turn back for the – thankfully – downhill trek home. Somehow the sweat and the freezing drizzle have silenced my brain. I'm not thinking unhappy thoughts; I'm no longer thinking at all beyond how to put one foot in front of another. By the time we reach Primrose Hill again I'm feeling weak from the exertion. Igor pulls ahead, back on familiar territory, eager to get home and sleep probably. I know how he feels.

We turn the corner and I stop when I see a familiar figure standing on my doorstep.

Tall. Long, straight, dark blonde hair. Sneery expression. She probably barely recognizes me, having only met me once, but I know every inch of her face. I've been picking over her photos on social media like I was a forensic scientist and she was blood spatter. I think about turning away, walking back the way I came. But she's seen me.

'Lou?'

'Can I come in?' she says. 'It's fucking freezing out here.'

Chapter 29

'Have you been waiting long?' I say as I open the front door. What do I care if she has? What is she actually doing here? How does she know where I live? Has she been here before? It occurs to me briefly that this is like the opener to one of those true-crime TV shows. Hapless wife allows scheming mistress into her home and is never seen again. At least my fearsome hound will protect me. I let him off his lead and he rushes over to Lou, tail wagging as if she's his long-lost mother.

'Hello, handsome,' she says, putting out a hand and stroking his head. I want to tell her to get her mitts off my dog. I know where those hands have been.

'I only just got here. It's my lunch hour so . . .'

'So, to what do I owe this honour?' I interrupt. I should probably offer her a drink or to take her coat or something but I don't want to give her the impression that she can stay. She peels her damp layers off anyway, draping them over the banister, leaving her in a tightly fitted jumper and snugly tailored trousers. She has an incredible figure. It's impossible not to notice. I look away.

I'm desperate for a coffee. Anything hot. A sit-down. My feet ache and I'm soaked through. But I don't want to invite her in any further, so I stand there in my wet things, waiting to hear what she has to say.

'I'm not having an affair with Nick.'

'Right . . .'

'I know you think I am. Or Siobhan. She's not either.'

'And you've come all this way to tell me this? Protesting too much, don't you think?'

'I have no idea what that means. But yes, I have come all this way, on my lunch hour, when I'd much rather be eating or shopping or even sleeping at my desk, to tell you that I think you're wrong. I don't think Nick is seeing anyone, if I'm being honest.'

I don't know what to think. Do mistresses do this? What would it achieve?

'And how would you know that?'

'The state of him. He looks like death and it's affecting his work. Badly. And the rest of us are running around like blue-arsed flies having to cover for him. Listen, I know you don't like me – for whatever reason – but I'm worried about Nick and this was the only thing I could think to do.'

I'm so confused. If I didn't know better I would think that this woman was totally genuine. I'm racking my brains, trying to think what she could gain from this visit.

'Can we sit down somewhere? You look like you need to anyway.'

'Downstairs,' I say, letting her go ahead while I take off my coat and throw it over hers.

She turns back and looks at me. 'When did you last see him?'

'How is that any of your business?'

She stops on the stairs and I almost walk into her. 'Because he's my boss and he's falling apart and that's affecting my work and everyone else's. Because I've been working for Nick for four years and I'm really fond of him actually. Because it just fucking is. You made sure of that.'

'I was told . . .' I say.

'That he was shagging me?' She throws herself down at the table, takes off one painfully high shoe and massages her bare foot. Pink toenails. Who wears heels and no tights in this weather? I turn on the kettle. I want to hear what she has to say now.

'That he was sleeping with one of his department. That whoever it is she was there the night I came to the pub.'

'That's bollocks.'

'Oh well, if you say so . . .' I hold up the coffee jar, somehow making it an aggressive act. She nods.

'Listen. I didn't come here for your sake. I don't know you; I couldn't give a fuck about you . . .'

'Well, this is nice,' I say, sploshing milk into the coffee without even asking her if she wants any. She ignores me. 'We should do it more often.'

'. . . I came because Nick's my friend, as well as my boss. And because I don't want our team to all look bad because his eye's off the ball.'

'How selfless of you.' I plonk the coffee down in front of her.

'You know what?' she says. 'If I thought he was playing around I'd take great pleasure in telling you because you really are a class-A bitch.'

'Takes one to know one.' I've never spoken to another woman – another person – like this. I'm finding it strangely liberating even though I know I'll probably hate myself for it later.

'Oh, forget it,' she says, standing up. 'Think what you like: I couldn't care less. He'll probably soon realize he's better off without you.'

I close my eyes briefly. Tell myself to calm down. I might never get an opportunity like this again to ask the questions I need to ask. 'Wait. Don't go yet. I apologize.'

She huffs and plonks herself down again, face like a sulky adolescent.

'This isn't me,' I say quietly. 'I'm not like this. Jealous. Nasty. Tell me what you came to tell me.'

She takes a long sip of her coffee. 'Here's what I know about Nick at work. He's a nice bloke. Well thought of. And I've never in the four years I've worked for him seen him so much as flirt with anyone. I mean, literally no one. There's never any gossip about him. No one's ever said they think he's a player or a sleaze or that he's come on to them. Nothing. He talks about you all the time. And not in a "my wife's a pain" eye-rolley way. I swear on my life that I'm not having an affair with him and I'd put money on the fact that no one else is either. The only person even less likely than me is Siobhan because she's completely loved up with Colin and she doesn't even notice other blokes exist.'

I'm momentarily distracted by the fact that the Viking's name is Colin. It seems so unlikely. But then I think about what Lou is saying. It sounds as if she means it.

'Apparently not everyone at Diamond Leisure thinks the same.'

She leans back, big grey eyes fixed on me. 'See, this is what I don't get. Obviously I don't know half the people who work there – nine-tenths, probably – but I imagine

224

if this person knows Nick as well as they're making out, I would have come across them. He said you think it's an Emma? Emma who?'

'I don't know.'

'So she didn't tell you directly? You don't actually know her?'

I shake my head. 'She's a friend of a friend.'

Lou looks at her fingernails, which are painted a deeper pink, hand splayed. 'Surely you've asked your friend? So you can check her out?'

'It's complicated,' I say. 'But, no.'

'There's no Emma in the London office, I can tell you that much.'

I rub the back of my neck. I can feel a migraine creeping in. 'She could work anywhere.'

'I can only tell you what I know. This Emma definitely said it was someone in our department? That he was seeing?'

I nod. 'She said they were gloating about it the next day.'

'Absolutely no way. I mean, really. No way. You've met them all . . .'

'Camilla . . .' I say, even though I know it's supposed to be someone who was at the pub that night.

She looks at me with a confused frown. 'Camilla's gay.'

'Ah.' I sit back. I've got nothing else. 'You couldn't know for sure, though, that it wasn't true. Why would someone . . . ?'

'Perhaps she thinks it is true for whatever spurious reason, I don't know. She might be confusing Nick with someone else, or, maybe someone made up a rumour about him to be spiteful and she believed it.'

'She heard it from the woman he's sleeping with herself apparently . . .'

Lou shakes her mane of hair emphatically. 'Then maybe Emma's the one making it up. Whoever she is. Either way it's not me. Or Shiv.'

I exhale slowly. 'How did you know that I thought it was you . . . ?'

'What? Apart from the fact you practically accused me in the pub? Because I forced it out of him. I'm worried about him. He's falling apart. I mean, I never really understood what people meant when they said that but with him I can actually see it. I made him tell me what was going on.'

'He must trust you,' I say sadly.

'He does. Because we're friends. Just not the kind of friends who want to socialize outside of work particularly. And definitely not the kind of friends who secretly want to bang each other either.'

'I believe you.'

She pushes herself up, standing. 'Well, hurrah for that. I have to go. I'm due back at two.'

'It still doesn't explain things though. I still have no idea what's going on.'

'You and me both. If you ask me this Emma has just made the whole thing up. She's looking for attention or something.'

I get up too. The fight has definitely gone out of me. 'Maybe. I wish I knew who she was. Does Nick know you're here, by the way?'

'Jesus, no. Please don't tell him – he'll probably fire me. I had to sneak into HR to find his address.'

'I won't. And I'm sorry again.'

'Yeah, well.' She smooths down her trousers at the front. Leans down and pats Igor's head. 'Maybe just give him the benefit of the doubt? Anything. Just a little bit of hope. Or he's going to end up losing us all our jobs.'

'Could I give you my number? In case . . . if you come across an Emma and you think it might be her, you know . . .' I stare at the table. Given how offhand I've been with her it feels like a big ask. No, 'offhand' is a massive understatement. Rude.

She reaches in her bag for her phone. 'Sure. Why not?'

I watch her sashay down the street in search of a cab. I don't know what to think. It makes no sense for her to come all the way over here if she was lying, but how can Lydia's information be so wrong? She can't know though, Lou. I mean, she can know he's not sleeping with her, obviously, and that I do now believe. But can she categorically know he's not having an affair at all? No. The minute she's left I wish I'd taken her number too. I have so many more questions.

I sit down at the kitchen table, put my head in my hands. There's only one thing I can do. I need to send Nick a text. I notice he's replied to my earlier accusations: *And again, I have no idea what you're talking about.*

I ignore it. *Can you come over tonight? I promise I'll hear you out.*

Fine, he texts back almost immediately. *See you 6.30.* No kiss.

Chapter 30

I'm so nervous when he shows up that I'm shaking. I've had a shower and dressed in my soft pale blue yoga trousers and a fitted T-shirt – I don't want to look as if I've made any effort but I also know he thinks this outfit is cute. I don't know why I care.

He's five minutes early. He looks dishevelled. Grey. He rings the bell even though he has a key. Shuffles in hesitantly, like a reluctant visitor, not someone who co-owns the place. He hardly has the swagger of someone who is in the throes of a passionate affair. Igor does his Igor thing. I can't believe it's only a matter of weeks since we first clapped eyes on the dog. How excited we were. How happy. It's like the world was hit by a meteorite a few days later and became unrecognizable.

'Thanks for coming. Come through,' I say as if he's a job interviewee. He follows me downstairs, ditching his coat over a chair when we get to the kitchen.

'What's this about?' he says, sitting at the table in his usual spot.

'Do you want a glass of wine?' I definitely do.

'Sure.'

I pour us both a large Cabernet Sauvignon. Sit down across from him. 'Are you OK?'

'What am I doing here?' he asks, not ready to indulge in small talk.

'I'm confused . . .' I haven't really thought through what I want to say. I just know that something's not right. Lou's visit threw me.

'Welcome to my world,' he says. It's an attempt at a joke, which gives me hope. But it's said with a sneer, which takes it away again.

I breathe in and out slowly. Stay calm. 'Has Lyds said anything to you about her friend who works at Diamond Leisure?'

This clearly isn't the question he's been expecting. 'So this *is* another interrogation session?'

'No. I'm just trying to get to the bottom of where it all came from. I'm . . . Please indulge me. This isn't about trying to catch you out or put you on the spot . . .'

Something in my tone must get through. He swills his wine round in his glass. 'She doesn't know anyone there.'

What? Why would she lie to him? It's not as if she was the one who told me he was seeing someone – well, she did, but not knowingly. 'You asked her?'

'I wondered if that was where this stupid rumour came from. But she didn't know what I was talking about.'

'She has a friend. Called Emma. Who works at Diamond Leisure.'

He shakes his head. 'She told me she doesn't know anyone there apart from me.'

It's so frustrating that I can't show him the proof – Lyds's messages to Patricia. Without that I just sound paranoid.

'Do you know any Emmas? Honestly.'

He looks as if he's about to snap at me but in the end he shakes his head. 'No. I think there might be one at Margate. I've seen her name on something. And there's one in Catering at Blackpool. But I've never had any dealings with either of them.'

'How would Lydia even know them?' I say, more to myself than him.

'She doesn't. I told you. She doesn't know what you're on about.'

'Is that what she said?'

He nods. Igor rests his head on his knee. Sighs when Nick strokes his muzzle.

'Do me one favour,' he says. 'Tell me who told you about this in the first place. This supposed friend of Lydia's? Because Lyds knows nothing about it.'

Shit. I wish I could just blurt it out. 'It came from Lydia's friend, yes.'

'She actually told you? Face to face? This Emma who Lydia is claiming she doesn't even know?'

'No. Not exactly.'

He thumps the table and I jump. 'Then who? Stop playing games, Georgia. This is my life. Our life. I deserve to know who's saying this shit about me.'

'Lydia told me. But she didn't mean to. She actually told someone else, but I overheard. Sort of. Don't be pissed off with her.'

A look of pure confusion crosses his face. 'Lydia? She doesn't even believe it.'

'Of course she does.'

He shakes his head again, more emphatically. 'She told me she didn't. You're saying she's the reason you even heard this story in the first place?'

Oh God. 'Inadvertently.'

'What if you misunderstood? She was talking about someone else? Did you ask her about it?'

'No. Well, kind of. I got someone else to ask . . .'

He rubs his hand over his face. 'So you heard your best friend telling someone that I was having an affair and you didn't even ask her about it? This is the biggest load of bullshit I've ever heard. You and Lydia tell each other everything.'

'I know it doesn't make any sense. But just trust me that that's what happened . . .'

He sighs. 'Like you trusted me, you mean?'

We sit there in silence for a moment, punctuated by Igor's snores. Something's not right. Something's off.

'So, let's get this straight,' he says. 'You overheard Lydia telling some random person that someone I work with told her I was having an affair, and, instead of asking her what she was talking about, you got some other random person to do that. Have you and Lyds fallen out or something?'

'No. It's nothing like that. I shouldn't have been listening in in the first place. I didn't want her to know.'

'Who was she telling?'

I feel the hole I'm digging for myself get deeper. 'I don't know.'

'OK.' He taps lightly on the table with his index finger, something he always does when he's trying to work out a puzzle. 'So who did you get to ask her about it?'

Shit. I lean forward on my elbows and rest my head on my hands. I knew this was a bad idea. But I can't let go of this feeling that everything is not as it should be.

'Please, please, please promise you won't say anything to Lydia. Promise.'

'Surely it's better for everyone if we all get everything out into the open?'

'No!' I say loudly. Igor's ears stand to attention.

'I'm just saying what you would usually say. Isn't that what you always told the kids?'

'I'm serious. If you tell Lydia what I'm about to tell you she'll never forgive me. Please, Nick . . .' Stupidly I start to cry. I have no idea how I've got myself in this mess when I'm the wronged party here. I can't risk losing her friendship.

He softens. 'I won't. I promise, OK?'

I look him right in the eye. 'Never, Nick. Whatever happens between us.'

He holds my gaze. 'I promise.'

So I tell him everything. About Patricia. I go overboard to make him understand that it was done from love. To give him credit he listens without comment until I get to the part where Lyds tells Patricia what she's heard about him.

'So she just ups and tells a complete stranger that I'm having an affair? Out of nowhere?'

'That her friend's husband was. Remember, Patricia wasn't supposed to know who any of us were. Lydia wasn't gossiping, she just needed advice.'

'From someone she met on Twitter?'

'I know, Nick. I'm just telling you what happened, OK?'

'But . . .' he starts. I give him a look and he clams up again.

'So you see why I can't just ask her for the details?'

He nods. 'This is crazy, though, you do know that? I can't even defend myself properly.'

'You promised.'

'I'm not going to say anything. Can I at least see exactly what she said?'

I nod. Go on to Patricia's Twitter account and scroll back to the beginning of her exchanges with Lydia. I want him to see how innocently it started.

'Do you want something to eat?' I say as I hand over my mobile. I need to distract myself while he reads and cooking is as good a way as any. 'I'm making something anyway.'

'Sure. Thanks.'

He buries his head in the phone. I can't bear to watch his reaction so I chop garlic and basil. Dig some fresh pasta out of the back of the fridge. Check the use-by date – I've been eating random crap since Nick left. Lacking self-care. Toast and more toast. Occasionally a bag of crisps to spice things up. I look over and watch a frown form, lines puckering his forehead. He shakes his head. I put on a pot of water to boil, slosh olive oil into a pan, trying to distract myself.

Eventually Nick puts the phone down. 'This . . .' he says, a look of confusion on his face. I can tell he's not acting. 'None of this makes sense. Why is she saying this stuff?'

'I guess she believes what this Emma has told her . . .'

'Not even that. I mean, let's give her the benefit of the doubt and say that she does indeed know someone called Emma who works at Diamond Leisure that for some reason she's pretending to me that she doesn't, and that that person really did make up a load of stories about me and fed them to Lydia . . . Even if that were true, the rest of it, the conversations she describes when we met up . . . it's all made up, George. It's all lies. All of it.'

I can't take it in. I don't know what – who – to believe. Why would Lydia lie? There has to be a rational explanation. I take the oil off the heat. Sit down opposite him. 'OK. Let's go through it.'

He nods, picks up the phone again. 'Here's what she says about us meeting up – *Met up with Georgia's husband tonight to try and prise the truth out of him* – maybe that's poetic licence but she told me straightaway she believed me. She seemed to think you were being irrational, if I'm being honest . . .'

I have no idea how to react, so I just nod. In the background the water starts to boil.

'It's as if he couldn't care less about Georgia any more.' He swallows noisily. 'And then you – Patricia – asked her if I owned up to the affair and she says yes. Never happened. I swear on my life. Even if I was . . . why would I admit it to your best mate and not you? Wouldn't I think she'd go straight back and tell you?'

'I don't know,' I say with a heavy feeling. I don't like where this is going.

'I begged him to talk to her . . . She told me not to! Told me I should leave you alone till you'd had time to calm down. That I should go round when I knew you were out. And here's my favourite – I apparently said what if my *girlfriend* had been there when Joe came round? What the fuck? None of this is true. None of it. Fuck. This is all Lydia, Georgia.' He knocks back the rest of the wine in his glass. Pours us both another. 'I don't know what she's up to, or why, but this whole thing started with her.'

Lydia? My best friend since I was nineteen? I've known her longer than I've known him. 'Why . . . ?'

234

He stares at the table for what seems like an age. 'What's the ultimate outcome of her telling you this? That we split up? So maybe she just wants you to herself. Maybe she can't stand me and she thinks if you're single she can see more of you?'

'No way. Although it does feel as if she's been avoiding bumping into you lately, but I thought that was because she felt awkward.'

His finger taps on the table again. 'What else could it be?'

'Wait,' I say loudly. 'It can't be that. If that was what she wanted then she'd have told me. Georgia. But she told Patricia, didn't she? She told a complete stranger.' Feeling energized, I stand up and turn the gas on under the oil again. Lydia isn't trying to ruin my marriage. She had no way of knowing I would ever find out what she'd said to Patricia. I throw some garlic into the oil and tip the pasta into what's left of the boiling water. Really I should top it up with some from the kettle but instead I poke around with a fork, trying to make sure it all gets covered.

'Shit,' Nick says. I look over. 'She knows that Patricia is you.'

Chapter 31

Time seems to stand still for a second. I feel lightheaded, reach out and steady myself on the counter. 'That's impossible.'

Nick shakes his head emphatically. 'That's the only explanation.' He scrolls back through the messages frantically. 'Right. Here's the first time she mentions you. All that stuff about her feeling unfulfilled and you being successful. My guess is that she knew by then or why start talking about you at all? Either way she definitely knows by the next exchange because that's when she starts on about feeling awkward around you and knowing something she shouldn't. So, something before that gave you away . . .'

'Let me look,' I say, grabbing the phone out of his hand. 'Drain the pasta, will you?'

He stands up and peers over my shoulder. 'You always do that.' He points at the screen. 'That *xoxo* thing.'

'Everyone does that.'

'Do they? I don't.'

'Everyone who watched *Gossip Girl* then.'

'Do you think Patricia watched *Gossip Girl*? In between cutting patterns?'

I watch as he pours the oil over the pasta in the pan, stirs it round, adds chilli flakes. 'Probably not. It can't be that simple though. How would you go from *xoxo* to that person must be a fake created by my best friend?'

'Read those first few exchanges out. Everything, punctuation and all.'

So I do, cringing at how they sound. When I get to a conversation we had about football – Patricia's eccentric passion – he stops me.

'Read that again.'

'It's about Wycombe Wanderers. There's no way she could guess anything from that.'

'Just that last bit . . .'

'What? "I have a bad feeling we're going to lose . . ."?'

'How did you spell "lose"?'

I double take at the screen. 'L-o-o-s-e.'

'*Loose*,' he says. 'That says *loose*. You always spell it like that.'

I stare at it. 'That's how it's spelt. Fuck, isn't it?'

He shakes his head.

'That's ridiculous. No way would she guess just from that.'

'Maybe not. But there's something.'

I keep reading. Stop dead, heart pounding. 'Shit, Nick. I know what it is.'

He looks at me expectantly. 'Lydia told Patricia about a mad Uber driver she had and then I asked her about it next day. Me, Georgia. Only she hadn't ever told me about him. That was right before . . . Fuck, I'm so stupid.'

'That'll be it . . .'

'Shit. Fuck. Why, though? If she knew it was me why go along with it? Why bring you up at all?'

'That's what we need to work out.' He helps himself to the Parmesan from the fridge, brings it all over to the table. It feels weirdly normal. That's the only thing that does, though. I'm hit with a vision of how things might have been – how they were meant to be. Me, Nick and Igor playing happy families now our kids were grown. What if he's been telling me the truth all along? What if there is no other woman? Have I ruined everything?

'Maybe she couldn't bring herself to tell me face to face. So she saw this as a way of letting me know . . .'

'Except it's not true, remember? And all that stuff about me admitting it to her . . .'

I clutch at the nearest straw. 'Could she have misunderstood? Misheard?'

Nick reaches a hand across the table and briefly touches one of mine. I can't help it, I flinch. He snaps his back. 'I know she's your best mate. I know you don't want to think the worst of her.'

'Are you saying she might have made the whole thing up? Lydia?'

He rubs his palms up and down over his eyes, something he always does when he's stumped. 'I don't know what I'm saying, to be honest.'

We finish the bottle of wine as we eat, and I open another. At some point Edie calls me and can't keep the happiness out of her voice when I tell her that her father has come over for dinner. Whatever happens I need to make sure the kids see us being civilized with each other. While he chats to her I reread the Patricia messages on my laptop for the hundredth time, trying to work out if I really believe I could have been caught out. If I really believe Nick is innocent after all. It makes no sense. Fucked up doesn't even come into it. As I'm staring at our exchanges I realize there's a new box at the bottom. Unread.

How's my friend Patricia today?

I hear myself squeak. Look over at Nick but he's deep in conversation with Edie, laughing at something she's said, and I don't want to ruin the moment. But Lydia is online now, waiting for a response. It seems like too good an opportunity to miss. I slide the computer across the table, raise my eyebrows when Nick looks at me. He flicks his eyes to the screen and his own eyebrows shoot up to the top of his head. I feel such a moment of connection with him, such a feeling of 'We're in this together, whatever this is' that I almost start to sob.

He wraps it up with Edie but she wants to say goodbye to me too so he hands the phone back and I try not to give away that my mind is elsewhere.

'Is everything going to be OK, Mum?' she says in a very un-Edie-like moment of vulnerability.

'Of course, sweetheart. Whatever happens,' I add in case she thinks I mean me and her dad are back together already.

'Fuck,' I say to Nick once I end the call. 'What shall we do?'

He's looking more upbeat than I've seen him in ages. High on adrenaline. 'OK. There must be a reason she's getting in contact now. Some bit of information she wants to feed you.'

'I'll just let her know I'm here. See what she says.'

I was just thinking about you. I'm well. How are things going?

I hold the phone out and let Nick read what I've typed. He nods. 'Good.'

I press send. 'Now we wait. Sometimes she comes straight back, sometimes I have to wait for hours.'

He starts to clear our plates away and I let him do it. I sit staring at my mobile. Igor follows Nick back and forth from the table to the dishwasher, and when Nick's hands are empty he trails his fingers down and scratches between the dog's ears. 'Message!' I shout as something comes through. Nick drops the cloth he's holding and comes and leans over my chair.

'*Good*,' I read aloud. '*Isn't this weather awful?* No way has she got in touch just to talk about the weather.'

'I guess it would look too suspicious to launch straight into the juicy stuff every time.'

Ghastly, I type. *How's life treating you?*

'I can see why Lydia likes Patricia, she's a scintillating conversationalist,' Nick says. I reach back and thump him on the arm.

'She's old-fashioned. Polite.'

We wait, both staring at the phone as though we think it contains the answer to the meaning of life.

OK, I guess. Finding it all a bit much at the moment, if I'm being honest.

My instant reaction is to worry. Worrying about Lydia is a default setting for me. Is she happy? Is she losing too much weight? Is her insistence that she's content on her own a front? Nick's eye roll brings me back to real life though. Back to the Lydia who's behaving very oddly.

Oh no, Lydia, what's wrong? Do you mean the situation with your friend? 'Might as well ask right out now,' I say to Nick before I press send. He nods. Her reply comes back in seconds.

Yes. It's really getting to me. All the deception.

A couple of days ago – this morning even – this comment would have floored me. The idea that Lydia was feeling so bad because of me. That she cared enough about me to insert herself into my mess of a life. Now I'm not so sure which deception she's talking about. 'What shall I say?' I ask Nick, who has taken looking sceptical to a whole new Olympic level. 'I've already said she should tell me – the *real me* – what she's heard countless times.'

'Ask her if anything new has happened. I can't wait to hear what I'm supposed to have done now.'

So I do. And then we wait some more. Nick and Igor wrestle on the floor like two drunken sumos and I wonder if I've let my dog down by not indulging him in this behaviour before. I've fed him, walked him, hugged him, thrown things, played tug of war with his cow but I haven't actually got down on the floor and tackled him before and apparently that's one of his favourite things to do. A boy needs a dad, I think, and that makes me laugh out loud.

Nick stops, red faced from effort. 'What?'

'I was just thinking about my mum. Do you remember when we had the twins and she took you aside for "the talk"?'

'"Don't even think about going off anywhere now you've got a son. A boy needs his dad,"' he quotes, doing a perfect impression of her husky voice. My mum always sounds as if she's about to have a coughing fit, courtesy of ten cigarettes a day until a couple of years ago when she and Frank both went cold turkey.

'And you said, what about Edie, didn't she need a dad too?'

He snorts. 'And she said it wasn't the same. "Joey needs a role model."'

It had become a running joke in our little family of four. 'Joey needs a role model,' I would say whenever Nick wimped out of doing something, and the kids would fall about laughing. Edie still says it to him sometimes.

Igor jumps on his chest, desperate to restart the game. 'Ow. Does she know . . . ?'

I shake my head. 'Not unless one of the kids has told her. I couldn't face it.'

'Thank God,' he says lightly. 'She'd have had Frank set one of his cronies on me.'

I look down at my phone. A family is all about in-jokes. Shared language. History. A private club that will never accept new members. Until any grandchildren come along, that is, and I'm not holding my breath there. I feel a lump in my throat.

'Message!'

Nick scrambles to his feet. 'What? What does it say?'

Apparently 'she' is now talking about her and Nick moving in together. So that's that, I suppose. She told Emma they were looking at flats. They're going to see a couple tonight!!

Nick looks at me. Touché. 'Fuck,' I say. Understatement of the century. 'She took a risk there, though. How could she know you wouldn't come round?'

'Because she told me not to, remember? She told me to give you space for a while. And I agreed with her because I thought she was genuinely trying to help.'

It finally sinks in. What he's telling me is true. I have no idea what Lydia is up to but I know it's not good. 'I'm so sorry,' I say.

He nods and I see he's biting back tears. 'So long as you believe me now . . .'

'I do. Shit.'

We sit there in silence for a moment. I can't look at him. Have I really been so wrong? All those accusations. The things I've said to him. The absolute shit show I made of myself at the pub that night. 'She said something odd. Lyds,' I say, remembering. 'She said you'd always been a flirt. Like it was accepted that everyone thinks you are.'

'Jesus, George. I'm the least flirtatious person ever. I didn't even flirt with you before we got together.'

He's right. We met at a running club. I was newly into my 'embracing my physique' fitness drive. I remember Nick was just always around and eventually I struck up a conversation with him because I liked the look of him. It was only later that he told me he used to hang about near me in the hope that that might happen because he was too tongue-tied to take the initiative himself. Even with Felicity I always assumed she made all the running. It was one thing to imagine Nick sleeping with someone else, but quite another to imagine him sweet-talking her into bed. 'I know. Listen, I have to tell you something else. Not a bad thing. But in the interests of us being totally upfront . . .'

I fill him in on Lou's visit. Make him swear never to let her know I've told him.

'She's actually all right, you know,' he says when I finish.

I shut my eyes. 'I feel awful.'

Nick reaches a hand across the table, puts it on mine. 'It's OK. We'll get past it.'

I can't say anything. I don't know what to say. I grip on to his fingers like I'm about to fall off a cliff and only he can save me. Eventually I wipe my eyes with my other hand, give him a watery smile.

'I need to find out what Lydia's up to first, though.'

'Too right,' he says. 'Whatever it is, she's not getting away with it.'

Chapter 32

'How about this?' I hold out the phone and show him the reply I've composed. We're still sitting at the kitchen table but now we're nursing whiskies alongside our wine. A celebration that we've made up even though my heart is now breaking in a hundred other ways.

How sad. You were expecting that, though, weren't you, from the way he was talking?

'Good,' he says. I press send.

I suppose so. It just feels so final now.

At least she has you, I write and Nick snorts.

Always. She's better off without him, actually.

'What a bitch,' he hisses and it's such an un-Nick-like thing to say I actually laugh. I'm feeling euphoric, empowered, out of control.

That's the spirit, Lydia. 'Shall I encourage her to meet up with you again? Do you think you can get through it without giving yourself away?'

Nick and I have decided to carry on as if nothing has happened. That is, he's going to move back in but we're not going to let Lydia know. As far as she is concerned, her plan – whatever that might be – will still be going ahead. And we're going to find out what her motives are, what she's trying to achieve, by whatever means necessary. Together.

245

I'm amazed, delighted, relieved at how easy it is for us just to decide we're a couple again. I can't quite believe it. After everything that's happened we're going to be OK.

'Good idea.'

You shouldn't let him off the hook though. Give him a piece of your mind. For Georgia's sake.

'Thanks,' Nick says, wryly.

Oh, don't you worry about that!!! she responds almost immediately. *I intend to!*

'OK. That's enough, I think, or I'll slip up.'

I stand up and walk round the table to him, lean my arms over his back and rest my head on the top of his.

'I believe you owe me big time,' he says, hugging my arms in closer with his. 'Sexual favours, that kind of thing.'

'Good luck with that,' I say, smiling. 'Igor sleeps on your side of the bed now.'

When I wake up in the morning – having had the best night's sleep I've had in weeks despite Lydia. This being real life there was no hot make-up sex that left us sweating and exhausted, merely a three-way, dog-breath-filled hug that cocooned me to sleep – I daren't move for fear of breaking the spell. Nick is still out cold, arm round the dog, and I lie motionless for a while, taking him in. I have no doubts left. None. I should have trusted him when he told me it wasn't true. I should have had his back.

The other thing that's happened is that Nick has a message from Lydia. I see it when I accidentally nudge his phone when I sneak downstairs to make a coffee. For the first time ever Igor doesn't follow me, he's too blissed out to move.

If you fancy another drink I'm around!!! it says. I check my own: *How are you doing? Call you for a catch-up later!* She's been busy. I reply with a heart emoji because I don't know what to say. Make two coffees and take them both and Nick's phone back up to the bedroom. He stirs when he hears me come in. Gives me a slow smile that melts my heart. Igor springs off the bed ready for action, but I'm prepared and I've brought him a couple of biscuits to keep him going till breakfast.

'Lydia,' I say as I hand Nick his phone.

He reads the message, squinting in the semi-darkness. 'Shit. I should go, shouldn't I? See if I can find out any more.'

'Definitely.'

He texts her back saying he can meet her at half six. Suggests a hotel bar in Bloomsbury that is equidistant between their offices and usually quiet. While we wait for her response my own mobile beeps.

Nick just texted me to ask me to meet for a drink!!

And if any more proof were needed that Nick is not the one lying here, there it is.

Chapter 33

Lydia changes out of her work clothes in the office toilets and redoes her make-up at the sink. She knows she's a bit on the thin side at the moment, living on adrenaline and not much else, but she has to admit it looks good in photos. She snaps a picture in the mirror – voluminous wide-leg trousers, heels and a snugly fitted pale coral cardigan, cropped at her tiny waist. She's about to post it on Insta when she realizes Georgia might see it and wonder why she's made such an effort just to meet Nick. She'll save it for tomorrow night, make up a glamorous date. She does that sometimes – more and more recently – when she can't be bothered to go out, can't bring herself to say yes to another play or exhibition. She gets all dressed up, takes some pictures and then puts her PJs on, opens a bottle of wine and stays home.

She wraps herself up in her big coat, scarf round her face to prevent her nose going red. Thankfully it's stopped raining. Part of her hopes she and Nick will arrive at the same time so he'll see how cute she looks in her oversize outer layers. So he'll get the full effect when she peels them off and reveals how good she looks underneath. But she also wants to get there first and scout for the most intimate table. There's no point them having to shout over noisy people; that would defeat the object somewhat.

On her way up Southampton Row she thinks about Georgia. She doesn't allow herself to do that too often. Not now. Not when she's making so much progress. She's been wondering if she should distance herself. It would make her quest easier. But it's unthinkable. She needs her. Loves her. None of it makes any sense, she knows that, but she's powerless to feel any other way. She needs to take her out, cheer her up. Make her see that she'll be better off without him. Georgia is struggling to finish her new book, she told her, although how it's possible to have writer's block when you only have to write about a hundred words, total, Lydia doesn't know. Maybe this will be the end of Wilbur. Maybe Georgia's run at the top is over, the natural cycle of things. Lydia received another rejection today. Her fourth. Always nice, always complimentary, but still saying no. There's no gap in the market for her faeries and trolls. But maybe her time is coming.

She reaches the hotel on Russell Square with five minutes to spare. Gives herself a quick once over in the Ladies and then settles at a table by the window. It's waiter service so she orders a vodka and tonic and explains that she's waiting for a friend. She snaps another selfie with the dark wood and low orange lighting of the bar behind her.

'Instagramming already?' a voice says and she almost drops her phone. It's Nick. Of course it is. She stands up and gives him a hug.

'Never miss an opportunity, that's what I say.'

He waves at the waiter and shrugs his coat off in one smooth move. She tries to analyse how he's doing from the way he looks. Still a bit haunted, a bit grey, but maybe not so bad as he was. He's coming to terms with it, she thinks. He's accepting that it's happening. He orders himself a lager, sits down opposite her, gives her a smile that makes her heart stop.

'How are you?' she says, all sympathy.

He nods. 'OK. Same, I guess. I think I'm outstaying Dom's hospitality though.'

'Shit. What will you do?'

He shrugs. 'I think I'll have to rent somewhere. That seems so final though. Like I've given up.'

She sees an opportunity to twist the knife. Sighs theatrically. 'You have to move on sometime. I mean . . . if she won't . . . you need to start thinking about you. Plan the future. If you want me to help you look for somewhere, I can . . . I mean, if you want a second opinion or whatever . . .'

She leaves it hanging there. She needs to keep coming up with reasons for them to meet. He won't be needing a shoulder to cry on forever. At least, hopefully not. And she needs to be the first thing he sees when he looks up from his misery.

'Thanks,' he says. 'That'd help. I haven't got a clue. Do you really think I shouldn't try and talk to her? What do I have to lose at this point?'

Georgia is obviously still at the forefront of his mind. She needs to tread carefully. If this situation were real what reason could she possibly have for advising him that it was better to walk away without trying? 'Of course try and talk to her if you want to. I just worry it might be counter-productive at the moment. You don't want to push her away even further because she feels cornered.'

'Getting my own place just feels as if I'm saying I've moved on for good. I don't know. Maybe I'm overthinking it.'

She considers for a moment whether she could offer to put him up at hers but she doesn't know how she'd ever explain that one to Georgia. And she knows she can't rush him. Not if she's in it for the long haul. 'Get somewhere with a short lease. I can explain to her that you're just giving her space. It might be a positive, anyway, that she sees you're getting a place on your own. If you really were having an affair wouldn't you be looking to shack up with the mistress?'

'She'll probably assume that I am.'

'Well, that's where I come in. I can tell her you're definitely not. Especially if I've been helping you.'

'That's true. OK, see, you've made me feel better already.'

She beams the full force of her smile at him. 'I missed my calling, obviously.'

'How's work?' he asks. At last. They've got the Georgia talk out of the way and they can have a proper conversation.

'Fucking awful,' she says and he laughs. He has always had a surprisingly booming laugh, especially when something catches him unawares. 'My soul is being sucked dry bit by bit.'

'It can't be that bad.'

'It's that bad. You wouldn't believe the egos I have to deal with. The arrogance of people who think that because they somehow persuaded someone that their crappy drawings were better than everyone else's they're something special. When we all know it was just a case of them being around and available when I needed something done quickly.' Too close to home? She needs to be careful not to look as if she's having a dig at Georgia. The Lydia Nick knows would never do that.

'Can't you just commission yourself?' People are always asking her this. As if it's that simple. She screws up her face in what, she hopes, is an appealing fashion.

'Even if that didn't look totally dodgy I wouldn't be the right person. Honestly, there's no art in these illustrations. They just have to be accurate. Factual.'

She tells him then about her personal project. The trolls in their netherworld. She shows him some pictures on her phone and she can tell he's impressed.

'These are beautiful. Surely someone would want to publish them?'

'Not so far. I was hoping Georgia might show them to her editor . . .' She gives a little half-laugh.

'Oh. Well, I'm sure she would . . .'

'I think she thinks it would be a bit awkward, maybe. I don't know . . .' What she really wants to say is that perhaps Georgia feels threatened. That she's so insecure in her own success that she daren't jinx it. But she leaves him to draw his own conclusions.

'Well, someone will snap them up at some point. They're incredible.'

She basks in the praise. Can feel it warming her body as if he's given her a hug. Waves a hand at the waiter, indicating one more round.

'I think she's jealous of you,' Nick says when he calls me from the taxi on the way home. I've spent the evening pacing around, unable to settle to anything. I tried, half-heartedly, to do some work – Bibi sent another email today. *Hi, Georgia, how are you getting on? Not sure if you got my note yesterday but maybe we could have a follow-up chat?* I've ignored it so far; head in the sand, I don't know what to say. Instead, I did a few sketches of Igor.

'That's ridiculous. No way. I mean, a bit envious maybe . . .'

'I'll try and remember everything she said. Present my case when I get home.'

'Are you going to stop at Dom's and collect your stuff?' All Nick's work clothes are still at Dom's. I want to know he's fully back, dirty washing and all.

'Yeah. I'll keep the cab running. He's packed it all up for me.'

'That was nice of him,' I say begrudgingly. 'You should invite him over one night, so we can say thanks properly.'

Nick laughs. 'It's OK. I won't subject you.'

When he arrives at the house I've already got the wine open. Nick grimaces when he sees it. 'I think I'll pass. I've had three pints already.' I flick the kettle on instead. He talks me through the whole evening, trying to remember every detail.

'Wait, when she went to the loo I made notes,' he says, poking at his phone. 'Oh yes. "You have to move on some time." She said that when I talked about renting a flat. "You need to start thinking about you." And then she basically said she didn't think you wanted to listen to anything I had to say because she'd tried and you weren't having it.'

'I probably have said I don't want to talk to you about it any more, to be fair . . .'

'But has she put my case across? That's what she was saying.'

'Definitely not. None of this explains why you think she's jealous, though. Tea or coffee?'

'Sod it, I will have a drink,' he says, reaching for the wine and filling up the two glasses I'd got ready. 'Nothing concrete but she's very bitter about her career not taking off. She talked about people who didn't deserve it getting commissions. I don't know . . . It was just a feeling I got. Maybe I'm wrong. She's offered to help me find a flat; how am I going to get out of that one?'

'Let's find you some places to look at.' I pull the laptop over to my side. Bring up Rightmove. 'Where do you want your fantasy home to be?'

'Here?'

'Idiot,' I say, although his comment makes me want to cry happy tears.

He moves round to the seat next to me, drapes an arm around my shoulders and plants a kiss on the top of my head. 'I've really missed you.'

'Me too. I'm sorry.'

'Stop saying you're sorry. It's fine.'

'I am though,' I say.

'I know. You've told me five million times. Jesus.'

I look at him and he cracks a smile. He can never hide when he's joking. He's too pleased with himself. I marvel again at how quick he is to forgive. How much I could have thrown away.

'OK, I'm not then. Right, where were we?'

'Finding me a bachelor pad. How about Chelsea or Knightsbridge,' he says with a twinkle in his eye. 'Somewhere to suit my suave man-about-town status.'

'Somers Town. Near Dom.'

'Can you at least find things to look at where I won't get stabbed on the way there?'

'Beggars can't be choosers. Divorce is very expensive. You won't be able to afford much. And you need to make sure it definitely looks as if you're going to live there on your own, not like somewhere you're setting up your happy new life. And then see what she reports back to me.'

'Do I actually have to go and see them? It feels like such a massive waste of time.'

'Just the outside. Just so she knows what you're after.'

'Here, look,' he says, pointing at the screen. 'King's Cross. Near my office. Affordable. Slight shithole by the looks of it. How about that?'

I scrutinize the listed price. 'Perfect. Download the details.'

We find a couple of others in the same area and he fires off a text to Lydia. *Have found a couple of flats. Was thinking maybe tomorrow night. I might check out the area. Are you still up for coming along?*

We both stare at his phone, waiting for an answer.

Of course! Let me know when and where. I'll treat you to a pint after x.

'That was quick,' I say.

'Shit,' Nick says. 'Am I really doing this?'

Chapter 34

I can't keep my head buried in the sand ignoring Bibi's emails forever. I take myself and my laptop up to the office in an effort to be professional. I open up a document where I've been noting all my ideas for book seven (*Hammer and nails and a bucket of snails*, it says. *Knee-high boots and some champagne flutes. No!* I've written beside that one. *I don't want to write books for three-year-olds who already know what champagne flutes are! How about 'two bandicoots'? or 'an owl that hoots'?*). It's uninspiring to say the least, especially in the light of Bibi's notes. I stare at the screen for a while. Nothing.

I start to sketch Igor sleeping. His comedy proportions make it easy to capture him. Big ears. Big feet. Big everything. I fill in the background behind him, everything just a little too small. I add layers of detail and give him a tiny girl companion. I base her on Edie when she was about four or five, with long straggly hair and a self-curated outfit of multi-coloured stripy leggings with a frilly purple tutu skirt over the top. Tiny Doc-Marten-style boots. I work on giving her expression attitude. It occurs to me that maybe Igor would make a good book character? *Mummy, Why Is That Dog So Big?* A kid literally said that to her mother on Primrose Hill the other day when she saw him. I told her it was because he ate all the other dogs' food when they weren't looking.

There's a ping to tell me I have a new email. I curse myself for not turning the notifications off, but I'm powerless not to check who it's from.

Shit. Bibi.

I almost don't open it, but I know I have to face up to my responsibilities sometime.

I click on her name.

The email is entitled *Wow!*

Confused, I read the text.

> Your friend's book is stunning! The illustrations are superb. Does she have an agent? If not could you let me have her details?
>
> P.S. We still need to have a chat about the next Wilbur. Could you call me today? Thanks.

Fuck.

'Listen . . . don't be upset but Nick is looking for a flat to rent.'

I nearly didn't answer. Bibi's email has thrown me, and I'm not sure I can trust myself not to blurt out what I've just read.

'Oh,' I say carefully. 'Do you mean with her?'

There's a pause. 'I think so. I offered to go and look at some with him so I'll get a better idea. I'm so sorry, George.'

I remember waking up this morning, Nick still sleeping beside me, Igor on his back between us. The absolute wave of love I felt when I looked at them. The complete certainty that we were OK.

'Shit.'

'I know. I hate being the one to have to tell you . . .'

Yes, of course you do, I think, surprising myself with the thought. Is Nick right? Is she jealous of my success and wanting to hurt me?

'When . . . um . . . do you know?'

She sighs theatrically. 'He's looking at a couple tonight. I get the impression he wants to get it sorted soon.'

'I wonder why he's not taking her to view them with him,' I say because I can't resist.

'Oh,' she says, momentarily caught out. 'Maybe she's busy. Or maybe it's because I just announced I was going too so he feels he can't bring her along.'

'He didn't ask you to?'

'No,' she says with a fake laugh. 'I was very forceful. You'd have been proud of me.'

Of course I don't call Bibi all day, I'm so thrown by her response to Lydia's book. I don't even reply to her email until about five to six in the hope that she'll be rushing to leave for home and notice that I've been in touch but decide not to even bother reading my response till tomorrow. I've been torturing myself all day with what I should say. This could be a fantastic in for Lydia. Not a certainty by any means, but a chance. But Lydia is not Lydia any more. She's an alien. A replicant. A stranger.

Possibly even an enemy.

Sorry I missed you when I called today, I say, a bare-faced lie. *All going well with the new Wilbur. That's great that you like Lydia's book! She doesn't have an agent but I'm giving her your details so she can get in touch.*

I'm not. Obviously. Not until I find out what's going on.

Chapter 35

The area is a bit rough: there's no getting away from it. She walked from the tube with her head down, and now she's pretty much cowering in the doorway of the three-storey, three-apartment terraced house, bag clutched to her chest, preparing to do battle with anyone who tries to take her on. She hopes he doesn't end up moving here; she's not sure she could bring herself to visit however much she might want to. She's been picturing herself helping him make a flat a home, adding personal touches and a few creature comforts. Throws and candles. A carefully placed lamp. Maybe framing a couple of her drawings for him to put on the wall. She can't quite imagine doing that in this bleak side street with its discarded cans and charred tinfoil crowding the pavements and the smashed windows of the empty shop opposite.

She jumps as she hears a voice. 'Jesus, they should put scratch and sniff on the photos. We could have saved ourselves a lot of time.' Nick emerges from the gloom, smiling at her, her knight in shining armour.

'You can't live here,' she says as he kisses her on the cheek and her heart races. He's in the same wool coat, beanie hat pulled low.

'No, probably not.' He has a pile of papers in his hand. Rips one up theatrically. 'Right, that's that one off the list.'

'Good.'

He takes his gloves off and blows on his hands to warm them up. 'I should have met you somewhere else. Sorry you've had to hang round here.'

'It's fine. It gave me an adrenaline rush. Fear of imminent death and all that.' She gives a little laugh, her breath white as she exhales.

'Is this a stupid idea, walking round looking at the outside of places?'

'Not at all,' she says, although it is a bit. She'd much rather be sitting somewhere warm.

'I just thought it would save time later. I don't know this area very well but it's near work so . . .'

'It's a nice night,' she says, and it is. Crisp and clear.

'OK, next one is just round the corner . . .' He shows her the printout. A small, clean, anonymous box of a flat. It actually looks tiny.

'Is it big enough? I mean . . .'

They turn a corner into a small square of Georgian terraced houses. On one side is a pub, a tiny food store and a pizza takeaway. Outside a teenage boy flips his skateboard over and over again.

'I just need somewhere to sleep and eat. That's it. It's hardly going to be a place for entertaining.'

'No, right . . .'

He refers to the papers again. 'It's this one. Number eighteen. Second floor.' They stop and look. 'This looks OK.'

She laughs. 'You do need to see inside, you know. You can't trust the pictures.'

He gets out his phone and takes a photo of the building. 'I know. But in all honesty I'm not that fussy. I'll phone up about it tomorrow.'

'You need at least one more, for comparison. I'm not going to let you take the first place you see. Let's have a look.' He hands her the documents. There are three more flats, all close by. The boy flips the skateboard. 'And you need to find out if he's local because that would drive you insane in a couple of days.'

She's gratified to see Nick smile at that. 'I'm used to living with noisy kids,' he says.

'That would be more like living near an angry woodpecker. OK, this one is right over there. Let's just look for the sake of it as we're here.'

They head around the square. She considers suggesting they walk through it but it looks a bit forbidding. Not exactly the place for picnics but handy if you want to smoke crack. There's a small side street of similar houses next to the pub.

'What number?'

He peers at the details. 'It doesn't say. This one, look . . .'

She checks the photos. The street is short, maybe ten houses each side. 'UPVC windows, black window boxes on the first floor . . .' They walk up one side and down the other. There's only one house that fits the bill.

'Top floor,' he says. They stand and gaze up. 'Looks OK. I'll make an appointment to see those two.'

He snaps a photo of the outside. Lydia loves how Nick's way of remembering anything is to take a photo of it. Phone numbers, restaurants he likes the look of, book reviews he thinks sound interesting. His phone is a perfect map of his life.

'Can I help you?' The front door opens just as he's getting ready to take a close-up of the upper-storey windows. It's a woman in a slightly shiny suit. Late thirties, smart bob. Lydia shivers in her many layers just looking at her. Maybe she has thermals on underneath.

'Sorry,' Nick says. 'We were just . . .' He waves the details at her. 'The top floor is for rent . . .'

'I'm the agent,' the woman says, holding out a hand for them to shake one after the other. Her hands are incongruously warm. She looks at Lydia. Smiles. 'Katherine Carver. I could give you a quick tour now. I just popped in to turn the heating up. Awful, isn't it?'

'Freezing,' Lydia says. 'That's really kind of you. We might as well, mightn't we? As we're here . . . ?'

'Oh,' Nick says. 'No, I don't want to put you out. I'll make an appointment . . .'

Lydia rolls her eyes comically at the agent. 'Don't be silly. We're here now . . . we'd love to have a look. Thanks.'

They follow Katherine Carver back into the musty hall. 'I should just take some details,' she says. 'Name?' She looks at Lydia expectantly.

'Lydia Somers, but I'm not . . . The flat's for Nick . . .'

'The couple who just moved out loved it here,' Katherine says, not listening. She starts up the stairs slowly, huffing after every step so that Lydia almost trips over her. She has to resist the urge to overtake.

'We're not . . .' Nick says. 'The flat is just for me . . .'

'Oh, sorry,' Katherine says, stepping on to the first

half-landing and wheezing as if she's just conquered Everest. 'I just assumed . . . I'm usually pretty intuitive about stuff like that . . .'

'Can you believe she thought we were an item!' Lydia laughs as they wave goodbye to Katherine. She wants to relive the moment. Plant the idea in Nick's head as a possibility.

He shrugs. 'Easy mistake to make, I guess. What a shithole.'

'Ghastly.'

'We could try that pub,' he says and her heart soars. They walk round to the square and peer hesitantly into the local. A couple of old men glare back at them from their seats at the bar like a pair of elderly gunslingers. The only other customers are locked in an intense game of darts.

'How about Russell Square?' she says. She can't really imagine their intimacy blossoming here.

'Jesus,' he says. 'I don't think I'll be popping in there after work every night.'

'Let's head to that hotel.' She likes the idea of them having a regular haunt. Their place.

'Great.'

He walks slowly so she can keep up in her heels. He's always been considerate. Not just to her but to everyone. One of those people to whom it comes naturally. It's not an effort. Not a conceit. Not done to impress others.

She steels herself, fakes a slip and makes a grab for his arm.

'Oh my God, sorry. It's so icy again.' She laughs as if she's embarrassed. Leaves her hand tucked into the crook of his elbow.

The table they sat at the last time is free and she heads

straight for it. They're building a foundation. Things that are just about the two of them. Our bar, our table. 'This'll have to be your local,' she says, slipping off her coat. They order drinks. They both want red wine, so she suggests a bottle.

'How do you feel about it, getting a flat?' she asks once the waiter has poured them each a glass.

He sighs. 'It's not exactly where I imagined myself at forty-five.'

She gives a rueful laugh. 'Well, join the club. What a pair of saddos.'

'She'll come round, won't she?' He looks at her so hopefully that it's all she can do not to give him reassurance. It would be so easy to give him his life back. All she has to do is tell Patricia that it turns out her friend had got it all wrong, had mixed Nick up with someone else, and the whole episode has been a ghastly mistake. But this is not about giving him his old life back. It's about giving him a new one. With her.

'I don't know.' She reaches over the table and lays a hand on his arm.

It's time to move things up a notch.

Chapter 36

Nick texts me to say that they are stopping for a drink, post flat-viewings. *Can I come home yet? I'm knackered.*

No! You have work to do! Unless you think you've found out what she's up to already?

This is exploitation, he writes. *I'm calling the union.*

Call them when you get home. Meanwhile get on with it!

Igor and I have already been for a long walk and he's settled down by the wood burner for the evening. He's a lazy boy at heart. I try to occupy myself by reading a book that Anne Marie lent me, the latest big domestic noir, but I realize I've skimmed a whole page and not taken in anything that's happened so I give up. My phone beeps, I assume with a reply from Nick. It makes me so happy that we're back to our easy banter, our teasing and in-jokes. How many years does it take to get that with someone? How would I ever have found it again?

There's a message, but it's not from him.

I stare at the name at the bottom. *Lou.*

What can she possibly have to say to me now? I read the text nervously.

Do not tell anyone I sent you this! I thought it might be helpful. This is all of them.

I look at the picture that's attached. It's a list of names and phone numbers. Seven in total. All for women called Emma who, I assume, work at Diamond Leisure.

That's fantastic, I text back. Obviously I no longer feel the need to check up on Nick, but Lydia is a whole other story. *I really appreciate it, thanks.*

That's my evening sorted then.

I get myself a glass of wine, settle down on the kitchen sofa, phone in hand. I've copied the numbers on to a piece of paper and I start to work my way through them. The first one answers almost immediately. I can hear a TV in the background and the sound of kids arguing. I have my spiel prepared. I need to get it out quickly so she doesn't hang up thinking I'm some kind of phishing call.

'Hi, is that Emma? Sorry to bother you but I'm trying to contact a friend of mine, Lydia Somers, and I remember her mentioning that she had a mate called Emma who worked at Diamond Leisure . . .'

'Lydia . . . ?' she asks hesitantly. She's probably trying to work out what the scam is.

'Somers.'

'No. Not me. There are a few Emmas though . . .'

'I know, thanks. Sorry to bother you.'

I cross Emma Bartlett off my list. On to the next. Two voicemails later (I didn't leave messages; I didn't think they would ever call me back) I get through to Emma Thornberry and basically have the same conversation. Then with Emma Sanders, Emma Sharpe and Emma Thurlow-Witt. They're all very pleasant, very helpful, and I believe them all when they say they don't know Lydia. Why would they lie?

While I'm waiting for a bit of time to pass before I try the two final candidates again my phone rings. Nick.

'Are you on your way home? Did you find anything out?'

'I'm in the toilets,' he says, so quietly I can hardly hear him.

'Why are you whispering?'

'I don't know,' he says, back to his normal voice. 'Just in case.'

'How's it going?'

'Something weird is happening—'

'Well, we know that,' I interrupt.

'No. I mean, I think she's flirting with me. It's making me really uncomfortable.'

'No way. She wouldn't,' I say, struggling to get the words out. Would she?

He tells me how she linked her arm through his on the walk to the hotel ('She supposedly slipped but then she just didn't let go') and how, while apparently being sympathetic, she put her hand over his on the table and left it there until he moved ('Which was quickly, trust me').

'And now I feel as if she's giving me meaningful looks. Honestly, George, I just want to get out of here.'

No. Not that. Whatever else Lydia might do I can't believe she'd do that. Could she have contrived this whole situation just to try to get Nick for herself? Knowing that he would never look at her so long as he thought he still had me? I'm fuelled with anger and my heart shatters in two at the same time.

'I can't . . . She wouldn't do that to me . . .'

'I don't know,' he says. 'I think she is. You know I wouldn't tell you this if I didn't really believe it . . .'

'This is like a nightmare.'

Once I've said goodbye, Nick telling me he's going to make his excuses and leave, I try the other two Emmas again. I get through to both. I go through my prepared speech. They both tell me that as far as they know they've never even met a Lydia Somers.

So it's true then. Lydia has made this whole thing up.

She has tried to sabotage my life.

And it looks as if she is trying to steal my husband.

Chapter 37

I feel as if I've neglected Anne Marie the past few days. So much has been happening. Not that I think she's sitting at home wondering why I haven't called, but everything that's going on with Lydia has made me realize how important real friends – true friends – are. Nick and I decide to invite her and Harry over. That is, I will invite them over and we'll surprise them with the fact that Nick is here. Swear them to secrecy just in case one of them bumps into Lydia. Although as that has never happened in all the time I've known them it seems unlikely.

Nick was full-on PTSD when he got home last night. Try to imagine it. Your husband or wife's best bosom buddy making a play for you. Not even a drunken pass to be bitterly regretted as soon as they open their eyes next morning. A calculated move with careful preparation to leave the field clear.

'Are you really, really sure?' I asked him for the third time as we sat drinking tea in the kitchen. 'She wasn't just trying to be nice? Sympathetic?'

He shook his head. 'I wish you could have been there to see it. Although obviously then she wouldn't have been doing it.'

I filled him in on the Emmas, made him swear not to mention it to Lou. 'It was kind of her to send me the list,' I said. 'Given how I treated her.'

He nodded. 'It was.'

'So what do we do now?'

'Fucked if I know,' he said, pulling me on to his lap as I walked past. Igor sat up, excited, clearly thinking it was wrestling time.

Today both Patricia and I have received reports of last night from Lydia. To me: *He was giving nothing away about whether he's moving in on his own or with her. Sorry! I'll keep trying!*

And quite a different story to Patricia: *So, he told me that he wants a lease for at least a year!! He's definitely not thinking he's going back home any time soon. And I'm sure I heard him saying something to the agent about his girlfriend needing to give notice on her flat when he thought I wasn't listening!!*

Drink tomorrow? To me, obviously. And, although I would rather do anything else, I say yes.

Harry and Anne Marie arrive promptly at seven, wine, a box of my favourite salted caramel chocolates and a jar of home-made chilli pickle in hand. Going overboard to make me feel that someone is thinking of me, even if my husband isn't. What they don't know is that he is currently shivering in the back garden, waiting to jump out and surprise them like a snowman-themed strippergram. Igor, of course, gives it away.

'What is he looking at?' Harry says, going over to check it out for himself. 'Is there a cat out there, boy?'

'Probably a fox,' Anne Marie says, joining them. 'What . . . Is that Nick?'

'Surprise!' he says, emerging from the shadows and flinging

open the patio door somewhat half-heartedly, knowing he's been rumbled.

Both Anne Marie and Harry turn to look at me. I slip my arms round Nick to warm him up. 'We're back together,' I say. 'I've found out it was all lies.'

'I knew it!' Harry says emphatically.

'He did,' I say to Nick. 'Harry never really doubted you.'

'Oh God, this makes me so happy,' Anne Marie says, and then she starts to cry and laugh at the same time.

We tell them the whole story while we wait for our pizzas to arrive. Their expressions change from delighted to horrified disbelief when we start to outline Lydia's guilt, tripping over each other's sentences to get the story out.

'We're only telling you two. No one else. And the kids know we're back together, obviously.'

'So, what now?' Anne Marie licks margherita topping off her finger. For someone with so much colour in her life her taste in pizzas is very vanilla.

Here's the thing. I have no idea where this is going. None. If Lydia is making a play for Nick, trying to ruin my life, then our friendship is over, obviously. I could never trust her again. I feel as if it rips my heart in two thinking about it, but it's the truth. I have to face up to it. But do I confront her or just pull away? Stop returning her calls? Ghost her? It's unthinkable. I might have got Nick back but lost Lydia in the process. It's not a choice I ever thought I'd have to make. I almost don't know which loss is worse: I've spent my whole adult life so enmeshed with the two of them.

'Shit!' They all turn to look at me. 'The awards do! I invited her when I thought Nick and I were over.'

'You uninvited me?' he says. He's pretending to be hurt but he probably really is underneath.

'Well, obviously. Sorry. If I'm not telling her we're back together then how do I get out of her coming with me? She's already planned what she's wearing and everything.'

I don't say anything but it's also just occurred to me that if she came she and Bibi would be in the same space. How could I get through a whole evening without Bibi realizing who she was and all but offering to publish her book on the spot? I haven't even told Nick about Bibi's request to be put in touch with her. I don't want anyone to think I'm that person who deliberately sabotaged their friend's chance at their life-long dream. Even if she's not my friend any more. Even if I now know she'd have no hesitation about sabotaging mine.

'I think we have to tell her,' Nick says, looking serious. 'Let her know we've caught her out. What's the point of dragging it on forever?'

'I agree,' Anne Marie says. She gathers our empty pizza boxes and tips the discarded crusts into Igor's bowl before stacking them up. Why does everyone feel the need to feed my dog? He's eaten them before they've even landed. 'Now you know what she's doing, cut her off. She's unhinged, if you ask me.'

I look over at her. 'I thought you got on OK with her, didn't you? When you met.'

Anne Marie shrugs. 'She was always a bit territorial about you. I felt as if she thought we were in competition.'

I think about how snippy Lydia was the first time I introduced them. I'd always hoped Anne Marie had been oblivious to Lydia's rudeness.

'I just want to look her in the eye,' I say decisively. 'It's as if, if I don't, I'll never accept that it's real. I'm not saying I don't believe you . . .' I say quickly to Nick. 'It's not that at all. It's like, if I don't see it for myself, I worry I'll be taken in by her again. I'll never be able to cut myself off completely.'

I close my eyes, steady my breath. 'I want her to have to face me.'

Chapter 38

She's meeting Georgia at the Princess Louise. She'd offered to go over to Primrose Hill – even though it was further from both work and her flat it was somehow less hassle. She was tired of being out night after night and – however weird this might sound to an outsider – Georgia's home still felt like her home. Somewhere she didn't have to try too hard – but George had pushed for the pub. 'I never go anywhere these days,' she'd said. 'And besides, I have to be in town earlier so I might as well just hang around.'

Georgia seems a bit better. As if she's getting used to the idea that Nick is gone. Moving on. Lydia raises her umbrella in the doorway of her office. The doorman steps out to cover her as she does and she rewards him with a big smile. It's all coming together. She can't quite believe it. Now her job is to make her friend feel whole again. Give her hope for a new and happy chapter of her life.

Leaving work always feels like an escape. Her days are interminable. Endless. A drudge from beginning to end. She has a good job, she knows that. But she isn't cut out to sit in an office. She isn't cut out to spend her days showcasing someone else's talent (or lack of it) while her own atrophies. Her life is passing her by. She's thought about trying to change jobs, of course she has. To move to a company that would actually interest her. With a big children's department. But she's afraid she would have to listen to her new colleagues discussing the phenomenal success of Wilbur the Wallaby and how could they find their own Georgia Shepherd to try to capture some of that market for themselves?

And now Georgia has been nominated for the fucking Gordon's Book Emporium award which, even though most people had probably never even heard of it, is pretty prestigious. Certainly in the industry.

She's eaten up with fear that Georgia will win. She's not a jealous person by nature but surely no one could fail to see the injustice here? It's hard enough that Georgia is published, let alone a bestseller. It's actually mind-blowing that legions of the three-to-fives are obsessed with Wilbur. That he's shaping their childhood. But the fact that she might win a fucking award? It doesn't bear thinking about. It's a joke. It really is.

She calls Georgia's mobile as she walks along Theobalds Road.

'Hey,' she says when Georgia answers. 'Do you fancy the Fitzroy Hotel instead? I'm not sure I can face the Princess Louise. It's always so packed.'

She wants to be in her and Nick's place. To feel close to him.

'I've just got off at Holborn,' Georgia says, slightly huffily. 'It's a bit of a trek and it's pissing down, in case you haven't noticed.'

'It'll be much nicer when we get there, though. You'll thank me.'

Georgia laughs as Lydia knew she would. 'I'm not sure I will. See you in fifteen minutes. Find towels.'

She'd worried she'd moved a bit too fast when she put her hand on his arm. Nick's. He'd looked a bit shocked. And then he'd pulled away, but gently. Reluctantly. Hopefully she'd styled it out. Played up the sympathetic-friend angle. She didn't want to scare him away before he was ready. But then again, she didn't want to be so slow on the uptake that he moved on with someone else before she registered her interest. It was a minefield. She's pretty sure there had been a moment when he looked into her eyes for a fraction too long while she sat with her hand over his. She's pretty sure there had been a spark, however faint. She just needs to keep it alive so she can rekindle it when the time comes.

She smiles at the waiter as she walks into the bar, shaking the drops from her coat. He clearly doesn't recognize her even though she and Nick have spent two whole evenings being served by him. Is she becoming invisible? Is this what happens? She's always heard that women over a certain age feel as if they disappear into the background, ignored by barmen, shop assistants and cat-calling builders. She's always thought she'd escape that fate somehow. Not that she wants the cat-calling builders – in fact, she isn't sure that even happens these days. Building sites all have notices up about how considerate they are, and phone numbers to call in any bad behaviour – but she isn't ready to be written off just yet.

She settles at a table just as Georgia arrives, wrestling to contain her umbrella as she tries to close it. Lydia takes her in for a moment without Georgia noticing. She's looking better. Less haggard. Human resilience is amazing. Or maybe it turns out that Georgia isn't as in love with Nick as Lydia has always thought. That would make life so much easier. That would be the fairy-tale ending.

She stands up to greet her. 'I'd hug you but I'm soaked,' Georgia says, putting up a hand to keep her away.

'You look good,' Lydia says. 'Apart from the half-drowned rat bit.'

Georgia waves the waiter over. 'I actually am. I'm much better. Surprisingly so.'

She should have known then. Alarm bells should have rung. But she wasn't paying attention to the right things.

They order drinks. A gin and tonic for her and a red wine for Georgia. Georgia nibbles on a couple of nuts from the bowl on the table. Lydia is always too aware of how many fingers have rooted around in there during the course of the day – and where those fingers might have been – to ever indulge herself. She'd read a statistic once about the amount of human faeces on communal snacks that had left her gagging. They sit for a moment in a silence that is usually comfortable but tonight, she realizes, feels a little off. It's her own feelings of guilt, she assumes, getting in the way of their usually easy flow of conversation.

'Your friend Emma,' Georgia says out of nowhere. 'What's her surname?'

'Um . . .' Lydia says, taken aback. Stalling for time. 'Emma?'

'The one who works with Nick.'

'Oh.' Shit, she has to think fast. 'Do you know, I don't even know. That is, it used to be Baker but she got married a couple of years ago and I can never remember what her second name is now. Cook? Cookson? Something beginning with a C, I think. Or it might be an S.'

Georgia nods. 'Could you maybe put me in touch with her?'

'Why?' Lydia says, way too quickly. 'I mean . . . I don't know her that well . . .'

'I just thought it might be useful to talk to someone who works with Nick, that's all. She might know something.'

'I thought you were feeling better . . .'

'I am,' Georgia says, brushing a strand of damp hair from her eyes. 'But I still don't have all the details. Not even the name of the woman he's gone off with. And until I do I can't fully get over it. It's the last piece of the puzzle and then I can move on. Does that make sense?'

'Sure.' Lydia has to think quickly. 'I don't think she'd know anything though. It's not as if she sees him all the time.'

'Where does she work?'

'One of the regional sites. I can't remember which one; she moved recently. Why don't I call her? Ask her if she knows anything?'

'That would great.'

OK. She might have got away with it. Georgia is looking at her expectantly though.

'Could you do it now?'

'Now? Um . . .' She has an idea. Probably a terrible one. 'Sure. I'll try her.' She looks in her phone contacts – making sure Georgia can't see the screen – and hits the number for her aunt Susan. She bought Susan a mobile a year ago but she has never even turned it on, so far as Lydia knows. Susan is Lydia's dad's much older sister and, now in her eighties, she firmly refuses to embrace any new technology. Lydia likes to comfort herself with the fact that at least Susan has it in her possession in case of emergencies, but, in reality, she knows that the house could be burning down around her aunt and she wouldn't even know which button to press to power it up. As expected the call goes straight through to the generic voicemail message.

'Not there,' she says, holding the phone away from her ear so that Georgia can hear. 'I'll leave a message.'

Georgia nods, smiling.

'Hi, Em! It's Lydia. Could you give me a call back when you've got a mo? I've got a quick question for you. Thanks! Bye! Right,' she says, putting her phone back in her bag. 'I'll let you know what she says.'

They chat about nothing much. Work. The twins. A show they've both started watching on the TV. There's something off though. For someone who claims to be feeling much happier Georgia has a slightly manic energy. There's a tightness around her jaw, a tiny muscle twitch that betrays her. Lydia feels a rush of guilt. Georgia can protest all she likes but she's clearly still hurting.

'So, what do you honestly think? Is she moving in with him?' Georgia says, bringing the subject back around.

'I don't know,' Lydia says carefully. 'I think so.' Shit, what has she told Georgia before and what has she said to Patricia? She really should have made notes. Something about Georgia is making her feel flustered.

'Didn't you say he said something to the agent about his girlfriend having to give notice?'

Did she? Not to Georgia, she's pretty sure. She had saved that nugget for Patricia so Georgia wouldn't feel she could confront Nick with it. She screws up her face. 'No. He was just vague, I told you.'

'So, he didn't say that?'

'No. I mean . . .' Why was Georgia pushing the issue? She was in danger of giving away again that she had read the messages that only Patricia should have read. Lydia doesn't like the turn this conversation is taking. Doesn't feel she can keep the two parts of her dual narrative separate in her head and not give herself away if pushed.

'Right. Of course not. And your friend Emma doesn't know? The office gossip machine hasn't given away that particular gem?'

Lydia clears her throat. Takes a sip of her drink. Her mouth is dry. 'Let's talk about something else. Let's not let Nick dominate our whole evening. I hardly ever see you as it is.'

Georgia looks right at her. It's so direct that Lydia feels herself blush. 'I know what you're doing, Lydia,' she says. 'I know this is all you.'

Chapter 39

I can hardly get the words out. Even though I've rehearsed them in my head over and over they still sound stilted. As if I'm reading from an autocue. All the colour drains from Lydia's cheeks.

'Know what?' she says, an attempt at bluffing it out.

'I know you know I'm Patricia. I know you've been feeding me a load of lies.'

'Who's Patricia?' she says, but her expression – fear mixed with a touch of defiance – gives her away.

I look at her. Say nothing. Let her sweat it out. Eventually she gives a nervous little laugh. 'George, you're freaking me out. What's going on?'

'Nick's moved back in with me.' I wait for that to sink in. Clearly it's the last thing she expected me to say. She can't hide the shock on her face. 'I don't know why you did it,' I say, 'but I do know that you set out to make me think Nick was cheating on me. Based on nothing. Lies. There is no Emma, is there?'

She gets a steely look in her eye, one that I've seen before. The Lydia who is defiant, who won't take any shit from anyone. The same look she gave one of our lecturers when he accused her of plagiarizing an essay (she had. In fact, we both had, but I'd managed not to get caught) and an ex-boyfriend who was insisting he had seen her share a brief kiss with one of his friends (again, she had. There's clearly a pattern emerging here).

'Of course there is. Why would I make up something like that?'

'So that I'd believe you.'

'Believe me about what? Wow, George, you really have lost it. What would I have to gain from upsetting you like that? Are you saying I was trying to split you and Nick up?'

Last night I debated long and hard with Nick, Anne Marie and Harry. They were all for me accusing her of making a play for Nick, flushing the whole sorry mess out.

'She's done some pretty shitty things but that is the absolute worst,' Harry said. Igor was wedged on the sofa between him and Anne Marie. If they were uncomfortable squashed into the corners while he noisily licked his non-existent balls they didn't say so.

'I don't have any proof of that bit though. I need to stick to the facts.'

'I know I'm right,' Nick had said emphatically.

'She'll just deny it and we'll get sidetracked. She'll turn it round so it looks as if I'm jealous. Irrational . . .'

'You tell me.' I say to her now.

Lydia's eyes fill with tears. I was expecting it. She should have been an actress really, with her ability to cry at will. Even though I know they're fake it's almost impossible not to be moved by them. Not to reach out a hand to comfort her. Tell her I'm sorry and it was all a big mistake.

'Georgia . . . what are you saying? I don't understand. You think I've . . . what? Lied to you about something? Made up a friend called Emma? I know you've been going through a hard time but none of this makes any sense . . .'

Keep calm, I tell myself. Stay focused. 'Let me see your phone.'

Her forehead creases a little and then her hand shoots out to grab it from the table. I get there first.

'What the hell are you doing?'

I hold it up to her face to unlock it. 'Give that back to me,' she says, raising her voice. Two men at a nearby table turn and look. It distracts me just long enough for her to snatch the mobile back. She gathers up her coat and bag.

'I'm going. Whatever this is, it's not funny.'

'I've got it all on my own phone anyway, obviously. I'll send you screen grabs just to refresh your memory.'

'Don't send me anything. Not till you've calmed down.' She struggles an arm into her coat.

'Nick's not interested,' I say as she walks off. So much for not going there. 'He said it really creeped him out, you throwing yourself at him.'

If anyone in the bar wasn't listening before, they certainly are now.

Lydia and I have only ever had one big fight before. We've had squabbles, obviously. There have been times when we've both taken a step back when something was simmering. Taken a couple of days out from contacting each other. But an all-out shouting match that threatened to ruin our friendship? Only once. We were sharing a flat in Camden. A rundown first floor above a dry cleaner's that reeked of ether. This was pre Nick, pre Wilbur. Only just post college. I don't even remember how it started now, but we'd been living on top of one another for a few months, struggling to make ends meet. We both had a complicated arrangement of part-time jobs to stay afloat, coming and going at all hours, sleeping whenever we found ourselves at home. I remember us standing in the tiny kitchen, hurling every buried resentment and stifled irritation we could dredge up at each other. From the mundane – 'You never clean up after yourself in the kitchen' (her to me); 'You make no fucking effort to be quiet when you get in from work in the middle of the night' (me to her) – to the truly personal – 'I'm sick of you whining on about how hard done by you are all the time' (her); 'You always act as if everything was about you. You're not the centre of everyone's fucking universe' (me). It was cathartic but it was scary. It left me bruised and shattered. Desperate to make up but unwilling to forgive. We didn't speak for almost a week. I hid in my room until I heard the front door close, only emerging when I knew she had gone to one of her three jobs. When I came home from work I would hear her holed up in her bedroom, listening to music at a volume that said 'Don't come near me.'

But – and I think I can speak for her here too – neither of us ever took steps to move out. We knew that whatever had happened it wasn't terminal. We wouldn't let it be.

Unlike this time.

I can't even remember how we made up. Who took the first steps to reconciliation. I just have an image of us hugging in the kitchen. Both laughing, both crying. And the feeling of utter relief.

That won't be happening this time either.

*   *   *

I pay the bill and manage to leave with – I hope – a modicum of dignity. In the taxi on the way home I delete Patricia's account.

I no longer care if Lydia admits it or not. It's enough that she knows she's not fooling me any more. That I'm on to her.

It's over.

Chapter 40

I have one last thing to do. I send Bibi an email.

My friend Lydia has decided to self-publish (I tried to persuade her you would be better but she'd made up her mind!). She says thanks so much for your interest. Sorry to have wasted your time.

I'm fucked if I'm going to help Lydia get a publishing deal now.

Half an hour later I get a reply back saying no problem and, by the way, any news about Wilbur?

Going well! I lie. *Should have something for you any minute now.*

As a distraction I allow myself to get caught up in excitement about the awards. I feel lost without Lydia. Completely adrift. But I try to focus on the positive. At least now I can all out revel in the moment without worrying that I'm upsetting anyone. Anne Marie fakes a sick day ('The kids will not die from lack of music tuition') and comes clothes shopping with me. She's as excited about my nomination as me. If not more.

'How are you and Harry?' I ask as we browse our way round Selfridges, her steering me closer and closer to the Vivienne Westwoods even though I've said ten times that I don't want to spend a fortune on something I'll probably get no wear out of.

'Really good.' She smiles. 'I need to thank you. You jolted me out of . . . whatever it was . . . before I did something totally irreversible. If you hadn't told me you'd seen us . . .'

'You were already putting the brakes on. Don't torture yourself.'

'I have no idea who that person was. None. I look at Jez now and, you know, he's a nice bloke and all that, but . . . just . . . no . . .'

'Think of it as a brief midlife crisis. Some kind of peri-menopausal madness.'

'Oh my God, look at that . . .' she says, grabbing my arm. It's a stunning petrol-blue ruched sleeveless dress. It's got just enough edge to stop it from looking as if you're trying too hard to look sexy. It's beautiful. Anne Marie paws at the fabric like a needy cat. I indulge her by trying it on. Which is a mistake because I love it and it does everything for my figure, but it's nearly a thousand pounds so there's no way I'm even going to consider it. She looks at me with her mouth open.

'You have to . . .'

'I absolutely don't.'

'Look at it though.'

I turn back to the dressing room. 'You try it on. It'll look amazing on you.'

'Don't be stupid. I could never afford it.'

I grab her hand, pulling her behind me. Grab two other random outfits off the racks as I go. 'We're not going to buy anything. We're just going to play dressing up.'

I snap photos of Anne Marie in the outfits of her dreams – we tell the officious shop assistant who is eyeing us with suspicion that she is the one who has a big occasion coming up.

'She's a famous musician,' I mutter while Anne Marie's trying on a pair of wide-leg pin-striped trousers. The assistant's – Lee, her badge declares – eyes widen.

'Have I heard of her?'

'Definitely,' I say, enigmatically.

'Right, let's go to Primark,' I say once we're out of earshot, having told Lee we'll be back once we've done a quick circuit to satisfy ourselves we're making the right decision. I text Harry one of the pictures – Anne Marie looking stunning in a floor-length black number. *Just picking our outfits for next week! Anne Marie is applying for a second mortgage as I type!* I have actually managed to wangle two extra tickets so that our best friends can come along to the do. I keep warning them it'll probably be really boring and that I definitely am not going to win, but they're still doing a good impression of being delighted.

'If it's really bad we can sneak out after my category and go for a drink somewhere,' I said as I asked if they were up for it.

'Oh no. I am going to milk the free champagne for all it's worth,' Harry declared. 'I mean, I'm not going to embarrass you by getting drunk or anything . . .' he added hastily.

'Oh God, I am,' I said.

Both Anne Marie and Harry are being extra solicitous since my confrontation with Lydia. I'm trying to act as if everything is OK, but the truth is I feel as if I've had a limb removed. I hadn't realized how often I think about Lydia each day, how many times I pick up my phone to text or call her. I've had a couple of pleading texts: *Please George let's talk about this, don't cut me off* and *You have to believe me. I would never make a play for Nick, never!! You're my best friend!* It's taken everything I've got to ignore them. A couple of days ago I was coming back from a late-afternoon walk with Igor and I saw her standing on my doorstep, bundled up in her big grey coat. Of course the dog saw her at the same time and started straining on the lead, anxious to go and greet his friend. I had to drag him with both hands to pull him the other way before she spotted us. When I realized she wasn't going anywhere soon I took myself round to Anne Marie and Harry's and texted Nick to meet us there after work. She'd looked gaunt even from a distance – even more so than ever. Huddled in on herself. We ended up staying out all evening just in case she was still there. Later I looked at her Instagram page and there she was, pouting at the camera. *Date night! Theatre and champagne!!* It reeked of desperation. I deleted the app. I couldn't allow myself to feel sorry for her.

She texted Nick too. *Why would you tell Georgia that? Why would you ever think I was making a pass at you? I was trying to be a good friend. How fucking arrogant must you be to think I fancied you! All I was ever doing was trying to help you and Georgia!!*

He ignored it.

I decide I have to give Bibi something so I work on some more sophisticated words and actually spend an enjoyable afternoon drawing a tall pangolin playing a small mandolin and a fat raccoon with a towel for his guest bathroom. Eminem I am not, but at least the pictures are cute. I email them to her as a peace offering. *How about something more along these lines?* She emails straight back. *These are better.* Just that. No elaboration. Not even an exclamation mark to emphasize the point. But it's something.

Life – if I don't examine the edges too much – is good.

There's just one more thing I have to do.

Chapter 41

I'm back at the Lighterman. This time I've warned Nick I'm coming. I think he's terrified I'm going to embarrass him again, but, if he is, he's too nice to say so. He thinks it's a bad idea, that much he does say, because he worries it'll bring back all my feelings of shame and embarrassment. And, to be fair, he's probably right. I have to do it though. I have to at least try to replace a terrible memory with a – hopefully – slightly less terrible one.

I text him when I get out of the taxi as agreed and he meets me at the front door. 'OK?' he says, hugging me.

'Yep,' I say, which is code for not really but I'm trying.

He squeezes my hand. 'They're all here.'

I follow him in, smoothing down my hair. My stomach leaps into my mouth as I spot them. Lou, Siobhan, Jasmine, Sue and the rest. There's a woman I don't recognize who I assume is Camilla. She's probably the only one who doesn't hate me. Or maybe she does just by reputation.

Once again all eyes turn on me. Nick clears his throat. 'You remember Georgia?' The only ones who even attempt a smile are Elaine and Anil. Camilla just looks confused. 'She wanted to . . . um . . .'

I put him out of his misery. 'I wanted to say something to you all. To apologize for the other week . . .' I spot Jess raise an amused eyebrow at Si. I'm probably never going to like her, let's face it. It's OK, though. It doesn't matter. We don't all have to be friends. I'm not expecting to go on holiday with them; I just want to explain myself. Maybe make things a bit less uncomfortable for Nick at work.

'I don't want to hijack your evening. I'm only staying for a second. Nick can fill you in on the whole story later if you want to know but . . . just before I came down last time, someone I trusted had told me that he was sleeping with one of the women here . . .'

That gets their attention. Theirs and the three people at the next table. I try to ignore them.

'She had details. Proof, supposedly. Just no name. That's why I was so . . . why I acted so badly . . .' I glance at Lou and she gives me an encouraging half-smile. 'And then, of course, I had about six vodkas because I was so nervous.'

'Understandable,' nice Abigail butts in, but I'm on a roll with my speech and I don't want to be distracted.

'I was rude. I know I acted appallingly, but in my de-fence I thought my life was falling apart and I had absolutely no reason to doubt what this person was telling me. Even though it was hard to believe and I should have known bet-ter. But she was my closest friend. My sister practically. She went out of her way to convince me. It's a long story. But the bottom line is I apologize to you all . . . That's it.'

There's a hiatus where, I assume, they wait to see if I've finished.

'Good on you,' Elaine says. 'That took a lot of courage.'

I smile at her weakly. 'OK,' I say. 'I'll leave you to it. Thanks for hearing me out . . .'

'Why would someone do that to you?' Jasmine says, just as Siobhan screws up her face and says, 'That's awful.' The questions come at me from all sides: Who was it? Why? How did I work out she was lying?

'Nick'll fill you in,' I say. 'I'm not staying. I don't want to hijack your evening.'

'No way,' Elaine says, pulling out a stool. 'You can't leave us hanging like that.'

I glance at Nick. He's smiling at me. 'They're all basically nice people,' he'd said when I told him I was planning to say my piece. 'If you give them a chance.' I look round to see if any of them are looking at me as if they'd rather I just left but every one of them is hanging on my last word.

'OK. Just one though. Really. If I try to order a second someone punch me.'

When we leave half an hour later I know I've done the right thing. To a person they were sympathetic. Even Jess. The general consensus seems to be that I have been a victim of a great wrong and that any of them would have acted as I did under the circumstances. Not one of them makes me feel awkward. In fact, they're practically offering to form a militia to take out Lydia on my behalf. It's tempting.

'I owe you a bigger apology than anyone else,' I say to Lou as we get ready to leave.

'Forget it,' she says. 'There's only one baddie in this scenario.'

'That seemed to go well,' I say to Nick as we cross the square, hand in hand.

'They love you.'

'That might be a bit of an exaggeration, but thank God. I feel better.'

I ignore the four heartfelt texts from Lydia when I look at my mobile in the cab. I can't trust myself not to get sucked back in if I let myself. I've spent half my life in tune with her feelings, worrying about whether or not she's happy. Not any more. I block her number.

'New start,' I say to Nick, shakily. He leans over and pulls me towards him. Kisses my forehead.

'New start.'

Chapter 42

This was never part of the plan. She'd been playing a long game. At least, that had been the intention. Maybe she made her move too soon. She curses herself for that moment of weakness, for laying her hand over Nick's, giving herself away. But how could she ever have anticipated that he and Georgia would reconcile? That somehow they would get together and compare stories?

This was the worst of all possible scenarios. And now Georgia has ghosted her. Which is ridiculous because Lydia knows where she lives, obviously, so it isn't as if she can hide forever. Not that she's intending to stalk her. That would be too sad. Too desperate. She just wants one last chance to explain herself.

Mostly what she feels is hard done by. Sometimes she thinks that the universe is against her. That she's powerless to do anything about it. She's talented, she's gorgeous (if she says so herself, ha!), she keeps herself in amazing shape, she's smart, she's funny, but none of this seems to be enough. You can be dealt all the best cards but still not have a winning hand, it seems.

She tries on a couple of dresses. There's a new one from Zara that she hasn't worn yet but it's actually looking a bit big on her now. Not so flattering. She does clever things with a bulldog clip, pulling it in at the back to show off her waist, checks her make-up. Puts her phone on timer and takes a photo. It takes eight more attempts to get it exactly right.

She plays around with filters, adds it to her story. *Another night out!! #Grateful #BeYou #LuckyGirl.*

She doesn't really want to go. It's Wes again – he of the truncated graffiti exhibition evening. He's asked her if she fancied a rain check a couple of times (God, she hates that term. When did everyone start saying that?) and she's ducked the question. But she needs something to occupy her mind, and sitting in the cinema with someone beats watching a film on your own. Just. She remembers to unclip the bulldog clip, not caring that the dress reverts to being a bit sacklike. It's not as if Wes is really even going to see it. She'll arrive at and leave the cinema in her coat, after all. And it'll probably be freezing in there from overactive aircon even at this time of year, so she might well end up wearing it all evening. She's already decided they're not going on anywhere after. She's heading home. On her own.

She puts the coat on now, checks herself in the hallway mirror. Tells herself to fake it. Georgia's mum once told her that if you fake a smile your body releases chemicals that actually do make you happy. Serotonin maybe. She tries it now. Tries not to think about what Georgia must have told her. That she probably hates Lydia for what she's tried to do to her daughter. That she probably, in all likelihood, will never want to see Lydia again.

When her parents were killed and Susan had gone back to America, Georgia and her mother – Auntie Irene, she had insisted Lydia called her, although the Auntie had always jarred a little – had saved her; she had no doubt about it. She was twenty-one, an adult, but barely. Not old enough to be all alone in the world (Susan didn't count. She was kind but self-absorbed. Fragile. Needy. And besides, she was thousands of miles away across the Atlantic). Too young to spend Christmasses all alone. Irene had made it clear that she was always welcome, any time. With or without Georgia. And she had taken her up on it too. When she'd needed an escape and a bit of home comfort. It wasn't home, it never would be, and in a way it had almost made her feel worse, reminding her of what she was missing. But knowing that the offer was there had made all the difference. She was no longer unmoored. She was anchored.

She can't bear to think that that safety blanket has been taken away.

She thinks about how lucky Georgia is. She still has her mum. Not that she bothers to see her very often. Her fabulous career. Her beautiful twins. And now Nick is back and her nest isn't even empty any more because they have the dog. Their big dopey surrogate baby. It's like a fucking Richard Curtis film. She doesn't wish her any harm, she really doesn't. It's just so unfair. Life is passing Lydia by and she has none of the pieces in place. She doesn't even own her own flat.

All she has is a date with a man she has no interest in.

She closes her eyes briefly. Tries the smile again.

Leaves the house, head held high.

Chapter 43

Edie gives me a make-up tutorial via FaceTime. Halfway through I look as if I've joined the SAS but she assures me that contouring is the key.

'You need to take time getting the base right.' Big sigh. 'I could come home on the day and do it for you if you want.'

'No. Don't be silly. So, what do I do next?'

'Blend it in,' she says. 'Blend, blend blend.'

I do what I'm told. Now I look as if a toddler has gone to town on my face with a brown wax crayon. 'Can't I just put two lines of blusher under my cheekbones like we used to?'

Edie rolls her eyes. 'Do you want to look hot or not?'

'I think hot is too much of an ask. Lukewarm. Tepid.'

'And you need to get some baking powder . . .'

I stop blending, brush in the air. 'I don't think I have time to make a cake.'

She screws up her face. 'It's make-up . . .'

'I know. I was joking. I'm not a complete idiot.'

'If you say so. We'll do eyes tomorrow. Keep practising this.'

'Yes, ma'am.'

Nick walks into the bedroom just as we're saying goodbye. Double takes. 'Did something happen?'

'This is my look for the awards. Good, huh?'

'Nice. You might want to add a bit of green in there for full camo.'

I scrub at my face with a wipe. Nick and I have got into a routine of walking Igor as soon as he gets home from work, weather permitting. I think he's worried that I spend too much time home alone during the day, picking over the ashes of my failed friendship. And he's probably right. I'm working though. Spurred on by Bibi's faint words of almost-praise I have done more work in the last few days than I have in the past month. At the back of my head the words 'Award Nominated Author' run on a loop like a mantra. I may as well revel in it while I can.

Still Lydia tries to get in touch. There's a note through the door. 'Please call me, George!! Please hear me out.' I'm actually in when she posts it, having ignored the doorbell five times, watching her staring at the camera, knowing I'm probably there, Igor barking up a storm. I know I can't hide forever but I'm going to try.

'We're going to have to move at this rate,' I say to Nick now as we huff up the hill. It's been raining for days. Non-stop. Relentless. Freezing.

'We can have plastic surgery. Change our names,' he says, trying to make me laugh.

'It might come to that.'

'She'll give up,' he says, stumbling as Igor spots a squirrel and jerks forward. 'Don't let her get in your head.'

On the morning of the big day I open the front door and there's a woman standing with the most beautiful bunch of sunflowers wrapped in brown paper and tied with bright red string. The first thought that pops into my head is where did she get sunflowers at this time of year? The second is that maybe they're an attempt at a peace offering from Lydia. Either way they're gorgeous.

'Who are they from?'

The woman smiles as if she's handing me a lottery cheque. It strikes me that being a flower-delivery person would be a lovely job. Everyone is always pleased to see you. No one ever put a notice on their front door: 'No Junk Mail. No Interflora'.

'There's a card.'

I take them inside, root around and find it: 'Congratulations from us all at Phoenix Publishing'. I can't decide whether they know something I don't (have I won?) or they're hedging their bets and sending these now before the inevitable bad news tonight. The latter seems more likely. I arrange them in a vase and put them on the kitchen table. Send Kate, Bibi's assistant, a gushing email saying thanks.

I have a list of things I'm supposed to do and in what order, courtesy of Edie: Wash hair. Face mask. Exfoliate. Moisturize. Fake tan. Paint nails. I was supposed to do the first five yesterday but I didn't get round to any of them, so I've thrown everything out of whack already. Looking presentable is too much like hard work. I finally get round to washing my hair – the only task that feels achievable – after lunch. I'm wrapping my head in a towel when I hear a key in the lock downstairs. Igor barks and I hear a high-pitched squeal. When I get to the hall Edie is there pinned to the wall, Igor standing with two giant paws on her shoulders.

'Ede!'

'Mum! I wanted to surprise you! Call him off.'

'Igor, sit. He's just checking you out.' He gives her face a big slurp before he obeys my request. 'See, he likes you. What on earth are you doing here?'

I gather her in a hug. Even on first glance I can tell she's well. She exudes happiness. I take her all in. Her long hair dyed a lilac grey, silver nose stud, earrings snaking up the side of her left ear. 'You look gorgeous.'

'I came to help you out. Why have you only just washed your hair now?'

'I didn't get round to it yesterday. Come down for a cup of tea. How long are you staying? Maybe I could get you a ticket . . .'

'Stop changing the subject. My train back is at half eight. I've got a tutorial first thing so I can't stay. What did I tell you about freshly washed hair? It's too silky to do anything with. We'll have to dirty it down . . .'

She allows me to make her a drink and then she takes charge, every now and then chastising me for having failed to follow her programme. I'm so happy being ordered about by her I could cry. By four o'clock my hair is blow dried in artfully messy waves and I'm the colour of a sun-kissed beach babe.

'I smell funny.'

'That's why you should have done it yesterday, so you could have showered this morning and got rid of the smell. Too late now. Just rub some more moisturizer over the top. Something that smells nice.'

She chatters away while she paints my nails a vivid purple, having dug the bottle out of her own dressing-table drawer because the orange I bought is 'Too matchy matchy' with my dress. 'It's so uncool to coordinate everything like that.'

'I need to tell Dad you're here, so he can make sure he gets back in time to see you.'

She looks me straight in the eye, her cornflower-blue eyes wide. 'You're definitely OK, right? You're not just trying to fob me and Joe off?'

'Definitely.'

Now that Nick is no longer the villain I tell her the whole story. She's going to wonder why Lydia is suddenly absent from our lives if I don't.

'Jesus Christ, Mum. Are you sure you're OK?'

'I am. I will be. She's been my best friend since I was your age pretty much . . .'

'I'm never going to speak to her again.'

I reach out a hand to stroke her hair and she flinches back, shouting, 'Nails!'

'Oh yes, I forgot. Listen, if you want to keep in touch with her that's up to you. I would never tell you not to . . .' Edie and Lydia have always been close. As godmothers go, Lydia's always been a good one. Involved. She has been there for all the big events of the twins' lives: the school plays and sports days, their christening and their eighteenth birthday party. I'm sure she's been a confidante for one or both of them more than once. I wonder if she considered them when she made a play for Nick. It occurs to me suddenly that she must really be in love with him to be prepared to detonate a bomb under her life like this. Either that or the bonds were never as strong as I thought.

'No way. God,' she says, screwing her face up. 'She'd better not try and get in touch with me.'

I send Nick a message. Get one straight back. *Leaving now!!!* I hold it up to show her.

She smiles. 'Is there food there or are you going to eat before you go?'

'Oh. I don't know.'

She rolls her eyes indulgently. 'Didn't you always ask me that question whenever I went anywhere?'

'Well, yes. But annoying questions are my prerogative as a mother.'

The doorbell rings. Edie jumps up. 'I'll get it. Don't touch anything.'

Thirty seconds later she reappears. 'Look what I found on the doorstep . . .' She stands aside and Joe peers round from behind her.

'Joe!' I throw myself at him as Edie shouts, 'Nails! Careful!'

'Did you know about this?' I say to her. My twin babies in one place. I couldn't be happier.

'Course.'

'I feel like I want to cancel this evening and spend it with you two . . .'

'Which would entirely defeat the object of us coming home in the first place,' Edie says.

'I'm just here for moral support,' Joe says. 'She's in charge.'

By the time Nick gets home they have me in an eye-brightening mask, reclining on the kitchen sofa. 'You look good,' he says. 'Should I wear a matching one?' Both kids throw themselves at him and I see the relief in his face that they obviously believe in his innocence. They're both huggers but they're not usually this demonstrative. I bat away a pang of guilt. It wasn't my fault, it was Lydia's (Nick says this to me several times a day, like a cult leader trying to indoctrinate me). Igor, not one to be left out, throws himself into the mix. I grab up my phone and take a picture.

I want to savour this moment.

Chapter 44

By the time Anne Marie and Harry arrive, promptly at a quarter to seven, I'm looking – if I say so myself – probably the best I ever have. Edie has done an amazing job, especially on my eyes, which glitter with gold around the smokey-brown edges. My dress is perfect. Burnt orange. Slimly fitted on the waist. Cap sleeves. Short but not too short. My fake tan is glowing, even if I smell like a packet of Hobnobs. I feel like a goddess. Possibly a bit OTT for warm Prosecco in a church hall but who cares?

'Blimey,' Harry says when he sees me. 'You look incredible.'

'You really do,' Anne Marie – looking resplendent herself in black cigarette trousers and a red halterneck top. 'We definitely made the right choice with that dress.'

'Not too much?'

She beams at me. 'Definitely not too much. Joe! Edie!' she shouts when she sees them. I leave them all hugging and go upstairs to get my bag and coat. Nick is running a comb through his hair. He's elegant in a dark suit with an open-necked pale grey shirt.

'Excited?' he says when he sees me.

'I wish we could spend the evening with the kids.' I give myself a final check-over in the mirror.

'Do you think Meryl Streep says that when she's on the way to the Oscars?'

'I'd put money on it,' I say. 'Right, let's go.'

Edie and Joe head off to the pub together, to kill time before their trains, while we wait for our Uber. I watch from the window as they round the corner, both creased over laughing at something. Nick comes up behind me and puts an arm round my shoulders, pulling me in towards him. He smells of figs and dark wintery foliage.

When we pull up outside the vast Gothic building my first thought is that I'm glad I made the effort I did. It's not so much church hall as a vast looming stunner of a structure. Two large torches burn either side of the huge wooden door, which is decorated with woven gold branches and twinkly lights. A projection on the wall reads 'Gordon's Book Emporium Children's Book Awards 2020'. I recognize the well-known author of a fantasy series for the eight-to-tens being photographed next to it. A couple of autograph hunters wait patiently for him to finish. No one recognizes me, obviously – I may be successful but I'm a million miles from a household name, let alone a famous face – but, when I give my name and am handed a badge saying 'Georgia Shepherd. Nominee' I feel like a superstar. We all drop our coats off at the cloakroom and then I'm guided to a bank of three photographers. Someone hands me a copy of the most recent Wilbur (*Wilbur's Christmas*, in which he buys 'green mistletoe and a bucket of snow' among other things. I told you it makes no sense. He also makes friends with a turkey, a duck and a goose and invites them all round to share his nut roast on Christmas Day. How can Bibi say he's not woke?) and I hold it up, beaming, while the flashbulbs pop.

I help myself to a tall flute of champagne from a tray and

look round to locate Nick and the others. They're watching me with the same expression I know was always on my face whenever one of the twins appeared in a school play. Pride with a hint of indulgent amusement. A splash of fear that they might embarrass themselves at any moment and it all end in tears. We stand around in a huddle. I'm so thankful they've all come along. My gang of three. No way could I have coped with this on my own. Young waiters and waitresses in smart black shirts sweep around with canapés. I daren't accept any in case I dribble food down myself or end up with spinach in my teeth. Harry takes one of everything. At one point he's holding five used cocktail sticks, awkwardly looking round for somewhere to put them. Budget Edward Scissorhands. The room is cavernous. Subtly glowing with candles – I assume fake or a clumsy gesture could wipe out most of the UK's children's publishing industry in one fell swoop – and dramatic uplighters that highlight Gothic features. It smells like the church it once was. A string quartet plays quietly. Something soft and barely there. Achingly melancholic. At one end of the room is a stage of sorts. A lone microphone rising from a stone pulpit, dramatically uplit. I see several other authors I recognize. Big hitters. Surrounded by photographers and smiley PR people. It's pretty overwhelming, if I'm being honest.

'Well, this is better than takeaway round at ours,' Anne Marie says, looking about her.

'It's actually rather fab, isn't it?' My default setting generally is to pooh-pooh these events – mainly, I've realized, because I never thought I would be invited to one, let alone nominated. But I've left my cynicism at home tonight.

'Amazing. You do know how proud I am of you, don't you?'

Usually I would bat the comment away, make a joke. Tonight I just accept it. I put my free, non-champagne-holding arm round her waist. 'I do. And thank you. Wait . . .' I prise my phone out of my little clutch bag (bought specially for the occasion and just slightly too small to be practical), hold it out and snap a selfie of the two of us. WhatsApp it to the kids. For a brief moment I wish I hadn't deleted my Instagram account. A very brief moment.

We stand there, looking round, taking it all in. Eventually I spot a familiar face. Kate, Bibi's assistant, pushes through the crowd and greets me with a huge smile. It's a bit like seeing one of your teachers in Sainsbury's on the weekend. It's hard to compute that they actually exist outside the context of work, or that they might – in the case of Kate – actually be a bit of a babe. 'Firstly you look fantastic,' she says as we hug. 'Definitely up for "Most Glamorous Author". Did you meet everyone?'

'What? No. I'm hiding.'

'You have to meet the other nominees,' she says, taking my arm. I look round and raise an apologetic eyebrow at Nick and he smiles indulgently.

'Come with me,' I mouth and he shakes his head, indicating Anne Marie and Harry.

'I'll stay with them,' he mouths back. 'Have fun.' I pull a face.

The next half-hour or so is a blur. I'm introduced to a couple of my writing heroes, one of whom has heard of me, which blows my mind. She tells me she has a four-year-old daughter who has declared that kangaroos are her favourite animals, so much does she love Wilbur. I daren't say he's actually a wallaby. To be honest, I don't know if I even know the difference. Which suddenly strikes me as massively disrespectful to my creation. But then he collects Tesco Clubcard points so I'm hardly trying to pass myself off as David Attenborough.

I meet countless industry people and forget half their names immediately but they're all lovely. Everyone congratulates me (Kate introduces me to them all as 'Georgia Shepherd, author of the Wilbur books. She's a nominee'), most of them tell me about some young child they know who enjoys my books. Whether it's true or not it's a massive ego boost. Usually I'm not a fan of being the centre of attention but I'm not going to lie, I'm enjoying this. I say hello to my rivals: Sian Hepburn, writer and illustrator of *Why? Said the Pig*; Ian Tranter, who both writes and draws the *Digby the Digger* series about an anthropomorphized excavator that lives on a building site; and Jan and Peter Seymore, who together created *Ferdinand the Flea Joins the Circus*. We all gush over each other's books; tell each other they're bound to win. Only Jan and Peter seem to believe this is true. They are supremely full of themselves. I make a silent wish that one of the rest of us steals it from under their noses. Eventually we wheel back round to where we started. Nick, Anne Marie and Harry are still huddled together, chatting away animatedly. I tell Kate I'll see her later and start to make my way back to them.

And then I see her.

Standing near the doorway, looking around as if she's just

arrived. Dark hair swept up in a tight bun. Figure-hugging dress with a mandarin collar. Vivid red lipstick. She looks amazing.

Lydia.

Chapter 45

She had had to beg, borrow and steal to get a ticket. Her shared assistant, Lana, has a friend who knows someone who works for *The Bookseller* and they had pulled a chain of strings and managed to find someone who wasn't using their plus one. It was a hot ticket in the publishing world, apparently. So she shows up alone. She's bound to know people here and, if she doesn't, she'll just chat to whoever she comes across. Making new friends has never intimidated her. Casual friendships are easy. It's the deeper ones she finds it hard to sustain. She knows exactly what a therapist would deduce: that's why she has never been to see one. That she has commitment issues because of the fear of that person being taken away from her suddenly. Irreversibly. No shit, Sherlock. Georgia was different. Their bond was already formed before the crash. Before she put the walls up.

The walls that have stopped her ever getting too close to a man. That she had been prepared to tear down for Nick because it turned out he had already been inside them before she even realized.

No way can Georgia refuse to hear Lydia out in front of all these people. Her admiring peers. She won't dare cause a scene. Lydia asks one of the doormen to hold her coat and snaps a photo of herself outside the church with the stunning illuminations behind her. She had taken a day's holiday and had her hair and nails done. She's wearing a skin-tight dress in a deep purple. Her highest heels. She had wanted Nick to see what he could have had, but now that feels a bit cheap. It's Georgia she's here for. She steps into the foyer, showing her invitation. Hovers in a corner adding a filter that makes her pale skin look even more dramatic.

How lucky am I when this counts as work!!! she types, hashtagging the name of the awards. She's pretty sure Georgia has deleted her Insta – not that she ever really looked at it anyway – so she won't see it. She doesn't want to lose the element of surprise.

Inside the space is packed. Fragrant with candles and that church smell, infused into the walls from hundreds of years of burning incense. She plasters on a big smile, accepts a glass of fizz from a young waiter and steps into the crowd. Another woman is hovering on the periphery too, looking around awkwardly.

'Intimidating, isn't it?' Lydia says. 'I can't see anyone I know.'

'A bit. I don't think any of my colleagues are here yet. I knew we should have met up beforehand.'

'Oh well, we can keep each other company till someone shows up,' Lydia says. 'That way we won't look like a pair of saddos.'

Her companion's name turns out to be Sara. She works in the marketing department of one of the bigger publishing houses, and has headed up the campaign for a couple of the nominated books. Lydia hates saying what she does, the dry factual company she works for. 'I'm an illustrator too, though,' she adds. She elaborates a bit on the book she's working on, failing to add that the work is purely speculative.

'I'm working towards giving up my job completely,' she says, which isn't entirely untrue. She just omits to say that she's made zero progress so far.

There's a tap on the microphone. She turns towards the stage as everyone gradually falls silent. A children's TV presenter – mostly famous for having a mouthy alligator puppet as a sidekick – is standing in the pulpit.

'Good evening, everybody . . .'

As he drones on, making lame book-related puns, she looks round the room. People are standing in groups, clustered around the nominees, most of whom she recognizes. She likes to keep an eye on the competition. She scans the groups, looking for Georgia. It strikes her that she has no idea what Georgia will be wearing. They have always planned for big events together. She had even been involved in every tiny decision about Georgia's wedding dress. Pale grey, not white, to complement her dark hair. Sleek and fitted, the opposite of a meringue. Cap sleeves to show off her toned arms. Lydia had steered her towards an antique lace overlay on the bodice, tapered down to a V where the skirt flared out – just a little – from the hips. They had scoured websites for hair inspiration together and, in the end, Lydia had suggested she just leave it long, maybe weave in a few tiny jewels. She had cried when she watched Georgia walk down the aisle (they had necked down a glass of champagne each in the hotel room just before the cars arrived, and then Georgia had manically brushed her teeth to get rid of the sickly-sweet odour). Georgia had looked radiant. Of course this was long before Lydia fell for

Nick so her feelings on the day had been of unequivocal joy for her friend. And, if she was being honest, it had been a huge relief that she liked the man Georgia was marrying. She had lost a few friends to relationships with bores or idiots over the years but the loss of Georgia would have been too much to bear. She can't think about that now.

And then in the sea of faces she suddenly sees her. She had read somewhere once that the feeling someone was looking at you was innate. A defence mechanism that enabled you to outwit predators. Give yourself time to get away. When she locates Georgia, Georgia is looking right at her. It must have been her gaze that subconsciously drew Lydia's eyes. There's a split second where they both just stare. And then Lydia gives a nervous little half-wave. She sees Georgia turn away, whisper something to Nick. His head swivels in her direction. Next to him Anne Marie and Harry gawp round. She's hurt momentarily that Georgia has invited them as her guests although interested to see that their relationship has survived Anne Marie's dalliance. She's pleased for them. She's only met them a couple of times but they seem like nice people. A bit pleased with themselves maybe, as Georgia's mum Irene might have said. That was one of her favourite put-downs. Anne Marie is a music teacher and he's something in web design. Too many kids, all with jazz-musician-inspired names. She hates themed names for kids. Like they're all part of a music-hall act. The Singing Siblings. When she was young Lydia had spent a disproportionate amount of time deciding on the names she would give her future children. She kept a list in an old diary that had been ever-changing as her tastes matured. The last entries just before she realized it was never going to happen, that there was only one man she wanted to have babies with and he was taken, were Gus and Lulu. She could picture them in her head. Twins (Joe and Edie came from Nick's side of the family. He had twin uncles, he had told her once). Nick's height and green eyes. Her bone structure. Beautiful over-achievers with her artistic streak and Nick's kindness and humour (of course Joe and Edie had both those qualities of Nick's and Georgia's own artistic streak but looks-wise she and Georgia brought very different things to the table). Gus gentle and thoughtful; Lulu feisty, taking on the world. It saddens her that she isn't a mother. That she has failed to make her tiny family any larger. But she never met a man she thought was good enough to be the father. She had frozen her eggs a few years ago, when she was worried time was running out, and had told herself that if all else failed she would give herself till forty-five (the oldest she could imagine dealing with a baby and not going completely insane, hormones permitting) and, if no suitable candidate had popped up by then, she would beg a friend, pay someone, anything. The fact that she has now accepted her motherless state speaks more about her dedication to Nick than anything. As soon as she realized how she felt about him she knew there was no point having another man's child. She has given up so much for him. She doesn't blame him. He'd had no idea, after all. But now he did and he'd rejected her.

Georgia is looking stunning. Bright orange dress, glowing bronze skin, hair cascading down her back. She carries her height so well – not like when Lydia had first met her, hunched in an oversized jumper in the college canteen, as if she were trying to blend in with the walls. Hair over her face like a curtain. Lydia had been looking around for a friend to sit with, but seeing no one and spotting a spare seat opposite a girl she recognized from class she had sat down and introduced herself. She'd expected Georgia to be shy but it had turned out she wasn't, just awkward in her skin. They'd bonded over making fun of one of their lecturers, who punctuated every other sentence with a mention of a book he had illustrated. Georgia had looked it up, it turned out, and discovered that it had been published some twenty years earlier and garnered neither attention nor sales. 'When you're an established talent,' he would say before rattling off a self-aggrandizing anecdote about his own career. 'He's been living off that one failed book since the seventies,' Georgia had said, laughing. 'How sad is that?'

Lydia had been a ball of ambition. She'd had a five-year plan for when uni was over. Work for a publisher, get a foot in the door, draw in the evenings, be right under their nose when they were looking for the next big thing. She had achieved the first three but number four was still eluding her decades later. Georgia had had a much more laid-back approach. She just wanted to draw. If she could make it her living somehow, then great. If not, then so long as she still had time to do what she loved, that would be fine too. Lydia had wanted the destination. Georgia would have been happy just to be on the journey. And look how things had turned out.

After that lunch they had become inseparable. BFFs. And Georgia had blossomed, lost her self-consciousness, started to stand up straight. All with Lydia's encouragement. Unfurling like a sunflower reaching for the light.

The TV personality is still burbling on. The room is getting a bit restless. In half an hour or so three-quarters of these people are going to be disappointed. Losers. Their chance gone for another year. They don't want jokes; they just want to know the results. She sees Nick place his hand in the small of Georgia's back. He's looking good; she's noticed a couple of other women give him a second glance already (publishing is not an industry that's awash with handsome men, to be fair, or many men at all, for that matter). She feels a lump in her throat, seeing him be so attentive.

But if there's one thing she's realized since Georgia cut her off, it's that their friendship is the thing she can't do without. Her fantasies of a life with Nick always had the caveat that Lydia and Georgia somehow survived it intact. She'd rather have Georgia and not Nick than the other way round.

Lydia smiles at Sara and edges away through the crowd. She isn't going to confront Georgia now; she'll wait till the awards are over. But she doesn't want to lose sight of her either. She doesn't want Georgia to leave without speaking to her.

Finally the first category is announced. The crowd hushes. There are cheers, an interminable speech by a nervous writer. Lydia looks around for another drink. Waves to a waitress. She sees Anne Marie scowl at her as she notices how much closer she's come. The second category comes and goes. This time a national treasure takes to the stage to rapturous applause. He holds up his trophy – a row of golden books – and thanks everyone he's ever met. And their mothers. Pontificates on about his own brilliance, managing to make every thank you some kind of barely disguised boast.

This is interminable. She's starting to lose her nerve. Georgia is steadfastly looking at the stage, at Nick, at the bar. Anywhere but at her. But the rigid set of her shoulders says that she is all too aware of Lydia's proximity. Lydia feels bad. She hasn't come here to ruin her evening. All she wants is the chance to speak to her, to apologize. To make it clear she temporarily lost her mind but that things could go back to the way they were. If only Nick hadn't betrayed her. Fucking Nick. She has tried every way she could but Georgia has shut down every attempt. She never answered her phone, ignored texts, closed her social media – even Patricia has disappeared into thin air, for God's sake. Lydia knows that Georgia had been there when she'd called round to the house in Primrose Hill. Even if the dog hadn't given it away, she would have been able to tell. And now, short of camping on the doorstep waiting for her to arrive or leave, she doesn't know what else to do. She has to say her piece. Convince Georgia that she did what she did from a good place. That she really did believe Nick was having an affair for some reason. That she'd had no idea Patricia was actually Georgia. That the idea she'd been making a play for Nick was ludicrous. She'll tell whatever lies she has to. Whatever it takes. Georgia is her family. The only one she has.

She drifts back a little. Still within sight but not so intimidatingly close.

The TV personality has got the alligator out now, one hand up its back end making it gurn. There are four more categories to go, according to the programme. And Georgia's is next.

'And here . . .' he says, alligator looking up at him, big-eyed,

'. . . are the nominations for "Best Illustrated Book for Age Six and Under" . . .'

Pause for dramatic effect.

'. . . Sian Hepburn for *Why? Said the Pig*, Georgia Shepherd for *Wilbur's Christmas*, Jan and Peter Seymore for *Ferdinand the Flea Joins the Circus* and Ian Tranter for *Digby the Digger*.'

There's a small round of applause after each name. Lydia feels her heart in her throat. She can't bear it. Much as she wants things to be back to normal with Georgia, for them to be friends again, the idea of her winning is too painful. Is there any dream of Lydia's that Georgia is not going to achieve first? Is the seesaw always going to be so loaded on one side?

'And the winner is . . .'

Even longer pause for even more ominous dramatic effect. Lydia holds her breath.

The presenter and the alligator wrestle with the envelope for comic effect. There are weak titters. She has to restrain herself from shouting 'Get on with it!' and she's pretty sure she's not the only one.

'. . . Georgia Shepherd for *Wilbur's Christmas*.'

Lydia's heart shrivels. She actually thinks she can feel it contract. A group of people nearby cheer and whoop. They must be from Phoenix, Georgia's 'team'. Nick swoops Georgia up in a hug and lifts her off the floor. Harry and Anne Marie jump up and down. Georgia herself just looks shell-shocked. Stunned. Lydia fakes happiness with as much enthusiasm as she can muster.

Which isn't much.

Chapter 46

My first reaction is that I've misheard. That, for some reason, they're reading out the list of nominees again but in a different order. Then I hear Anne Marie shriek and Nick whirls me round. Bibi and Kate scream. As it sinks in, my first thought is maybe Bibi will stop trying to make me reinvent Wilbur now. And then I think, Fucking hell, I've actually won!

I've barely been concentrating on what's been going on. The sight of Lydia unsettled me to say the least. There's no way she's come for any legitimate reason. She's here because she knew she'd see me. Or Nick. Nick, Anne Marie and Harry stand round me like a human shield. I was so looking forward to this evening and now all I want to do is to go home. Except that I seem to have won.

'The judges felt Wilbur has an instant appeal to a young audience, Georgia's illustrations perfectly convey his character and the book is a useful tool for widening vocabulary and inviting discussion,' Bobbi the host reads from a card that his alligator puppet is holding in its mouth. I have a sudden sad thought about how much Lydia and I would have laughed about that later. The desperation.

I somehow find myself on the stage. A couple of people snap pictures. In the sea of faces I pick out Nick; Anne Marie and Harry; Bibi and Kate, along with the rest of the Phoenix gang; Jan and Peter, sour-faced; Lydia. I know I need to be

320

quick – Don't be one of those arseholes that drones on about herself, the voice in my head says. Everyone's just waiting for the next category. For the awards to be over and the celebrating and commiserating to begin.

I clear my throat. 'Wow,' I say. 'I was so convinced I wouldn't win that I didn't write anything down and now I can't remember my own name, let alone anyone I need to thank . . .' There's a ripple of laughter and I relax. 'I feel like a bit of a fraud. All the other nominated books are beautiful. Works of art. Wilbur is . . . well, he's Wilbur . . .'

'We love Wilbur,' someone, a girl I recognize from Phoenix – Marketing, I think – shouts. I'd already noticed she was looking a bit tipsy. Several other people cheer.

'Thanks. I love him too.' I realize as I say it that I do. He might be simplistic but he has character. He's alive. He's just not necessarily what I want to spend the rest of my life drawing. 'I mean, I wish he'd get help for his shopping addiction but otherwise . . .' More laughs. I rattle through some thank yous while I have their attention. Everyone I can think of at Phoenix. My agents. I've never been a fan of those people who credit God and their children at awards ceremonies but then I see Nick standing there, beaming with pride, and I can't help myself. 'I want to thank my husband, Nick. Not because I think he deserves any credit for my work' – yet more titters – 'but for putting up with me. We've been through some . . . stuff . . . lately and it can't have been easy, but he's my rock. I don't know what I'd do without him.'

I turn and look straight at Lydia then, give a huge 'look how happy I am' smile. Fuck her.

* * *

Afterwards I am whisked off for a photo clutching my stack of gold books, my award. It's surprisingly heavy. My name is engraved on one of the spines, the title of the book and the category and year on the others. I'm trying to enjoy the moment but I'm distracted wondering what's going on in the other room. We should, I decide, cut our losses and leave. Go and celebrate somewhere else, the four of us.

I get back out there as soon as I'm able. My little group is intact. Unassailed. The three of them look as happy as if they'd just won something themselves. I can't see where Lydia is. But then, just as I'm about to rejoin them, she steps out in front of me.

'George! Congratulations!'

I have nowhere to go. Plus we're in public and surrounded by my peers so I have to be polite. 'Hi, Lydia,' I say through gritted teeth. 'I wasn't expecting to see you here.'

Someone walks past and pats me on the back. 'Congratulations.'

'Thanks,' I say, without even looking to see who it is.

'I managed to blag a ticket. You know, because I'd bought the dress and everything when I thought—'

'Great,' I interrupt. 'Well, I should go and join the others . . .'

She reaches out and puts a hand on my arm. Perfect deep blue nails. Gels. I know where she will have gone to get them done. I know the name of her favourite technician. I know everything about her.

'I want to talk to you. Please . . .'

'Fucking hell, not now.'

'When then? You don't answer the phone. I know you were in when I came round the other day . . .'

'We really don't have anything left to talk about.'

Her eyes fill with tears. 'Please, Georgia.' But, of course, I've seen this party piece before.

'I'm going. You shouldn't have come.'

'Please, George. Please. I know you think I've done something awful, but I haven't. I can explain everything. You know I'd never set out to hurt you . . .'

I turn to walk away but just as I do Bibi appears out of the crowd.

'Georgia, darling!' She grabs me up in a hug. Now I'm an award-winner she loves me suddenly. 'I knew you'd win!'

I have to stop myself saying, 'But isn't Wilbur the Boomer of the children's book world? Doesn't he need to be dragged kicking and screaming into the 2020s?' It's nice that she's so pleased for me, even if it's only because she thinks she's somehow responsible. 'I didn't,' I say, just as Bibi sticks out a hand to Lydia.

'Hi. I'm Bibi Welbeck, Georgia's editor. Isn't it fantastic?' Behind her the alligator is ripping open another envelope.

'Lydia Somers.' Lydia shakes her hand with a professional smile.

'Lydia Somers!' Bibi says, eyes wide.

Shit. No. This can't be happening.

Chapter 47

'Lydia of the wonderful trolls?' Bibi gushes. Lydia looks at her, confused. Fuck. I want to walk away but I can't just leave them to it. I have to derail this train somehow.

'What happens after the awards?' I say slightly desperately. 'Is there a party?'

Someone in the crowd shushes me. Bibi is not to be put off. 'I'm not going to lie, I was gutted when I heard you were going to self-publish. They're pretty special.'

Lydia looks between me and her. I look away. I have no idea what to say to end this. 'You've seen my work?'

The author on the stage wraps up his speech. I need to get out of here but I can't leave Bibi and Lydia talking. 'Bibi, shall we go somewhere and celebrate? Everyone from Phoenix, I mean . . .'

'Yes, let's,' she says and I breathe again. She turns back to Lydia. 'I told Georgia I really thought we could have made something of them. So marketable. But, good for you. Self-publishing can work if you've got a large social media presence. Of course you don't have the marketing or distribution back-up that you'd get going the traditional route . . .'

I practically take her arm to drag her away. We need to leave. Go somewhere else. Somewhere Lydia is not. I reckon I have seconds to pull that off.

'I'm a bit . . .' Lydia says. 'Maybe you've mixed me up with someone else. I mean, I do draw trolls . . .'

I look over at Nick, Harry and Anne Marie as if they might save me. They're laughing at something. They haven't noticed that I'm right here, juggling with an unexploded grenade.

'Lydia Somers? The book with the faeries and trolls? The black and white ink illustrations?'

'Yes,' Lydia says with a question in her voice. 'That's me. But . . .'

I am fucked.

'Georgia gave it to me. I thought she told you.'

They both look at me. The only thing I can think to do is fake a heart attack but I'm not sure I could pull it off. Out of the corner of my eye I see that Anne Marie has noticed me. Noticed Lydia. I raise my eyebrows at her. Help me.

'Um. No . . . Did you?' Lydia fixes her stare on me. Behind her Bobbi the host is wrapping up. Telling us all to go and enjoy ourselves.

'Ages ago,' I mutter. 'I really should get back to my friends. Are you coming, Bibi?'

'So,' Bibi says, not allowing me to steer her away. 'How are you getting on with the self-publishing? I know it can be a minefield.'

'I'm not . . . Did Georgia tell you I was self-publishing?' Lydia asks as the penny finally drops.

'I was very disappointed, I can tell you. It's not often a book really grabs me like that. Seven-, eight-year-olds, I thought?'

'You really liked it?' Lydia says.

'Loved it. I'm actively looking for something for that age group now. But edgy, you know . . .'

'*Game of Gnomes*,' Lydia says.

'Ha!' Bibi shrieks. '*Game of Gnomes*! Perfect. Is that what you're calling it?'

'Yes. I mean . . . I'm not sure why Georgia gave you the impression I was self-publishing—'

'I thought you said that . . .' I butt in.

She flares her nostrils at me. 'I think you know I didn't.'

'You're not?' Bibi says. I don't know how to stop where this is going. I notice Anne Marie weaving through the crowd of people, Harry and Nick following. The cavalry.

'No,' Lydia says. 'I'm looking for a publisher, actually.'

'Congratulations!' Anne Marie says loudly, getting between Lydia and me. I don't know how to communicate with her that it's actually Bibi she needs to keep Lyds away from. 'Oh, hello, Lydia, I didn't know you were coming.'

'This is Bibi, my editor,' I say. If I can just keep Bibi talking to someone other than Lydia until I can get her away. 'Anne Marie, Harry, Nick, my husband . . .' They all say polite hellos. Lydia shows no sign of moving on. I see her look at Nick. He looks away. 'I was just saying to Bibi we should go on somewhere and celebrate with all the people from Phoenix.' I raise my eyebrows at the others for them to pick up the baton on this.

'Great idea,' Anne Marie says. 'We should go now. Otherwise everyone'll be leaving at once and there'll be no taxis.'

'I'll get the coats,' Nick offers. I imagine he's a bit confused about why I'd want to go anywhere with Bibi but he knows me well enough to understand I must have my reasons. He grabs all our tickets.

'Shall we gather up all the others?' I say to Bibi. She's looking a bit bemused by the urgency.

'Sure,' she says. 'We'll meet you at the front door. Nice to meet you, Lydia.'

I breathe a sigh of relief. But then Bibi roots around in her miniature gold bag and hands Lydia a card. 'I'd love for you to call me.'

'I definitely will,' she says. 'It's lovely to meet you.'

'Right,' Anne Marie says decisively once she's gone. 'Let's go. Bye, Lydia.'

Lydia ignores her. Fixes her stare on me. 'What the fuck was that all about?'

I shrug. 'She must have got her wires crossed.'

'You told her I wasn't interested in talking to her because I was going to self-publish?'

'Of course I didn't,' I say. But Lydia has always been able to tell when I'm lying.

'You tried to sabotage my shot at a publishing deal? When you know that's been my dream all my life?'

'Steady on,' Harry says. 'I don't think Georgia would ever—'

'Oh, shut up, Harry. You know nothing about this.'

He stands there open-mouthed, not used to such rudeness.

'Of course I didn't. She would never even have seen your book if it wasn't for me.'

'My book that she loves,' Lydia spits.

Nick appears with a heap of coats. 'Come on, they're all waiting for you.' Neither Lydia nor I look at him. We're locked in our battle, swords drawn. I don't want her to cause a scene here of all places but I also have to stand my ground.

'Well, that's good then, isn't it?' I say. 'You've managed to ingratiate yourself with my editor.' I don't know why I say that last bit. I should just leave it. She's right, after all: I did try to sabotage her. But she deserved it. And it was self-preservation as much as anything else.

'Managed to ingratiate myself with her? You heard her. *She* approached *me*. She loves my work. Are you jealous? Weren't you worried that she didn't really rate you? That she thought Wilbur was outdated and simplistic? A bit Middle England, isn't that what you told me?'

'OK, that's enough.' Anne Marie takes her arm. Lydia shakes her off. People are starting to listen in. Pausing their conversations to better hear what's going on.

'Let's just go,' I say.

'Are you worried she's found something she can be much more passionate about? Wait . . . are you worried she thinks I'm more talented than you are? You couldn't bear that, could you? For me to become the successful one. That's not how it's supposed to be, is it? Not in your world.'

'Lydia, that's enough,' Anne Marie says in the voice I imagine she uses for her year sevens. 'This isn't the time or the place—'

'Sorry, is this anything to do with you?' Lydia spits.

'Stop being such a bitch,' Anne Marie says. I turn away. There's no point in allowing this to escalate. And the truth is that what Lydia said stings. I am worried about exactly those things.

'That's good coming from you,' I hear Lydia say. I turn back. Harry puffs up like an angry cat.

'OK, that's enough,' he says. 'Leave Anne Marie out of this.'

'Aah, how gallant, coming to her rescue. I hope she appreciates it.'

'You're pathetic,' Anne Marie says. 'Trying to ruin Georgia's big night like this.'

'Come on, let's go. I don't know what you were hoping for coming here tonight, Lydia, but if it was for us to forget everything and move on then I wouldn't say it's been a great success,' I say. I put my hand on Anne Marie's back.

'I might have come away with a book deal, though, so I'd say it was worth it.'

'Someone giving you their card and saying they like your work is hardly the same as them offering you a contract.' Anne Marie is refusing to budge. My lanky Rottweiler. 'I bet she's given twenty people her card tonight.'

'Sorry, I'm going to ask again . . . what exactly does any of this have to do with you?' Lydia snaps.

'They really are all waiting,' Nick says to no one in particular. There's actually a small crowd gathered round us now, all pretending they're not listening, but you could hear a pin drop.

'I'm being a good friend,' Anne Marie says. 'But I guess you wouldn't know about loyalty . . .'

'Oh, and you do? That's rich.'

An alarm bell rings in my head. Suddenly I know what she's about to say and I'm powerless to stop it.

'We really are leaving now,' I say, yanking Anne Marie's top.

But it's too late.

Chapter 48

It's as if it happens in slow motion.

Anne Marie is actually turning to go, Harry and Nick along with her. We're so close to it being over. A little uncomfortable; a few curious looks from my peers. Nothing I can't get over. I didn't embarrass myself. Lydia is the one who looks like the crazed, bitter troublemaker. I'll almost certainly be the object of sympathy in the story. *Did you see poor Georgia Shepherd having to deal with that madwoman?* I can live with that.

But then the words come out. Not aimed at me, the cause of her anger, but at the friend who dared defend me. You couldn't get a lower blow.

'I wonder how loyal Harry thinks you are. Or doesn't he know about that bloke Georgia saw you with? In the school playground, wasn't it? Bit tacky.'

Everything stops. It's like a game of statues, the world frozen. I hear someone across the room laughing loudly at a joke, oblivious to the carnage going on in our corner.

Anne Marie's face gives her away. She looks at me, betrayed. Out of the corner of my eye I see Harry, head whipping round from her to me. Confusion. Fuck. I need to step in and try to defuse the situation. 'For God's sake, Lydia. You really must be desperate to start making things up. Leave Anne Marie out of it though. She hasn't done anything to you.'

She sneers at me. 'What was it you said? You were so embarrassed you had to get out of there? You said they were basically rubbing up against each other like a pair of randy cats.'

'Lydia—'

'And where was it you said the actual deed happened? Oh yes, the fake conference. Pretending to dedicate themselves to the welfare of young people while actually holed up in a Premier Inn screwing each other senseless. Nice.'

'Don't listen to her, Harry,' I say, trying to play it down. 'She'd basically say anything at this point.'

But Harry is only looking at Anne Marie.

Chapter 49

She didn't mean to say it. It wasn't Anne Marie she was angry with after all, although Anne Marie had inserted herself into something that was none of her business and so couldn't really complain when it rebounded in her face. Lydia could remember Irene once telling her not to fight anyone else's battles. 'Life's hard enough, love,' she'd said. 'And in the end no one'll thank you anyway.' But when she found out what Georgia had done – that Bibi had liked her work enough to ask to be put in touch only to be told she wasn't interested – well, all bets were off. Lydia had been waiting for that validation all her adult life and her best friend, the one with the career and the success and the whole fucking fairy tale, had almost stolen it from her. No, she actually had. But she'd been caught. So of course Lydia had lashed out. Just at the wrong person.

And the truth is she likes Anne Marie. Harry is as dull as dishwater. Nice but wet. Probably a great dad and a kind husband. But, other than that, just a bog-standard bloke. Nothing to make him stand out from the crowd. When Georgia had told her about Anne Marie, it had made sense. Who wouldn't want a little excitement on the side when surrounded by all that sensible reliability?

'Remember she told me Nick was having an affair,' Georgia says now, still trying to get Harry's attention. 'It's what she does when she feels like she's losing.'

She's about to retort when Bibi appears, coat on. Whatever happens, Lydia doesn't want to show herself up in front of her new contact. She keeps quiet.

'Are we going?' Bibi says, sounding a little irritated. 'Only Kate's holding a couple of cabs outside.'

Georgia grabs her coat from Nick. 'We are.' The rest of the group just look sideswiped. Unable to move.

'Are you coming, Lydia?' Bibi says and Lydia almost laughs. She has to stop herself from saying 'Yes, I'd love to' just to see Georgia's face.

'No, I should get going. I have to work first thing.'

'Well, give me a call,' Bibi says. 'Tomorrow maybe? I'll be the only one in the office without a hangover. Or maybe just the only one in the office.'

'Definitely,' Lydia says, smiling sweetly. 'Night, everyone. Have fun. Oh, and congratulations again, Georgia.'

None of them say goodbye as they leave.

By the time Lydia gets home – after two more glasses of champagne – she's feeling deflated. This isn't how the evening was supposed to have gone. She had wanted to repair their friendship, not fall out even more and drag Anne Marie under the bus with her. But she knows now that it is beyond repair. What Georgia has done to her can never be forgiven. Fuck her. It's Lydia's time.

She can't think about Anne Marie. Or Harry. His look, like a puppy who has just been kicked by an owner it worships. They're collateral damage.

Chapter 50

Anne Marie won't look at me. She and Harry trail behind as we leave, her staring at the ground, him giving her anxious sideways glances. Nick clutches on to my hand as if I need holding up, which I probably do. I have no desire to do anything other than go home, get into bed and hide. I definitely do not want to go on to a bar with Bibi and Co, even though I was the one who suggested it.

I have to stop every few metres when someone congratulates me. One woman asks for a selfie with me to show her little girl, which ordinarily would have blown my mind. This has never happened before. Ever. I paste on a smile – more of a grimace, to be fair. My little fan will probably be put off for life.

When I catch up with the others Harry and Anne Marie are already heading off up the road. I look at Nick quizzically and he shrugs. Harry turns back. 'We're . . . sorry . . . See you soon. Thanks for a lovely evening.'

'Bye,' I say, waving a limp hand. Anne Marie just keeps walking.

'What the fuck is going on?' Nick hisses. 'She's been cheating on him?' Bibi, Kate and the others are clambering into one of the two waiting taxis.

'I'll tell you in a minute. Can we just go home?' I look at him pleadingly.

'We can't now, can we? It'll look rude.'

'I can't . . . I'll tell them I'm not well. Hold that other cab, will you?'

I walk over just as Bibi shouts, 'See you at the Hospital Club, guys! Endell Street. I'll leave your names at reception,' and slams the door. They pull off before I can reply. I stand there, deflated, award in hand.

'Fuck. What do we do now?' I say to Nick. I can't go and pretend to have fun. All I can think about is Anne Marie.

'Follow them, I guess.'

'I can't face it. Shit.'

He puts his arms round me. In the cab the driver is getting restless, tapping his hand on the outside of the door. It starts to drizzle. 'Are you coming or what?' Nick waves a hand, hold on.

'This is meant to be your big night,' he says into my hair. 'You're an award-winner.'

'I've ruined everything,' I say quietly.

I tell him what I know about Anne Marie and Jez on the way back to Primrose Hill. I've sent Bibi a text – *Really sorry. Not feeling good. Too much champagne and excitement! See you soon. Thank you so much for everything! x* – and then turned my phone off. There are more important things.

'Fuck,' he says. 'Poor Harry.'

'It was just once,' I say as if that's going to make the blow any softer. 'I mean . . . it's still awful but, you know . . . she wasn't thinking straight. She ended it.'

'And Harry had no idea?'

I shake my head, tears welling up. 'No. She knew it would

devastate him, and it was never going to happen again, so . . .'

'Why the hell did you tell Lydia? I mean, sorry, I'm not having a go but . . .'

'I don't . . . It's complicated. Obviously I never thought she'd say anything. She barely even knows them.'

He rubs his face with both hands. 'Anne Marie? I just can't . . .'

'I know. But you have to believe me that it was a moment of madness. Don't judge her.'

He sighs. 'I'm not.'

'Oh God, poor Harry,' I say as the cab pulls into our road.

'This is Lydia's fault, not yours.'

'I know. Shall I send Anne Marie a text? Fuck, she must hate me.' It strikes me that I might have gone from having two best friends to none in the space of a few days. I can't bear the thought of losing her. But more, I can't bear the thought of her losing Harry.

'Now's maybe not the best time.' He squeezes my hand. 'I'd leave it till the morning.'

I bite back tears. 'Oh God, Nick, what have I done?'

I don't know how to say what I need to say in a text, and I don't want to give Anne Marie the chance to cut me dead, so at lunchtime the next day I'm hovering outside the school reception, trying to get up the courage to go in. I know my way around from when the twins went here – both of them left to do A levels at college though so it's been a couple of years, but nothing has changed. Neither of them took music, thankfully; Anne Marie didn't have to teach them. They probably would have been scarred for life by one of their teachers getting mildly drunk in their living room on a regular basis. I keep my head down and try not to draw attention to myself. There's little security, which suddenly strikes me as a dangerous oversight. We all send our kids off every day to be taught by a bunch of strangers in a building where literally anyone could walk in and do anything.

I head for the canteen first, jostled along by a tidal wave of hungry teenagers. I can't just walk in but, luckily, it has windows on three sides and, even though it's crowded, it's easy enough to see she's not there. I'm loath to try the staff room. Someone is bound to question my reasons for being there. I decide to check out the music room first.

Unlike some teachers, whose form room changes every year, Anne Marie has been in residence in the same space since she joined the school five years ago. I imagine the two pianos were the clincher. Over time it's become like an extension of her home. Instruments of all sizes and shapes stacked up in heaps. Glass jars of plectrums and clarinet reeds. Lamps with vibrant scarves draped over them ('Do they know how much of a fire hazard you are?' I asked her the first time she showed me round). Misshapen pottery animals that Nina has made. A still life by Billie. A photo of Gino in fancy dress as Albert Einstein. It's cosy and warm and, for a lot of the kids who don't have much to go home to every night, an oasis of comforting calm, I imagine.

As I approach the door I can hear someone playing the piano. Something haunting and beautiful. Anne Marie sometimes gives free lessons to gifted kids who couldn't afford to have them any other way. It's one of the reasons she's still here. While the vast majority might be indifferent to, even dismissive of, her importance, a vocal few fight to keep her with a passion so intense it's hard to ignore.

All I can do is wait. I sit on a plastic chair in the corridor. At least she's at work. That's something. Eventually the piano stops, halfway through a piece. I strain to hear voices. It's difficult against the noise of children shouting and playing outside. I get up and lean in towards the door. Nothing. Silence. For the briefest second I panic that Jez is in there with her and they're having a lunch-break quickie. But I know there's no way that's true. It's just Anne Marie on her own, losing herself in her piano-playing instead of eating lunch.

I tap on the door, heart pounding.

'Yes,' she calls. But faintly. Uncertainly.

I steel myself and go in. She's sitting on the piano stool, hands on her knees, looking up expectantly. When she sees it's me the shutters go down.

'What are you doing here?'

She looks terrible. Dark shadows under her eyes as if she's been up all night crying. Her always pale face is grey-white.

'I'm so sorry,' I say. I've planned my speech but I can't remember a word of it. 'I should never have told her—'

She interrupts me. 'I thought we were friends. I trusted you. And you treated what I told you like a piece of gossip?'

'No. It wasn't like that.'

'You knew how much I regretted it. How fucking . . . shit . . . I felt.' Tears are suddenly pouring down her cheeks. It seems so wrong. My strong, capable friend.

'I'm so sorry,' I say again. I don't know what else there is to say. I go over and wrap my arms around her and she lets me for a second before pushing me away roughly.

'I'm at work. You shouldn't have come here.'

'How's Harry dealing with it?'

She looks up. 'How do you think?'

'I think Nick was going to call him . . .'

'And say what? That it never happened? Because it did. And there's nothing I can do to change that.'

'He'll come round,' I say, not at all sure I believe it.

'Like you did when you thought Nick had strayed?' she snaps. 'And that wasn't even true.'

'He loves you,' I say.

'He loved who he thought I was. But he doesn't think I'm that person any more. Thanks to you. You know I never would have done anything like that again? For as long as I lived? I hated myself. I could barely look in the mirror.'

'I know . . .' I say quietly.

'But I decided that if I told him I would be doing it because I couldn't live with the guilt, not because it would be better for him. Because it wouldn't be. It would ruin his life. And now it has.'

'I never thought she'd say anything. Never . . .'

'Forget it. If I'd never done it in the first place there wouldn't have been any gossip to tell. It's all my own fault – I know that.' She doesn't say this as if she's absolving me. More as if she wants to punish herself.

'Anne Marie . . .'

She stands up. I know it's impossible in less than twenty-four hours but she looks thinner, frailer. All the vibrant life that made her who she was has drained away.

'Please go now. I have to get ready for my next lesson.'

'Please talk to me,' I say desperately.

'I need you to go,' she says and I know that the conversation is over.

I walk home and get Igor, take him straight out for a walk to the top of the hill. I need to clear my head. The brief euphoria of last night is completely gone. I have nothing to celebrate. I'm furious with Lydia. She knew what she was doing, however cornered she might have felt. She knew that what she was saying would change Anne Marie's – and Harry's – lives forever. But she still decided to counter a slap with an atomic bomb. She pressed the big red button.

The truth is, though, that if I'd never shared what I knew with her in the first place, she would have been unarmed.

And that's on me.

Chapter 51

Nothing can shake my mood. My phone is buzzing with messages congratulating me on my win. Flowers and champagne arrive from Antoinette and more from Phoenix. Last night we WhatsApped the kids and my mum to tell them the news, me holding up the trophy, gurning. I forced myself to look happy in the photos. It should have come naturally. I'd won an award. It's a massive validation for me, and for Wilbur. And a giant middle finger up to Lydia which, I'm not ashamed to say, gives me satisfaction. But I couldn't feel it. I felt hollow.

There was even a tiny mention in one of the papers today. Just a list of the winners. I take a screen grab and send it to my mum. *That's a first!* she sends back. *One of us in the paper for something to be proud of!* She adds a smiley face to let me know she's joking. I assume it's Frank's shady past she's referring to. I don't ask.

As I'm dragging Igor up the hill again to try to clear my head Nick sends me a text. *Harry coming over later, hope that's OK.*

It's the last thing I want. Poor devastated Harry.

Of course, I send back. How can I say no? I divert up Regent's Park Road to buy some food, assuming he might stay for dinner. The idea of Harry being so unhappy he's off his meals doesn't bear thinking about. I buy fresh tortellini

341

and pesto and fragrant baguettes. A chunky block of aged Parmesan. Two expensive bottles of Chianti Classico. It's ridiculous, I know. I imagine the last thing on his mind at the moment will be the quality of the wine or the maturity of the cheese but, like when your kid has been bullied at school and you comfort them with usually forbidden junk food, I want to make him feel better in the only way I can think of. I keep my eye on Igor tied up outside. Nick and I have a rule that he's never left alone in public. Too many stories of dognappers stealing pets to sell on Gumtree, and fighting gangs looking for bait. But this constitutes an emergency. I put him where I can see him from all the corners of the shop and stick my head out of the door every few seconds to reassure him. He seems to be making a new friend every time, basically offering himself up to would-be thieves. Look at me! I've been abandoned! I'm wasting away here! I'm pretty sure the assistant behind the counter – new since I was here last – thinks I'm a would-be shoplifter trying to build up the courage to make a run for it. I try a smile on her. 'I hate leaving him outside.' She blanks me.

When we get home, thankfully unscathed, I tidy up a bit and then put clean sheets on Joe's bed in case Harry decides to stay the night. At about twenty past six I get another text from Nick – *Running a bit late. Sorry! Won't be long xx* – and then the doorbell rings. Shit. I really wanted to avoid being on my own with him. I'm scared he's going to press me for details and I have no idea what Anne Marie has told him.

Like Anne Marie, Harry seems as if he's shrunk. His coat suddenly two sizes too big. He looks, well, shattered. Devastated. Broken. I give him a hug. To my absolute horror he starts crying on my shoulder. Big, heaving sobs. My heart breaks. He's such a good man. No one deserves this less.

'Come and have a drink,' I say, once he's calmer. He nods, red-eyed, follows me down to the kitchen, petting Igor on the way. I try to think what to say. Everything feels trivial under the circumstances. 'How are you?' is the best I can come up with.

'You knew?' he says.

I clear my throat. Nod.

'When?'

'A few weeks ago . . .'

He steadies himself with a hand on the counter. 'So we've seen you since? We've all been together? Making jokes. Having fun. Celebrating Nick's fucking fidelity.'

I pour him a glass of red, my hand shaking. 'I didn't choose to find out, Harry. And then I didn't know what to do. It wasn't my secret to tell.'

'I'm one of your best friends . . .'

'You both are. Me not telling you wasn't me sanctioning what she'd done. It was me not having a clue how to handle it. And it's not as if it was still going on . . .'

'So the idea was I would just never know? Poor dopey old Harry, stupidly thinking his marriage was perfect . . .'

'No. I don't know. I mean, yes, I think she wasn't intending to tell you. Because she regretted it. She hated herself. And she knew it would never ever happen again.'

'I bet if you'd asked her six months ago if she thought it could have happened in the first place she would have said never too.'

I sit at the table. I don't know how to handle this for the

best. I'm out of my depth and terrified of making things worse than they already are. 'What has she said to you?'

'That it was a mistake. A one-off. A midlife crisis. All the clichés.'

'They're clichés for a reason, I suppose.'

He flops down opposite me. 'I thought we were happy . . .'

'You were. You are . . .'

He laughs a fake laugh. 'Yeah, looks like it.'

We sit there not saying anything for a moment, me willing Nick to walk through the door. I have to do something, a distraction, so I jump to my feet. 'I need to make a salad. You'll stay and eat, won't you?'

He shakes his head but says nothing. I get tomatoes and spring onions out of the fridge and lay them on the chopping board. Start slicing them half-heartedly.

'What else did she tell you?'

I stop, knife in hand. 'Nothing. I mean, just that she felt awful. That she wished it had never happened.'

'Why did she even tell you anything? That's what I don't get. Just to unburden herself? Because she thought you'd be impressed?'

Fuck, so she hasn't told him I saw her and Jez together. But Lydia did, didn't she? This is a fucking minefield. 'No. God. I don't know. Maybe because of what I was going through with Nick.'

My mobile starts ringing. I pick it up. Edie. I can't exactly talk to her now, but I can't ignore it either. I wave it at Harry as if to say I have to answer this, and he shrugs.

'Ede. I'm right in the middle of something. Can I call you back in a bit? Are you OK?'

'Yes, of course. And yes. All good. I just wanted to congratulate you!'

For a second I wonder what she means. Last night seems like years ago, so much has happened since. 'Oh, yes. It was the make-up that did it.'

'That's what I assumed. Talk to you later. I want all the goss.'

I'd like nothing more than to settle down for a chat with her now, but I know that's out of the question. 'Great. Bye, love.'

'My kids go to that school,' Harry says as soon as I hang up. 'That fucker teaches Billie.'

Shit. I hadn't thought of that. 'They don't know, do they . . . ?'

'Of course not. But I don't want him anywhere near them.'

'No.'

'And Anne Marie must see him every day . . . Oh God, it doesn't bear thinking about . . .'

I remember how I felt when I thought Nick was sleeping with someone he worked with. How that made it so much worse – the idea that whatever happened they would still be connected in that way. There would be no question of a clean break. I put the knife down and go and sit on the chair next to Harry. Put a hand on his. 'I am so so sorry. I can't even imagine . . .'

He puts his big hand over mine. 'I know. I'm not having a go at you . . . You must have been in an impossible situation. I just want to know the details. I have to, do you understand?'

I do. That was one of the worst parts. Feeling lied to. Stupid. Duped. Knowing that there was no way of dealing with the fallout because you weren't armed with all the facts. The constant attempts by your imagination to fill in the blanks.

'I do.' So I fill him in with everything I know. Yes, I probably underplay the obvious sexual tension that I witnessed between Anne Marie and Jez in the car park, but I give him the hard facts. He nods along, and I realize, thankfully, that I'm not telling him anything Anne Marie hasn't already shared. I'm just confirming that whatever he's heard from her is true.

'Thanks,' he says when I finish. 'I appreciate that.'

'She made a mistake,' I say, just as I finally hear the front door open. Igor jumps up and runs up the stairs. 'There's nothing she can do to take it back now but I know she would if she could. So you just have to decide if you can live with it.'

'It's not that simple though, is it? Not while she still sees him every day . . .'

We're interrupted, thankfully, by Nick, coat half off, appearing at the bottom of the stairs.

'Haz,' he says, chucking his outerwear on a chair and throwing his arms round his friend.

'Did you know too?' Harry says into his armpit. Nick shakes his head emphatically.

'No. Not a clue.'

'I'm just going to . . .' I say, indicating the stairs. I want to leave them alone for a bit. Get away from Harry's ravaged face. In the living room I send Anne Marie a text. *Harry's here. Just in case you're wondering where he is x.* Then I sit on the sofa, head in my hands.

Chapter 52

Of course she calls Bibi first thing. She can hardly make herself wait until nine thirty when she hopes the offices might open, only to be met with a recorded message telling her the phones are manned from ten till half six. She's feeling a touch delicate this morning. Not that she had a particularly late night – she didn't. But she did have one glass of wine too many, taking a nightcap to bed because she was worried she would lie awake due to a combination of excitement about Bibi, fury with Georgia and guilt about Anne Marie. In the end she'd slept like a baby.

She distracts herself by checking the illustrations in the final proofs of a book about aneurisms. Luckily Aldwych Press is a small company and still housed in a rickety old terrace house, so she has a tiny office to herself and doesn't have to suffer the indignities of an open-plan space. It's literally the only thing that makes her job bearable. She can shut the door and be doing pretty much anything. At exactly four minutes past ten she calls again. Asks to be put through to Bibi Welbeck.

After a moment she's transferred to an assistant. Kate, she thinks she says her name is. Lydia is so nervous she hardly hears. She waits to be told that Bibi is in a meeting or out for the day or otherwise indisposed but what Kate actually says is 'Oh, Lydia, great. Bibi was hoping you would call. Let me just get her.'

Lydia's heart starts to pound. She gets up and checks that her door is closed; she wouldn't want her colleagues to hear.

'Lydia!' a voice booms through the phone, making her jump. 'Wasn't last night a blast? You should have come to the Hospital with us; it was insane. So, tell me everything. What do I have to do to persuade you to sign with us?'

'Oh,' Lydia says, overwhelmed. She'd thought this would just be a 'Hello, how are you, would you like to come in for a meeting?' kind of conversation. Her head feels fuzzy but she mustn't fuck this up. 'Really?'

'Really. I mean, assuming you're up for it. Who's your agent?'

'I don't have one. I mean, I haven't actually committed . . .'

'You'll need to find one. For your own sake, I mean. Unless you're a lawyer on the side and you can negotiate contracts . . .'

Lydia feels a wave of dizziness. This is actually happening. 'I will. Can I tell them . . . ?'

'That Phoenix are interested? Too right. Meanwhile, do you want to come in and say hello properly? Meet the team? Allow me to persuade you we're the ones for you? At least let us see if we all get along?'

'Yes,' Lydia says, trying to keep the shake out of her voice. 'I'd like that.'

Mind blown, she runs through a list of the agents she deals with. Most of them small fry, happy to accept whatever she's offering for their clients' work. And most of them just deal in illustrators for hire. Not writers of actual books. The backing singers, not the star. She wants to aim higher. She googles

Franklin and Carter, Georgia's representatives. She's met Antoinette a couple of times over the years, just casually. At Georgia's fortieth and once when she and Georgia were having lunch in Charlotte Street. She's not sure if Antoinette would remember but it's an in at least. A way to get past her assistant.

She knows that Georgia would be horrified. Well, tough. You had to make use of any contacts you had these days. She takes a long swig of coffee and dials the number. Someone answers immediately.

'Antoinette Goodison, please.'

'Who's calling?' the plummy-voiced receptionist asks and Lydia almost loses her nerve. She's definitely called Tamara and lives in a flat in Knightsbridge that her parents Hugo and Annabelle pay for. She probably has a brother also called Hugo. Who plays polo. She's almost certainly judging Lydia by the miniscule variant in the poshness of their accents.

'Lydia Somers. I'm a friend of Georgia Shepherd. We've met before.'

'Let me try her.'

She's put on hold with tinny classical music playing in her ear. A few seconds later she hears a click.

'Lydia? It's Antoinette. How are you?'

She can tell from Antoinette's voice that she can't quite place her; she steadies her breath. 'Hi! Good, thank you. Listen, I'm sorry to bother you, but something rather un-expected has happened. I think Phoenix want to offer me a book deal – Bibi Welbeck said I could say that – and I don't have representation . . .'

'Oh,' Antoinette says, sounding interested now. 'Tell me all the details . . .'

Ten minutes later Lydia has an agent and the sniff of a book deal and her life has changed in a million ways in a split second. Not for the first time, of course. But maybe this lightning bolt will help obliterate the memory of that other one, all those years ago. She allows herself to think about her parents for a second. Something she rarely does. She can't imagine how much this would blow their minds. There is no one in her life now who would ever feel such pure pleasure when something good happened to her. You can't underestimate the loss of unconditional love. You can't replace it.

She wants to tell someone her news but there's no one. Susan, of course, but it's way too early in Florida and, besides, she wouldn't really understand the magnitude of what's happened. She thinks about sending Georgia a text – *Guess what?* – but it already feels like an empty victory. She doesn't want to gloat, she wants someone to celebrate with. Lydia knows that she's still a million potential missteps away from being published, let alone successful, she's not delusional. Bibi could change her mind, be overruled, offer her such an insulting deal that Antoinette advises her not to take it (she would ignore that one, to be fair), but she's closer than she's ever been before. There's only one thing she can do. She retouches her make-up in the little mirror she keeps in her desk drawer, smooths down her hair. Snaps a selfie with a wry, knowing smile.

Stand by for some BIG news!!! All your dreams can come true! #Blessed #LivingMyBestLife #NeverGiveUp #AuthorsOfInstagram

Hits share.

Chapter 53

Harry refuses my offer of Joe's room for the night, and I'm relieved. He needs to go home to Anne Marie. Try to sort things out. He's much more sad than angry. In fact, he's not angry at all, just broken-hearted.

'What can we do?' I say to Nick as we get ready for bed.

'Nothing,' he says, reaching out a hand and squeezing my shoulder. 'Just be there if either of them needs us.' The implication is there: don't interfere.

He has no need to worry, I have no intention of ever interfering in anything ever again.

I feel the loss of Anne Marie like a bereavement. Lydia goes deeper, but I'm used to sometimes not seeing her for a few weeks. Anne Marie is my everyday, just-around-the-corner-if-I-need-her friend. My uncomplicated, no-baggage, no-agenda, no-tiptoeing-round-the-awkward-stuff buddy. History versus daily life. I unblock Lydia's number, send her a text: *Why the fuck would you do that? What's Anne Marie ever done to you? You're so fucking self-obsessed, you don't care whose life you ruin. Don't ever contact me again.*

It doesn't achieve anything but it makes me feel better. Until five minutes later when it makes me feel worse.

* * *

Igor and I hover in the street outside the school. Igor always elicits a reaction. He's not the kind of dog you can ignore. People either cross the road to avoid him or throw themselves at him for a hug. I now judge people on which category they fall into. Jez, it seems, is of the 'cross the road' variety. That tells me everything I need to know.

I didn't mean to speak to him. I'm here to try to talk to Anne Marie again. To see if she's OK. She may not want to see me but I'm not going to let our friendship die without a fight. And I'm not going to stand by and watch her and Harry fall apart either, whatever I've promised Nick. I'm keeping half an eye on the car park when I see him, heading for his blue Toyota. Despite the signs saying 'No Dogs Beyond the Gates' I'm over there before I have any idea what I'm doing. I feel irrationally angry with him. What was he thinking, breaking up my friend's marriage? Of course, she was the one who owed Harry loyalty, not him, but why split hairs?

'Jez,' I say loudly as he's about to open the car door. He looks round, sees Igor and jumps, actually jumps. Holds a hand out in front of him as if to say 'Keep your dog away.'

'He's friendly,' I say. 'It's fine.'

'I'm, um, sorry, do we know each other . . . ?'

'Georgia Shepherd. I'm Anne Marie's friend.'

Up close he looks older, more lived in. That's not a bad thing. It makes him more interesting if anything, but he still has the leather-elbow-pads, bad-American-movie-teacher vibe going on. He's good-looking – in a bland kind of way – but it's not easy to see what Anne Marie saw in him. Why she would have risked everything.

'Oh,' he says, warily. 'Er . . . nice to meet you.'

I have literally no idea what I'm doing here. What I'm going to say. And Anne Marie coming out and spotting me talking to Jez would hardly be the quick fix for our friendship that I need. We both stand there in silence for a moment. It starts to drizzle. I fish a scrunchie out of my coat pocket and tie my hair up in a ponytail.

'Um . . .' Jez says, making a vague motion that he should go.

'Did she tell you Harry knows?' I say. 'It's not good.'

'Er . . .' he says, colouring up. His bumbling nature is starting to irritate me. 'I . . . erm . . .'

'You've met him, I suppose. You teach Billie, don't you? He's lovely. The nicest man. I don't know why I'm telling you this . . .'

'It's all over and done with,' he says, stroking his beard nervously. 'She . . .'

'Regrets it. I know. Maybe . . . I mean . . . Could you get Billie transferred to another class? So Harry doesn't have to think about bumping into you?' Is that even possible? And what if Billie loves him and thinks he's the greatest teacher ever (unlikely, I feel. Billie and enthusiasm for anything beyond music don't generally mix).

'I . . . um . . .' I have to stop myself interrupting him to tell him to get on with it. 'I'm leaving at Easter. I've handed in my . . . um . . . notice.'

Oh. Well. 'Where are you going?'

'I don't know yet. I'm applying. When she said she didn't . . . um . . .'

I wonder if he's a serial hopeless Romeo. Waffling about like a harmless old bumble bee before making his move.

Falling in hopeless, inappropriate love and then on to the next. I want to ask him if that's why he left his last job but it's clearly none of my business. 'Right. Does Anne Marie know?'

'I don't know. We're not . . .'

I wait. Does this man never finish a sentence?

'Well, it's for the best, I suppose,' I say eventually. I catch sight of a familiar tall figure over by the main doors. 'Fuck. I don't want her to see me talking to you.' I start to move away. 'Good luck. I'm sure you'll find something.'

He half raises a hand goodbye. I hurry across the car park towards the front gates. Anne Marie is just up ahead, striding fast, head down. I catch her up at the main road.

'Hey.'

She turns. Turns back. 'Oh. Hi.'

'I . . . um . . .' Christ, now I'm starting to sound like Jez. 'I came to meet you.'

She looks drained, miserable. She puts the hood of her black coat up. It might be the rain but it also might be to create a barrier between us. Igor recognizes her though and jumps up, happy to see her. She reaches down a hand and strokes his head.

'I don't really want to talk to you,' she says flatly. 'I'm not trying to be horrible but there's nothing you can say to make anything better.'

'I can't bear it. I can't bear to see you and Harry like this.'

I expect her to say 'Well, you shouldn't have told Lydia then' but she just shakes her head. The lights change and we cross, me shadowing her, surfing her shoulder. 'Jez says he's leaving,' I say desperately. Anne Marie stops in her tracks.

'You've been talking to Jez?'

'No. I mean, yes, but . . . I saw him just now, I . . .'

'What? Wanted to check up that it really was over?'

'No! God, Anne Marie, no. I thought I should tell him Harry had found out. Just in case . . .'

'In case what? Do you think Harry's the type to storm into the school and pick a fight? I almost wish he was, so he could get it out of his system that way. I can't bear that I've made him so sad. That I've shattered his fucking heart.' She strides off again and I hurry to catch up. Suddenly she stops dead again. 'Did Jez really say he was leaving?'

I nod and then realize she can't see me. 'Yes. At Easter.'

'So, I've messed his life up too.'

'I think he knew what he was getting into,' I say. 'He decided to sleep with a married woman.'

She starts walking again. 'I appreciate you trying to make me feel better about this, Georgia, but there's nothing you can do to help, OK? I'll see you soon.'

'Anne Marie . . .' I say, hopelessly. 'There must be something I can do.'

She turns back. 'There isn't. Please don't follow me all the way home.'

Chapter 54

Wilbur book seven is finished, dashed off in a couple of manic days and delivered yesterday. He's the same old Wilbur. His rhymes are as unsophisticated as they've always been. 'If it ain't broke, don't fix it,' my mum said on the phone last night when I told her I wasn't going to bow to Bibi's pressure. Another one of her favourites. Joe has started doing a great – affectionate – impression of this one since she said it to him when he told her he was gay on the phone at Christmas. 'What does that even mean in this context?' he'd said to her through gasps of laughter. I could picture her chuckling along. My mum adores her grandkids. Bibi might not like it but I'm hoping that now he's an award-winner she'll have a sudden change of heart. And if she doesn't, well, that's just too bad.

I haven't spoken to Anne Marie in days. That is, she's replied to my texts, she hasn't cut me dead, but they're formal, polite replies. Answers to questions, not a conversation. Harry has been a sad presence in our house most evenings, heading home to the flat slightly earlier each night. He just can't bear not to be there, whatever's happened. He was buoyed up by the fact that Jez is leaving. Out of sight, out of mind. Anne Marie told him, not me. I'm keeping well out of it.

I throw myself into work on the drawings for my Igor book. When I showed them to Nick, he'd said – after exclaiming that he thought they were 'fantastic' – 'Is Igor you in this situation' and I'd suddenly realized that that was what I was doing. How had I not seen it? I was writing about myself as a child. The big outsider who all the others stared at. The one who was teased for being different. Sad doesn't even come into it. But, in fact, once that became clear, it was obvious that that was what I needed to do. Write a book for all the kids like me who were being ostracized for being slightly outside the norm. I decided that the little girl – who I called Evie because, you know, creative genius – would be the friend I had never had to stand up for me. And she would fight Igor's corner every time someone stared at him or pointed. She would be the sidekick every child deserves.

I'm excited to show it to Bibi. The illustrations are packed with details and bright vibrant colours. Turquoise-blue skies and lime-green grass. Butterscotch-yellow sunflowers and raspberry-red poppies. A heightened world. I'm stupidly proud of them. And the message – the celebration of difference – surely that will be right up her street? As if she can read my thoughts, my laptop buzzes with an email from her: *Kate is going to call you to arrange a time for you to come in and discuss Wilbur 7. B.* I pre-empt Kate's call by ringing her first and fix a meeting for tomorrow.

'Ultimately you're the author, Georgia, but I can't say I'm not disappointed. I thought we were on the same page.'

I was expecting this, obviously. In a weird way, hoping for it almost. It makes what I have to tell her easier. Bibi picks up the string of her teabag and swirls it round. 'I know. I tried, I really did, but it didn't work. Wilbur is who Wilbur is. I don't think it's right to try and shoehorn him into being someone else.'

'I see. I was just hoping we could broaden out his fan base. I mean, the sales are good but they plateaued a couple of books ago . . .'

'But he does have loyal readers. What's the point of losing them in order to try and gain new ones?'

She nods slowly. 'Are those the readers we want, though? Are those the readers that are going to propel us through the 2020s?'

I'm not going to get into an argument about whether Wilbur's fans are the right kind of fans. There's no point. 'The thing is, this is going to be the last Wilbur. I've decided it's time to move on to something new . . .'

A few days after the awards ceremony – a week ago now – my agent, Antoinette, called me to tell me that Bibi had been on the phone keen to discuss a contract for books eight and nine. It's the call every author hopes for. It means you're wanted, you have security for another two years. I had been about to tell her about *Mummy, Why Is That Dog So Big?* when she dropped her other bombshell.

'Oh,' she said in her clipped voice, just a hint of the South African accent she grew up with. 'Thank you for sending Lydia to me, by the way. I think *Game of Gnomes* is going to be huge . . .'

'You're representing Lydia?'

'Yes. Has she not told you?' Antoinette had had to miss the awards ceremony because her little boy was sick but she'd called me first thing to congratulate me – I had been too wrapped up in Anne Marie and Harry to really register – and then sent over the flowers and champagne later in the day.

'Um . . . no. I haven't seen her . . .' *Thank you for sending her to me* could only mean that Lydia had told her that I had. That she'd used my name to get a foot in the door.

'Yes, isn't it exciting? Phoenix have offered her a contract already . . .'

I didn't hear the rest. I knew Bibi was interested in Lydia's book, of course, but to have put a deal on the table already . . . ? I was in the kitchen, in the middle of making a moussaka for that evening's dinner, and I reached out a hand to steady myself on the counter.

'Oh . . .'

I got off the phone as quickly as I could. I didn't want to hear about Lydia's success. Her using me as a stepping stone to propel herself up. That night I'd talked it through with Nick and come to a momentous decision. I needed to follow my passion, my heart. There was no point sitting around moaning that I had way more talent than I was showing the world, quietly seething as Lydia got recognition and praise. ('It might never happen,' Nick had said, trying to talk me down. 'How many people get book deals and are never heard of again? Most of them, probably.' I knew he was right but the possibility was eating me up.) I could either become one of those embittered bores who drone on about how they could have been a contender, or I could put my energies into trying to prove what I was worth.

Bibi raises her eyebrows at me. 'Antoinette didn't mention this . . .'

'She doesn't know. I haven't had a chance to tell her.' I scrabble round in my bag for the artwork for *Mummy, Why Is That Dog So Big?* 'This is what I'm working on.' I tell her the story – the giant awkward canine who hates how people react to him, and his feisty friend who teaches him that being different is OK. 'I have more sketches. Here . . .' I pull out my iPad and find the photos I took before I left home. Bibi studies them closely. I'm a bag of nerves. A defendant waiting for a verdict.

'So, you see, it's all about diversity. Embracing who you are.'

'Yes,' she says, peering at the drawings. 'Yes, I see. I love this . . .'

My heart starts to race. Validation for your work never gets old. And nervousness, waiting for that validation, doesn't either. 'Oh, thank goodness.'

'It's very good,' she says, scrolling backwards and forwards through the pages. 'But the new contract offer is for the next two Wilbur books . . .'

At first I think I don't hear her correctly. 'It's for . . . ?'

'The next two Wilbur books. Yes.'

I pick at a bit of fluff on my leg, anxiously. 'It's . . . um . . . it's just for my two next books, isn't it?'

'On the understanding that they are Wilbur eight and nine.'

What? 'I thought you didn't even like Wilbur.'

'It's not really about what I like, Georgia. Wilbur is a franchise. If we can just get this latest one working then it would be crazy to stop producing them now.'

I lean forward in my chair. Outside there's a view across the rooftops of Bloomsbury towards the Old Bailey and the

Inns of Court. On a normal day I would be happy to gaze at it for hours. 'But I don't want to do more Wilbur. It's time for something new. And you said you loved these,' I add, indicating the drawings.

'I do. But here's the thing. We did some market research recently, and while Wilbur the Wallaby is a name a lot of people recognize, Georgia Shepherd isn't really . . .'

'That's OK. It might take a couple of books to get a new series off the ground but it's an investment in the future, right? I mean, you said yourself that Wilbur can't go on forever.'

'And we already have a franchise with a dog for that age group. You know *Scaredy Dog*?'

I do. They're cute books about a nervous basset hound trying to negotiate going to school. Nothing like mine. 'They're very different . . .'

'We're not really in the market for another dog.'

'What if it was a cat? Or a rabbit?' I say, somewhat desperately.

'Georgia, we love you at Phoenix,' she says. 'You'll always have a home here.'

'So long as I keep churning out Wilbur books?' I know I should be trying to tell her what she wants to hear, at least just to get me through the meeting so I can call Antoinette and regroup, but I've spent the whole night psyching myself up for this. It's not a decision I've taken lightly. And I know it's the right one.

'So long as the relationship works for both of us.'

'Right,' I say. 'I see.'

'Have a think about it.' She pushes my iPad and pages back

across the desk towards me. 'Meanwhile, let's try and knock Wilbur seven into shape . . .'

'Why didn't you talk to me before you went in?' Antoinette sighs.

I have to stop myself from saying: 'Because you probably would have banged on about how brilliant your new client Lydia was.' Instead, I mutter, 'I don't know . . .'

Bibi had spent the rest of our meeting taking apart every line of the new Wilbur book and telling me why it wasn't 2020 enough. I had sat there, submissive, not fighting my corner. All my bravado gone. At one point I'd said, 'What if I made the illustrations more complex?' and she'd shaken her head. 'The kids love the illustrations as they are. It's the words that need to evolve.'

I let her do what she wanted. I was past caring. So what if Wilbur wanted to drink kombucha and take up holotropic breathing? I'm sure those things are huge with the three-to-fives. At least the ones Bibi's friends have sired.

'It's going to make negotiating this deal harder now,' Antoinette says. I'm lying on the sofa in my kitchen under a throw, Igor on the floor beside me. I almost went straight back to bed when I got in, but that seemed like a step too far at eleven thirty in the morning, so this is the next best thing.

'I'm not doing another Wilbur,' I say. 'I don't care if that means they withdraw the offer.'

'You need to be absolutely sure because they probably will.'

I sit up. Igor stands to attention. 'Really? Just like that?'

I can hear her bite into something. 'Can't you just keep on

producing Wilbur books and I'll try and sell this other one on the side?'

'I don't know,' I say. 'I don't know what to do.'

I can't really afford to turn down a contract, obviously. We have a big mortgage. Nick earns well but I earn more. We'd be all right for a while but it's not a decision to take lightly. What if I move on but no one is ever interested in anything I draw again and I just become 'that woman who used to do Wilbur the Wallaby'?

What if it's the end?

Chapter 55

Nick tells me I have to do what I need to do. We'll manage. 'You don't want to end up like Rod Hull.'

'I have no idea what that means,' I say, laughing. I had been in a fug when he got home, having barely moved all afternoon, going over and over the decision in my head. It felt good to laugh.

'Didn't he hate the emu? I'm sure I read that somewhere.'

'I think that was Keith Harris and Orville.'

'Whoever. You know what I mean. Come here . . .' He pulls me to my feet. I think he's going to give me a hug but he leads me up the stairs and then up again to the first floor. Into my office. Igor pads along behind us. Nick points at a framed poster on the wall. Wilbur three. *Wilbur Moves House.*

'Look at him. Look at his little face. Look how fucking cute he is.'

I look reluctantly. He is – Nick's right. 'I just wish he wasn't so simplistic. I wish I'd pushed to do proper backgrounds in the first place. I can do so much more, Nick.'

'I know that, but the thing is, Wilbur is as successful as he is because he's exactly like he is. If you'd made him different in any way he might not have appealed to kids like he does. He's perfect. And he's bought us this . . .' He waves his arm around, indicating the house.

'Well,' I say, 'he got us a huge mortgage anyway.'

'Yes. Bastard.' Despite myself, I smile. 'But you know what I mean. Whether you retire him or not no one can take that away from you.'

'We'd have to move though.'

'I can cover the mortgage till you get another publisher. If that's what you want to do.'

I reach over and pull him towards me. 'I love you.'

'I should hope so,' he says, laughing. 'What's not to love?'

I lie awake all night going over and over my options. Nick's support has freed me up to make the decision I want to make, but I have no idea what that is. Anne Marie is the person I would always have talked it through with. Not Lydia. Lydia's own agenda would always have got in the way. She would have said, 'Have you any idea how lucky you are to have a publishing deal at all?' and that would have been that.

But I can hardly go to Anne Marie and say, 'Sorry your marriage is falling apart but can I talk to you about my own problems?' Even if she would hear me out I don't think it would go down too well. Yesterday Harry went straight home from work rather than hanging out at ours for a bit first. I hope that means that things are getting better.

In the morning I get a message from Antoinette: *Let me know what you want to do x.* I don't look at my emails for the rest of the day. Put my phone on Do Not Disturb. I lose myself in the illustrations for *Mummy, Why Is That Dog so Big?*, trying out different styles, different versions of Igor. Bibi may not want to buy it but she definitely liked it. It's worth pursuing.

In the late afternoon I put my trainers on, grab Igor and head out for a run. Pounding up and down the hill has become my therapy. I've practically worn a groove in the path. Today it's dark, dingy, wet. More like a punishment. Igor is sulking, longing for the warmth of the wood burner and a snooze on his bed. He lags back so I unclip his lead and let him do his own thing.

Suddenly he hares past me at lightning speed. Squirrel, I assume. He's never caught one – thank God – but he lives in hope. He races towards a lone figure sitting on a bench at the summit. It is most definitely not sitting-on-a-bench weather. He greets them enthusiastically and I see a hand reach out and pet his ears. For a second I wonder – irrationally – if it's Lydia, but I know the awards do was her big finale. She must know that I will have heard her news from Bibi and from Antoinette. I'm thinking about turning back. It's a bit creepy up here after dark in the mist, especially with Igor's new friend, hood up, looming at the top.

I call him just as the figure unfurls. I see wisps of familiar blue hair.

'Anne Marie?' Why is she sitting up here alone? I stop in my tracks. I'm so happy to run into her but I doubt the feeling will be reciprocated.

'Oh. Georgia,' she says. 'I was just . . .' She waves a hand around as if that'll tell me what I need to know. She looks frozen through. I feel a pang of anxiety that she and Harry might not be edging towards a reconciliation after all.

'Are you OK?'

She gives me a half-smile. 'Absolutely. Just getting some air. Clearing my head.'

'Do you . . . I mean, would you like to come to mine for a coffee? Dry off a bit?' I have to try. To my surprise she accepts. We walk slowly back, her trailing behind, Igor running between us. We don't say a word until we get through the front door. She hangs her coat over the banister.

'Do you need a towel? Dry off a bit?'

She shakes her head. 'I'm not too bad, actually.'

'Come on down then.' It's a bit like inviting a vague acquaintance in, not one of my – former – best friends. We're on eggshells around each other.

'How are things?' Usually Anne Marie will just flick the kettle on in my kitchen. Help herself. Today she leaves it to me. Flops into a chair by the radiator.

'We're OK,' she says. 'At least we will be. I don't think he's going to get over it any time soon, but you know Harry. He's never going to get angry or make me feel bad. I don't know what I did to deserve him really.'

'Oh, thank God,' I say, feeling tears forming. 'I couldn't bear it.'

'You and me both.' I look at her properly for the first time then and I'm overwhelmed with the urge to hug her. I'm pretty sure she wouldn't accept it so I hold back.

'You?'

I nod. 'We're good. I can't quite believe it.' I carry our coffees over. Sit opposite her.

'Nick told Harry you were struggling. With a work thing,' she says eventually and I actually burst into tears. I've been so desperate to talk to her about it. About anything. And the idea that she's been thinking about me with everything she has going on kills me.

'I've missed you,' I sob.

'I've missed you too,' she says quietly. 'I'm sorry I had a go at you . . .' I start to protest but she carries on. '. . . when it was me who was in the wrong. No one else.'

'And Lydia . . .'

'OK. Yes, Lydia was a bitch. But I shouldn't have taken it out on you. It was guilt. Panic.'

'It's OK,' I say through tears. 'Of course it's OK.'

'Tell me what's going on. Harry said you might be giving up Wilbur.'

'Oh God, it's such a mess.' I wipe my eyes with the back of my hand and fill her in on my meeting with Bibi. 'So they basically want Wilbur more than me, that's the gist of it.'

'And can you afford to just walk away?'

I sigh. 'Not really. I mean, yes, for a while, but what if no one ever picks up the Igor book?' I tell her about Lydia. My fears about her outshining me. I feel stupid but I know Anne Marie won't judge me. I can be honest with her – show the ugly sides of me – in a way I can't be with anyone else. Not even Nick. Not about this.

'What if Lydia's books are a huge success?' I say. 'What if everyone says she's brilliant and she wins awards and all I've ever done is draw a fucking wallaby? What if she has a bestseller and she goes on chat shows and . . . and don't say it might not happen because I know that, but what if it does?'

I'm full out crying again now. Big ugly tears. Anne Marie leans over and takes my hand and I grab on to her long fingers. 'What happens to Lydia has no reflection on you. Her being a success wouldn't mean you weren't. Imagine the most extreme scenario. Lydia's book is published and it's a huge success. She sells a million copies and wins awards and . . . I don't know . . . the Queen says they're her favourite books . . .'

I laugh despite everything. 'Would that be cool?'

'Beyoncé then. Does any of that happening take away from what you've achieved?'

'I suppose not.'

She shakes her head vigorously. 'Not at all. Nothing can take that away from you. Forget about Lydia. Think about what's going to make you happy. What's the best version of your future you can imagine, forgetting about anyone else?'

'I love you,' I say. I lean over and hug her. 'I'm so happy you're here. And about you and Harry.' She hugs me back and we just sit there for a moment, arms round each other, listening to the thump of Igor's tail on the floor.

'I have a confession to make . . .'

I lean back and look at her.

'Nothing scary. I just . . . I've been sitting on that bench every day after school hoping to bump into you. It wasn't a coincidence . . .'

I'm almost rendered speechless. 'Why didn't you just come round?'

She shakes her head. 'I don't know. I couldn't face the thought that you wouldn't want to see me . . .'

'Oh my God,' I say. 'I would never . . . I didn't know what to do without you.' I squeeze her hand again. 'Please say we're OK. I can't bear it . . .'

'We are. Of course we are.'

I smile at her through my tears. I'm overwhelmed with happiness. Relief.

'Now,' she says decisively. 'What are you going to do about Wilbur?'

We go back and forth, exploring all the options. It's such

a relief to talk it through with someone who genuinely wants what's best for me with no agenda. Even Nick has a horse in the race and so can't be completely impartial, however much he wants to be. Every now and then I get overwhelmed by how happy I am to have her back in my life and have to tell her. First Nick, now Anne Marie. Me two, Lydia nil.

By the time she leaves I know what I have to do.

Chapter 56

'So, let me make sure I've got this right before I call her,' Antoinette says. 'You'll sign up to do Wilbur eight and nine if they don't mess with him—'

'That doesn't mean no notes,' I interrupt. 'But no changing his style, no trying to make him some kind of woke poster boy . . .'

'Got it.'

'And the same with the latest one. I need to take it back to what it was before Bibi stamped herself all over it. Again, she can give me notes but I'm not going to bend it to her agenda . . . Don't say it like that, obviously.'

Antoinette laughs. 'I'll try not to.'

'And we have to be allowed to try and place the other book somewhere else if they definitely don't want it. What do you think?'

'It sounds like a plan. It's possible, obviously, that they'll walk away. Are you prepared for that?'

'Absolutely,' I say. 'It's non-negotiable.'

While I wait to hear what Phoenix have to say I lose myself in drawing ideas for my Igor book, inspired like I haven't been since, well . . . ever. I'm almost grateful to Lydia. I needed something to jolt me out of my comfort zone. Push me into scary territory where I might actually fail. Thankfully the real Igor is happy to pose, sleeping on a bed by my desk while I draw version after version of him, trying to get him exactly right.

Anne Marie and Harry come over for the evening and, while they're a little subdued, it's enough like old times for us to believe those old times will come again eventually. I catch her looking at him sadly at one point, and he does too, and he squeezes her hand. She gives him a smile that's full of love and gratitude. And I know they'll be OK.

Step by step life goes back to normal. Antoinette calls me and tells me that Phoenix love me and Wilbur, and I obviously misunderstood their intentions, which were never to change him. She tells me that Kate is being promoted to editor and will look after me from here on in. Bibi is going to concentrate on other projects (*Lydia*, my evil head voice says, but I channel Anne Marie and drive the thought away, concentrating instead on my own success). They're not sure why I think they wouldn't be interested in *Mummy, Why Is That Dog So Big?* because they only have one book in production with a dog hero and it's nothing like what it sounds as though I'm proposing, so could they take a closer look?

The relief is immense. A crashing flood that I didn't realize was on the horizon. I call Nick, laughing and crying and shouting all at the same time.

I don't think about Lydia again. Not if I can avoid it. At least, not until I'm forced to.

'Lyd's birthday!!!' The words scream out at me from the page. At the beginning of every year I always take a moment to go through and enter special dates I don't want to miss on the paper calendar I keep in the kitchen – this year from the

Mayhew in honour of Igor. Birthdays, anniversaries, school and now uni term times. For the first time ever I wish I hadn't bothered. It's inevitable that I start to wonder what she's doing, who she's celebrating with this year.

I take myself out shopping as a distraction, down to Kensington High Street, where I can easily spend an hour pottering around Whole Foods, examining every product. So much more satisfying than browsing for clothes. I'm gazing in wonder at the loose nut selection when my phone rings. It's a number I don't recognize, a landline. I'm tempted not to answer, but I know if I don't it'll probably be someone saying: 'You've won the lottery but because you weren't in we're giving it to somebody else.' It would be just my luck. I rest my overstuffed basket on the corner of a counter and take the call.

It's a woman. But I can't understand what she's saying because she's crying. My immediate thought is that something's happened to one of the twins or Nick. Or my mum.

'What?' I say, panicky. 'What's happened? Who is this?' A man holding a large loaf of fresh bread double takes and then hovers close by, unsure what to do. I hold a hand up to say I'm OK, although I don't know if I am, and turn away slightly.

The woman says whatever she's saying again, and I catch a couple of words but not enough to make any sense out of it. 'Slow down,' I say. 'Please.'

'It's me, George,' she says and I realize it's her. Lydia. I'm tempted to cut her off, but I know I can't. Not until I know what's up.

'What's happened?'

'I just realized I'm older than they were,' she says between sobs. She doesn't have to say any more. I know exactly what she means. It's Lydia's forty-sixth birthday and her parents were both forty-five when the car crash cut short their lives.

'Oh God. I'm sorry.' I've never really thought about how young they were, only ever seeing the tragedy from Lydia's viewpoint. They were the age that parents were. Not people with hopes and dreams still to accomplish. Not people with everything to live for. 'I hadn't . . .' I stop. I don't know what to say.

'There's no one else who would understand,' she says quietly.

'I know.' My arm is aching from supporting the basket, so I push it further on to the counter. 'Where are you?'

'At work. I'm shut in my office; it's fine. Sorry. I shouldn't have called. I didn't know who else . . .' She starts crying again.

'It's OK.' Would I have called her if I'd put two and two together myself? Realized how significant it was? Would I have put my anger aside for a moment and checked up on her? I don't think I would. I'm not proud of that fact.

I abandon my basket of goodies and head up to the street, phone pressed to my ear. I don't say anything because there's nothing I can really say that doesn't sound like a platitude. I walk up and down Church Street, listening to her pour her heart out. Despite everything I feel broken-hearted for her.

'I have nobody left who loves me unconditionally,' she sobs at one point. Once I would have said 'You have me', but it had turned out that there were conditions after all. There was a limit. So, instead, I say nothing.

'I'm sorry. For everything,' she says, once she's cried out.

'I know,' I say. 'It's OK.'

I don't have it in me to hate her any more. I have my own life to live.

Chapter 57

Lydia dries her eyes. She hates crying at work, it's so obvious even hours later, even after you've splashed cold water on your face and reapplied your make-up. Despite her new, thrilling book deal there's no way she can give up her day job just yet. She's an unknown. Phoenix offered her a tiny advance and Antoinette didn't bat an eyelid. It was the norm, she said. The more books she sold the more money she would be offered next time. There was probably an algorithm somewhere. Lydia doesn't care. She's knows Georgia's first big advance was for Wilbur four and five, once she'd proved her worth. And if Lydia is being honest she'd do it for nothing. Just for the honour of being able to call herself a published author.

But God, she wishes she could hand in her notice.

To be fair, when she told her co-workers about her book deal they'd brought out the champagne and toasted her good fortune. She'd showed them her illustrations and her boss said something like 'How have you kept that talent hidden from us all these years?' – which was sweet. But there was no one there who knew what it actually meant to her. Who really understood.

She'd missed her parents more than ever that day.

And then this morning it had hit her. She had often thought about what age they would be if they were still alive, what they might look like. But it was as if she had suppressed the idea that she might one day be older than they had ever got to be. It was unbearable. Gut-wrenching. She'd looked in the mirror in the office's bland, white-tiled toilets, searching for her mother's face. Everyone had always said how alike they looked, as if she'd given birth to a clone with no input from her husband. And Lydia saw her clearly, as she always did, only now she would become more unfamiliar with every passing day. Lydia would lose her all over again.

Before she knew what was happening tears were running down her face. She locked herself in a cubicle but she couldn't stop. Eventually she knew she had to make it back to her own office before anyone discovered her. Before anyone started being sympathetic and wanting to make her cups of tea and listen.

She shut the door, put her head on her desk and wept.

She needed Georgia. Georgia was the only one who could understand. Who knew what their deaths had done to her. Susan had loved her brother – Lydia's dad – but she'd hardly known her mum. She'd hardly known them as a family. How happy they were in each other's company. Lydia and Georgia might only have been friends for two and a bit years when the accident happened but she got it. And she had been the person Lydia had turned to ever since.

Before she knew what she was doing she picked up the phone. Georgia's was one of a handful of numbers she knew by heart. She had no idea what she was going to say, no desire to get into an argument or even a discussion of what had gone wrong with their friendship. She just needed to talk and for someone who understood to hear her out.

Afterwards she felt drained. Raw. Empty.

Georgia had let her get it out of her system. She still cared enough to indulge Lydia as she'd cried herself out. She had given her all the time she needed. But as they said goodbye Lydia knew with absolute certainty that that was it. There was no way back.

She has a date with a man she met in the café at the National Portrait Gallery: Pavel. He's a bit younger, a barista at a coffee shop off St Martin's Lane. He spends every lunchtime wandering art exhibitions, he tells her. The location is the only benefit of his job. He has ambitions to paint himself, doing the occasional portrait on the side. He seems nice enough. Sweet. Harmless. She hasn't told him it's her birthday because what kind of a saddo would that make him think she is? Spending the evening with a virtual stranger instead of celebrating with friends or family. She buys herself a little cake and a half-bottle of champagne on her way home from work. She'll celebrate on her own once the date is over.

She showers and changes into a pair of skin-tight skinny jeans and her new Ted Baker top. High open-toed shoes. Spends an age doing her make-up and teasing her hair into waves. She takes a photo in the bedroom mirror. Then another. And another. She's going to be late at this rate, but who cares? Pavel will either wait or he won't. She picks the best photo, works her magic on it. Puts it up on Instagram (she hasn't told Pavel her surname yet, let alone her Insta details, and if he sees this tomorrow she won't care anyway. It's not as if they're going to be meeting up again. He's not Nick. He can never be Nick. So what would be the point?).

She tags Edie in, as she often does, hoping, but knowing there will be no response. Joe has already blocked her but Edie is still there. Silent, but there. The chink of light in the doorway. *Birthday girl!!!* she writes. *#Blessed #LivingMyBestLife #DoYou #AuthorsOfInstagram.* Then she changes her heels for her favourite clumpy boots and leaves for the tube.

Chapter 58

Eighteen months later

I clutch a glass of warm champagne. Even with all the windows open the room is airless. Stifling. There's a sheen of sweat on everyone's face, turning them all to liquid. A woman I don't know stands in front of one of the large fans, her arms lifted from her sides, laughing as she feels the breeze. There are about sixty people here in this beautiful panelled room overlooking the river near Tower Bridge, celebrating with me.

This is the launch for my new book. Due out at the end of the month, published by Phoenix, edited by Kate. I'm so proud of it I could burst. I look round the room, packed with people who only want the best for me. I pick out Nick, his pale yellow shirt bright against his tan, chatting to Edie and Joe, Anne Marie and Harry with Nina and surprise baby Nat, chubby and smiley at seven months. Igor, the guest of honour, the muse for *Mummy, Why Is That Dog So Big?*, sits panting by my feet, his smart collar and tie wilting in the heat. I reach down and pat his head, check that his water bowl has been refilled.

We've only been back from Spain a week, the four of us. A fortnight on the Costa del Crime. My mum was beside herself when I told her we all wanted to come. I've been three times on my own, and they came to us together for the first time a couple of months ago. Frank, it turns out, has a daughter, Joni, living in Farringdon. How did I not know this? Because I had never bothered to ask, that's why. I mean, I knew he had a daughter but nothing else about her. It seems like beyond rudeness now. Anyway, she came over. She's a couple of years older than me. Divorced. Riotously funny. Wary of Nick and me at first, I thought, because (I imagine) she knew we (I) hadn't exactly welcomed her father into our family with open arms. But by the time she left in a cab at eleven o'clock that night (she had only been intending to come to lunch) we were promising to meet up for a drink in a few weeks. And we did. And we have several times since. We're stepsisters. How weird is that?

I hadn't expected the twins to join us in Spain – Edie was working in a vintage shop in Bath for the holidays and Joe had been home in London doing shifts as a lifeguard at the lido on Parliament Hill – but the potential for comedy value made it an irresistible prospect. We opted to rent our own villa a few minutes away, rather than stay chez Irene and Frank, so that we could have our own space when we needed it, but Joe insisted we say yes to every one of Mum's suggestions, so we spent half our nights at the club playing bingo or watching dodgy tribute acts (my favourite was Britney Houston who performed to songs of both Ms Spears and Whitney with an equal lack of authenticity). I don't think I've ever laughed so much in my life. My mum was on form; Frank bent over backwards to makes us feel welcome, especially his stepgrandchildren. ('They're at university. Waste of bloody time if you ask me, but they're smart as whips. They don't take after you, do they, Reen?') And then at the end of the night we would share a nightcap back on our terrace looking over the mountains and go over the highlights, Edie and Joe acting out the juiciest bits of Mum and Frank's conversations:

'Remember Nobby?'

'Nobby?'

'From the golf club.'

'Oh, the fella with the bald head?'

'No, that was Kojak. Nobby. Geezer with the head that looked like a knob. I mean, he *was* bald, but you were thinking of Kojak . . .'

We had the best time.

One day Mum and I went shopping and to lunch alone while the others – Frank included – amused themselves on the beach. ('It was like looking at one of those peat-bog people they dig up from archaeological sites,' Nick had said to me that evening, describing wiry Frank's deeply tanned, sinewy torso in his red budgie smugglers. 'Imagine if you put Santa's head on Iggy Pop's body. I'm scarred for life.') Frank was, thankfully, over his prostate scare. ('All back in working order, thank God,' my mum said, and I'd asked her, laughing, to please never tell me anything like that again.) When we stopped for a coffee in a fragrant little square she asked me about Lydia as she always did: it was almost a reflex – mostly, I had realized, to ensure I wasn't caving in and trying to re- kindle our friendship. And I told her, truthfully, that there was no chance of that. I hadn't spoken to Lydia since her tearful call over a year ago and I wasn't about to.

'I actually miss her,' she said gruffly. 'How mad is that?'

'I do too, Mum. But it's better, isn't it . . . ?'

'It is,' she said, and I knew from the purse of her top lip that she was trying not to cry. 'Whoever would have thought.'

Her first book – *Game of Gnomes* – came out a few weeks ago. I had been obsessively googling both the title and her name for months until I finally gave in and asked Antoinette when it was being published. For weeks before I woke up every night in a cold sweat, imagining her being hailed as the new Quentin Blake, storming the charts, appearing on breakfast TV, the new big thing. As the date grew closer I scoured the internet for reviews. I was trying to concentrate on Wilbur eight (Wilbur seven – *Wilbur at the Zoo* – having come out at the end of last year and done nicely enough to keep everyone happy), but all my old insecurities started flooding back, threatening self-sabotage, and I took to dragging Igor out on ever longer and more arduous walks to try to distract myself.

So far there have been no reviews. No TV appearances or spreads in magazines – she's an unknown author in a crowded market; there was no big fanfare at all. A week or so ago, once I finally accepted my darkest fears hadn't yet been realized, I ordered a copy and, when it arrived, I sneaked it up to my office guiltily and pored over it secretively. It was a thing of beauty: there was no doubt about that. The illustrations were pure Lydia. Dark and intricate. Layer upon layer of detail. Black and white. I turned it over and over in my hands.

On the fourth or fifth time of flicking through I noticed the dedication.

'For Georgia, my sister'.

Having Anne Marie be at home on maternity leave with Nat has been a joy. We meet up almost every day as she tries to negotiate having a new baby again eleven years after she did it last. Her pregnancy had been a complete shock to both her and Harry. She had panicked that she was too old, too settled in her career, too relieved that those small-baby days were over for good to go through it all again. But in the end she knew it was the right thing. Nat was a happy, contented bundle. A mini-Harry. And a living, breathing symbol of the fact that they were OK.

Jez had left the school at Easter last year as he'd said he was going to, but not before Harry had been to see him. In typical Harry fashion, as soon as he knew that everything between him and Anne Marie was going to be all right again, he'd started to worry about his rival. Was he sabotaging his own career by leaving so soon after he'd arrived? Did he already have another job to go to? He'd started to fret about it so much that he'd found out from Billie where Mr Grey lived and turned up, unannounced, one day after work.

Apparently, Jez had gone into panic mode when he found him on the doorstep, and ummed and aahed his way through an attempted justification of his behaviour. Harry had told him he didn't care about any of that any more, he just wanted Jez to know he didn't have to leave on account of him. They were all grown-ups; they could work it out. He'd been relieved to hear that Jez had found a post at a private school in Berkshire and also – he told me and Nick, asking us not to say anything to Anne Marie – that he really was going to be leaving. There was no doubt it would make the healing process easier. Once Jez had realized Harry wasn't there to hit him he'd apologized profusely, taken all the blame on himself ('I . . . um . . . should have . . . er . . . backed away. I did all the . . . erm . . . running') and promised – unasked – that he would never darken their door again.

'I'm really pleased you've . . . um . . .'

'I can't really see what she saw in him,' Harry said when he told us.

You and me both, I thought, but I wasn't about to own up to my own chat with Jez. 'I don't think it was about that,' I said. 'It was about her feeling invisible. It could have been anyone. I mean . . . that came out wrong . . . I think he was just there at the right time, paying her all this attention . . .'

Harry had wished him luck in his new job. He felt sorry for him, he said. Jez's flat was in a tired block with no lift and broken windows on the stairways. There was an Asda Macaroni and Cheese for one ready to go on the kitchen counter. *The One Show* on the TV with the sound down.

'I don't think he's got much of a life,' Harry said. I was doubly glad Jez was moving away because otherwise I'd have worried Harry was about to take it upon himself to befriend him.

'Don't you think that's a bit . . . weird?' Anne Marie said on the phone later when I told her about the dedication. I could hear Nat burbling away in the background.

'I can't decide. Maybe she's just trying to be nice. Make a big gesture.'

'There are easier, less attention-seeking ways.' Anne Marie was never going to forgive Lydia; I knew that. Not just for what she did to her but for what she tried to do to me.

I was sitting at my desk, feet up, leaning back in my chair. 'I've realized it's just another book. A beautiful book, I'll give you that, but it's not going to change the world.'

'Exactly. So all your worst fears came true and – what? Nothing, that's what.'

'Well, not exactly all of them . . .'

'A big one,' she said. 'One that's been eating you up for years.'

I reached down and petted Igor's ears. 'I know. I don't know what I thought was going to happen.'

'Maybe now you can have more faith in your own fabulousness,' she said and I laughed.

'I'm getting there.'

And I actually think I am. Slowly.

Chapter 59

It's been years since I went out on publication day and scoured the shops for books bearing my name, but this time Nick has taken the day off work and insisted we go on a tour of all the bookstores we can think of in easy public transport access of Primrose Hill. We're fine, Nick and I. I worried that my accusations might have destroyed our hard-earned trust, that Nick would feel he could never live down his old mistake after all, and so what was the point in trying? And for a while I did have a homeopathic trace of distrust. I would wake up in the night sweating, heart pounding, and think that something was wrong, that I had something to worry about, before remembering that it was all a lie.

We take Igor with us, so he can pose for pictures next to his image. It's a few days since the schools went back so there's a hint of autumn in the air, even though it's nearly eighty degrees outside. Nina started secondary school on Tuesday although, happily for her, her mum won't be back at work till after Christmas, so she doesn't have to be labelled 'the teacher's kid'. At least, not yet. But the bigger news is that Gino left for Boston a week ago to start what will undoubtedly be his brilliant academic career – after taking a hastily arranged, unscheduled gap year to get some life experience first. ('I've realized I've been very sheltered, Georgia,' he said the night before starting work at a hostel for the homeless) and Anne

Marie and Harry have been mired in a swamp of anxiety ever since, despite the fact that he's called home almost every night with news of the chess club he's joined and the like-minded friends he's made. Billie, who, against all the odds, has fallen hard for her new little brother, has moved into Gino's old room and allowed the baby to move in with her, 'at least until he starts toddling around, then Nina can have him'. All is well in their world.

We find *Mummy, Why Is That Dog So Big?* on a display table in the first shop we visit, in among the other new releases. Nick props the top copy up and we snap a few pictures of Igor looking at it, bemused. It turns out he's the best sales boy ever, because a kid makes a beeline for him and, when I explain that he's the dog on the cover of the book I'm holding, she insists her mum buy it for her.

'He can finally earn his keep,' Nick says as we head off in search of shop number two. Here the book is on the shelf, but not on a table in a prominent position. Nick grabs the three copies and plonks them down on top of a pile of someone else's opus while the assistant isn't looking. I can't help myself: I scour the shelves for *Game of Gnomes*. I know from Kate that Phoenix have offered Lydia a deal for a second book, and I know from always indiscreet Antoinette that while she pushed for a contract for two more titles Phoenix didn't feel they could make that big an investment at this point.

'Is it bad that I'm relieved?' I said to Anne Marie. We were sitting in my patio garden with Nat bouncing on her knee.

'It's human,' she said. 'That's what it is.'

At shop number three (the novelty is wearing off. I'd like

to go and sit somewhere and have lunch and a glass of wine, but I don't want to rain on Nick's parade. He's so proud of me. So thrilled on my behalf), I spot a copy of *Game of Gnomes* on the shelf. Shepherd and Somers being in close proximity alphabetically. Nick sees me looking. He pulls it out and puts it back spine first.

'No,' I say, righting it. 'I want to play fair.' Now I've been able to show what I can do I'm actually OK with it if she ends up becoming a success. I don't care. There can be room for us both.

We snap another photo: me holding the book like a trophy, Igor next to me. The girl behind the counter looks over quizzically. 'She's Georgia Shepherd,' Nick says and I cringe waiting for the inevitable 'Who's Georgia Shepherd?' Thankfully she's too polite.

'And this is the dog, look.' Nick holds the book up next to Igor's face.

'Oh, well, in that case you should sign them,' the assistant says to me. 'And we'll put them up front with "Signed by the author" stickers on. People love that.' I do as I'm told and let her snap a few pictures before suggesting that Igor is a better subject. 'Good idea,' she says. 'I can put him on our Facebook page.'

'OK,' Nick says as we leave. 'Covent Garden next.'

'We don't have to do this,' I say hopefully.

'Only four more on the list,' he says cheerfully. I suggest maybe we could stop for sustenance and then pick up again after but he's not having it. 'Igor could do with some water,' I say and he produces a bottle and a foldable rubber bowl from somewhere.

'It was genius bringing him with us,' he says, leading me towards Seven Dials. I'm getting a bit grumpy; my feet are hurting and I need a drink.

'Where are we going now?' I say sulkily.

'There's one just up round this corner. I forget the name.'

'The thing is, no one knows who I am and we can't keep—' I stop dead as I spot Joe sitting at a table outside a restaurant up ahead. I thought he was on his way back to Brighton today; we said goodbye this morning before Nick and I left for our epic quest. 'What . . . ?' I start to say, and then I see Edie – who returned to Bath a week ago – sitting next to him, and then Anne Marie and Harry, Antoinette, Kate. Finally my gaze lands on my mum and then Frank. Last spotted on FaceTime the day before yesterday sitting by their pool, glistening with oil, roasting themselves slowly.

'Surprise,' Nick crows just as Mum spots me.

'Here she is!' she shouts at the top of her voice and, inevitably, I burst into tears.

I hear the pop of a champagne cork. I'm swallowed up in a sea of hugs from the people who mean most to me in the world. I can't even fathom the logistics. Kate hands me a glass and then raises hers. 'Here's to *Mummy, Why Is That Dog So Big?*,' she says. 'And to Wilbur, of course. Let's not forget Wilbur.'

'You sneaky bastard,' I say to Nick as we settle ourselves at the table, Igor plonking himself down between Anne Marie and Joe, historically the most likely to feed him snacks. Nick beams at me, proud of himself for pulling it off.

The sun is shining; London is at its best. I look around the table at the happy, smiling faces toasting my good fortune. I wonder, briefly, who Lydia celebrated with. Who was in her corner cheering her on when *Game of Gnomes* hit the shelves.

Every now and then I look at her Instagram page. I can't help myself. It's still the same old, same old, with a few added shots of her posing with the book. There are dates and nights out and she's still living her best life and blessed and it still looks like perfection.

But it turned out it was never true and I'm pretty sure it isn't now.

Later on we all go back to ours – minus Kate and Antoinette – a little bit merry and a lot overemotional. Nick opens more champagne, and it's like Christmas except there's no arguing and no one's trying to make me play charades. There's nobody else I would want to be here; my whole world is in my kitchen.

Eventually they all start to drift off: Anne Marie and Harry to relieve the babysitter; the twins to get their trains; Mum and Frank to the hotel they've booked near Heathrow ready for their early flight home. I collapse on the sofa, Igor beside me. Nick flops at the other end.

'We could do those other bookshops tomorrow, if you like,' he says, and I don't have the strength to do anything other than throw a cushion at him.

'Best day ever,' I manage to say. I mean it.

He raises his eyebrows. 'Better than the day we got married?'

'Oh God, yes. Much. Today was just about me.' I wriggle round so my head is in his lap. Close my eyes. He strokes my hair.

'Do you think you can make it to bed?'

'Nope,' I say. I don't think I've ever been so comfortable.

My phone beeps with a message. I dig around in the sofa cushions till I find it. It's from a number I don't know. A mobile.

Congratulations on the new book, it says. *It's gorgeous.* There's no name, just an initial. *L xxx.*

I hold it up to show Nick. He rolls his eyes.

Thanks, I reply. And then I block the number.

Acknowledgements

Thank you to the stellar team at Michael Joseph who make me feel both completely supported and trusted to get on with it alone at all times. Most especially to the wonderful power-house that is Louise Moore and my brilliant editor, Maxine Hitchcock (who couldn't be less like Bibi if she tried). And to everyone at my agents, Curtis Brown, particularly, of course, Jonny Geller. I'm indebted to Charlotte Edwards for her eagle eyes and to my gorgeous friend Anna Higginson who always listens to me panic that nothing in my first draft is working and never says 'You say this every time'.